Q AWAKENING

G.M. LAWRENCE

VARIANCE

Published by Variance LLC (USA).
www.variancepublishing.com

ISBN-13: 978-1-935142-53-9
ISBN-10: 1-935142-53-4
e-ISBN: 978-1-935142-46-1

© Many Rivers Press, Langley, Washington. From the collection *Songs for Coming Home*. Printed with the permission of Many Rivers Press, *www.davidwhyte.com*.

Interior format by Stanley J. Tremblay
Cover Illustration by Steve Stone
Cover Design by Stanley J. Tremblay

Find G.M. Lawrence online at www.gmlawrence.com

For Katherine and Greyson

ACKNOWLEDGMENTS

Q: Awakening would not have been possible without the support and encouragement of many individuals. While it is impossible to list them all here (and I ask the forgiveness of all those not mentioned expressly by name), I would be a poor fellow indeed if I did not at least endeavor to acknowledge some of them.

First and foremost, I wish to thank my wife and my son who endured the long days of writing and the extended periods during which I was away from them, often without means of communication, while I conducted my research in distant and sometimes dangerous lands. They, above all, have been my inspiration in this project.

I also wish to thank my extraordinary editors, Ed Stackler, Shane Thomson, Christine Knecht and Rich Klin. Their dedicated labors, thoughtful comments and superb insights greatly enhanced the original manuscript, adding depth and dimension to the plot, characters and texture of my story. My agent, David Hale Smith, who was with me from the beginning and stayed the course for a debut novelist, made it possible for an intriguing idea to become the book that you are now about to read. And, of course, I extend my heartfelt gratitude to the remarkable team at Variance, including my publisher Tim Schulte, assistant publisher Stanley Tremblay, and cover art designer Steve Stone, all of whom willingly embraced the unique challenges of bringing a new voice and a different kind of thriller to market.

I also wish to acknowledge that this book (which in all respects is a work of fiction) is built on the scholarly and literary efforts of a wide range of experts, historians, theologians, researchers and authors. While any errors, omissions and misinterpretations are mine alone, I thank all of those whose research and publications shaped and inspired this novel. Among those whose work I consulted in researching this book are Burton L. Mack, professor of New Testament at the Claremont School of Theology; John Kloppenborg, Chair of the Department and Centre for the Study of Religion at the University of Toronto, and Middle East historian Kamal Salibi, to name only a few.

Lastly, I wish to thank my friends Abraham Paskowitz (who first taught me to surf and shared with me his deep, abiding love for the sea), Bruce Hopkins (the actor who portrayed Gamling in the *Lord of the Rings* movies and who traveled beside me in my research on the South Island of New Zealand), and the brave Bedouins, Israelis and others who made my Middle East research possible even in the midst of revolution and turmoil.

G.M. LAWRENCE

To: Jim

Happy Father's Day

Best,

QAWAKENING

In these waves
I am caught on shoulders
Lifting the sky

Each crest
Breaks sharply
And suddenly rises…

And the spark behind fear
Recognized as life
Leaps into flame

From "Out in the Ocean"
By David Whyte

NORTH ISLAND

176°

36°

Auckland   Tauranga
Hamilton

40°

Wellington

SOUTH ISLAND

Christchurch

44°

172°

Queenstown

NEW ZEALAND

PROLOGUE

MIDIAN DESERT
SOUTHERN SINAI
38 AD

On the far horizon, beyond the shifting grey dunes, a lone jackal howled, fell silent, then howled again. Silver strands of lightning flashed within the towering bank of storm clouds. The date palms groaned as the gusting wind bent them low over the swirling sands. To the east, beyond the scattered clumps of salt bush, restless waves, driven hard by the coming storm, pounded the boulders of the chiseled coast. The scent of brine mingled with the sharp aroma of camel, driftwood smoke, and the dying autumn blooms of juniper.

But still, the rain did not come.

Only the campfire—its glowing embers racing fitfully into the night sky—pierced the onyx fabric of the darkness.

From the shadows, a gaunt robed figure half walked, half staggered, toward its warmth. In the shimmering red light, the crescent scar that ran like a river across the high ridge of his cheek seemed for an instant to disappear into the shadows of his beard. He tossed the folds of his robe over his shoulder, knelt down beside the fire, and cast another branch into the glowing circle of flame.

The pain was always at its worst on cold nights when the winds blew strong and the sky filled with clouds. But he would make do. He always had. Besides, it wouldn't be much longer now. Soon he'd be aboard the galleon, beyond the reach of the wind and the rain that was sure to come. Then he could rest, but not sleep. Not yet. Not until it was safe.

He stood up from the fire and suddenly the earth shook beneath his feet. Grasping the gnarled branch of the juniper tree, he steadied himself. He closed his eyes and whispered the warm breath of a prayer.

A zephyr rose up and around him, engulfing him, lifting his robe like the wings of a giant kestrel. The enchanted wind gave him flight and sent him sailing high above the desert and out toward the sea. He granted the wind dominion over him and surrendered himself to it. In gratitude, the wind banished the crippling pain and made him whole again.

He was floating now, like an angel, high above the waves of the churning sea. He reached his hand out and spiraled downward, sailing ever closer to the pulsating depths beneath him. The soft utterings of a voice wrapped around him like a vapor. It was the Damascene who had saved him and returned to him his sight, the one who had interpreted the vision and revealed his destiny to him. The voice was hollow and distant but pierced him like an arrow, its words exploding in a brilliant shower of jewels deep inside him.

Follow the sea. Let it guide your path.

Then as abruptly as it had come, the zephyr vanished. The Damascene's voice faded and his words scurried away into the void of night. Only the sound of restless fronds, crashing waves, and the gathering winds of the pounding storm remained.

The billowing, dusty robe gradually descended as he returned to earth. The illusion was gone, its spell broken. He drew a breath, then opened his eyes, standing alone in the light of the fire beneath a canvas of brooding purple clouds.

The smuggler was late. Perhaps he wouldn't come. Perhaps, like the frightened young Bedouin before him, he had allowed his fear to overcome him, to cause him to push the tiller away from the haunted coast and toward a less foreboding shore.

Only time would tell.

Just as he had with the Bedouin, the voyager had chosen the smuggler for his knowledge of these isolated sands and shores. No one, not even the Midians, knew these deserts better than the Bedouin tribes. But, as with all men, what they knew and what they had the courage to undertake were not always the same.

Each evening, after the blood-red sun had melted into the melancholy dunes, the Bedouin's trembling hand had traced in the sands around the fire the sacred symbols his father had taught him. But even the talismans of a Bedouin elder held no power to crush the seed of fear that had begun to grow inside him. As their journey drew them deeper into the sinister void, the Bedouin cast fragrant offerings of incense sealed in beads of dried honey onto the glowing embers of the evening fire. But the sweet smoke proved as impotent as his father's ancient symbols. And so the seed of the Bedouin's fear took root and grew within him until at last, when the storm clouds swallowed the silver glow of the moon, the fear entangled him and made him its own. When that moment came, the Bedouin simply rose, grasped the worn leather reins of his camel's bridle and the bag of silver he'd earned for his service, and walked northward toward the safety of Bier Mousa. The voyager offered no protest as he sat in the amber glow of the fire and watched the Bedouin's image first fade into shadow, then at last dissolve into nothingness.

What if the smuggler doesn't come? he asked himself. But as quickly as the doubt had risen within him, he cast it aside. The smuggler's galleon, its patchwork sails taut in the quickening winds, would come. It would come because the Damascene had said it would come. It would come because the treasure was too precious. It would come because it was the destiny of them all, and no man was powerful enough to escape his destiny.

From the pocket of his *jalabiya*, the voyager withdrew a soft swatch of goatskin, unfolded it, and removed a small, flat tentmaker's needle. As was his habit in times of contemplation, he laid the broad side across his knuckles. Absently, he set the tiny piece of iron in motion, undulating like a wave across the back of his hand. Left, then right, then left again. Over and over, as if daring the needle to pierce the scarred leather of his hands. The simplicity of the motion freed his mind to contemplate . . . what, exactly? The vastness of the universe spread out before him? Yes, that. Always that. And the *ruach*, the divine breath of God that animates everyone and everything—that as well. But now, in this hollow land, amid the windblown dunes and the echoing waves beyond, surrounded by danger and uncertainty, there was something more. Something he remembered from a dream. Something familiar, but just out of reach. Something vague and obscure, yet very real.

A bolt of dry lightning flashed on the horizon.

In its white light the voyager at last saw what he had been waiting for, the image the Damascene had promised. A galleon with pale grey sails floated impatiently in the darkness beyond the rocks. And in that instant of relief and joy, he felt another sensation, an awareness of something lurking in the darkness, not on the near horizon, but so close beside him that he could feel its breath on his skin. It was something the Damascene had not foretold, but it was not a stranger to the voyager. He knew its purpose. He could call it by its name. For the first time since he'd left Damascus, he was afraid.

The Bedouin had sensed its presence from the beginning. He had seen it for what it was. Dark. Malevolent. Eternal. And when he had learned that he could neither banish it with his sacred symbols nor placate it with his fragrant offerings, he fled. But the *djinn* hadn't wanted the Bedouin. They had come for something much more precious and powerful than a man. They had come for the treasure. The treasure the voyager now sought to protect.

A long, unwelcome shiver ran down the length of his spine. For an instant his fear gripped him, as it had the Bedouin before him. The oasis of Bier Mousa taunted him. Its high stone walls beckoned. Comfort, food, and sleep awaited him there. Peace and safety awaited him there. *Come*, it cried. *Come and find peace*. But the voyager knew it wasn't Bier Mousa that called to him. It was the djinn who had come to keep him from his mission.

He shoved the needle back in his pocket and leaned over the fire. With a quick, jabbing motion, he ignited a torch then turned to face the sea. Over his head, in a wide, sweeping arc, he waved the billowing flame three times. Seconds passed as he stood alone in the darkness. Then, as if it were an echo, the signal was at last returned. Three flashes of light from the waters beyond the jagged rocks. The sign had been given. The sign had been received. It was time to go.

As the first pregnant drops of rain tumbled onto the desert sands around him, the voyager doused the fire. From the shadow of the juniper tree, he reclaimed the leather bag and the precious treasure hidden deep within. The blue and gold flame of the torch leapt wildly as the wind quickened. Shadows swirled around him, stirring the desert into a frenzied, stinging cloud of sand. He drew the fold of his heavy robe across his face and strode toward the shore. Only the flickering torchlight penetrated the darkness of the night. Its dancing flame etched a pale, unsteady circle at his feet. The torch alone would guide his footsteps to the sea, and those of the djinn who now walked beside him.

CHAPTER I

BRITISH MANDATE PALESTINE
WORLD WAR II

The silver bombers rose like ominous shadows on the horizon of the still Palestinian morning. Abandoned shovels and pickaxes littered the ancient ruins like driftwood on a deserted beach. Hapless laborers, their *keffiyehs* flying behind them like sovereign banners in retreat, rushed for shelter from the coming storm.

Only Dr. Emile Zorn, the white stubs of his coarse beard shimmering like snowflakes on the saddle-brown field of his face, refused to run. He leaned hard onto the tattered leather pad of his crutch and watched the Savoia-Marchetti SM-81 bombers and their Fiat G35 fighter escorts bring fear and confusion to his little encampment in the place the world had once called Capernaum.

As Zorn gazed up into the brilliant blue fire of a morning sky that had unfurled itself like a flag above the dry hills and rolling plains of Palestine, it occurred to him that a man in his lifetime should not have to come face-to-face with the dogs of war twice. Once should be enough. As he shielded his eyes from the sun, Emile Zorn felt a queer sensation. He had the sense that the minions of this brash new war the Germans had started were coming for him, and that this time they meant to take more than just a leg.

In the Great War, he'd aimed his blazing tripod-mounted Maxim at the Kaiser's soldiers and mowed them down like blades of grass. He hadn't spared any of them, not the *Hausfrau* sons who had been fish mongers, nor the cobblers nor the wheat harvesters. He'd pulled the trigger and unleashed six hundred rounds a minute. In that merciless hail, he'd sent them all tumbling over the barbed wire and into the mud like the broken dolls of spoiled children.

How many had he killed? Hundreds, certainly. First, at the Ardennes in August 1914. Then again at Ypres in October, and at Neuve-Chapelle the following March. But when the last of the spring rains came, the tables turned. The Kaiser's bright blond boys came and took their measure of revenge. They hurled a Howitzer shell right beside him and blew off the leg. Just as he had done to the *Hausfrau* sons in his own remorseless season, they left him crumpled and broken, crying in the sludge and mire of a hard April rain.

Zorn unsnapped the pocket of his jodhpurs and withdrew a flask. The cool, dry air was heavy with the scent of ripe olives, diesel fuel, and the grilling of spiced meats. A lazy breeze ambled up from the south, along the banks of the Sea of Tiberias. It took an edge off the rising temperature, drying the beads of sweat that dotted the high furrowed plain of his forehead. The silver wings of a Fiat fighter flashed above him as it swooped down over the camp.

"Take a good look at what you've come to make war on—a cripple and a handful of Bedouin boys," Zorn roared, shaking his fist at the sky.

With an air of jaded indifference, he uncorked the flask and took a drink. He liked the sour aroma of warm Scotch whiskey that wafted up into the autumn air. In a gesture of disdain or defiance—he hadn't yet quite decided which—he tipped the flask skyward and offered a toast to the Fascist armada. Then he took his second—or was it his fourth?—drink of the still-young day. Zorn knew it was an even number because his mind worked in even numbers. The odd ones never seemed to matter.

A boy, flustered and out of sorts, suddenly appeared at Zorn's side. He waved his arms and chattered as if a school teacher were close behind him with his whipping cane. The boy spoke in his native Farsi, as he often did when he became agitated or excited.

"My uncle says to tell you that they are bombing *everywhere*, Professor!"

Zorn smiled and gazed down at his little Persian who had drifted into Arab lands.

"My uncle says there are many women and children dead in Haifa and Tel Aviv and that the oil pipelines are burning. He says the coffins line the road from the Balfour School all the way to the cemetery."

"Yes, bad business, this, Shari. But please, speak Arabic or English. You must learn that emotions are dangerous things, especially when they control the tongue. Always remember, Shari, *intellect*, not emotion, is the pathway to treasure." Zorn dusted the boy's thick brown hair then tapped the cork back into his flask and returned it to his pocket.

Shari worked to control his breathing. But the planes that troubled the skies entranced him. Like a siren, they called to him. Anxiously, he turned and glanced into the burning bright sky that rumbled as if in the grip of a storm. Then just to prove to himself that he had learned his master's lessons, he methodically drew a crumpled yellow paper from his pocket and shifted to English.

"The museum has sent a telegram, Professor:

Terminate project immediately STOP

Abandon dig STOP

Secure all artifacts STOP

Return to Zurich END."

"Now that's much better, Shari. Much better. There's promise in you, my little Persian. Yes, great promise indeed."

A glimmering green scarab scuttled across the toe of Zorn's boot. In a moment of whimsy, he reached for it, but the high plane of his crutch held him back.

"Do you see how magnificently its shell sparkles in the morning sun, Shari? It's unconcerned with our troubles here. There's a lesson somewhere in that, I think. I shall contemplate the matter over a drink one day."

"Please, Professor. My uncle says you must read the telegram. He says we must leave." Shari shoved the telegram under Zorn's nose. "My uncle has many sources and knows many things. He says tanks and soldiers will come. He says you are a *cousin*, Professor, and that I must not be found with you. He says it will mean the camp in Morocco for me and worse still for you."

Zorn had fallen under the spell of the beetle. There was something curious, alluring, even comforting, about the glimmering green creature. But it took no notice of Emile Zorn. As suddenly as it had appeared, it slipped inside a tiny black hole in the ground and vanished. The scarab, it seemed, sensed the coming war.

"A cousin? Ah yes, your uncle means a Jew, Shari. I see your point."

In a gesture of courtesy to the boy, Zorn drew a pair of glasses from the pocket of his safari jacket and pretended to read.

"My uncle says that the old house of the Christians has been buried for two thousand years. He says the soldiers do not come to dig in the sand for scrolls or broken pottery. They come to make history, he says. They come for land and oil. They come for power. The stones will still be there when they are gone, will they not? They will keep their secrets, will they not?"

A fresh wave of bombers appeared overhead. In the deep roar of their engines, Zorn heard not so much the howling of war as the clarion call of yet another season of an old Jew's migration.

"Yes, my little one, perhaps you're right. Perhaps it is indeed time to gather up the pickings from this fine field of poppies and move along. As Jews have always had to do. Harvest a while, sojourn a while. Then when the latent threat awakens from its slumber and bares the fangs of its discontent, scoop it all up into a pouch like so many diamonds and move along."

Zorn wadded the telegram into a ball and tossed it to the wind. Absently, he scratched the thinning hairs of his head.

"What, after all, is the point? We've found all we're likely to find here. Nothing but the remnants of a few squalid dwellings. Dried mud huts and a few scattered stones and nothing at all of Q. That's hardly enough to satisfy the museum. It's all so unfortunate. But when planes come and kill children at play in the streets, perhaps it is indeed time for a wandering Jew to pack his bags and ease along."

"What is Q, Professor?" Shari seemed no longer to notice the bellowing of the engines overhead.

"The Christians say it's the word of God, my boy, an ancient manuscript undefiled by the hands of men. They believe its revelation will trigger the return of their savior and unite the world under the cross. The Muslims, of course, don't care much for that outcome. While they too believe Jesus will return, they believe that it must be the Mahdi, the last of the sacred twelve Imams, who unites the world—not under the cross, but under the crescent. So for them, Q is a threat of unimaginable proportions. And the Jews? Well, take it from me, they don't like anything that suggests anyone else's messiah is coming back to do anything. So they fear and hate the idea of Q as much as the Muslims. But one thing's for sure, Shari, whether one's a Christian, Jew, or Muslim, or even just a treasure hunter like you and me, it's a powerful thing indeed. That's why men will always dig in the sand in hopes of finding it."

"It is a great treasure then? The greatest treasure?"

"If it is anything at all, it is surely that. If Q really exists, my little helper, it would be more valuable than any archaeological find in the entire history of mankind. Indeed, it would be the greatest treasure, the greatest source of power and wealth in all the world."

Shari pondered Zorn's words then whispered softly, "With a treasure such as that, a man might have everything."

"Indeed so, my boy. If we ever managed to actually find Q, you and I would be farting through silk."

Zorn nodded toward the sound of thunder above. "But enough of myths and legends. We can dream our dreams later. Go tell your uncle to gather the artifacts and pack them up. It's time for us to go." Zorn spit once then rubbed his beard. "And tell the old thief no deductions for carrying charges. Do you understand me, boy?"

Shari nodded. "Yes, Professor. But that is what he sent me to tell you. The crates are already packed. They are loaded on the lorry. He only wants to know should he drive them to Haifa."

Zorn reflected for a moment then replied.

"No, not Haifa. The Italian bombs have made a mess of Haifa. I think Beirut's the place for us now. The Fascists shouldn't have much interest in launching a campaign there, at least not yet."

Zorn drew the flask from his hip and touched it to his lips. It was dry.

"Tell him that when he gets to Beirut, he's to take the crates to the warehouse, not the shipyard. I want to be sure we collect our fee before we send our meager harvest on to Zurich. It would be foolish for us to forget the first rule of our ancient tribes, would it not? Never deliver the goods till the payment is in hand."

"Yes, Professor," Shari smiled, inching along beside the old cripple, never shifting his gaze from Zorn's face.

Zorn smiled then reached inside the pocket of his jodhpurs.

"Of course, what was I thinking? Another rule of our tribes, is it not? Always get a little something up front." Zorn pressed a glimmering gold coin into Shari's outstretched hand.

"But will you not come with us, Professor? Will you also not be safer in Beirut?"

"Ah, the question of the ages, Shari. Who can say where safety lies when the world's in flames? But don't worry. I won't be far behind you."

Shari bowed then scurried off like a frightened hare, running pell-mell toward the lorry.

As he turned and walked toward the tent, Zorn whistled an old tune from the Great War, one he had nearly forgotten before the planes had come to stir it from the attic of his mind. He felt a tingle of excitement work its way up his spine and into his consciousness. For the first time in many years, he felt bright and alive. The world seemed rich not only with danger, but with possibilities.

Zorn lifted the tent flap and pressed himself, crutch first, into the darkness. He opened a fresh bottle and filled his mouth with the familiar warm smoke. Then he heard the roar of the Fiat engines behind him and knew he'd been right all along. This time they had come for him. But he didn't run. He was too old, too broken, and too jaded to run. He simply smiled, whiskey dripping from the wispy strands of his white moustache, and waited for destiny to play its hand.

Like the summer rain that comes in an instant, a shower of bullets tore through the canvas, struck his torso, and shattered his crutch, splinters swirling like a swarm of insects in the dark, musty air. Like the Kaiser's boys he'd mowed down with his flaming Maxim gun—six hundred rounds a minute—the old cripple tumbled to the earth, a broken doll covered in blood. Then as if to put an exclamation point on it all, the tent exploded in a ball of fire. Emile Zorn's account was settled, invoice paid in full.

As the blood filled his lungs and his consciousness faded to black, he wondered about his little Persian and what might become of him now.

וְיִדְעֲלַבְמוּ וְדִי־לַע הָיֶהַנ לְ
יֶחְ־וְיֶה וּב הָיֶהַנ רְשֶׁא־לָכ הָיִ

CHAPTER II

PHOENICIAN DOCKYARD
TARTUS, SYRIA
PRESENT DAY

Dante Falchetti didn't believe in omens. Like his father before him, he spit on them. They were fables told to children by frightened old hags. Omens were not for the *malviventi*, who fought their battles in the hard streets of Palermo. Omens were not for men.

Still, the ominous vapors of the damp yellow fog, smelling of death and decay, made him uneasy. They swirled in menacing, billowy clouds beneath the gallows trees of rusting gantries then settled in impenetrable sheets of mist over the tarmac of the deserted Syrian dockyard. Dante didn't believe in omens, but that didn't mean that he liked the blinding fog that filled the lost hours of night.

It had been ten years since he had wandered in such a fog. He had gone to Venice in his customary disguise of a restorer of ancient manuscripts. But his true purpose was to steal the Carta degli Apamea for the Instituto Centrale delle Biblioteche Italiane and leave his perfectly crafted forgery in its place. That had been in the early days of his career, and it had nearly been the end of him. His mother, who had come of age in Caserta where the women had powers the men could not understand, had warned him even then. "The fog is always an omen, *cucciolo*. Never challenge the fog."

But it wasn't the fog that had been his problem, he told himself. It was the manuscript itself. Papyrus was never easy. Coarse and brittle, it made the work all the more demanding and risky. After that, he'd left papyrus to others. After that, he'd only forged parchments, and then only the best ones. That was where the money was. In a codex like the one the Egyptian monks had hidden away in the bowels of the scriptorium at Wadi al-Natroun. There his forgery had been perfect—so perfect that the fools in their dark brown robes had paid him a bonus thinking his restoration work a miracle. But in Venice the papyrus had taunted him. Each time he touched it, a corner crumbled or another fiber disintegrated into dust. That was the doing of the fog, his mother warned him. It was the fog, she said, that had come and closed in on him like the walls of a coffin and squeezed the air out of his lungs. It was the fog that had knocked him down on the Corte Vecchia and left him like a fish out of water laboring for his breath.

But this time it would be different. This time he would spit on the Syrian fog as his father spit on the Sicilian fog, as they both spit on his mother's omens. That was the way the malviventi dealt with superstitions and magic.

But he had to admit that it was strange. The fog hadn't been there when the liveried doorman at the Shahin Tower Hotel, his red uniform coat fraying at the sleeves, hailed the cab. "You are sure, *Sayyidi*? Those docks are deserted, sir. There is nothing there now. Better to go to the Old City. Better to pay for the girls," he said, smiling.

Dante merely shook his head and spit. Without a word, he entered the taxi and sped away.

It wasn't until the battered diesel Mercedes turned onto the cobblestones of the abandoned pier that the fog had appeared. In an instant, it dropped like a stage curtain, smothering the street lamps as if they were candles.

"*Basta!*" Dante whispered to the fog as he paid the driver then strode away, the heels of his black boots echoing across the hard, wet tarmac. Beside a gantry, he paused and adjusted his leather jacket. He checked the 9 millimeter subcompact Ruger he had tucked inside the waist of his pants. The feel of cold steel in his hand gave him a sense of indestructibility. *Let the fog and omens come,* he told himself, as he patted the pistol's hard rubber grips. *I spit on them.* Then the wind stirred, and he heard his mother whisper into his ear. "*Attento, Dante.*"

"*Che cazzo stai dicendo!*" Dante scolded himself. Then for luck he touched himself and squeezed tightly. "To hell with this old Persian. I'll take him *veloce e facile*—fast and easy—just like all the others. Why should this one be any different? Never once has my forgery been discovered. Ten years, never once! Veloce e facile."

From the darkness at the end of the pier deep within the maze of fog, a beam of amber light flashed twice. Cautiously, Dante edged toward it.

"Shari, are you there?" Dante's voice ricocheted off the cold metal walls of the cargo crates and disappeared into the night.

Again, the diffuse yellow beam flashed twice. Dante touched the butt of the Ruger and adjusted the leather portfolio, squeezing it tightly under his arm and inside the jacket.

"Shari, *dove siete?*" he bellowed again. A gust of damp wind pushed along the docks and sent a chill down his back. The fog swirled. For a moment he was blinded. Like gunfire, his breath came in short quick bursts. The billowing yellow clouds had coiled about him like a serpent. Then in the distance, he saw the shadowy contours of a black Mercedes sedan. Its image floated in and out of an undulating cloud of fog.

The sedan's headlights flashed again, but this time they stayed on, suspending Dante in a damp yellow column. Nervously, he wiped the moisture from his brow, cursing the fog. With his palm turned outward, he shielded his eyes against the bright beam of light.

"Dante, *buona sera*." The voice was comforting and warm. "But, you are late. For a moment, I feared that you might have failed me. It is good to see you. You have my package, of course?"

"*Si, signore*. It is here," Dante tapped his fingers against the bulge of his jacket then strode briskly toward the Mercedes. A driver, straight and silent, stood beside the door.

"And you have mine, signore?"

Shari smiled. His snow-white hair danced in the maritime breeze. "But of course, Dante. And in cash, as is our custom."

The Persian stepped into a pool of sodium light and glided toward the sedan. He was dressed as he always was, in a double-breasted worsted suit, a white linen square peeking out from behind its lapel. The silver grenadier, knotted in a Prince Albert, hung as straight as an arrow from the center of his starched white shirt.

"Come then, Dante. Shall we bid farewell to this lovely veil of fog? I confess that I find a strange comfort in it, but we'll be more secure inside the cabin, I think." Shari ducked his head and slid into the car, the Sicilian close behind.

The driver closed the passenger door and returned to his seat behind the wheel. In the rearview mirror he glanced at Shari. The Persian, his black eyes sparkling against the olive grain of his face, nodded his head once, then looked away. The driver pressed the button. As the panel of smoked clear glass ascended, he removed a stainless steel Glock from the shoulder harness beneath his jacket and discreetly placed it beside him.

וּ וַ יִ שְׁ וַ נֵ

ל וַיִ דָֽעְֽלַבִמֹּו וְדִי־לַע הָיֶהַֽן לַ

יְחֽוְיָהֽ וֹּב הָיֶהַֽן רְשֶׁאֽ־לָכ הָיֽ

CHAPTER III

GHOST SHIPS BREAK
SOUTH ISLAND, NEW ZEALAND

Brother Ibrahim thought for a moment that he might throw up. He
would have liked to blame the rugged road, the rattling old taxi or
the long days of travel past the endless stream of security checkpoints in his journey from the deserts of Syria. But he knew it wasn't
any of those things. It was the prospect of seeing Declan Stewart
again after ten long years.

Biting down on his tongue, he tugged at the plastic grip of the
handle. In a rapid-fire stream of circular motions, he lowered the
window, leaned his head out, and took a breath. A breeze rich with
exotic scents rushed in to greet him. He closed his eyes and swallowed hard. He redoubled his efforts to ignore the churning
sensation in his stomach. Gradually, the nausea subsided. Then the
taxi hit a deep pothole and lurched to the left. He felt a warm stream
of acid rise into his throat.

"Sorry, Father. It's a bad road, this. Not much used. Nothing
much down this stretch of coast."

Ibrahim managed a smile as he studied the broken ridge of the driver's crooked teeth in the smudged glass of the rearview mirror.

"Not to worry, my son. Better than what I'm accustomed to at home, I assure you."

Had it been only a week, he asked himself, since he'd placed the images in his leather portfolio, mounted the limping old stallion at the monastery called Dier al-Shuhada and waved goodbye to Amala and little Issa?

"It's only a bit further, Father. Just a few kilometers. Not much more."

Ibrahim closed his eyes and swallowed again.

"Father, can you hear me?"

"Yes. Forgive me. I sometimes daydream. It's a common habit among old men."

"Not to worry."

At last, the driver brought the taxi to a stop. A dirt and gravel road cut a serpentine path from the asphalt up a steep ridge then disappeared beyond the rim of a high plateau.

"It's straight up the crest here and down the road along the sea," he said, pointing up the rugged hill. "But it's a ways and a bit of a challenge. I'd take you to the door myself, but this old wagon couldn't manage it to the top of them high sea cliffs. It takes a four-wheel drive or a horse for that, even on a good day like this. Besides, Dr. Stewart's not known for his hospitality. He don't like visitors. Been known to shoot at them, some say."

Brother Ibrahim handed the driver three crisply folded bills and stepped out into the brisk wind of the mid-afternoon. It gusted in from the road behind him and stirred the russet folds of his heavy woolen robe.

"Interesting wind, that," the driver barked, looking back over his shoulder, his words caught like leaves in the strong draft. "Wind usually flows from the sea to the land on this part of the coast. Never seen it blow from the east such like. Odd that." The driver lifted his cap and scratched the scattered strands of his faded red hair. "Anyway, just follow along the edge of the gravel road. Then walk to the south. Keep the sea on your right, and you'll be fine." He pointed a nicotine-stained finger and gestured toward the shimmering blue horizon. "You'll pass a reef where the waves break big and hard. You can't miss it. They call it Ghost Ships 'cause of all the sailing ships lost there in the old days. You'll see what I mean when you get there." He perched the cap back on his head and adjusted the bill.

"Mind you, there's no sign. But his is the only cottage up there. Stone and timber, it is. If he's not there, he'll likely be on a board riding the waves. He's a right hermit. Mostly keeps to himself." The driver coughed then spit a yellow bolus on to a boulder. "Now, you're sure you don't want me to walk a ways with you? I don't mind it, you know. It'll be dark in another few hours. You don't want to be on that ridge then. It's black as pitch out here unless there's a moon."

"No, my son. I've come this far alone. I think I can make it a bit farther."

"As you wish, Father."

Ibrahim smiled. The driver touched two fingers to the jagged edge of his eyebrow and saluted goodbye. Then he slipped back behind the wheel, turned the dusty cab around and headed for home.

For nearly an hour, Ibrahim dug his cane into the hard-packed dirt and clawed his way to the peak at the far end of the ridge. When he at last reached the top, his skin was covered with sweat, the tight muscles of his back and legs aching with the effort. Gently, he slipped the brown leather satchel from his shoulder and rested against a boulder. The strong breeze caught the powdery strands of his beard and made them dance like the tendrils of the willows that dotted the wide, flowing meadows of flax behind him. He closed his eyes and amused himself with the sensation of cool wind drying the beads of sweat that dotted his brow.

"Not long now," he confided to God. The words came easily, as if he were speaking casually to an old friend.

"*A few months . . . perhaps less,*" was what the oncologist in Damascus had said when he looked at the X-ray that revealed the contours of Ibrahim's destiny. "*But there will be no suffering. The end will come swiftly, like a summer storm.*"

Ibrahim had found the news unremarkable. In many ways, he was happy at last to be moving on, and with God's good speed. But for reasons beyond Ibrahim's ken, God had given him a final mission. Only when it was done might he surrender his broken body and at last go home. Ibrahim had to search out Declan Stewart. He had to tell him what Amala had found buried inside the ancient crate. He had to call him out of his exile.

Surely God had known that would not be an easy thing to do. Declan Stewart had lost everything, even to the point of descending into madness. He had sacrificed all he had ever loved to the consuming fire that was the quest for *Q*. And yet, somehow, a dying monk from his distant past must find a way to bring him back.

A hundred meters farther along the trail, in the shadow of the cliffs, Ibrahim came to a packed dirt trail. He followed its winding path along the face of the cliffs until at last he came to a rustic stone cottage on an open plateau above the sea. It was a sturdy structure built from local greywacke and mighty oak timbers. Its broad slate roof, covered in a carpet of blue-green lichen rosettes, projected beyond the wall and made an encircling porch nearly as expansive as the space within. The cottage faced eastward, its rear portico looking out over the sea and sky.

The enormity of the solitude astounded him. But then, that was what had drawn Declan Stewart here in the first place. He had come to this place stripped of everything, barren in soul and physically broken. And somehow this land and sea, this sturdy cottage, had brought him back from his madness and made it possible for him to live with, or at least to endure, the burdens no man should have to bear. Here he had found just enough to buffet his beaten body and soul from the memories he carried.

With the gnarled handle of his cane, Ibrahim rapped twice on the door. For a long moment he waited, his heart pounding inside his chest. In the distance, the sea, a great desert of indigo and aquamarine, reflected in piercing silver arrows the fading sunlight of the antipodal spring. When he received no answer, Ibrahim slowly made his way around to the back of the cottage, edged up the broad plank steps, and eased onto the porch. Raising his eyes up from the steps, he felt as if he had entered an enchanted world, a place of peculiar and wondrous things, and each of them a clue to what Declan Stewart had become.

On either side of the door, surf boards leaned lazily against the greywacke walls, and no two of them were alike. Some had three sharp, translucent green fins at the rear. Others had only two or none at all. The tall ones nearest the steps bore the logo of a breaching whale and the insignia "Wyland" in brash, contrasting lettering. The ones farther along the wall were marked "9 Fish." The one nearest the plank timbers read "Firewire." Some shimmered with a coat of fresh acrylic. Others bore ugly gashes and scars. Still others were burnished grey by a thick coat of coarse, sandy wax. One was broken squarely in two.

On the other side of the porch, where the vista opened to the sea, lay a jumbled stack of sea harvest and the tools used to fetch it. Giant pink and granite sea shells hung from the rafters, suspended by nearly invisible bits of pale blue nylon fishing line. Beneath them sat three aluminum diving tanks and a tattered black harness covered in D-rings and carabiners. Everywhere there were masks, fins, lures, a spear gun and devices he did not recognize. For a long moment, Ibrahim leaned hard on his cane and simply took it all in, trying to decipher their secrets and what they said about the man he had come so far to see.

"So Father, this is what has become of the true genius of Tell

Nebi-Mend and of the ossuaries. The one who unveiled the fraud of
the *Secret Book of Mark*, the man who recognized the *Lost Gospel of
Waraqah Ibn Nawfal* for what truth it held. He's left the desert behind
him. Let us hope that I have not come too late."

On the wind, Ibrahim smelled the scent of brine. It conjured
memories of the past for him, memories of another coast and
another shore.

They had set up camp in the Wadi Dababir less than two kilometers from the Dead Sea. Salt and sand had filled their every breath
and a harsh summer sun had burned like a furnace in the cloudless
sky. Declan had been electric then, filled with the energy and elation
of conquest.

It had been the codex's script of course. Declan said it was *always*
the script that revealed the truth or the lies. That was how he'd
known that it was genuine, that it was the work of Waraqah ibn
Nawfal and not of a forger. That finding, like so many others of the
infamous Dr. Declan Stewart, had controverted everything the
experts at the Israel Antiquities Authority had asserted frequently,
loudly, and publicly. But, as always, Declan took no position regarding the matters of faith, and that, at least, had saved him from their
fury. He declined to offer a view regarding whether the epistle's
author had been a Christian Ebonite priest or the first monotheist to
believe in the prophecy of Muhammad. His abstention had been
enough to give the IAA sages a partial victory. And that was fine
with Declan. To him, those were sideshow issues that didn't matter.
The parchment was all that mattered. It was everything—the skin,
the words, the ink. Those were tangible. A man could touch them,
read them, and hold them in his hand.

Declan had no religious bias, no doctrine to inflate or diminish.
He only sought the truth. And that was what had made him different. It was why so many feared him, and why some even hated him.
But the tragedy of Khirbet Qumran had come, and everything had
collapsed around him. Then he vanished. "In an asylum, I heard.

Bloody well where he belongs," the IAA wonks had boasted. And they simply forgot him.

Ibrahim turned toward the steps that led down to the beach path. *"If he's not at the house, he'll likely be on a board riding the waves."* That was what the gentle driver had said, wasn't it? But as he turned, he tripped. The tip of his cane caught on something and threw him off balance, but he did not fall. At his feet, he found a pair of tattered leather sandals. Simple bindings, well-worn, and covered with the pale, grey dust of the earth. He recognized them immediately. They were desert sandals made for desert sands, not for the beaches of the South Island of New Zealand. Declan had bought them from a Bedouin in Ein Gedi in the days before the red rain fell. Like Ibrahim, they were a relic of the past, a reminder of things now long buried beneath the sands.

In that idle moment of aimless recollection, Ibrahim felt a powerful surge, crystalline and uncontaminated, run through him. He knew it and could call it by name. He had felt it many times in the last five days. It was fear. The fear that he might fail in what he had come to do. That after traveling so far on such an important mission, he would fail to awaken this complex, wounded man from his dream. That he would be too weak to stir him from the solitary dungeon into which his tragedies had cast him. That in the end, Ibrahim would prove himself inadequate to the tasks his God had set before him. That in the end, the fallen world might never find its way into the light.

The wind gusted as if it meant to hold him back, to keep him from what he had come to do. But that only stiffened Ibrahim's resolve. He stepped off the porch and leaned hard into the wind. Step by step, digging the tip of his cane into the coarse, rocky soil, he pulled himself closer to the brink of the precipice until at last an epic vista of sea and sky appeared before him. As he reached the edge of the cliff, Ibrahim whispered a prayer. "Father, if it be thy will, uphold thou me that I may uplift thee."

On the great reef far below, a solitary man bobbed atop a board in the roiling grip of the sea. All around him water raged. Waves as tall as buildings, ominous and alluring, rose in the distance then crashed into the phalanx of jagged, jutting boulders. The man was a long way off and Ibrahim's vision was not what it once had been. But even after ten years, there was no mistaking him.

Fear and excitement rose in equal measures inside Ibrahim as he filled his lungs with air. In mournful bellowing cry he called out: "*DEC-LAN . . . DEC-LAN STEW-ART . . .*"

The man on the board appeared to glance up toward the cliff, but just as quickly he turned back toward the churning mass behind him. A towering wave streaked toward him. *What is he waiting for?* Ibrahim wondered. *Why doesn't he paddle toward the shore in search of shelter?* And then he had his answer.

In a single motion, fluid and smooth, the man turned his board, pivoting toward the shore. He lay down on his chest. For a moment he waited. Then flexing his powerful shoulders, he drove the board forward and let go of the rails. He plunged his arms deep into the boiling tempest, cupped his hands, and began to paddle.

"He'll never make it," Ibrahim whispered to himself, touching the rosary in his pocket.

One stroke . . . two strokes . . . three . . .

Mindlessly, Ibrahim counted them, praying that he would not drown. The wave moved ever faster toward him. Like a stallion, it bucked and reared, determined to throw the man who sought to harness it.

Four strokes . . . five . . . six . . .

Still the wave was faster than his board.

Seven . . . eight . . .

Then at last, he had it. The thundering force of the water lifted the tail of his board and swept the man forward. Suddenly, he was moving as fast as the wave itself. They had become as one. The man gripped the rails again then sprang swiftly to his feet, crouching low and shifting his shoulders to the left, right foot forward, left foot back, the way he always rode the waves. He leaned forward into the wind and picked up speed. There was no stopping him now. He had taken the sea and bent it to his will.

For two hundred meters he carved the face of the wave with the edge of his board. He pivoted right, then left, always running just ahead of the breaking, roiling crest of spiraling water. Then like a spent lover whose lust had drained her energy away, the wave melted into the sea. The mighty wall of water bowed down to its master, collapsing in a soft, churning mass of blue and white foam. Slowly the man began to paddle toward the shore.

Ibrahim clambered down the steep, winding trail and stepped at last onto the grey sand beach of the barren cove.

In the placid shallows, the man stood up in the knee deep foam. His weather-beaten black O'Neill—a tattered 3/2 too thin by far for the cold waters of Ghost Ships—glimmered like seal skin in the surging wash of the Tasman Sea. He scooped up the Wyland, wax side out, adjusted the ankle leash to unwind its kinks, then strode cautiously ahead.

"Ibrahim," he uttered as he laid his board down on the firm ribbon of sand and unstrapped the leash from his ankle. The utterance came with neither warmth nor hostility. But there was an unmistakable coolness in Declan's demeanor.

The old priest sensed it. Indeed, he had expected it. So he simply stood beyond the water's edge and waited for whatever might come.

Declan snatched a faded red towel from the open canvas bag that sat atop a half-submerged boulder. Mindlessly, he buffed the cascading strands of his hair then reached behind his back and unzipped the collar of his wetsuit. Cautiously, like the wild thing he had become, he stepped forward, glanced up toward Ibrahim, and paused. As Declan pushed a shock of wet hair back behind his ears, Ibrahim caught the outlines of the ragged crescent scar then quickly looked away. But it was too late. Dark images were already filling his mind, bringing back a past that he, like Declan, had tried hard to forget.

Declan took a seat on the rocks, slipped out of his neoprene boot-ies, and stepped into a threadbare pair of Toms. At last he spoke. "What the hell are you doing *here*? And how in heaven's name did you find me?" Once again the tone was cool but devoid of any dis-cernible emotion.

Ibrahim conjured a smile. *"Man plans, God laughs*, Declan. That's what our Jewish friends say, isn't it? Two months ago, my plans were simple. I had the monastery. I had my work and my routine. What more could a man want? To be surrounded by his brothers, to be busy. But God, it seems, had other plans. And so now I am here."

Declan coiled the leash around the tail of his board. "Look, Ibra-him. No offense, but you know I'm not much for small talk. I never have been. Why don't you just get to it and tell me what could pos-sibly have brought you fifteen thousand kilometers across the planet to see an old surfer who has absolutely nothing left to say to any-one."

Ibrahim ran the calloused palm of his hand across his beard, debat-ing his odds. How much should he say now and how much should he hold back and save in hopes of finding a better moment? There was no way to know.

"Forgive me for coming unannounced, Declan. But you're a very hard man to find. And even once found you're a harder man to reach. If I was to speak with you, I had no choice but to come here myself."

Declan dabbed the edge of the crumpled towel across his neck and chest. "It's hell and gone from Dier al-Shuhada to New Zealand, Ibrahim. And with the Assad regime about to fall, it couldn't have been easy for you to get out. It must be something pretty damn important for you to have come all that way under those circum-stances."

Ibrahim was cold and tired. He felt dizzy. It wasn't supposed to happen like this. Not so curt and formal. Not so rushed and disorderly.

He had to find a way to break through, to make an opening. But Declan's mood offered him no quarter.

"It is. But it was a long drive from Graves Bay, Declan. And a rather challenging hike up from the road below. I'm not as sturdy as I once was. This old body of mine"—he tapped his cane to his knee—"is nearing its limits. I suppose I should be embarrassed by my frailty. But I tell you plainly, I am tired. I promise that I will tell you everything. I want to tell you everything. But isn't there some place we can sit down together and take our rest while we talk?"

The softening around Declan's eyes and the slow exhalation of his breath signaled a kind of surrender to the inevitability of it all. "Not much of a host, am I? That happens when you've lived alone as long as I have. You lose the art of hospitality, even of common courtesy, if you aren't careful." Declan tossed the damp towel across the opening of his crumpled canvas bag.

"You've come half a world to see me. I suppose the least I can do is to give you a seat, a warm fire, and a decent meal. My place isn't exactly the King David or the American Colony, but there's coffee and fruit and most of the comforts of home, at least the simple ones. It's not far. Just up the trail." Declan lashed the bag to his board then tucked it inside a long, narrow crevice in the cliff.

"Come on. Take hold of my arm. We'll make our way together. Mind the sand and stones though. They take a little getting used to. We'll walk bit by bit. There's no rush hour here. We just want to be up the trail and settled well before the sun sets."

Declan draped Ibrahim's arm over his shoulder and took a measure of the old monk's weight on himself. Carefully he led him to the cottage path. The sun, low on the horizon, emerged from behind a bank of clouds. Gentle rays warmed Ibrahim's face. Unconsciously, he smiled. He sensed at last that somehow everything was as God meant it to be.

As he climbed the winding trail, Declan felt an unwelcome sensation move along his neck and down his spine. He paused and glanced up toward the high ridge beyond the rugged stone cottage. But there was nothing there, only a blanket of tall shrubs undulating in the wind, a wind strangely tinged with the faint scent of diesel fumes. Declan pursed his lips, studied the ridge again, then with Ibrahim close beside him, turned around and headed for home.

וַיְדָעֲלַבְמוּ וְדִי־לַעַ הָיְהָנ לְ
יַחוְיָה וּב הָיְהָנ רְשָׁא־לָכ הָיַ

CHAPTER IV

PHOENICIAN DOCKYARD
TARTUS, SYRIA

Dante lowered the zipper of his leather jacket, withdrew the portfolio, and handed it to Shari. The pungent aroma of sweat filled the cabin.

Shari pressed the silver button on the console beside him. The halogen reading light above his shoulder cast a circle of light on the package. He untied the portfolio then removed a pair of white cotton archivists' gloves from the pocket of his suit coat. He slipped them over his hands and gingerly reached inside. Carefully, he removed the contents he found inside.

For a long moment, Shari held the manuscript in the bright circle of white light. Then adjusting the half-moon glasses on his nose, he drew the parchment closer and began to read.

"It is beautiful is it not, signore?"

Imperceptibly, Shari winced. He closed his eyes and took in a deep breath before offering a reply. "Yes, Dante, it is indeed a beautiful work."

"*Grazzi, signore.*" Dante suppressed a smile. <u>*Veloce e facile*</u>.

Shari slid the manuscript back inside the protective cover and placed it on the seat beside him. With the fingers of his white gloved hand, he delicately probed the inside of the portfolio. Tilting it into the beam of light, he gazed inside. There was nothing else.

"Where is the map, Dante?"

"Si, signore. This is what I wish to tell you."

Subtly, Shari's expression shifted. His voice was soft, but beneath its veneer lurked something ominous and intimidating. "I must have the map as well as the manuscript."

"Si, signore, this I wish to explain. This job has not been easy. Not like other jobs. When I stole the Essene Codex of Levi ben Yehoshua from St. Catherine's in the Sinai, the old monks there slept the day away. I had the freedom of the library with no one watching over me. Sadly, this is not the way of Dier al-Shuhada. The monks there, especially the keeper of the library, are vigilant. Just to remove the manuscript, this itself was nearly impossible. But the map, I am not even certain it is at the monastery. No man can steal what he cannot find."

By force of will alone, Shari holstered his anger. But it wasn't easy. He forced himself to close his eyes and recall the images of the past. An old Jew with a rugged, white stubble scattered across a leather tanned face. A bowed and fraying crutch. A flask of whiskey. "*Intellect, not emotion, is the path to treasure, my little Persian.*"

Shari eased the titanium rimmed reading glasses from his face and held them up to the light. From his pocket, he removed the crisply folded square and began methodically to polish the lenses. He could hear the sound of the Sicilian's breath and smell the garlic he had eaten for dinner.

"But such was not our arrangement, Dante. Our terms were quite clear, were they not? It is the manuscript *and* the map. Only days ago, you were eminently confident of your ability to deliver them. Both of them. Many plans have been made, Dante. All of them require that I possess both the manuscript and the map. That is what you agreed to deliver to me. That is what I agreed to pay you for. Not one. Both."

"*Si, certo*, but as I have told you, signore—"

"You say the map may no longer be at the monastery, but surely that is impossible. The monks would never knowingly let the manuscript or the map slip from their grasp."

Dante began to worry. He stared at the old man then, for reassurance, touched the leather of his jacket where the pistol lay hidden.

"Si, signore, but it is true. The problem is the old monk who's the guardian of the manuscript and the map. The one called Ibrahim. He has left Dier al-Shuhada. He has taken the map, of this I am almost certain. How could any man stop such a thing without being discovered?"

Shari returned the square to his coat pocket then folded his hands into a tent and placed his elbows on his lap. Contemplatively, he gazed out the window into the swirling mist of fog.

"That is very curious, Dante. Why would a monk leave his monastery? Where would he go? And if he did leave, why would he take the map and not the manuscript? You appreciate my confusion, do you not?"

"Si, signore, this question I can answer. He has gone in search of someone."

"He goes in search of whom, Dante?"

"A man, a scholar of manuscripts and maps. He told the girl. I heard him say it."

"And does this man have a name, Dante?" Shari bounced the tips of his fingers.

"Si, signore. I listened well. I always listen well. His name is Declan Stewart."

Shari's fingers froze and the hard edges of a grimace formed at the corners of his mouth. For the first time in many years, not even the counsel of Emile Zorn could keep Shari from revealing the contours of the emotions he felt inside.

"Declan Stewart? You must be mistaken, Dante."

"No, signore. No mistake. Declan Stewart."

"Are you quite certain?"

"Si, signore. There is no mistake. It is *Doctore* Declan Stewart. I heard this name clearly. No mistake. I even saw one of this man's books in the scriptorium. The old monk had a copy on his desk."

Shari rubbed his hands together, drew a filtered Dunhill from the pack inside his pocket, and calmly lit it. A cloud of fragrant blue smoke filled the cabin.

"How very extraordinary." Shari's eyes peered out the window into the fog.

"You know this man?"

Shari ignored the question. He took another deep breath from his cigarette and held the smoke before blowing it out. The fog was heavier now, more like a blanket than a veil. Its color, too, had changed, shifting from yellow to a foreboding shade of grey.

Dante eased a hand inside his jacket and touched his fingers to the butt of the Ruger. He could feel the beads of sweat pooling under his arms and along the tip of his spine. "If you please, signore, if you must have the map, then I will arrange it for you. We will find it. I will bring it. Sure, no problem. I have friends in Palermo. This can be arranged, no worries."

"And how exactly would you do that, Dante? If you are correct, the guardian and his map have vanished. As you said, a man cannot steal what he cannot find."

"Sooner or later the old monk will return to the monastery, no? If he took the map with him, it must return with him. If he has not taken it with him, then he will know where it is. And so when my friends show him the knife, he will give them the map. Either way, I get you the map. Sure, I can arrange it, just a small fee. Very small, for you."

Shari studied the thin line of perspiration that ran from Dante's temple to the crest of his jaw.

"Have you ever been to Beirut, Dante?"

"Beirut? No, signore. Not Beirut. No manuscripts there."

"Like Tartus, it is a city by the sea. And in that city, Dante, a golden watch ticks. The man to whom it belongs studies every movement of the small black hands as they sweep relentlessly around its dial. He does it a hundred times a day just to remind himself that time is precious. I find his affliction tedious at times, but it's a good lesson for us all. Time is indeed a luxury. I don't have time to wait in hopes the monk will return. I don't have time to wonder where my map has gotten to. I need the map now."

Shari took another breath of smoke and returned for a moment to the fog. He found it alluring and inviting. Its shadows and vapors softened the edges of a hard, industrial world. Fog to hide the ugliness. Fog to keep the secrets of this night.

In slow, measured movements, Shari shifted his stare to the rearview mirror. Almost imperceptibly, he touched his thumb to his chin, then nodded faintly. The driver nodded in return. A sign had been given. A sign had been received.

"But he will not be gone long, signore. The girl said five days. He will return tomorrow, maybe the next day, yes?"

"And your fee for the map, Dante? The small fee, just for me, that you mentioned."

"For you, a modest amount. Just enough for expenses, si? Just enough to pay my friends from Palermo who must perform a service such as this."

"Yes, just enough."

Shari pursed his lips, then pressed a button beside him. Slowly the smoked glass panel between the cabin and driver descended. "My friend Dante has important matters to arrange. Please bring his payment now so that he may be on his way. Time, after all, is short." The driver nodded, adjusted his black leather jacket and stepped out of the car.

"Grazzi, signore."

"*Prego*, Dante."

The driver opened the passenger door. Dante pivoted on the black leather seat and stepped out into the night. He watched the fog as it swirled in dense grey clouds at his feet. He recognized it immediately and sensed its omens. It was the fog from Venice; the fog that had nearly taken his life on the Corte Vecchia. He lowered his head and stepped out into the mist. But as he did, something hard struck him across the back of his neck and sent him tumbling down on to the hard, wet pavement. The taste of sand, grit, and oil filled his mouth.

"*La nebbia. Basta, la nebbia!*"

Dante tried to focus. He had to reach the Ruger. Quickly, he worked his hand inside his jacket but before he could draw the weapon, the driver kicked him in the ribs, driving the air from his lungs and leaving him gasping for air. He felt the hard, cold barrel of a Glock tight against his temple. With a jerk, the driver grabbed his collar, pulled him to his feet, and banged his head into the hood of the sedan. He twisted Dante's arm behind him and pressed it up between his shoulder blades. Something snapped. Dante bit his tongue, refusing to cry out, because the Marcantonios of Palermo never cried out. The driver grabbed a fistful of hair and jerked Dante's head toward Shari.

"You're very foolish, my young friend." Shari shoved the wadded pages of the manuscript under his nose. "You ignore the most important rule of the tribe. You must never cheat your partners. And above all, you must never cheat me."

Shari adjusted the collar of his overcoat, placed both hands on the hood of the sedan, and leaned down, placing his face next to the Sicilian's.

"I've sought the treasure that this manuscript and map reveal for my entire life, boy. No man alive knows more about them than I do. You think you can fool me with the forgeries you use on weak-minded monks in forgotten deserts who know nothing?" In a gesture of disdain, Shari flicked his cigarette into the wind. It vanished into the fog.

Dante bit down hard on his lip. He snorted in the cold night air and slowly regained his consciousness and his breath. He had to reach the Ruger, but there was no room for error. A quick thrust of the hand, two shots. Then he would spit on the fog.

"Let me put it in terms a boy from the streets of Palermo can't misunderstand. You picked the wrong mark, cucciolo. I don't play games. Did you really think that your pitiful bag of tricks could deceive me?"

"*Va all'inferno, checca!*"

With a hard, explosive jerk, Dante freed himself from the driver's hold. In a flash, he drew the pistol and turned to fire. But the driver was faster. He regained his feet and with a lightning strike, slapped the pistol from Dante's hand. The cold blue steel made a clattering sound as it tumbled down on to the wet pavement. The Ruger came to rest in a pool of dark water beside the crumpled remnants of the forged manuscript. The driver spun round again and this time struck Dante hard across the face with the barrel of his Glock. He grabbed the Sicilian by the collar of his jacket and slammed his head into the door of the car, then flipped him over and pressed him down onto the hood of the Mercedes.

"That was rude, Dante. I dislike rudeness immensely." Shari made a gesture toward the driver. "Please teach him some respect."

The driver made a tight lipped smile then slurped Dante's ear into his mouth. Using his teeth like pincers, he bit deeply into the flesh, severing the cartilage just above the lobe. With a ferocious jerk, he tore off Dante's ear then spit it back into his face.

This time the Sicilian could not restrain his cries. Warm blood cascaded down the side of his neck and pooled in the hollow of his neck beneath his leather jacket. The fog at last had defeated him.

"We have so many more methods, Dante, but they are crude and painful. I rather prefer to avoid them when possible. Must we use them? Or will you resign yourself to the situation and cooperate with me?"

Dante bit his tongue against the searing flame of pain. Almost imperceptibly, he nodded.

"That is much better. Better for you, and better for me." Shari drew a cigarette from the pack inside his coat and lit it. He blew a long, steady stream of smoke into the dense cloud of fog.

"You know more about all this than you've told me, isn't this true, Dante?"

The Sicilian stared helplessly into the night, but did not answer.

"Please don't compound your mistake by continuing to assume that I'm a fool. It will only cost you additional measures of suffering and pain. One way or the other, I will have my answers. You can give them to me here or, if you prefer, my driver will take you aboard the yacht behind us. There he will deliver you to a man known as the Syrian. And I assure you, Dante, you will experience fearsome, awful sensations when you are in his private room and under the ministrations of his skilled hand. It pains me to think of them. I so very much dislike the sight of blood. Now I want to know two things, Dante. First, I want to know where the manuscript is— the *original* manuscript. And second, I want to know where the old monk has gone."

A long moment passed. Then Dante managed to find his voice. "The original," he mumbled, struggling against the pain "is in my room at the Shahin Tower Hotel."

"And the room number, Dante?"

"*Quattordici undici.* Room 1411. It's hidden inside the lining of my bag."

"Good. Very good. And now what of the monk?"

"I don't know. As God is my witness, I don't know what has become of the monk. Declan Stewart, that is all I heard. I swear before God. Only Dr. Declan Stewart."

"Oh that won't do at all, Dante. Perhaps the Syrian can improve your recollection."

"Wait," Dante coughed, then swallowed, "the girl said something to her boy. She said 'New Zealand.' That is all I heard. The monk went to New Zealand. That was where Declan Stewart lived. That's all I know. I swear before my mother's grave that is all I know."

"That's better, Dante. Much better. Assuming it is true."

"Before God, I swear to you—"

"And you wish me to believe that you would lie to me, cheat me, take my money, and deliver me a forgery. But you would not lie to God?"

Shari adjusted the drape of his coat then turned back to the driver. "Take him to the Syrian then go to the hotel and make sure the manuscript is there as he claims. If indeed it is there, take great care with it. Bring it immediately back here to me. And make certain the Syrian knows that this one is to stay alive until I have personally confirmed that we have the original manuscript. Make sure he understands. He may take his liberties later, but not now, not until I am sure."

The driver nodded then smashed the butt of his Glock into Dante's head. The Sicilian's legs crumpled beneath him. Like a broken puppet he slumped across the hood of the gleaming black sedan.

"Do you know the words of another more famous Dante?" Shari asked his driver. "His observations are so very informative and often so very true. '*Superbia, invidia ed avarizia sono, le tre faville che hanno i cori accesi.*' Three sparks—pride, envy, and avarice—have been kindled in all hearts. Do you know the literature of the West?"

"The caliph says a man has need only of the Koran, Sayyidi."

Shari shook his head slowly. "Yes, such is the wisdom of the caliph."

The driver heaved Dante's limp body up onto this shoulder and made his way up the gangplank. Shari stepped back inside the sedan and closed the door. He lifted the handset of the phone from its cradle and quickly punched in a series of numbers.

"What resources do we have in New Zealand?" he asked, drawing deeply on his cigarette then expelling a soft blue cloud of smoke. "There is someone there I need to find, and quickly."

CHAPTER V

GHOST SHIPS BREAK
SOUTH ISLAND, NEW ZEALAND

Clouds of steam corkscrewed through the cool afternoon air as Declan filled Ibrahim's cup and then his own with fragrant black coffee. He then sat down across from Ibrahim and studied the crimson sun as it melted into the deep blue void of the Tasman Sea. For an awkward moment, they sat in silence and stared out to the sea.

Restlessly, Ibrahim adjusted the folds of his robe then rearranged the fruit in a bowl. He had spent every hour of his long journey from the chaos of Syria to the quiet of this fine green island contemplating just how he would begin. And still he wasn't sure. This deep, quiet man who had risen from the ashes of Khirbet Qumran was an enigma to him now, a stranger holed up in a soli-tary fortress in a strange land.

Trust your heart, the voice inside him said. And so, he folded his hands together, pressed his fingertips against his beard, and began.

"I have imagined this precise moment many times, Declan. I imagined where we might be when we had this talk, what I would say, and how you might respond. One would expect that after so much contemplation I should have it all worked out by now. But I don't."

A tieke glided in on the sea breeze, flapped its russet wings, then settled on the rough timber railing that separated the porch from the vast panorama of sea and sky. Its feathers glimmered in the sunlight. The pale henna and deep orange stripe that ran along its back glowed like a band of embers. Softly, the little bird began to sing.

The space around them filled with the pulsing, staccato rhythms of the bird's morning song. Ibrahim closed his eyes and surrendered himself to the sweet, lingering notes. *This is the way God intended the world to be. A place of beauty and repose. A place devoid of want and suffering. This is the world Q will bring when its secrets are revealed. The world will at last become what our Father always meant that it should be.*

The translucent image of the waxing moon joined the ebbing scarlet sun on the fabric of blue sky. A diaphanous veil of marine layer was already creeping onto land, bringing with it a chilly breeze from the south. Ibrahim breathed it in, then opened his eyes and stared at the man before him.

"So, you see, Declan, I stumble already, misdirected by so simple a thing as a song bird and a dying day. I suppose that I am nervous, my son. And to be honest, I am afraid that I may fail."

Declan gazed into the liquid canyons of Ibrahim's eyes then rubbed his hands together and wrapped them around his mug. Declan looked as if he might speak. But in the end, he offered nothing.

"I have come to tell you two important things, Declan. Or I suppose it is more accurate to say that there is one thing you must know and another which is not so important but which it would be wrong of me to withhold. The first, the thing that is not so important after all, is that I am dying."

As if it understood the language of men, the tieke fell silent. Its song vanished on the wings of the maritime wind. In its place came the echoes of waves crashing onto the rocks far below. A somber mood settled over the porch as the day melted into the sea.

Declan gazed at Ibrahim and again appeared for a moment as if he might speak. But like the tieke, he too had fallen under a spell and had lost his voice. He gently shook his head and stared down at the wisp of steam that rose from his mug.

"You must promise me that you won't grieve on my account, Declan." Ibrahim smiled, as if he were sharing news of the birth of a child or the coming of the summer after a long season of rain. "It's a blessing really. After all, I'm just a wayfarer heading home. How can I not welcome entry into my Father's mansions? How can I not cherish the freedom from this broken old body? But for my knowledge that you must now do alone what I would have helped you to do, I leave this world with no regrets or sorrow."

Declan gripped the smooth wooden arms of his chair and looked up. A deep feeling of emptiness and despair had taken hold of him and made him its captive.

"So now let me tell you the important thing, the real reason why I've invested so many of my dwindling days in search of you. I ask only that you hear me out with an open mind. Ask me anything you want. As I told you on the beach, I promise to give you every answer I have, to tell you honestly both what I know and what I don't yet know. But you must promise to hear me out. Is that a bargain you'll make with this old Palestinian? I promise you will not be disappointed."

Declan stroked the salt-and-pepper stubble of his day-old beard and looked out to sea. He filled his lungs with the cool salt air then twitched an almost imperceptible nod.

"In 1940, the Jerusalem Institute of the American Schools of Oriental Research, in partnership with the Swiss National Museum in Zurich, funded a small and entirely insignificant expedition in British Mandate Palestine. No one even noticed it. The war made sure of that. But even without the Nazis setting the world afire, I doubt anyone would have cared. The leader of the expedition was an obscure archeologist with a wooden leg, a man named Emile Zorn. Even you have never heard of him, have you?"

Declan reflected for a moment then shook his head.

"It's not surprising. He was a charlatan, a grant gypsy as they called them in those days. He'd convinced his sponsors that he'd found the house of St. Peter in Capernaum. He no doubt waved the Gospel of Matthew in front of them and with a con man's conviction sold them the romance that it was the refuge, the safe house, of the most extraordinary revolutionaries of all time—Jesus and his disciples."

Something in the way Declan cocked his head toward the monk told him he'd set the hook. He'd broken through the wall of ice and stone. He'd penetrated the first of Declan's fortifications, but he was certain there were many more yet to come.

"Then the Italians and their German allies, seeking to disrupt their enemy's lines of supply, attacked Palestine and its coastal refineries. Not surprisingly, Zorn's sponsors lost interest in his little project. After all, the entire world had turned its attention elsewhere, and the Swiss in particular had fallen under the spell of the Nazi riches stored in their vaults. And so, the excavation funding stopped."

Ibrahim removed a small briar pipe from the pocket of his woolen robe. Taking his time, so that Declan's mind might linger over the possibilities of his tale, Ibrahim struck a long wooden match and touched it to the bowl.

"It was no great loss to anyone, except Zorn, I suppose. They'd found only a few shards of ancient pottery, some sealed amphorae filled with oil for lamps, and insignificant household items. Zorn accepted his loss and prepared to move on. He crated the meager findings and sent them by truck to Beirut for trans-shipment on to the museum in Zurich. But unfortunately for Zorn, he didn't live long enough to complete that task or to undertake a new adventure. An Italian fighter strafed his tent, killing him as the crates were being taken away. So his findings vanished in the mists of war. As it turned out, Zorn's foreman sold them to a Turkish antiquities dealer in the Quartier des Arts in Beirut. The crates still remained unopened. And so they waited."

Ibrahim adjusted the pipe between his teeth, shifting it from one side of his mouth to the other. He reached down beside his chair and recovered a scuffed and scarred portfolio made of tan belting leather. He placed it on the table in front of Declan. Ibrahim intentionally let his fingers linger there a moment before reaching for his coffee. He nibbled at some fruit, then brushed the lint from his robe. The tieke flapped its wings then, arching its head, sprang into the rising winds that had come with sunset. Like a tiny colorful kite, the bird hovered between the railing and the sea.

Soon I will be like this little bird—untethered, an eternal thing unbound. Soon I will go home, Ibrahim said to himself. Gently he stroked the cracked brown leather of the portfolio, his hand a hypnotist's bauble to Declan's curious eyes.

His gaze still locked on the portfolio before him, Declan asked, "And after the Turk?"

Ibrahim smiled. Declan had at last found his voice.

"He died as we all must die. But in a most important twist of fate, he left no heirs behind him. And so his landlord, an Armenian and a patron of our order, sent his inventory, including Emile Zorn's crates, to Dier al-Shuhada. And once again they waited, lost in the shadows of a storeroom in the farthest reaches of the scriptorium. For more than fifty long years, they waited. Until the Israeli rockets sent me Amala and the boy. It was she who at last answered their call. It was she who opened the crate, who found the manuscript and the map. And so in a way, it is she who has brought me here to you."

Ibrahim pressed his hands together and stretched his legs. He rotated his head but felt nothing. With a quivering hand, he touched the muscles of his neck. The sensation was muted and irregular, registering only intermittently like a fluorescent bulb flashing on and off. "*First a loss of sensation, sporadic, unpredictable,*" the doctors had said. "*Then later, persistent. Then in the end, a single failure, total and devastating, as if a candle had been extinguished. Numbness and darkness. That is how you will know when the time has come.*"

Out of habit, Ibrahim glanced at the yellowed dial of his wrist-watch. But he already knew the time. The flickering sensations told as much. He had to hurry. He had to help Declan remember who he was. How he wished Val were there. She had a way with Declan like no one else. In her presence, all his defenses and his conceits melted away. She would have shown him the road ahead and made him understand it. She would have led him back to his destiny. But she was gone now, taken in a ball of fire. Gone and never to return.

Declan raised his mug and took a sip of coffee.

"Look, Ibrahim, I was rude when you first arrived. I don't want to be rude now. You're an old friend, and I owe you a lot. But people change. Life changes them. I'm not who I used to be. That man's dead and buried in the desert. So why don't you skip the history lesson and just tell me what this is all about. This portfolio, for example. You've been baiting me with it ever since you got here. I may have chunks of metal in my head, but I'm not a fool. So why don't you just tell me what's in it and what it has to do with me."

For a long, pregnant moment they stared at each other in silence. Then at last Ibrahim answered.

"It contains photographs."

"Okay. Photos of what?"

"A manuscript. The manuscript that Amala discovered hidden inside a sealed amphora packed in Emile Zorn's crates."

Declan leaned across the table. "And, so what's all that got to do with me?"

Ibrahim hesitated. "Surely you've guessed it already, Declan. Surely you know what I'm about to tell you. You sense it, don't you? I hear it in your voice. I see it in your eyes. You know this is about Q."

Ibrahim studied Declan's face. A dark, brooding storm had entered those liquid eyes that burned like black stars in a white sky.

"Do you understand me, Declan? *Q*. Not a rumor. Not another dead end. In that amphora that hadn't been opened in two thousand years, Amala found incontrovertible evidence that *Q* exists. And more importantly still, she found a map that leads to the place where it is hidden."

Declan rose again from his chair, turned toward the sea and placed his hands on the heavy timber rails. He leaned hard against them, pressing the full measure of his weight against them.

"Do you understand me, Declan? *Declan?*"

But Declan Stewart no longer heard him.

"Declan, I still say it's crazy for me to go to the hospital in Tel Aviv. The baby's two whole months away. And besides, there isn't any reason I can't have him right here. Women have been having children in the Judean desert for thousands of years. It would be so easy to arrange for a local doctor and a nurse, or if you insist, we could have them come down from Jerusalem. We wouldn't have to disrupt our work. We could keep the project on schedule. Besides, you need me."

"That's beside the point," Declan said, shaking his head. "First, I'm not having our son born in a caravan tent like a Bedouin. Second, it's not safe. You know that as well as I do. Even if we arranged medical care here, there's too much risk. Do you think we're the only ones looking for the manuscript? We've never been the only ones looking for it."

"But we haven't had any trouble in weeks now."

"That makes me even more nervous."

"But what about the security team the Israeli Antiquities Authority promised to send? Surely they will be here any day now. They'll set up some kind of cordon around the site. They do that sort of thing all the time."

Declan sat down on the cot beside her. "Look, Val, I asked for that team two months ago. I went straight to the top, all the way to the director's office. Smiles and promises, sure, but we both know that's all we'll ever get from them. They haven't liked this excavation from the beginning. They're scared to death we might actually find Q, and then what would they do? Hell, for all I know they're the ones who ransacked the camp the first time. They'd like nothing better than for this whole expedition to just go away."

"So we hire our own guards. Set up our own perimeter around the camp."

"With what? A university budget that's already twenty thousand dollars in the red? Half the Harvard faculty thinks my work is an embarrassment to the university as it is. Even old bin-Mahfouz sent a letter suggesting we consider shutting down for the season and come back to Cambridge. We've been over all this a thousand times. We both know that Tel Aviv is the place for you now. The baby has to be our first concern. We can't take chances. Q has been lost for two thousand years. I think Ibrahim and I are more than capable of holding things down till you're ready to come back."

"I know, I know. It's just hard. I have a premonition about this place. I can't explain it, Declan, but I feel it in my bones. That's what the Arabs say, isn't it, when they know a thing for sure but can't prove it? Something important is going to happen here. Right here, in this place. You feel it too, don't you? This time, we're close. We're so very, very close."

Declan took her hand in his and gazed into the green canyons of her eyes.

"Yes. I feel it too."

Without turning around, Declan answered him.

"Q. So that's what this visit is about. I should have known. Maybe

I did know and just didn't want to admit it."

"Yes, Declan. *Q*. Now you understand, don't you? The thing you've sought all your life. It's not only within your reach, it is within your grasp. The world is on the threshold of something truly monumental, an event unparalleled in all of human history."

Declan snorted his disdain. "You just can't let it go, can you? Maybe no one can. You're still convinced it exists. That there's a utopia somewhere out there on the horizon of mankind and that *Q* is the key to it all."

"I've never doubted it."

"Bullshit. Human life doesn't have great truths, Ibrahim. I woke up to that reality a long time ago. In the asylum, I gazed into the sun of human suffering, the chaos all around me. And at last, I saw the truth, the stark, cold, existential truth. It's all a lie. Everything. We're born, we suffer, we die. End of story."

"You sound like a man trying to convince himself of something he doesn't believe, my son."

Declan pivoted on his heel and confronted Ibrahim. "Sure. Go on. Keep telling yourself that if you want to. But you know as well as I do that even if *Q* does exist, it's only a brittle piece of crumbling parchment. It won't change anything. Not for those poor bastards in the asylum. Not for the Jews, the Christians, or the Muslims. Not even for a Palestinian like you."

Ibrahim bristled. "So that's it then? Your answer is no?"

"Answer to what? To packing my bags and heading back into the desert in search of a manuscript that has already taken everything from me? Look at me, Ibrahim! There's nothing left. I'm all hollowed out. Got it? An empty man in a stone cottage at the far corner of the world. I'm just waiting for the day the waves take me under and hold me down, because I don't have the courage to do it myself. And you? You should be ashamed, knowing all you know. You were there when it happened, and you still have the balls to come here with tales of lost crates, shattered amphorae, bullshit manuscripts and maps?"

Ibrahim placed his pipe on the table, stood up, and leaned onto his cane. Stiffly, he hobbled forward, closing the distance between himself and Declan until they were face-to-face.

"You mustn't allow your pain to blind you, Declan. Look at the fading sun there on the horizon behind you. That golden orb is more than a hundred million kilometers away from us, yet it burns so brightly that it warms our entire planet. A bit closer, we would all burn. A bit farther away, the earth would be a lifeless ball of ice. Tonight when the stars fill that glorious southern sky, gaze up into eternity. Billions of light years from here matter moves into nothingness at astonishing speeds expanding the very fabric of the universe itself.

"These are all miracles of incalculable greatness. Far more profound than water turned to wine or Lazarus brought out of his tomb. That we are even here, now, in this place and in this time, is a miracle so improbable that anything I believe about Q pales in comparison. Don't be afraid to see what you see, Declan. Don't be afraid to believe what your heart knows to be true. You know that is what Val would have said. She would have placed her hand atop yours, looked into your eyes, and told you the same thing I am telling you now."

Declan slammed his hand into the railing. "Don't lecture me, Ibrahim. I'm forty-five years old. I've made choices and paid prices. Say what you've come to say. But no lectures and no myths. No promises that can't be kept. And if you respect me at all, you'll leave Val out of this and never speak her name again."

Ibrahim brought his hands together as he did when he prayed.

"As you wish, Declan. I'll make my request, then I'll leave you in peace. I have come to ask you to return to Dier al-Shuhada with me. I've come to ask you to do what my illness makes it impossible for me to do. I've come to ask you to take the map, unravel the secrets I can't decipher, follow its signs, and set Q free from its bondage. I've come to ask you to bring light to a world lost in the darkness."

Declan shook his head. "Look me in the eye, Ibrahim. Tell me that you really believe that Jesus Christ is coming back one day and that an ancient piece of sheepskin is the trigger for his return. Look me in the eyes and tell me that you really believe all that."

"Does what I believe really matter so much, Declan? Why not just focus on what it is that I know? I have proof that Q exists, that it came into the possession of the Apostle Paul, and that he went to extraordinary lengths to ensure its safety. Precisely how all that came to pass, I don't know. Perhaps Paul stole the parchment while he was still a persecutor in the service of the Temple. Perhaps the Damascene who healed his blindness gave it to him or perhaps it came into his possession during his time in Arabia. Maybe even God delivered it to him divinely. Like my beliefs, none of that should really matter to you. What is important is that I have a map that will lead you to Q. It doesn't matter whether you share my vision that the end of time and the beginning of eternity is upon us. I am not even asking you to believe in God if that is no longer your conviction. I'm only asking you to decipher the map and recover the manuscript. You can decide for yourself what you believe."

Declan walked back over to the table. He picked up his mug, held it for a moment, then slammed it down. Broken pottery hurtled through the air, tear drops of black liquid scattering like rain.

"Riddles and myths, Ibrahim! It's always the same with the desert. It consumes a man's life with riddles and myths."

Slowly, Ibrahim approached Declan and placed his hand atop his shoulders. "Declan, why are you so afraid to imagine? You asked me your questions, and I gave you my answers. Allow me now to ask my own. Do you really believe that the universe in its all vastness and its diversity is only a cosmic accident? Do you honestly, deep in your heart, believe there is no purpose to the clockwork of it all? And what if Q really is as I believe it to be? Have you considered that possibility at all? What if the prophecy is real? What if the suffering of the world is at its end? Wouldn't you take that chance? Who among us has never dreamed of such a thing? Who among us would turn away even if there is only the faintest glimmer of a chance that it is true? And if I'm wrong, what then? You still will have made the most important archaeological discovery since the beginning of time. If nothing else, you will have closed a chapter of your life once and for all."

Stillness settled over the porch. There was only the sound of the crashing waves far below.

At last, Declan raised his head and turned to face the monk. "Look, Ibrahim. I'm sorry. I'm all spent. So let's not argue. Let's just end this now. We can have a nice dinner together. You can stay here a few days if you want to. Enjoy the sea and the countryside, then turn around and head back to Syria, assuming you can even get back before Assad falls and the place descends into chaos. You've said what you came to say. I listened, as I promised I would. So each of us has done what he had to do. No looking back over our shoulders. No regrets. But the answer is still no. I don't care if you have a manuscript. I don't care if you have a map. I'm not in the business any more. I'm just a surfer who wants to be left alone on his cliff above the sea."

Ibrahim placed his cane on the table and returned to his chair. "If that is your answer, I will respect it. God works in mysterious ways. Perhaps this is how it was meant to be. In any event, I no longer have the manuscript. That is why I have brought only photos. It was stolen by a thief parading as a restorer. But by the grace of God, I still have the map hidden safely away in the scriptorium. At least for now. But we both know it is just a matter of time before they send someone else for it. Someone else always comes."

The tieke flapped its wings and vanished into the darkening sky. Ibrahim's words made the final connection in Declan's mind. He walked toward the rail and studied the high ridge beyond the broad, undulating field of flax. He no longer seemed to be interested in what Ibrahim was saying.

"The wind's been queer all day, blowing offshore, not on," Declan said as he studied the ridge beyond the meadow. "But there's still no way for exhaust to make it up here from the road. Did you have a car wait for you or tell him to come back and get you?"

"No. The driver dropped me at the foot of the road and then returned to Graves Bay. He'll be back in the morning."

"I bet if you look in the canyon beyond that ridge you'll find a truck and someone in it watching us. Hand me the binoculars in the basket beside you."

Ibrahim recovered a battered pair of Steiner 10 x 40s from the wicker creel and passed them to Declan.

"Who else knows you've come here, Ibrahim? Who else knows about the manuscript and the map?"

"Only Amala and the Brothers."

"You're missing a few. The man who stole your manuscript knows. And whoever is behind that ridge knows. You said they always send someone. Well, my guess is they already have."

"But that's impossible."

Declan placed the field glasses to his eyes, studying the ridge. "No one comes on my land, ever. And there's no way to just wander off the main road and end up here. And even if you somehow managed to, you wouldn't sit behind a ridge with your engine idling. You'd come up to the house and ask for help. This is about Q, about what's in that portfolio."

Declan placed the binoculars on the table and went inside the cottage. When he returned, he had a 9 millimeter Beretta subcompact, three ammo clips, and a box of hollow point cartridges.

"What are you doing, my son?"

"I'm doing what the desert taught me to do. I'm being careful. I'm being smart."

Ibrahim pressed the palms of his hands together and closed his eyes. "But we can phone the authorities. Allow them to handle this."

"Why'd you fly all the way here from Syria, Ibrahim? You did that because I don't have a phone or an address. It's nearly two hours from here to Graves Bay to get the police station. That makes four hours round trip. Besides, what makes you think whoever is out there is just going to let us get in my truck and drive off?"

"But the gun, Declan. Surely that's not called for."

"What don't you understand, Ibrahim? Whoever's out there has followed you all the way from Syria. Nobody does that. I made the mistake of underestimating an enemy once. I swore I would never make it again."

Declan hastily slipped on a pair of oiled leather boots and laced them up. "There's a shotgun beside the fireplace inside my bedroom. It's loaded and ready to go. Three shot pump. Aim it at anything within thirty meters of you and you can't miss. Pump the handle, fire again. Get it now and wait here."

Declan finished pressing the cartridges into place, then, with the palm of his hand, popped the clip into the butt of the Beretta. He loaded the remaining clips then slipped them into the top pocket of his shirt.

"I'll come back for you after I find out what's out there. In the meantime, stay out of sight. If for any reason I'm not back in half an hour, take the shotgun, crank up the truck, and see if you can make it back into town. The keys are in the ignition. Keep it in low gear or it'll stall out. Follow the dirt road to the highway, then make your way north to Graves Bay. Find the sheriff and bring him back here. Tell him to bring weapons and men."

Declan slipped off the porch, rushed past the yellow kowhais, and waded into the thick brush of manukas. He was headed for the tall stand of flax and the smell of diesel fumes beyond.

CHAPTER VI

SYRIAN COAST, MEDITERRANEAN SEA
LATITUDE 34° N-LONGITUDE 35° E

"Hurry Mahmoud, finish it!"

The Syrian stood on the forecastle deck below the conning tower, his image floating in and out of the shadows. His voice was harsh and guttural, snapping and snarling like a hungry dog.

"As you command." The long grey ash of the boy's cigarette broke off and drifted down onto the stained red fabric of his t-shirt. Groaning, he lifted the corpse, pressed its torso against the railing, and readjusted his grip. The body was wrapped in rusted iron chains that clattered and clanged as they bounced along the gunwale.

The boy shifted the dwindling stub of his cigarette from one side of his mouth to the other. Then he shifted the angle of his hands and took hold of the chains where they crossed the body in an X pattern. Like wet paint, blood covered the metal and made it difficult for the boy to take a firm grip. A cloud of spent blue smoke streamed from his nostrils as he worked his hands under the chain. He took another deep inhalation, then mustering all the strength in his back and legs, he heaved the corpse up onto the ship's rail.

For a moment, the lifeless body teeter-tottered, threatening to fall back down onto the deck. But the boy knew he couldn't let that happen, not with the Syrian looking on. Decisively and with a hard, quick thrust, he pushed the load over the rail and watched as it slid down the white iron ribs of the yacht and disappeared into the sea. A door in the face of the waves opened, then just as quickly, closed again. Dante's small but important role in the quest for Q had come to an end. The boy snatched the stub from his lips and cast it into the sea.

The red conning tower light passed behind the Syrian. For a fleeting moment his shadow covered the boy in darkness.

"Now get below and clean the cell. There must be no traces of blood. Nothing. All must be in order before Beirut."

The boy wiped his bloody hands on the tail of his shirt. Then he drew a fresh cigarette from the crumpled pack and nodded once in the Syrian's direction. He struck a match, took a puff, then disappeared through the open hatchway and down the ladder.

For a long moment, the Syrian studied the surface of the sea. He never took chances if he didn't have to. That was how he had managed to stay alive so long. But the boy had done his job well. He'd wrapped the chains tightly. Soon the body would be at the bottom of the sea. There would be no trail for anyone to follow.

When he had satisfied himself with the result, the Syrian pivoted on his heel and strode swiftly toward Shari's cabin. Out of habit, he touched the razor sharp *jambiya* tucked into the scabbard on his belt. Only moments before, it had been wet with the Sicilian's blood. Something stirred in the Syrian's loins as he recalled how smoothly the knife had slid across the flesh and made the Sicilian cry like a woman. A shiver of excitement ran down his spine. It was the electricity of power. Power over men. Power over life and death. The power of the strong to subjugate the weak. The power of the knife.

But in his mind's eye, it was not the face of the Sicilian he saw as he drew the jambiya's blade across that throat. It was the Persian's. And in that moment of recollection mixed with fantasy, the sensations came again, but infinitely more powerful and fulfilling.

For the time being, he must let the Persian enjoy his dominion. He had the caliph's confidence. That the quest for the relic and the smoke of the opium pipe had blinded him was irrelevant. But soon all that would change. In time, the Syrian would find the Persian's weakness, exploit it, then return to his rightful place beside the man who would be the Mahdi. And when he did, the Persian would know the wondrous agony of the ragged blade as it scudded across his flesh in a thousand cuts. Then he would simply disappear forever into the eternal night, just as Dante had disappeared into the sea.

CHAPTER VII

GHOST SHIPS BREAK
SOUTH ISLAND, NEW ZEALAND

Declan emerged from the thick stand of manukas into the open meadow of tall toitoi grass. Dropping first to his knees, then to his chest, he crawled belly-to-the-ground toward the ridge.

Adrenaline surged within him as he made his way cautiously, quietly, through the sea of tall, dry grass. Nothing escaped his senses. He smelled the faint aroma of the sea and tasted the fragments of salt that lingered in the air. The muffled crack of a dry cabbage tree branch snapping underneath him sounded like a cannon shot in his ears. Even his skin was alive, the edges and contours of each rock and pebble beneath him registering precisely on the map inside his head. For the first time since his long, dark season of exile had begun, Declan Stewart felt alive.

Night had fallen, but the soft silver light of the moon, haunting and surreal, cast an eerie glow over the crests and canyons. He'd come nearly two hundred meters from the cottage. The crest of the ridge was now within earshot. Mingled with the sounds of the wind and rustling leaves, he heard voices and smelled the familiar scent of diesel that had first alerted him to the intruders' presence. Warily, he raised his head and peeked over the summit into the dark, vacuous hollow beyond. Halfway down the other side, beneath a groaning black beech tree, he could just make out a battered black SUV, its engine softly purring.

Then something moved to his right. Instantly, he froze. His heartbeat quickened, the breath coming in short, fast sips of air. Cautiously, Declan rotated his head toward the sound of the movement. From the corner of his eye, he saw first a shadow, then a discernible image. It was a man on the far side of the ridge, carrying a rifle and moving slowly across the open field back toward the vehicle.

How many were there? Declan quickly worked the math. He had twenty-seven hollow-tipped rounds among the three ammo clips. If he was smart and used them to their full advantage, he could handle at least six, maybe more. But first he'd need cover, and he needed it fast.

The intruders had set themselves up between two unused stone storage sheds along the backside slope of the ridge, with the SUV just behind them. If he could make his way unnoticed across the meadow, he would come up beside the northern shed. From there he would have both cover and an effective vantage point to assess the strength and numbers of his adversaries. He'd seen at least one weapon. He'd have to be careful, bide his time, then move when the opportunity presented itself.

"*Be patient,*" the voice inside his head whispered. And so Declan settled back down beneath the blanket of grass and listened through the sounds of the night. He tucked the Beretta into the gap between his belt and the small of his back. The sparse, fast moving clouds made the moonlight unpredictable. It faded in and out, casting the world around him in alternating windows of illumination and darkness. But the tall stands of flax and the manukas would give him

cover. Like artillery netting, they would make for a natural camouflage and obscure his movements. That might be enough to allow
him to make it to the shed undetected.

The sound of voices, louder this time, stopped him cold. The rustling of wind through the stalks of dry grass turned their words to
indecipherable gibberish, but they were unmistakably moving closer.
Declan flattened his chest against the ground and oriented his head
toward the sound of voices that came from the car. He closed his
eyes and forced himself to focus. Bit by bit, a comprehensible whole
began to emerge. One voice farther away, stationary. A second voice
growing progressively louder, coming closer by incremental measures to Declan's hiding place. They seemed to be bickering, but the
words themselves were lost in the sounds of gusting wind, rustling
leaves, and stirring grass.

"He could only discern bits and pieces. The rhythm of the speech
was steady and paced. The exaggerated diphthongs suggested Yemenis. *But what would Yemenis have to do with Q?* he asked himself.
Yemen was a dictatorship stranded in a dark era of illiteracy and
tribal feuds. There were no scholars there, not even treasure hunters—no one who would have ever heard of *Q*, much less come after
it.

Then the voices stopped. Declan pressed his head to the ground,
squeezing down into the moist soil. He could feel the vibration of
footsteps beneath him, the heavy thud of boots in a metrical cadence
of staccato movements. And with each step, the vibration grew
stronger. Someone was walking directly toward him.

Declan gradually moved his right hand toward his belt and
grasped the Beretta. Gently, he wrapped his fingers around the butt
of the gun. Beads of sweat ran down from this scalp and pooled in
the hollows of his shoulders. He'd been in firefights before. He'd
even shot at men. But he'd never killed a man. Never pulled the
trigger and watched one die. Could he do it? Could he kill a man? He
clenched his jaw and drew the Beretta. He sensed that he was about

to find out.

In that brief moment of self-reflection, Declan lost consciousness of the sounds around him. His heart raced as he realized that he no longer heard the footsteps or felt their vibrations in the hard ground beneath him. Now he had no idea where his adversary was.

Declan again forced himself to quiet his mind and focus only on the sounds around him. He heard the rustling of manukas in the quickening night breeze, the idling of an engine, and in the far distance, the muffled sound of crashing waves. Then only ten meters ahead of him, something new. A sound that he hadn't heard before, the splattering of liquid striking stone.

"I'm taking a piss, you son of a dog," the intruder groaned in Arabic, directing his words back over his shoulder.

Every muscle in Declan's body tensed. The man was so close that Declan could hear every word, clearly and precisely. He had been right. Yemenis. But that was of little comfort now. He tried not to breathe as he squeezed the Beretta tightly in the palm of his sweating hand

"*Waa faqri*," the Yemeni muttered, cursing. With his free hand, he slung the ancient Kalashnikov over his shoulder and redirected the stream of urine toward the grass and away from his boots.

"Get ready, Ahmed," he grunted half-heartedly as he finished relieving himself. "I'm tired of waiting. I'll miss my dinner if we don't get this done soon. This watching is a big waste of time. Three years we sit and wait for jihad. What do we get? We get a shack in the middle of bloody nowhere. We're errand boys, Ahmed. Nothing but errand boys. I came for action, not to look through binoculars and make a report. I say let's kill the tall one now, then we use the knife on the monk after he tells us where it is." He shook himself twice then spit. He zipped his pants and shifted the rifle back round. But he paused, studying the irregular shadows that ran across the high grass in front of him.

"What the—*Ahmed*!"

Declan knew instantly that he had been discovered. He had to act or die.

Now! the voice inside Declan's head screamed.

Every neuron in his body fired. Instantly, he sprang to his knees. He thrust the pistol forward and took aim. But just as he commanded his finger to squeeze the trigger, Declan saw the face of his adversary and he went tumbling through space and time. He was no longer on the ridge. He was in the deserts south of Ein Gedi, bleeding on the sand, deaf from the acoustic shock of the explosions, covered in drops of aviation fuel, his jacket on fire, his head pounding like the thunder of great weapons in war.

The shrapnel inside his head burned him, as if molten steel had been injected through a needle straight into his skull. He blinked his eyes and the scene shifted again. But something still wasn't right. The pace, the rhythm was out of kilter. Like a movie reel run in slow motion, every action and reaction registered at quarter speed. The boy in front of him fumbled with his Kalashnikov. His hand slipped slowly around the butt, his finger sliding into the trigger guard. Declan counted the movements until he sensed it was time to act.

He squeezed the trigger.

In a flashing series of still images, a hollow lead cylinder tumbled through space then disappeared into the man's chest. Gradually, a red dot appeared at the center of his stained white fleece. Incrementally, the circle grew and grew until at last it covered his whole chest and erupted in a great ragged oval of red. In rigid mechanical increments, the man fell backwards over his own heels. His finger slowly clamped down on the trigger of the Kalashnikov. Bullets rose haphazardly into the cool night air and disappeared into the darkness in a wide ranging arc over the meadow.

Declan squeezed the trigger again.

The slug tumbled in slow motion through a seemingly infinite expanse of space. This time it struck the center of the man's forehead. A diminutive black hole appeared. Then gradually it too turned to a ragged oval of red. The man dropped in faltering stages to the ground. In the milky light of a lover's moon, the remnants of urine that clung to the bushes smoked softly, their steam rising into the cool night air.

"*Nawaz! Nawaz!*" the angry voice roared like the harsh winds of a winter gale.

Declan's perception of time shifted again. Events no longer ran at quarter speed. Now they raced forward in double time. The world around him blurred. And then he was back on his feet, running. He was in an open field of high grass, the stone shed thirty meters away.

A bearded Yemeni with an assault rifle charged into the bush. As he sprinted toward his fallen comrade, Declan streaked across the meadow, closing the gap between him and safety. The intruder raised his assault rifle to his shoulder and quickly took aim. A blistering spray of gunfire erupted at Declan's feet. Shards of granite and clouds of dust spewed into the damp night air. A sharp pain ran from the toe of Declan's right foot up into his groin. He'd been hit.

A fresh surge of adrenaline coursed through him like the current of a thundering river. Rotating his torso toward the shed, Declan extended his arm behind him and rapid-fired without breaking stride. He emptied the clip. Automatically, he pressed the discharge button, snatched a new clip from his shirt pocket, popped it in, and racked the slide.

From the corner of his eye, Declan saw the shooter drop unevenly to one knee. Had he hit him, or was he merely positioning himself for a better shot? It was impossible to know.

Declan was close now. Only a few more meters and he'd have the safety of the stone walls to shelter him from the gunfire. He took two more giant steps then dove head first into the shadows. He hit the ground hard and rolled into the doorway as the earth behind him erupted in a swirling cloud of dust and stone.

"*Caliph Akbar!*"

Then absolute silence.

Declan's hands were numb and quivering, but for the moment he was safe. He looked down to see what damage the bullet had done to his foot. The front of his boot was gone but miraculously his toes were all still there. The shell had scrapped the skin and nicked the muscle, but nothing more.

The bearded figure with the Kalashnikov had vanished into the moon's maze of shadow and light. He could be anywhere. But at least Declan had the advantage of a number of clear sight lines now and a building to shield him. The moonlight, which only moments before had given him away, was now his ally. It illuminated all the areas he needed to see from the relative safety of the shadows. Now all he could do was wait.

As he scanned the horizon, Declan began a systematic analysis of his situation. He knew that one man was dead. The second, too, might be dead, the hollow-tipped rounds having flattened out and plowed a gaping hole through him. He might also have dodged Declan's fire and was in possession of his faculties and weapons. Possibility three: he was wounded, which might make him more dangerous still. Or four: regardless of his status, he was not alone, in which case the danger could not be calculated without more information.

The sound of a shotgun blast shattered the silence of the night.

Ibrahim! Instantly, Declan pivoted toward the ridge.

"For God's sake, get down! Get down! Get—"

The high-pitched report of the Kalashnikov smothered Declan's words. *Rat-tat-tat. Rat-tat-tat.* Declan turned back toward the sound. The muzzle flash came from a crease of shadow beside the SUV. Instinctively Declan sprang from the shed. Diving head first into the grass, he fired three rounds directly into the shadows from which the flash of the Kalashnikov had come. He heard a groan then the clank of a rifle falling to the ground. Then silence once again.

Rising slowly, Declan eased his head up above the top of the grass, the Beretta thrust forward, his arms locked and pointing toward the narrow crease of shadow. He waited five seconds then hurriedly made his way toward Ibrahim, advancing in a sideways motion, his body and weapon still pointing in the direction of the muzzle flash.

Ibrahim lay on his side at the top of the ridge, dark blood seeping from a gaping hole underneath his left arm. Red rivulets glimmered in the moonlight. Declan took a breath and lowered his gun.

"You fool, you crazy old fool. I told you to wait. To wait, dammit! Why the hell didn't you listen?" He placed his finger against Ibrahim's carotid artery. The pulse was still strong. That was good. But he needed medical attention and he needed it fast. Declan worked his hand under the crop of white hair and gently raised Ibrahim's head. A ribbon of blood ran from his pale thin lips down his cheek and disappeared beneath his robes.

"Why?" Declan uttered, shaking his head. "Why didn't you listen to me? Why didn't you do what I said?"

"I heard the gunshots. You were alone. You needed help." Ibrahim's words were wet and frothy as blood mixed with air inside him. "You are more important than you know. My part is done. All that matters now is you."

"Quiet. Don't move. We'll get you out of here and back to Graves Bay. Just hold on. All you have to do is hold on."

"I should have known you would be fine, Declan. Someone watches over you even now. Someone who will guide your steps and show you the way."

Declan slipped his thigh under Ibrahim's head. With the edge of his crumpled bandana, he mopped the beads of sweat from his brow. Then he took the old man's hand in his and squeezed gently.

"The ones who sent these men will send others. They will go to the monastery for the map. If I should not make it, Declan, you must protect Amala and Issa. They will be in danger. You must save Amala and the boy. Promise me."

Declan nodded.

"Do what you will about *Q*. Only you can decide."

"Listen, we have to get out of here. I have to get you back to the truck. You need a doctor."

Declan stashed the Beretta in his belt and lifted Ibrahim up into his arms. Then in long, purposeful strides, he sprinted across the field to the old Holden Ute parked in the drive. Hurriedly, he pulled the door open and placed Ibrahim inside. Together they vanished into the night.

In the distance beneath the faltering branches of a decaying karaka tree, a wounded man stirred. The warm pool of blood beside him smelled of sweat and damp earth. He had been hit twice, once in the abdomen by a bullet and once in the thigh by a spray of shotgun pellets.

He didn't know how much time he had, but he knew what he must do. He stripped his belt from his pants and made a tourniquet for his leg. Then drawing the pistol from its holster beneath his arm, he struggled to his feet and slipped behind the wheel of the SUV. Shifting into gear, he eased along the ridge and headed back toward the dirt and gravel road that led to the highway.

וַיִּדְעָלְבְּמוּ וּדִי־לַע הָיְהָנ לְ

יֲחוָיה֫וּב הָיְהָנ רְשָׁא־לְכ הָיְ

CHAPTER VIII

MEDITERRANEAN SEA
LATITUDE 34° N–LONGITUDE 35° E

In the ashen light of his oak-paneled stateroom, Shari sat alone. On the desk before him lay the most beautiful, the most perfect, and the most valuable manuscript he had ever seen—the final epistle of the Apostle Paul.

For another man and under other circumstances, that epistle alone would have been enough. It would have satisfied his quest for treasure. At auction it would command tens of millions of euros. On the black market of the antiquities trade, who could say? Eight figures was not out of the question. But what was a mere fortune when measured against the value of Q? Shari leaned back in his chair and smiled. How Emile Zorn would have laughed to discover that what had slipped through his fingers so many years ago had at last found its way into the hands of the little Persian boy who'd clung to him like lint. Zorn would have told him to sell and be done, but he wouldn't have meant it. The manuscript was half the puzzle. Now he needed the rest. To find the greater treasure still, to find Q, he would need the map.

It had been a long road spanning many decades. And there had been many sponsors and many false turns since Emile Zorn had first planted the seeds of Shari's desire. Most had been dead ends or, at best, way stations along the road of his quest. Then one bright spring day in Beirut, destiny had at last grown impatient and steered him into the camp of the caliph. Suddenly, the prospect of finding Q became infinitely more real. The goal seemed not only closer, but indeed imminent. But in the quest for Q, time was never linear. It moved in fits and starts. Days passed, then decades, then back two steps and forward one. And so even armed with the caliph's limitless wealth, power, and resources of a very special kind, the quest for Q had consumed another twenty years.

The legless prophet would have proved too dangerous for most. His fanaticism made him paranoid. And his paranoia made him lethal. The opium he consumed from morning till night and the visions it spawned only heightened the peril. But Shari had learned well from Emile Zorn. He, like his mentor before him, had mastered the art of manipulation. And so, like a grand puppeteer, he had taken the measure of his eccentric sponsor and plumbed the depths of his character. He knew his strengths and his flaws. He knew what buttons to push. And above all, he knew his passions and his desires.

Shari smiled as he took a sip of scarlet Merlot from the delicate crystal stem. He tapped the remote control. The cello of Yo-Yo Ma rose to a rhythmic crescendo. He closed his eyes and for a moment allowed himself to return to the Royal Albert Hall. He'd been dressed in a smoking jacket and supple leather pumps, with a private box, seated alone. As the music filled the auditorium, he drifted into that place of infinite peace all the power and wealth of Q would one day bestow upon him. Few men better appreciated the beauty and serenity of wealth well spent. The deprivation and hardships of his youth, it seemed, had taught him well.

A heavy knock on the cabin door wakened him from his reverie.

Shari opened his eyes, placed the manuscript inside the box, and removed his white archivist's gloves.

"Enter."

The door opened with a crisp, military snap. An inverted reflection of the Syrian glimmered in the polished crystal of the wine glass. Shari suppressed a frown. His quest for Q required him to deal with many vulgar and crude men, men with small minds and large egos. But the worst among them was the Syrian. He was the oldest, most respected and most feared of the caliph's fanatical warriors. If the rumors were to be believed, he had answered the call of jihad at thirteen and come of age in a dozen dangerous lands from the Khyber Pass to the Sudan. By twenty he'd killed as many men and become a master of military tactics, explosives, hand-to-hand combat, treachery, and torture. And now, at thirty-two, the Syrian might easily have been mistaken for fifty-two. Stooped, swarthy, and scarred, his physical appearance was the visible expression of all that he had become. He seemed to Shari a sponge that had absorbed the violence and bloodshed he'd encountered and incorporated them into the very substance of his being. Shari reminded himself that when the time came, he mustn't forget that this one was nimble and shrewd. This one, above all the others, would prove extremely difficult to eliminate.

"Forgive me, Sayyidi."

In the background, the supple strains of the cello rose again, but this time not quite so loudly. The Syrian bowed and waited for him to reply.

"Please come in. You're always welcome, Commander." Shari removed the half-moon reading glasses from the high bridge of his twisted nose and placed them atop the box.

"Do you know this piece, Commander? Can you not see the images the composer paints with sound? Are you not swept away?"

"Forgive me, Sayyidi. I am only a warrior in the caliph's army."

Shari paused as he noticed a stain of blood on the Syrian's *jalaba*.

Crude men and crude actions. They were part of the price of *Q*.

"Such a tragedy that rare beauty should pass so easily in the night and not be appreciated for what it is. Why is there no music in the *madrassas*, Commander?" Shari shook his head quietly, then, raising his glass, tested the bouquet of the wine.

"I do not know, Sayyidi."

Shari touched a button on the remote control. The amber tones of the strings vanished and in their place came the humming vibrations of a ship gliding across a windless sea.

"You've missed a spot. I do so wish that you and your men would wash away the blood before entering my chamber."

The Syrian clenched his jaw, but said nothing. Instead, he bowed in feigned apology.

"Not to worry. But you will remember next time, will you not? I'm certain that you will. In any event, I gather from the stain that you've put the matter to rest?"

"Yes, Sayyidi. His body is no longer on board."

"Thank you. But to be honest, Dante doesn't interest me now. His contribution to our endeavor is in the past. You and I, we must look ahead. We must go and take what dear Dante promised but failed to bring us. We must have the map. Time is short, Commander. The caliph awaits."

"It will take a few days, but no more, Sayyidi. We will come to the monastery by night. If what the caliph seeks is there, we will recover it."

"And the Jew, what of him?"

"All is arranged as you have ordered. You need only give the command."

"Excellent, Commander. Make it so. There must be no delay."

"*Insha'Allah*, it shall be as you have ordered."

Shari slowly lifted the silk square from the pocket of his smoking jacket and polished the lenses of his spectacles. It was a pointless habit, but the simplicity of the repetitive motion of a mindless endeavor comforted him.

"We dock at Antiyas at dawn. When I conclude my visit with the caliph, I'll meet you at Bi'ral Ulayyaniyah. Shall we say three days? Will you have the map and the Jew by then?"

"It shall be so, Sayyidi."

"Good." Shari nodded. "In three days we shall add the map and the Jew to our resources. Then it's a merely a matter of time until we have the relic. But remember, Commander, neither delay nor failure is an option in the service of the caliph."

"I have served the caliph long, Sayyidi. It is understood."

The Syrian touched his hand to his heart, then to his knife. He bowed from the waist, pivoted on his heel, and departed. Shari tucked the silk cloth back into the top pocket of his silk jacket and clicked the remote. The aural incense of strings and woodwinds once again filled the room.

Shari closed his eyes, took a deep breath, then leisurely released it. He contemplated for a while the immeasurable challenges and not inconsiderable dangers that lay ahead of him. In time, he would have to arrange an accident for the Syrian. But for now, he would have to endure his coarseness and vulgarity. He had a further role to play before his usefulness would be at an end.

But what of Declan Stewart? he asked himself. Shari didn't like surprises, and most assuredly the second coming of Declan Stewart was a surprise of rare dimension. Why had the old monk gone after him, he wondered? Why Declan Stewart and to what end?

When the movement ended, a shroud of stillness draped itself around the cabin. The only sounds that remained were the gentle lapping of the waves against the hull and a faint voice inside Shari's head that whispered softly, *Declan Stewart . . . how very extraordinary.*

וְיָדְעֲלַבְמוּ וְדִי־לַע הָיֶהְנ לַ

יֹחּ וְיָה וּב הָיֶהְנ רְשָׁא־לְכ הָיֶ

CHAPTER IX

PAPAROA HIGHWAY,
SOUTH ISLAND, NEW ZEALAND

Declan jammed his foot on the accelerator and sped into the darkness.

"Hang in there. Just keep pressing down on the cloth. It'll staunch the bleeding."

Declan hit the brakes as the Ute skidded around the curve. The front tires slipped off the pavement and ran onto the gravel shoulder. He tightened his grip on the wheel and slewed into the skid. Regaining control, Declan guided the truck back onto the rugged asphalt road. Again he jammed the accelerator. He was in a race against time, and he knew it.

"Find a place to pull over, Declan." Ibrahim gritted his teeth. With his free hand, he slid the portfolio onto the console between them.

"No time. We've got to get you to a doctor and the nearest one's in Graves Bay."

"We both know I'll never make Graves Bay, Declan. Find a safe place to pull over so we can talk. There is much you need to know, and I have little enough time as it is. Get us off the road and into shelter. Then all you need to do is listen."

Declan bit down hard on his lower lip. He knew that Ibrahim was right; they would never make it to town. It was too far and there wasn't enough time. And even if they did, Ibrahim's odds of survival were a million to one.

At the next bend in the road, Declan slowed the car then steered a hard left. He disappeared behind a stand of tall kauri trees and slipped onto a nearly invisible thread of winding loose gravel. Two minutes later he brought the Ute to a stop on a rugged butte above a hidden cove beneath the jagged cliffs of Paparoa.

Ibrahim slowly opened his eyes. "Look inside the portfolio, Declan, and thank God for Amala. Without her photos, the manuscript would be lost. Q would be lost."

Declan switched on the cabin light and quickly thumbed through the stack of photographs.

"There's no photo of a map."

"Forgive me, Declan. There isn't one. That was my trump card, you see. In case you faltered. To see the map, my son, you must go to Dier al-Shuhada. But destiny it seems has made my little ruse unnecessary. Now you must go in any event. You promised me you would, if not for Q then for Amala and little Issa."

Declan stared at the blood stained cloth. "Enough talk. Here, take a sip of this water." He lifted the crumpled plastic bottle to Ibrahim's lips, but the old priest shook his head.

"No one knows better than I, Declan, how much you've sacrificed. Forgive me, son. Had it been within my power, I would have left you in your exile. But that isn't the will of God."

Declan struggled against his emotions. He curled his lower lip over his teeth and bit down on it. Above them a restless moon troubled the western horizon. Below them the waves marched inexorably toward the guardian boulders then vanished into the darkness.

"Q is like opium. You know that, don't you, Ibrahim? It's not the parchment itself. It's the promises it makes. The promise that there really is a God and that all our suffering isn't wasted. That's the most potent opium of all. That's why no one who seeks Q can ever really be free of it."

"God calls men in the moments of their greatest despair, Declan. I am only the messenger. It is not I who calls you to your destiny. It is your Father in Heaven."

Declan slammed his hands on the steering wheel. He wished Ibrahim had never come. He wished that he could wave his hand, and like a conjurer in a circus, erase all that his coming had wrought. He wanted the theater of his life to be bare and unencumbered again. He could not, must not, allow Q back in. It would destroy everything he had worked so very hard to build up from the ashes the desert had left behind.

"Declan, search inside yourself. You know that even now, here in the emptiness of this land, after sacrificing all to the quest for Q, you still want it to be true. You still want to believe."

Ibrahim let go of the bloodied cloth and touched Declan's arm. "Take my hand, son. Let me feel the warmth of your skin before I die." Declan took Ibrahim's hand in his.

"You may think that I've grown delusional in the winter of my life, that my wounds and my illness play tricks with my consciousness. But I have seen the future in a vision. Do you still believe in God, Declan?"

Declan didn't answer. With his bandana, he wiped the sweat from Ibrahim's brow.

"Well if not God, then in evil? Do you believe that evil is real, that the djinn walk among us and cause the suffering of the world? Evil does exist, Declan. The djinn are real, and you must not underestimate the powers at their command. Even now dark forces drive toward a different destiny for the world. They seek Q for their own purposes, their own ambitions. And only you have the power to stop them."

Ibrahim coughed. A thin trail of blood oozed from the corner of his lips.

"An angel has spoken to me as clearly as I speak to you now. She has shown me the future, or at least fragments of it. The great awakening *is* upon us, Declan. Like Moses, I will not live to see it, but I know that you are to be the awakener. You will not only discover the window to the divine that you have always sought. You will be the first to pass through it, my son."

Ibrahim lifted his head, as if he had something more to say, but the words would not come. Then he closed his eyes and slumped back into Declan's lap. His breathing had stopped.

For a long moment, Declan sat in the darkness and cried. Like the gentle rain that comes in from the sea, his tears fell without sound, large clear drops cascading down the tanned plane of his face. Then, for the first time since he'd buried Valkyre, he whispered a prayer.

In the black hours before dawn, Declan buried Ibrahim on the high cliff above the sea where the rugged canyons of Paparoa fall away into the ocean. He buried him shallow, the way he'd buried Val's ashes, so that the sun, the rain, and the sound of the waves could reach him. Before placing him in the ground, Declan removed the rosary of onyx and silver the old monk had clenched in his fist. He'd take that with him to Dier al-Shuhada. He would give it to the boy.

How long would it take the assailants to return? he wondered. How long before the masters who sent boys posing as assassins would send more behind them to tie up the loose ends? And how long before they would strike the monastery and take the map? Declan closed his eyes and rubbed the crescent scar. He had to find a way into Syria now and somehow to make it without a visa past the checkpoints and the army and all the chaos of dictatorship in the throes of revolution. He'd find a way. He always did.

In the distance, storm clouds gathered on the western sky. Big waves were building, the kind that should only have come in winter. The kind that took a man and his board and drove them straight to the bottom of the reef. The kind that dragged them over the jagged stones while ten tons of water came crashing down like boulders on them. The kind that took a man's breath and, if he wasn't careful, his life. The kind Declan prayed one day might plunge him into the peace and tranquility of eternal nothingness.

Unexpectedly, everything in Declan's life had become infinitely complex. The simplicity of his daily rituals and his routine had vanished into the night. There would be no more placid sunrises with the waves rising at his back. No more freedom from the madness of men. Not for a while at least. Not until he had fulfilled his promise and found his way back. If he had any shot at all of making that happen, his only chance was to run as hard and as fast as he could straight into the storm and hope that at the end of it all, he could find his way home.

Declan knew what he had to do, but he didn't know if he had the strength to do it. This couldn't become about Q. It mustn't be about Q. He couldn't let that happen. It had to be about one thing, a promise to a dying man. It had to be about getting Amala and her son to safety.

וַיְדַעְלֶבָמוּ וְדִי־לַע הָיְהָנָ לְכ
יְחַוִיהְ וּב הָיְהָנ רְשָׁא־לְכ הָיְד

CHAPTER X

MARTYRS' SQUARE
BEIRUT, LEBANON

In the flaxen light of the fading Beirut afternoon, the caliph studied the dial of his tiny golden watch. Even in all his greatness, he held no dominion of the sweeping black hands that raced like charioteers around that infinite white circle. Time was not an illusion. Time was not replenishable. Time, in fact, was running out. He brusquely snapped the case shut and returned it to the pocket of his *jalabiya*.

In a smooth, flowing motion, he guided the motorized chair toward the desk, turned the key, and unlocked the drawer. He removed the long narrow pipe with the small metal bowl and the tiny orb of black tar that would held the power to show him his destiny. He drew a long wooden match, struck it, then touched the restless blue flame to the bowl. He drew deeply, holding the smoke for a long moment, allowing its vapors to penetrate deep within him. A pungent cloud of opium smoke drifted up to the ceiling, crawled along the walls like a spider, then vanished into the shadows. He struck another match and drew again. And with each draft, the caliph felt himself evolving into that which destiny had ordained that he must be.

When at last he'd exhausted the contents of the pipe, the caliph dutifully returned it to the long, narrow drawer and turned the key in its lock. Then he pressed the worn metal toggle with the calloused tip of his broad, flat thumb. With a hum as soft as a whisper, the wheelchair's motor whirred to life. Gradually, he pivoted. He touched the toggle again and rolled toward the open doors of the terrace. It was nearly time for the call to prayer.

The motorized chair seemed almost a part of him now, a prosthetic integrated into the whole of his person. He called it his "gift" from the Russians. They'd sent it to him as a mockery when their mine had failed to kill him. They'd taken the remnants of his limbs and placed them on display in the private offices of the Kremlin. In return, they had sent him the chair.

How merciless is Allah in his mercy. In the early days, long before the Russians had come to make an empire, he had been dashing and handsome, fast and strong. "Like a lion," said the men of the villages along the Khyber Pass from Jalalabad to Peshawar. "Handsome and mysterious," the *burqua*-clad women confided to each other in the quiet, squalid corners that the men permitted them to call their own. But then, of course, he was not the caliph. He was simply a warrior who had taken arms against the infidel invader. In time they came to call him Siddiqul Islam, the son of Islam. It was a name that he had chosen for himself. It had come to him in a vision, the gift of the opium.

Then the Russians took his legs, and he evolved again. He came to realize that not only could the poppies reveal his destiny to him, but they might make him rich beyond all measure, and in so doing, expand his power far beyond the mountains from which he had come. And so he wandered the road laid before him to see where it might lead. And lead him it did. Over time, just as the poppies had promised, his wealth and influence grew. And so did his stature.

His name acquired a kind of dark magic. Some refused to utter it aloud for fear that the syllables alone would conjure the djinn. His inky beard, olive skin, and penetrating green eyes became the fabric of legend, symbols of the name that could not be spoken. He had become a reclusive idol, icon, a man of great power and immeasurable wealth, and, so some whispered in the deep of night around the fires of winter, a prophet. He was feared by everyone—Tajik, Pashtun, Uzebek, Nuristani, Hazaras—from the Karakorum to the sea. But above all, he was feared by the hapless factory men and farm boys the Kremlin had sent to do their bidding in the tribal lands. At mountain checkpoints, the boy soldiers, their pale white skin cracked by the ceaseless wind and merciless sun, dutifully, if fearfully, conducted their inspections as they had been ordered to do. But none probed too deeply, for none truly wished to find Siddiqul Islam. None desired to return home in the coffin train that ran from Kabul to Ashkhabad. They had no desire to lie among the rows of honored dead on the squalid, somber platform of the Paveletsky Station, their grieving mothers come to fetch their remains.

Then at last, in the fading season of his life, it was the poppies that had given him the vision. The opium had opened his mind and revealed to him the prophecy. When he possessed the relic, he would no longer be the caliph. He would evolve yet again and arise as the Mahdi, the twelfth sacred imam, the portent of the end of time. He was to be Allah's chosen, the force that would capture Mecca, defeat all the armies of the world, and ascend the golden throne. By the force of his hand and the power of Allah, he would unite the world under the dominion of Islam. All would bow down in the shadow of the minaret. And then jihad would end. Time itself would end. He would have dominion not only over the world and all those who dwelt within it, but he would, at last, have conquered time itself.

The caliph touched the metal toggle. The chair rolled past the lazing curtains and onto the tightly mortared stones of a terrace that ran the full length of the building. In the foreground, so close it seemed that he could touch it, the cobalt dome of the blue mosque shimmered like the mirrored waters of a Himalayan lake. The polished slabs of the towering minaret glowed pearl white against the sapphire sky. For a quiet moment, the caliph absorbed the smells and sounds of the coastal city that had become his fortress and his prison.

In the near distance, a taxi honked then squealed to a stop. The Mediterranean breeze stirred briskly. On its wings came the fragrance of lamb grilling over charcoal fires. He wondered how long it had been since he had eaten. The opium played tricks with his appetites and his memory. He shuffled through the deck of hours in his mind. At dawn, he had taken olives, cheese, bread, and honey. Then through the long hours of morning, an endless stream of cigarettes rolled from fragrant black Turkish tobacco and cups of warm mint tea, its broth soothing and aromatic. He remembered the pipes, one in the morning and then again just now before prayers. But he couldn't recall a midday meal. He checked the watch then shook his head. His hunger would have to wait.

The caliph surveyed the line of the horizon, performing delicate calculations inside his head. Running his finger along the plumb line of the minaret against the pale blue sky, he determined that his chair was out of position by a few precious degrees. He tapped the toggle ever so slightly. The dull metal spokes of its wheels lurched forward a few centimeters then stopped. At last, he was satisfied. The gift of the Russians now faced squarely in the direction of the Quiblah and the Ka'bah, the sacred city of Mecca.

The muezzin's *adhan* rang forth from the minaret. Its dulcet tone pierced the fabric of the day like a tent maker's needle and magically the caliph's world came to a stop. To his ears it sounded like the voice of an angel. He closed his eyes. Magically, he floated like a spirit hovering before the azure tiles of the great dome. He no longer needed the chair. He no longer needed legs. He was free. *Blessed be the name of Allah.*

In the distance, a shadow appeared. It rose up and obscured the rays of the setting sun. Its image, in the shape of a man with a long, curving scar across his face, grew ever larger until at last it obscured the very mosque itself. It was always there, in every vision. A threat to his destiny. A threat to the mosque. A threat to them all. The shadow extended its arm toward the caliph, and the caliph in turn reached out. If only he could take hold of the shadow, then he would bend it to his will. But the harder he reached, the more elusive it became. It floated now over the sea, and again the image extended its hand. Magically, the relic appeared beside the shadow, a golden scroll, light emanating from within. The shadow reached for it, but it was just beyond his grasp. But with each vision, the shadow's hands came closer. Then, as suddenly as they had appeared, both the scroll and the shadow vanished. The wind gusted and sent the caliph sailing back to the terrace and the captivity of the chair.

A barely audible tapping came at the door of his private chamber. He opened his eyes and checked his watch.

"Come," he commanded in a voice that still resonated with power.

The door eased open, its dark wood panels shifting then disappearing into shadow. The caliph's son bowed. His keffiyeh hung loosely about his neck and shoulders, its diaphanous weave opaque in the tawny afternoon light. Pressing himself lower still, he whispered, "Peace be upon you."

"And upon you, my son."

"He has arrived. It was your wish to be informed."

"And it is now you who would tell the caliph his own wishes?"

He touched his right hand to his heart and bowed deeper still.

"Forgive me, father."

"Bring him."

"As you command."

He backed out of the room and eased the door closed behind him. With a subtle gesture, he signaled to the visitor then disappeared down the long paneled hall.

Shari wore a black matte suit and white shirt with banded collar sealed at the neck with a simple brass stud. Day-old stubble graced his cheek and chin.

"My Caliph," Shari said softly and bowed deeply from the hip.

"You say that as if you believed there was more than one caliph."

"There is but one caliph, my master." Shari bowed low, his eyes gazing into the complex matrix of the carpet's geometric pattern. His voice was soft and obsequious.

The caliph nodded in satisfaction. "It is well that you remember. Now, come. Sit beside me and tell me of the relic. Time is short. Everything depends upon your success." He caressed the golden watch but did not open the case.

Shari placed the sealed portfolio on the scrolled leather inlay of the caliph's desk. Alluringly, he slowly slid it forward.

"With the blessings of Allah, our mission continues well. We now have the manuscript. Soon we will have the map. The relic will be yours, Caliph."

"And the Jew who can decipher the map?"

"All is arranged, Caliph. When I arrive in Bi'ral Ulayyaniyah, the Jew will already be awaiting me."

The caliph smiled, still working his fingers across the smooth gold case of his watch. "You have done well."

Shari smiled and bowed again. "All is as you command it to be, Caliph. All is as Allah has willed it must be."

"Why do you make me wait? Come, show me what you have brought."

Shari bowed, then delicately withdrew a pair of reading glasses from his jacket and perched them on the bridge of his nose. From the pocket of his jacket, he withdrew a pair of soft white gloves and placed them on his hands. At last he removed the parchment from the portfolio and began to read.

Outside the open terrace doors, the wind rose up and stirred the dry fronds of the date palms, their red and golden fruit dancing like restless birds perched within. Shari paused in places to expound upon the subtle meaning of a particular symbol or phrase. And as he deemed it prudent, he enhanced its content for the satisfaction of his listener. The caliph hungrily consumed it all, as if the words and phrases were substitutes for the meals he had not taken. Slowly, he drifted under the Persian's spell.

As the sun disappeared behind the dome of the mosque, Shari returned the manuscript to its portfolio, removed his glasses and his gloves, then with a bow vanished as quietly as he had come.

For a while, the caliph meditated in silence. Like a lover's perfume, the lingering words of the Persian toyed with his imagination and fanned his paranoia. He contemplated the image of the strange threat from his visions, the shadow in the shape of a man who bore a scar. A man whose reach grew ever closer to the scroll.

Reaching beneath the edge of the desk, he pressed a tiny black button. Then he guided the wheelchair back toward the gently stirring curtains of the open terrace doors. The tantalizing scents of charcoal and grilling meat called to him from the streets below. He would take his meal now, but first there were arrangements to be made.

"Yes, Caliph. How may I serve?"

"Tell the Syrian I want to see him."

לְ וְיָדְעַלַבְמוּ וְדָי-לַע הָיֶהְנ לַ
יּחַ וְיֹה וֹב הָיֶהְנ רְשָׁא-לְכ הָיֶ

CHAPTER XI

ZURICH, SWITZERLAND

As he strode briskly past the old synagogue at Number 10 Lowen-strasse, Herr Dr. Judah Lowe felt as if he had stepped through the portal of a time machine and returned to his past. He did not enjoy the sensation.

Rarely these days did he stroll the narrow lanes west of the river and north of the Volkerkundemuseum. Why precisely he'd come that way today of all days, he couldn't imagine. Was it instinct, like the salmon who return to the waters of their birth to spawn? More likely, he imagined, he'd come on this day of particularly good fortune to show the moribund old building whose rouge-and-cream stone facade reminded him more of a synagogue than a temple that he was his own man and no longer was of the tribe; that he had erased it from the scrapbook of his past. But even that, he supposed, might be a tribute to its power over him.

He found it strangely comforting that the dwindling and decrepit temple looked so tired and ill at ease on what now had become a modern, leafy street filled with stylish shops and intimate cafes, their patrons and tables spilling out onto the bright lively sidewalks. But if he was honest with himself, there was no erasing its memory from his past. In some way he would never clearly understand, it had placed an indelible, if now invisible, mark upon him. Perhaps there was a perverse justice in the permanence of his indenture, he mused. Had he not, after all, passed through childhood and youth in the echoing halls that lurked beyond the black wrought-iron gates and heavy timbered doors? Like the invisible gamma rays that Herr Dr. Kistler was always rambling on about in the faculty lounge, the temple's scents and sounds and ritual seasons had penetrated him right through to the very core of his genetic structure.

But institutions are not men, Judah Lowe reminded himself. Institutions are what they are. They lack the ingenuity, the will-power, to reinvent themselves, and so must forever remain the same. Not so with men, he reasoned. With conviction and an iron will, a man might remake himself, just as Judah Lowe had done. It had taken him many decades, of course, but he had eventually managed to make himself into something of his own design. And so while the specter that haunted the Lowenstrasse might still have the power to lure him into the shadow of its decline, he no longer rightfully belonged to its tribe. Gamma rays and genetic codes be damned. He had proved himself stronger than them all. For Judah Lowe, that past was dead and buried. Only the bright horizon of the future remained.

He had attained his vaunted state of scholarly godlessness honestly, in the halls of academia where so many had trod the path before him. Ensconced in its ivory towers, he'd left behind the quaint rituals of circumcision and lamb's blood on door posts. Indeed, in those infrequent moments of self-doubt when he gazed more deeply inside himself than was his habit, he wondered whether he truly had ever been "of the tribe." Perhaps there had been an error in the maternity ward of the Universitatsspital in the Raemistrasse. Perhaps a name-plate had gone astray and two infants had been hurled into destinies that were not their own. Even when his parents had dressed him in black knee pants and fraying frock coat then clipped the grosgrain *yarmulke* like a crown to his thick patch of dusty red hair, he never truly felt that he belonged. He had always been a giraffe wandering aimlessly in a meadow of grazing cattle. And that feeling had only grown after he'd won the battle for tenure.

Nearly two decades before, and grudgingly so even then, they had granted him that distinction in a brittle ceremony at 190 Winterhurerstrasse, the Archeological Institute of the University of Zurich. The hall had been filled with false smiles and congratulatory utterings that hid emotions more akin to *"I suppose it had to happen one day. And if it must be, then as well Judah Lowe as another."* It was of course exceedingly rare for a Swiss Jew in those days, even a reinvented one who had gone to such lengths to obscure his origins, to attain permanency of his academic stature. But he'd managed it nonetheless. He had found a way. He was smart and ambitious. And when he set his mind to something, he did not make a habit of failing.

Why, he wondered, had the other Jews clung so tenaciously to it all? Being a Jew was so difficult and offered so few rewards in the lands of the Diaspora. One always had to tiptoe around the latent threat, convincing himself that in this time and in this place it would be different, only to find that when the demons at last woke from their slumber, the result was the same.

When Jews first came to Zurich in the thirteenth century, they were—for the consideration of a special tax, a commitment to keep within the confines of the *Judengasse,* and a promise always to wear the conical hat called *Judenhut*—tolerated. For those humiliations and countless others, the good townspeople of Zurich had agreed to offer a safe haven and refuge to their boarders. Provided they stayed in their own quarter; provided they wore the hat; and especially provided that the *Juden* tax should never be in default. And for a while things worked out, at least after a fashion. For a while they plied their trades and kept their sacred rituals unmolested by the *Volk.*

But then the Black Plague came and changed it all. It killed Jew and gentile alike, as if there were no difference between them, as if they were all of one tribe. But not even the universality of the suffering and death could save them from the beast. The crowds always needed a malefactor to explain such tragedy and suffering. And the Jews once again found themselves cast in a role for which they had not auditioned. The rumor spread quickly that the tribe had spawned the epidemic. They had come by night and with a secret potion known only by the elders of their tribe had poisoned the water wells of the city, it was claimed. And so the families of the Judengasse were forced from their homes and ordered never to return, but not until a dozen had been tortured and burned at the stake. The fantasy of security and safety, of a homeland between sheltering spires of the snow-capped mountains, disintegrated like the myth it had always been.

But none of this mattered to Judah Lowe on this day of all days. And so, as if he were a dry leaf swept along by the scurrying breeze, he exited the shadows of his past, made a left turn onto Talstrasse, and headed south toward the lake. He enjoyed the sound the heels of his scuffed brogues made as they clicked and clattered musically along the uncluttered concrete ribbon of sidewalk. Quite intentionally, he had captured precisely the look of a senior, respected, and very un-Jewish professor. He sported a worn tweed jacket with lapels too narrow for the fashion and a maroon stripped tie knotted in a half Windsor and pressed tight against the starched white collar of his cotton shirt. The sole of his left shoe displayed a not unsuitable pinhole of wear. The ash umbrella he carried against the promise of rain had one bent-but-not-broken rib.

A gust of moist mountain air swept down from the sheltering peaks and stirred the lush canopy of conifers. In the distance, he now could see the Quaibrucke and the milky grey waters of the Zurichsee beyond.

To think, he'd nearly refused to take the call because it was his off

Tuesday, and he never took calls on his off Tuesdays. But when he'd heard the words "sheikh" and "Arab Bank of Switzerland," he'd decided that even the tradition of his off Tuesdays might stand for some reinvention. And so he'd taken the call, and what a fortuitous decision that had been. *"A collector of rare manuscripts,"* the voice in its soft amber tones had said. *"A unique piece of uncertain provenance in need of review by an expert of the reputation and stature of Herr Dr. Judah Lowe."* And, of course, there would be a handsome sum as reward for his services, deposited directly by wire into an account at the Banque Privee. Ten thousand Swiss francs, to be precise.

He supposed that the sheikh had come into the possession of his map through something other than the usual channels, but such was the way of the world and not a proper matter of inquiry for a tenured scholar whose only relation to the affair was a consultation.

As he strode ever more brightly toward the Bar au Lac Hotel, Judah listened only half-heartedly to the voice inside him. It was a tiny voice that uttered things like, *"Gentlemen never walk so briskly down the streets of Zurich,"* sounding so very much like his mother. On most days, he would have minded its counsel. But not on this fine autumn evening. Not now. Not when ten thousand francs was waiting to be earned for a single visit to a suite overlooking the lake.

Judah glanced quickly at the yellowing face of his not-quite-genuine Vacheron Constantin wristwatch. Its new brown leather band quite effectively obscured its forgery. Was it nine o'clock yet? Without his reading glasses he couldn't tell for sure. Hurriedly, he glanced back over his shoulder at the old church clock. Its large black hands showed precisely seven minutes before nine o'clock. He would be right on time.

The menacing black Bentley waited patiently in a pool of shadow. In very un-Swiss fashion, the street light above it had gone out.

With the index finger of his left hand, the driver touched the tiny blue light on his wireless earpiece. For a moment he listened, then muttered something in Arabic, nodded his head, and disconnected.

"Is it time?" his companion asked.

"Soon. The caliph's plane is waiting. We have only to collect the package and deliver it to the landing strip. Then our part is done."

"Good. I'm hungry, and besides Renate does not like me to miss Khalid's bed time. If we don't hurry, he will be asleep before I am home."

"And is it not the same in my home, a wife who is never satisfied and children who cry if I do not kiss them goodnight? Let us hope this Jew is not late. But he probably will be. You can never trust a Jew, Ghassan."

Ghassan nodded his head absently and stared out the window toward the green awning of the café across the way. His neck was stiff. He was tired of sitting idly in the car. He was tired of the jihad that made him wait, tired of inconvenience and the endless complaints of his fat Swiss wife. But the servants of Allah must answer his call, he reasoned, vaguely recalling something the Imam had said in his Friday sermon. So Ghassan drew a filtered Marlboro from the inside pocket of his jacket and lit it, wondering how he would explain the lateness of his return to Renate and whether Khalid would cry when he did not come to tuck him in.

Across the street at a small table under a green striped awning, a man dressed in a black leather jacket, faded jeans, and scuffed white athletic shoes toyed with his mobile device. He sipped a glass of warm pilsner against the growing cool of the autumn evening. To the neighborhood locals, he looked nothing more than the usual Swiss student, cell phone in front of him, short locks of black hair curling easily behind his ear. Smoking. Overall in need of a good washing. When he ordered his beer neither the server nor the patrons around him detected the slightest hint of foreignness in his perfect Swiss Deutsch. His day old beard, while not precisely stylish, was unremarkable. It was in keeping with the bohemian fashion that appealed to the student classes. He was, in short, invisible to them all. It was precisely the way the caliph's camp had trained him to be.

At four minutes past nine o'clock, Judah Lowe rounded the corner and walked directly toward the freshly washed green awning that still smelled of disinfectant and mildew. A thin mist rose from the streets as cool air released the moisture gathered in the warmth of the day. The fading sound of a departing train echoed in the distance.

Judah whistled softly as he walked. His bubbly gait carried him, like a frog leaping across a field of lily pads, from one street lamp's circle of light to the next. As he approached, the man in the black leather jacket quickly downed his pilsner. He placed two coins on the table and slipped his mobile phone into his pocket. As Judah Lowe strode past, the man rose up from his chair and fell into stride a dozen steps behind. Quickly, he waved the glowing ember of his cigarette twice. The lights of the Bentley flashed in response.

"*Bitte*, Dr. Lowe," he called out softly "*Bitte . . .*"

Judah Lowe paused and turned around.

"*Ja*, it is Dr. Lowe."

"Sir, my uncle was unable to reach you by phone. He has encountered a slight change in his plans. He is profoundly sorry and doesn't wish to inconvenience you. But his accommodations at the Bar au Lac were not entirely satisfactory. He has relocated to the Dolder Grand. He hopes that you will be able to adjust your plans so as to meet him there instead. He has put his sedan and driver at your disposal." The student nodded toward the Bentley that lurked in the shadows on the far side of the street.

Judah paused and glanced at the car. He'd never been inside a Bentley.

"The Dolder Grand is a distance from my home, young man. I take it the driver shall be able to return me when we are done?"

"Of course, Herr Doctor. Yes, by all means. My instructions are that this inconvenience isn't to trouble you in any way. All that my uncle has is at your disposal. He's embarrassed by the circumstance and wants to make everything as easy for you as possible."

Judah pretended to consult his watch, smiled, then nodded his head.

They walked through the rising mists toward the pool of shadow. The student opened the rear passenger door. Judah leaned his head in. A strong hand took hold of his arm and shoved a needle into it. Instantly, his legs collapsed beneath him and sent him tumbling into a pool of darkness.

Declan gazed out the airplane window into an endless blue void dotted with sparse white clouds. Air Emirates flight 0903 from Dubai circled Amman's Queen Alia International Airport waiting for clearance to land.

Already he was working the math in his head. It had taken nearly twenty-five hours just to make it to Amman. It would be a four hour ride by hired car to the remote eastern desert at Mahattat al Jufur. With the Syrian army on full deployment against the uprisings, he would have to cross the frontier beyond the checkpoints, using currency, not visas, to make it through. That meant he'd need to find a Bedouin on the Jordanian side willing to take him by camel or four–wheel-drive across the desert under cover of darkness into Syria somewhere between Abu Kamal and At Tanf. He wasn't worried about finding a Bedouin. That was merely a matter of money and sensible precautions. But actually getting through without being discovered, that would be the tricky part. He would have to be very, very careful. No roads, no villages, and as few eyes as possible.

Every step of the way from New Zealand he'd had the sense that he was being followed. As he had waited to board the sea plane at Graves Bay, he noticed a man in faded black jeans sitting near him, glancing from time to time in his direction. He sipped the cold remnants of his coffee and pretended to read a crumpled copy of *The New Zealand Herald*. But still the man lingered. Declan quickly settled the bill and took a circuitous route to the gate. In Auckland, as he bought toiletries in the airport shop and then again as he washed his face at the restroom counter, Declan sensed a presence behind him. But each time when he turned around there was no one there. In Dubai, the passport-control officers made him wait, then asked meaningless questions while they whispered among themselves. But in the end they had stamped his passport and sent him on his way. Everywhere he saw omens and sensed danger. But who wouldn't? After all, two men were dead, maybe more. And when he added to the mix that whoever had killed Ibrahim most assuredly wanted him dead as well, it was no wonder he felt naked without the Beretta.

Every instinct told him to turn back, yet he knew he couldn't. He'd made a promise to a dying friend, and he was determined to keep it. But that was all he would do, he told himself. He would get in, find the girl and her boy, get them to safety, then turn around and go home.

Declan checked his watch. It had been only three days since he'd floated alone in the sea above the great reef, riding the waves, oblivious to the powerful forces that were hurtling toward him. A few simple rotations of narrow black hands around a dial. That was all it had taken to turn his life upside down and send him tumbling into the abyss.

CHAPTER XII

DIER AL-SHUHADA MONASTERY
SYRIAN DESERT

Near midnight a double clap of thunder shook the timbers of the ancient monastery. In the eastern sky, a vast armada of purple and black clouds growled like menacing hounds and hurled drops of rain as large as almonds onto the cracked, dry soil and the red clay tiles of the rooftop. Streams of rushing water cascaded down from the eaves and washed away great swaths of amber sand. It was the kind of storm that came only once in a lifetime to the remote Qualamoon mountains of the high Syrian desert.

In the flickering half-light of the scriptorium, Amala struggled with her aging laptop. For nearly an hour she had wrestled with it. The machine was slow and unpredictable under the best of circumstances. And the storm, with its power surges and unseen electrical fields, had only made things worse. She pushed her chair back from the crude wooden table and stretched the knotted muscles of her neck. Another clap of thunder rumbled through the darkened cavern and sent a cold, wet shiver down her spine. What had become of Ibrahim?

The brooding storm cast a dark spell over the room and filled Amala with a pervading sense of dread. She tried to shift the gears of her mind and alter the vector of her thoughts, but it was to no avail. How she wished that she had never broken the amphora and revealed the manuscript and map hidden within. If only the candle had not drawn her into the spidery maze of the storeroom and led her to the wooden crate. If only she had not, in her excitement, dropped the amphora and broken it into a thousand pieces, Ibrahim would not have gone in search of Declan Stewart. He would still be there beside her. And all would be as it once was, peaceful and safe.

But she had done those things, and there was no undoing them now. Time could not be made to run backwards. The hands of the clock moved implacably forward, never in reverse. Actions, like arrows, once loosed could not be recalled. And so a simple series of quotidian events, passing one upon the other in the span of time it takes to brew a cup of tea, had changed everything and brought them all to a perilous place of uncertainty and, perhaps, even danger.

Ibrahim had been gone for more than a week and she'd heard nothing from him since the day of his departure.

"It's a great distance, of course. But, I won't be long." His words had comforted her as she stroked the thick black mane of Issa's hair.

She recalled the moment of his departure as if it were a motion picture recorded inside her head. Even now, strangled by the cold despair of the storm, she could feel the warmth of his breath on her face and smell the hint of coffee and pipe smoke that always clung to him.

"Only a few days, my dear. It will pass before you know it."

"Issa will miss you badly, Brother. We both will." She reached up toward the saddle and squeezed his hand.

"There won't be time for you to miss me. Your cameras and your computer are calling. There is much work for you to do and those tasks are more important than even you can now imagine. But you're a wonder. I know you'll have everything in readiness when I return with Dr. Stewart."

"If he returns with you."

"Why don't you leave that part to me, my child? You just make sure the images and enhancements are ready for him when he gets here. With the theft of the manuscript, I fear that time is already short and will only be shorter still when we return."

"I promise, Brother. I'll have everything in order when you return."

"And whatever happens, don't let me return to find that Brother Crispus has filled my scriptorium with compost for his garden!"

Brother Ibrahim laughed roundly and nibbled at the corner of his ragged, white moustache. Then he raised the reins up to his chest and pulled them to the right, the dry red mountains looming over his shoulder in the distance. He shifted his weight from one side to the other, freeing the folds of his heavy brown robe from the saddle beneath him. He made a clicking sound with his tongue, the worn cusp of his incisor peeking out like an ivory tusk. The horse's hooves clattered across the stones of the trail as he rode into the blood red sun and made his way toward al Nabak.

"I will pray for you, Brother," Amala called after him, waving and pretending to smile.

"God will take care of this old monk. Pray instead for the man I ride to see. All our hopes rest with Declan Stewart."

"*Declan Stewart . . .*" Issa's enchanted voice echoed through the canyon, his left hand corkscrewing in the cool morning air as it danced its mystic dance.

"*Doctor* Declan Stewart," Amala scolded him. Issa smiled as the dancing hand twisted like a kite in the wind, carving the secret symbols that only he could translate.

Amala didn't like partings. Too often they had been omens of emptiness yet to come. On a warm summer's afternoon, she had waved goodbye to her father, her mother, and brothers. By nightfall, the Apache rockets had claimed them all. She had waved goodbye to her husband Jibril as he dutifully journeyed to his mother's home in Jerusalem to help her along. But on the very first day of his return, a Palestinian bomb had claimed him for the *intifada*. And so like a clock that ran in ten year spans of time that flashed like a motorist's blur, she had lost them all. Everyone she had ever loved, everyone except her son Issa, had perished on the heels of a goodbye. All she had left was the boy who kept a secret world inside his mind, a cocoon spun of ideas and images that she could not even begin to fathom, where the madness of the world could not come in.

Another clap of rumbling thunder shook the scriptorium then a bolt of lightning flashed. The screen of Amala's computer glimmered then went completely dark. She shook her head, expelled a long breath, and slapped the laptop shut.

"Three hours of work lost."

Without the computer, there was nothing else to be done. She had no choice. It was time for bed. She rose from her chair, took the lantern in hand, and turned toward the stair.

"I thought I might find you here."

Amala jumped at the sound of the voice that came from the darkness. But the smell of garlic reassured her. It was Brother Crispus, the keeper of the garden and of the bees. "Do you never sleep, child? I shall have to scold our good Brother Ibrahim for working you too hard."

"There's no choice, I'm afraid. Ibrahim needs this work done before he returns with Dr. Stewart. I'm already hopelessly behind, and I imagine he'll be back any day now."

"Yes, any day. I'm certain of it." Brother Crispus sat a small tray covered in a white linen cloth on the writing table beside them. "But in the meantime, you have to keep your strength, you know. I've brought you some warm tea and sweet biscuits. And as you have probably already guessed from the two cups and the two plates, I thought I might share them with you."

Amala smiled, beckoning him to sit down beside her.

"Everyone's been so kind to Issa and me, especially you, Brother Crispus."

"It's our custom. Hospitality is our calling. To serve is not only our duty but our great privilege. It has always been this way, even from the earliest days of our order."

"Still, it can't be easy having a woman and child in your way all the time."

"Not at all, my child. To give you and Issa shelter and sanctuary is as much a blessing for us as it is for you. It's been a long time since any of us heard the voice of a child at play. In any event, Gaza is no longer a good place for you. Too much trouble there these days."

Amala nodded then poured a cup of tea for each of them. She offered a cookie to Brother Crispus and took one for herself.

"One never knows for certain, Brother. Perhaps the Americans will decide someday that they can have more than one friend in the Middle East. Perhaps Hamas will decide that it can find a way to live with the Jews. Perhaps the Jews will decide that Jerusalem is a big enough place after all to share it. Perhaps then peace will come."

"The hand of God is everywhere. More impossible things than this have come to pass in the fullness of time."

Amala sipped the tea and let its warm embrace take hold of her. "God willing." She pressed her hands together. "But it seems that at least for now, everyone has become what the gun has made them. Even the children. Do you know that in the streets of Jerusalem they play games of war—Jew against Arab, Palestinian against Israeli? Peace seems to be so very far away."

"Yes, I sometimes wonder why God allows it all to be. But you never know. In all things there is purpose and meaning. In all things there is the hand of God."

Amala smiled then quickly finished her tea. "Well, perhaps the diplomats and the politicians will eventually sort it all out. But for now, it's getting late. I should check on Issa, then, as you suggest, get some rest myself. Tomorrow, even before the sun is up, I'll have to start again. Perhaps Brother Ibrahim will have made it home by then, and I don't want to disappoint him."

"Yes, child, I'm certain he will."

Amala took hold of the lantern and together she and Brother Crispus made their way cautiously through the darkness and back up the stairs.

As they passed through the heavy wooden doors and into the cool drizzle that filled the courtyard, Amala thought she saw a tiny flash of dim, yellow light in the high cliffs above them. She paused and studied the dark mountain. Did it flash again? A faint spark of quivering light in the far distance?

"What is it, my child?" Brother Crispus asked, the misting rain making a halo around him, droplets of water beading on the broad ridge of his forehead.

"I thought I saw a light on the ridge, just there." She raised the lantern and gestured toward the angled shadows of the mountains.

"I'm sure it's nothing, my dear. Just a trick of the passing storm."

Amala tilted her head upward, allowing the raindrops to strike her face. They were cool and refreshing, but in a way she couldn't quite comprehend, menacing. Whatever she had seen was gone now. Gone back into the darkness from which it had come. She lowered the lantern and returned her gaze to Brother Crispus.

"Of course." She smiled, then gently nodded. Together they vanished into the darkness.

וַיְדַעְלַבְמוּ וְדִי־לְעַ הָיְהָנ לִ
יְהֹ־וָיָה וּב הָיְהְנ רֶשָׁא־לֶךְ הָיָ

CHAPTER XIII

10,000 METERS ALTITUDE
SYRIAN AIRSPACE

Shari contemplated the stark expanse of nothingness that loomed beyond the large oval window of the Gulfstream IV as he waited impatiently for the call.

He rubbed his hands across his face then gently squeezed the bridge of his nose. He had not rested in three days. He was tired and soon would have to sleep. But not yet. Not now. Not when he was this close to the prize. He must not allow anything, not his fatigue, not the Syrian, not the caliph, and most of all not the unwelcome ghost of Declan Stewart to stop him now.

"Forgive me, Sayyidi."

"Yes, my daughter, what is it?"

"It is the call from New Zealand that you've been expecting. Shall I have the pilot put it through?"

"Yes, thank you, daughter. And kindly bring me a cup of Earl Grey and some cakes. I won't have time for food in Damascus. The helicopter's already waiting."

"Of course, Sayyidi."

Shari admired the way her full breasts pressed hard against the buttons of her bright red uniform. He especially liked the tall leather boots that stopped just beneath her knees, complementing the firm, tanned flesh that ran above them and disappeared into the secret places beyond the hem of her skirt. He wondered whether she minded his staring. The scarlet crescent of her smile assured him that she did not.

As she turned and slowly walked back toward the galley, he lingered over the undulating motions and the smooth skin of her long, muscular legs. The close-fitting skirt revealed the firm contours of her hips and outlined the delicate lingerie beneath. He allowed himself to imagine the feel of her skin against his own and the sounds she might make as he touched her. Perhaps she would whimper. Or more likely, he fancied, howl with desire and urge him on. Even in the late season of his manhood, so often filled with long days of exertion, his sexual urges were as powerful as they had ever been. And he had found it wise never to restrain them.

The encrypted phone tucked into the console beneath the window buzzed once. Shari picked up the handset and placed it against his ear.

"Speak."

"Sayyidi, I have news."

"Good news, I trust."

"Forgive me, Sayyidi. The mission has not gone as was expected."

Shari clenched his jaw and resisted the surge of anger that welled up inside him. He took a breath then watched the girl as she placed the tea and cakes before him.

"Thank you, daughter." She smiled, then turned and walked back toward the front of the elegant cabin.

"Tell me how it is, my son, that a mission against an old priest and a lunatic castaway on a remote and isolated island might not have 'gone as was expected.'" Shari was sharp and to the point. In the window of silence that followed, he sensed the fear and trepidation his words had produced on the other end of the line.

"Forgive me, Sayyidi. In the darkness, before we could strike, our brothers were attacked even as they prepared the assault. One brother was killed, another badly wounded. But, insha'Allah, he survived long enough for us to learn much that has been of use to us."

Shari forced himself to lift the porcelain cup and take a sip before responding.

"So what you are telling me is that both the priest *and* Declan Stewart have escaped. And that not only do you not have the map, you don't even know if they had it in their possession or where they now have flown?"

"No, Sayyidi. The old priest is dead. There is no mistake. Only the man called Stewart escaped us."

"And what of the map?"

"We are confident that either Stewart has the map with him or he never had it at all. In all events, we are certain it's not in New Zealand, Sayyidi."

Shari methodically returned the cup to its saucer.

"And you were certain that the old priest and Dr. Stewart would present no challenge for your jihadis. You were certain that you would take them both alive and recover the map for me. I have little confidence in your certainties, boy. Do you at least know where Declan Stewart has gone?"

"Yes, Sayyidi. He took the sea plane from Graves Bay to Auckland."

"Why would he go to Auckland?"

"We believe Auckland was only a transit point, Sayyidi, and that his destination lies elsewhere. Already our brothers have penetrated the bank and airline databases. We know he withdrew a large sum of money from his accounts. We do not know yet where Stewart has gone, but in an hour, I shall have that answer for you."

"Time is short, boy. I have to know where Dr. Stewart has gone."

"By day's end, we will find the trail. He will not escape."

CHAPTER XIV

MOUNTAIN CAVES WEST OF DIER AL-SHUHADA SYRIAN DESERT

On a high promontory under a starless sky, the Syrian gazed into a pair of infrared field glasses and studied the contours of the rambling compound called Dier al-Shuhada. The worst of the storm had passed. Only a foggy blanket of clouds and a gentle misting rain remained.

Setting the binoculars aside, he crouched on the heels of his thick-soled boots and drew a breath from the dwindling stub of his damp cigarette. With his finger, he carved an imaginary arc across the ancient stone walls, moving east to west, pausing just long enough at each structure to decide its fate. Two buildings stood at the very center of the Syrian's arc, the great basilica, its ornate bell tower crowned with a golden cross, and the library. The basilica would be the first to go. He would let the artillery shells turn it to dust. But the library he would save for the fire. That was the place where he would find what he had come for. Somewhere deep within the complex labyrinth of five thousand books, three thousand manuscripts, and more than a thousand ancient scrolls, was where he would find the map. It had taken the Crusaders and their progeny a thousand years to fill those shelves, but it would take the Syrian and his soldiers less than an hour to burn them all.

On the far side of the Syrian's arc lay the guest refectory, the hermitages and the cells where the monks lived. He would take care with those buildings too, ensuring that the rockets rattled but did not destroy them. He wanted the monks frightened, but he didn't want them dead—at least not yet. Not until they had told him where to find the map. To the east lay the Fatimid mosque, the monk's tribute to the twelfth-century Muslim regent who had demanded its construction in exchange for his promise not to destroy the monastery.

A half dozen well-placed rounds of artillery was all it would take to open the gates wide and strike a deep chord of fear within them all. The kind of fear that would loosen tongues. The kind of fear that would lead him to the map.

The Syrian tossed the trailing end of his keffiyeh over his shoulder and consulted the military watch strapped tightly to his wrist. Its luminous dial glowed softly in the murky darkness. Only four hours till dawn. They would be finished and on their way by then. Insha'Allah, they would also have the map.

Over the small rise behind him, sixteen of the caliph's jihadis checked their ammunition and tested their weapons. Among them they had eighteen Bulgarian-made Kalashnikov AK-47 rifles, five thousand 5.45mm rounds, and two PK 7.62mm machine guns. To breach the gates, they had two RPG-18 shoulder-fired anti-tank weapons with two dozen rounds of 66mm shaped rocket charge. The Syrian had come prepared.

Quickly, he rechecked his calculations, drew a final puff from the dwindling ember of his cigarette, and tossed it to the ground. He crushed the butt in the mud under the heel of his heavy boot then rose and walked back toward the cave.

The soldiers had gathered themselves together in a tight knot around the fire. The Syrian strode briskly into the cave, adjusted his rifle, then crouched down beside them. Slowly, according to his practice, he gazed into each of the faces floating in the pool of shadows and pulsing red light. The patchwork of beard and scars that defined the Syrian's face struck equal measures of fear and admiration in them all. They were all young and untested, but each had survived the rigorous training in the camps. But he sensed the trepidation of untested men. He chose his words carefully.

"It is good to be in the company of men, my brothers." He paused, allowing the tribute he had paid them time to do its work.

"Tonight we are the instruments of Allah, as foretold in the caliph's vision. Tonight, with the strength of our hands and the courage of our hearts, we proclaim the coming of the Mahdi, the savior of the world, the lion of Islam who will unite all the lands under the dominion of Allah." The Syrian spoke softly now, an elder brother counseling his siblings. These were village boys, thin and gaunt. Not so long ago, they had played cricket in abandoned fields on drab afternoons filled with nothing to do. But now they looked to him like creatures in a zoo, primates kept too long in captivity, absently pulling at their ears and scratching the matted clumps of hair that leaked out from the edges of their keffiyeh. Restlessly, they smoked their cigarettes and sipped the sweet nectar of sugared black tea. Crooked teeth, stained yellow and brown, flashed intermittently in the firelight.

"You know the Mahdi's prophecy as it has been foretold in the holy books. The sun and moon will descend into darkness, just as they have this night. Then the Mahdi will rise up from his place of hiding and lead the army of the righteous against the infidels. At the gates of Hudd in the valley of Ifiq, Dajjal—the liar and false prophet, the spawn of the djinn—will fall to the sword. Then the Mahdi will shoot his sacred arrows into the sky. The arrows will return stained with blood. For forty days it will rain on the earth, and the earth will be cleansed by the blessed water. Fog will cover the skies for forty days more. A night three nights long will follow the fog. After the night of three nights, the sun will rise in the west and then at last, from his golden throne in Mecca, the Mahdi will blow the trumpet. All the nations of the world will bow down as one before the minaret. Only then will jihad be at an end."

The Syrian rose from the fire and raised his rifle high into the air.

"As the prophet said to his disciples, 'Who will be my helpers to establish the rule of Allah?' You know the answer do you not, my brothers? You know that we say tonight what the disciples said then. 'We are Allah's helpers!' This night, we are the weapons of Allah. This night, we clear the way and declare the coming of the Mahdi."

The predawn desert exploded in an aurora of fire and light as the first volley of 66mm rocket shells struck the northern and western walls of the monastery.

The ancient stone arches and the pillars that supported them collapsed in a fog of masonry dust and black smoke. The mighty timber gates, eight feet thick at their center, erupted in flames, the cross beams and support rails reduced to splinters. Only the mosque was untouched.

The Syrian leaned against the boulder, steadying the view through his field glasses and smiled.

"Enough," the Syrian barked. "The gates are breached. Now place two rounds in the church. I want it gone and that cross on the ground."

The artilleryman nodded. Hurriedly he adjusted the settings, made a signal with his hands, then fired. The final rounds whistled in fearsome high pitch as they cut a path through the damp air of the predawn. As the Syrian had ordered, they struck each corner of the Basilica's foundations in carefully arranged increments, one following directly after the other. The bell tower fell. The golden cross tumbled end over end through the dark, wet sky and landed in the mud. Only rubble remained.

"It is beautiful, is it not?" the Syrian declared, watching it all unfold before him. He pressed the handset switch of the field radio and gave the command.

"Move in."

וְיִדָעֶלַבמוּ וְדָי־לַע הָיִהְנ לַ

יִחִ־וְיָה וּב הָיֶהְנ רְשֶׁא־לְכ הָיִד

CHAPTER XV

EASTERN DESERT
MAHATTAT AL JUFUR, JORDAN

As he paid the driver and waded into the buzzing cacophony of the souk, Declan had the distinct impression that he was being watched.

The market at the center of the remote Jordanian village of Mahattat al Jufur was a beehive of activity, filled with the sounds and pungent aromas of impoverished peasants going about the commerce of their daily lives. Lean, curious dogs darted in and out of the open stalls scavenging for bits of food or venturous rats that might make a meal. And everywhere vendors of fragrant grilled meats and sparkling trinkets called in high pitched sing-song voices, hoping to lure customers to their wares.

"*Marhaba, marhaba,*" they greeted one another, hands raised in the air, imploring Declan to buy something from their stalls.

Avoiding eye contact, he thanked them with a softly muttered *shukran* and moved deeper into the souk. The bitter smell of black tobacco and the dissonant sounds of humans chattering were omnipresent. Eerily, the dogs scrutinized him but neither moved toward him nor made any sounds.

The villagers weren't accustomed to a *khawaja* in these remote southeastern deserts, even one who looked vaguely as if he belonged and seemed at ease in his surroundings. But he looked like he might have money. And that possibility far outweighed any concerns they had about who he was or why he'd come.

Declan quickly inventoried the options. Bookending the market were a half dozen camel and donkey caravans and two trucks. Bedouins were busy loading them all with staples, readying themselves for the journey into the desert. Declan had a decision to make. If he joined one of the camel caravans, he'd be nearly invisible. He'd blend into the jumble of the convoy and draw little attention should they stumble across a Syrian border patrol, or worse still, the army. But that also meant more curious minds and loose tongues. And, above all, the camels were dreadfully slow. It would take nearly a week to cover the two hundred kilometers to al-Qusayr if he elected the invisibility of the camel caravan. That was a steep price to pay for a man whose goal was to get in and get out as quickly as he could. If he opted instead for one of the trucks, he'd cover the same distance in a single night. But trucks inevitably meant clouds of dust in the daylight and headlights at night. Both could be seen for many miles. With the Syrians in open revolt, there would be many eyes in every corner of the desert. The chances of a truck's passing unnoticed were not promising.

Time or an added measure of invisibility? It was a tough call.

Declan lowered the duffel from his shoulder and removed a half-dinar coin from his pocket. The winds of chance had brought him this far. He might as well let them take it from here. The king's head, he'd join the camel caravan. Tails, he'd hire a car.

The silver and gold coin sparked as it tumbled end over end in the softening sunlight of the late afternoon. Time seem to slow as it lingered in the air. Then, with a quick overhand strike, Declan snatched the coin in his fist. He rotated his wrist and opened his palm. A random geometric pattern stared up at him. He slipped the coin back to the pocket of his dusty brown jeans, hoisted the load back up on his shoulder, and moved decisively toward a battered white Toyota at the far end of the market.

As he closed the distance between them, Declan made eye contact with the old Bedouin who lounged beside the truck, a filterless cigarette protruding from the cracked brown parchment of his face. That was the one Declan wanted. Here was one old enough to know the hidden paths across the sands into Syria, wise enough to keep his mouth shut, and jaded enough to have no fear of the revolution or the danger it entailed.

Two hours after sunset, they were already deep within the desert and well across the border. But like the Syrians in the villages and towns they sought to avoid, his body was in open revolt. It had been two full days since he'd slept. He needed to rest, and the truck was as good a bed as he would have this night.

As the old Bedouin grinded the gears and skidded over the mounds of red sand, burrowing deeper into the darkness beneath the stars, Declan could no longer subdue his fatigue. Inexorably, he surrendered to it. He slumped, his head coming to rest on the back of the seat. As he drifted off into the warm, white haze, he thought for a moment that he smelled the scent of Val's perfume. But even his muddled mind, clouded by the mists of exhaustion, knew that it was only a dream.

"So you're Stanford's star swimmer?"

Val smiled, wiped the counter with her towel, and turned to the next customer.

Declan set the bottle of Stella back down on the counter, its translucent glass glimmering with beads of cold sweat. He couldn't quite make out the writing on her name tag, but he had an unforgettable view of the woman herself. Her skin was the cinnamon color of ginger snaps and her eyes flinty green like the leaves of a eucalyptus tree. She was tall and lithe and flashed a bright, playful smile. Her hair glimmered like the sand at San Onofre when the slanting rays of the summer sun struck it just right.

She turned back to Declan. "We're a little busy here. No special treatment for swim stars, or any other big jocks for that matter." That playful smile again.

"My name's Declan." He pushed the wet bottle aside and extended an open hand across the bar. Busy with her work, she ignored the gesture.

"I know," she said.

"And?"

"And what?"

"What's your name?"

"You can read, can't you?" She turned to give him a better look at her name tag. "Valkyre. First syllable *Val*. Next syllable *Keer*—long 'e'. Two syllables, not three—never three. Not a Norse 'Val-kyr-ie,' but a Dutch 'Val-kyre,' with a 'Stuyvesant' on the end of that. But you can call me Val."

"I don't make a habit of shortening names. It's a quirk I inherited from an old Marine colonel, my dad. I'm Declan, never Dec. So maybe you'll be Valkyre—two syllables, never three. "

"I like Val, but suit yourself, swim boy."

Someone called for a drink from the far end of the bar. Valkyre turned to leave, then paused and quickly jotted a note on her order pad. With a flourish, she ripped it from the booklet. As if in a single movement, she took hold of Declan's hand, squeezed the paper into his palm, and turned away. Glancing back over her shoulder, she said, "Call me sometime. Maybe we can get lunch."

Suddenly the busy cafe began to fade. The motions of the crowd—every footstep and gesture—slowed to a crawl. Then they simply stopped. Like watercolors in the rain, their images began to melt around him, blending all the colors into one. Then those colors turned to a soft, ashen shade of white. Declan saw the world through a veil of gossamer. He moved his hand toward the beer, picked it up, and touched the cold bottle to the scar on his forehead. But he felt nothing. Only the fire, the burning fire, of the shrapnel that throbbed inside.

"Declan."

The voice came from the across the room on a billowy cloud of soft perfume. Both the voice and the scent were somehow familiar to him. They spoke of something from his past, someone close to him. But the pain, the pounding, pulsing pain inside his head obscured his memory of them and kept him in his prison behind the veil.

"Declan, come. Sit with me a while. We have so little time."

Then all the agony and confusion vanished. The fire inside his head surrendered its grip. He could feel the cool dew on the glass of the bottle as it soothed the scar, tiny rivulets of icy water running along the creases of his face. The suddenly, like a cloud receding to reveal the sun, he at last recognized the voice and the delicate fragrance.

"Val."

"Hurry. Time is short. Come, sit beside me. I have important things to tell you. Things you need to know if you're ever to find your way home."

He pivoted on the toe of his sandal. The veil was fading now. He could see her, there in the distance, seated in a circle of warm white light. But she was different now. She was no longer a student working her way through school. She was his wife, the woman she had been in the days before the red rain came and took her away, pregnant with his child. Towering waves of emotion were rising up within him. He could feel them coming, but he was completely helpless before her. They were too powerful to be restrained. The foundations of the walls he'd built around himself, the walls intended to keep him safe, already were cracking. Soon they would tumble into the sands from which they had arisen.

"Take me home, Val. Please, take me home."

She reached out and took hold of his hand, drawing him closer to her.

"Sit with me. There is so little time and so very much you need to know."

The Bedouin had taken the dune too fast. The cab hit the sand hard, then bounced twice more for good measure. Declan's head snapped forward. Only the seatbelt had kept him from bashing into the dashboard.

For a moment he couldn't remember where he was. He glanced at the driver then at his own hands. They were ragged and dirty, like his clothes. Then the fog of his dream lifted. It was all coming back to him. Suddenly, he was filled with an overwhelming sense of dread.

Declan took a deep breath and leaned back into his seat. Outside the window the pink light of dawn was just stirring from its sleep. On the near horizon just beyond a low ridge of dunes, lay the village of al-Qusayr. Either they had been lucky or the old Bedouin had been that good. Either way, they'd made it over the border and across the desert without encountering a single Syrian patrol. He was now less than a day's ride by horseback from the sheltered canyon of Dier al-Shuhada.

"Shukran," Declan said, taking the coarse hand of the ancient Bedouin in his own and squeezing a fifty dinar note into it.

"*Aasalaamu Aleikum.*"

Declan nodded, snatched his duffel from the bed of the truck, and strode into the midst of a quiet village just coming to life.

He needed a horse, provisions, weapons, and ammunition. The last three would be the easy part. It was the horse that would be the challenge. In the old days, a fitting horse and saddle would have cost

400,000 Syrian pounds or nearly 8,000 U.S. dollars. But with the cities on fire and the government in turmoil, who could say what the price would be now? The only thing he could count on was that it would definitely be more. Even in the best of times, the local tribesmen valued horses more highly than people, and even more so in times of uncertainty and peril. They rarely sold the good ones even to a kinsman, and certainly never to a khawaja.

It took him most of the morning to find a right-minded dealer motivated by the promise of US dollars paid in cash. Then it took another three hours of haggling over tea and water pipes filled with stale black tobacco to make the deal. By mid-afternoon, he had a pistol at his side and the reins of a fine dappled grey mare in his hand. But by then, he had no chance of making the monastery before nightfall. He could either stay in the village overnight, where he would draw more attention than he cared to, or he could ride on and make camp somewhere in the desert before darkness.

"*Somewhere*?" the voice inside him asked. They both knew exactly where. Tell Nebi Mend.

Ever since crossing the border, he'd lied to himself. He'd said he wouldn't stop there. He'd press his heels low in the stirrups, gently tap the sides of the grey mare, and ride on past it. But he'd known it was a lie even then. Even when he was telling himself it wasn't. He knew he would ride into the depths of its desolation and quiet. He knew he would dismount and walk for a while beneath the jumbled masses of stone and columns that rose like broken teeth from the sand. He knew all that and more. The only thing he still didn't know was whether he would dig it up. And if he did, what he would do then.

CHAPTER XVI

THE MONASTERY OF DIER AL-SHUHADA

Amala's heart pounded in her ears. The weight of troubled dreams had made her groggy and disoriented. For a moment she thought it was thunder from the storm. But when she smelled the scents of burning sulfur and carbonized wood, she knew it was something much worse. Thunder didn't upset the furniture or rip pictures from the walls. Thunder didn't knock sleeping bodies from their beds. This was something else. Something from her life before the monastery. Something she'd learned about in Gaza.

Ibrahim had tried to warn her. "There is great hope in this manuscript, Amala," he had said, smiling joyfully as he clapped his hands together. "But others will seek to turn the power of *Q* to their own ends. That means there is also danger." She knew now that he had been right.

Amala sprang from her cot and woke Issa. He rubbed his eyes, staring blankly into the darkness.

"Hurry. We must leave now!"

"But *Ommy*—" He stared up at her from the small wooden cot.

Strangely, he seemed undisturbed by the danger and the noise that flared around him, only mildly curious as to why he couldn't remain in bed. Then his hand floated into the air and began to carve invisible images into the cool dampness of the desert's night air.

"No questions. Not now. We have to go."

"Don't worry, Ommy. The noise won't hurt us. You mustn't fear the noise." He uttered the words as if he were chanting at Eastertide in the old Latin Church on Zeitoun Street in Gaza.

"It's just like the time at Jaddah's house in the winter, remember Issa? It's not just fire. There are rockets and guns as well. You were smaller then, but you remember when the soldiers came. When that happens, we don't talk. Okay? We run and then talk later. We run from the guns and the men who carry them now."

Issa nodded.

Amala, the thin cotton of her night dress floating around her, wrapped her arms around Issa and pulled him from his bed. She took his hand in hers and together they slipped out the door and rushed into the hermitage courtyard. The horizon glowed red, tongues of flame lapping air filled with the bitter scent of gunpowder and burning timbers.

"Yes, good, Issa. Keep going. Follow Ommy now."

"We have to go to the library."

"No not the library. They'll go there first. We have to find one of the Brothers. They'll help us."

Quickly, the voice inside her beckoned. But where to go?

"But the library is where the storage room is. We'll be safe there, just like the crates you found." Issa spoke softly as if they were merely on an evening stroll through Brother Crispus's garden.

"Yes. Yes, that's where we'll go. The storage room. That's a very good place. It has darkness and a maze to hide within." She could feel the terror trying to overwhelm her and strove to quell it.

"Don't be afraid, Ommy. Everything will be fine."

"We have to be quiet when we get there. Do you understand? Very quiet, like two mice."

"Of course. We'll be quiet, won't we?" Issa inquired of the dancing hand. "You know, don't you, Ommy? You know they've come for the map."

"You must never speak of the map. Never! Promise me now. You'll never speak to anyone of the manuscript or the map."

Issa glanced at his hand, nodded, and then said, "I promise, Ommy."

"Good, now hurry."

They ran full tilt past the burning ruins of the Basilica and rushed through the darkened doorway of the library. Amala immediately began to count her footsteps. *One . . . five . . . seven . . .* It was a game from her childhood, counting the paces from one place to another then filing them away.

"It's forty paces to the stair, Issa. Count them with me."

"Thirty-seven . . . thirty-eight . . . thirty-nine." Amala probed the flickering red darkness with her naked foot and felt the floor fall away in front of her. She squeezed Issa's hand and drew him close to her.

"Good, Issa. You counted them perfectly. Now, we go down. But remember, quietly."

Then like two desert hares fleeing the gardener, they scampered down the stairs.

"It's twenty steps down. Let's count them too, but quietly."

Seventeen . . . eighteen . . . nineteen. Just as they reached the bottom of the stairs, she heard the first spray of gunfire.

Rat-tat-tat. Then quickly on its heels, another. *Rat-tat-tat.* The battle was coming closer, the distance between them and the danger was narrowing. The threat was imminent. In the empty space at the foot of the stairs, she paused and listened. Another spray of gunfire. *Rat-tat-tat.* Silence. Then voices, harsh and commanding.

"Hurry! We must be quick. Bring that one, the fat one. Bring him and two more. If he does not show us where the map is hidden, he'll taste the steel of the jambiya."

How could she help the Brothers? she asked herself. But she already knew the answer to that. She was powerless. She couldn't even protect Issa.

Move! the voice inside her cried.

But Amala couldn't move. She couldn't think.

Then Issa's hand rose from his side and began to dance again. Suddenly, as if swept along by the current of an unseen stream, they were moving toward the scriptorium. It was thirty-five paces, but in her confusion, she had lost count. She slid her hand along the wall as the invisible current inched them ever forward.

"It has to be close now," she whispered.

"I counted the steps, Ommy. Twenty-one, twenty-two . . ."

"Keep moving. Keep counting. We're almost there."

Then just as they arrived at the storeroom door, she heard the hammering, clattering footfall of boot nails banging on the stone steps behind them. The intruders were only two turns of the stair-well above, fewer than thirty paces behind. She grasped the iron handle of the door and pushed down. It didn't move. She pressed again, this time harder and more forcefully, but still it wouldn't budge. A mountain of fear was growing inside her.

"The key's in Brother Ibrahim's desk."

"There isn't time."

Issa consulted the dancing hand. "Then try again. The magic hand says it will open."

She leaned hard against the handle and with a jump pressed the full measure of her weight down on it. The door groaned softly. She jumped again. Grudgingly it opened a crack. She grabbed Issa's hand and together they slipped into the darkness, pressing the door closed them.

They were suspended in a sea of absolute black. Gradually, they inched forward, turning left then right as they squeezed through the narrow passages between the crates.

Then suddenly Amala froze in her footsteps. In the inky darkness at the back of the room, a flame flickered. They were not alone.

CHAPTER XVII

THE SYRIAN DESERT
EAST OF TELL NEBI-MEND

Declan noticed a faint, sweet smell as he clicked his heels and eased the mare into the tumbled ruins of Tell Nebi Mend. The sweet fragrance filled the dry air like sandalwood in a sanctuary. On the horizon the sky sagged with heavy clouds the color of coal.

"Hamal," he said, smiling at last placing the scent. "The pods must be bursting now, old girl." Declan spoke to the mare as if she were a companion, whispering in the manner horses enjoyed.

"They burst open like a harbor seal popping its head up from beneath the waves, then spray thin clouds of sweet pollen everywhere." Declan closed his eyes and savored the bouquet. "But you wouldn't know about harbor seals, would you, old girl? Never seen the sea or smelled the ocean air. That's a shame. A good girl like you; a shame to have lived all these years and never seen the sea."

Declan clicked his heels and pressed her up a winding trail littered with broken pillars and scattered shadows. That was all that was left of a once-mighty kingdom called Kadesh. Shattered stones scattered across the lifeless sands of a barren desert. Even the clear blue waters of the powerful Orontes had long since been swallowed by the sand.

"Look around you, old girl. All of this, you know what it is? It's a tribute to the folly of men. Three thousand years ago this nothingness was the site of a great battle, one of the greatest of the ancient world. No one knows how many died to control . . . *this*." Declan gazed at the lifeless expanse of sand and shook his head. "And now look at it. Only a hill covered in ruins. Even its name has been forgotten. Only the mound itself, Tell Nebi Mend, remains."

Declan and Valkyre had made their first excavation together here, along the eastern wall, burrowing into the sands in search of the past. But that was before *Q*. Before Ibrahim had planted the seeds from which great vines would grow, vines that in time would come to entangle them all.

"The Gnostic scholar Gerhardt Reichmann was the first," Ibrahim said. "But perhaps you both already know that."

"I for one have never heard of him," Valkyre said in her easy, straightforward way.

"That makes two," Declan added as he flipped through the stack of papers in his lap, picking intermittently at the plate of food on the table beside him.

"Well then, I shall explain. In 1897, Reichmann published an article in the *Swiss Journal of Archaeological Sciences*. It was not, shall we say, well received. In fact, it made him something of a pariah, the subject of extensive ridicule and disdain throughout all of academia. It wasn't that they had trouble imaging a proto-gospel predating any known manuscript. That part wasn't so controversial. They were all beginning to come around to that conclusion in one form or another. But to suggest that it was not only a gospel, but an epistle to the future written in the hand of Christ himself and heralding the Second Coming, well that was going much, much too far for any of them."

"I should say so," Declan mused as he nibbled the last bits of his dried fig.

Discreetly, Val shook her head, scolding him.

Ibrahim ignored the young scholar's quip. "In any event, Reichmann lost his position, bounced around Europe for another thirty years taking one second-rate professorship after another, still trying to convince his colleagues that they had it wrong and he had it right. But as is so often the way, they closed their ears tighter still and pushed him farther and farther toward the fringes." Ibrahim closed his eyes and rocked slowly in the canvas camp chair, as if he were not merely telling the story, but actually reliving it himself.

"There are hundreds of kook theories, Ibrahim. Reichmann's sounds like just another one to me. That's why nobody even remembers his name." Declan licked the sweet residue of the fruit from his fingers, then rubbed his hands over the warm, golden flames of the campfire.

"Perhaps. But there is far more to the story. Shall I carry on?"

"Sure."

"Reichmann discovered something. Something hidden and very important."

"What makes you think that?" Declan yawned. He'd worked a long day and was ready for bed.

"Many reasons. One is that in 1939, after losing his last university position, he left Berlin for Yemen where, like a hermit, he took up residence in the desert. Then two years later he hiked off into the mountains on the Saudi border and disappeared completely. He didn't show up again for more than three years."

"I can't imagine what would be worth three years of a man's life in those mountains. That's a big, desolate range. It runs all the way up the western coast of the Arabian Peninsula through a long expanse of nothing," Valkyre offered, loosening the laces of her boots.

"Perhaps. In any event, what he did there—what he searched for and what he found—no one can say. But what we do know is that in the late winter of 1944, he reappeared in a Berlin asylum, bearded, crippled, half out of his mind, claiming an incredible discovery that would prove to the world he had been right all along. But he refused to say anything more than that. He said he would tell the rest of it only to the Fuhrer. But the whole of Germany was in flames by then. By spring the city itself had fallen and the Fuhrer was dead. In the fires of war and the fog that came after it, Reichmann disappeared and was never heard from again. He left behind a few pages of scribbles, portions of maps yellowed with age, and many, many questions. His theories fell into obscurity and in time vanished altogether. Until I came along and began to follow his trail."

"Great story. Loved the ending," Declan quipped playfully as he tucked the last of his papers into a file. "Now if you both will forgive me, I'm headed to bed. It's been a long day, and I'm afraid if I listen to more of the mystery of Gerhardt Reichmann, I may not be able to sleep. It's all far too thrilling!" He patted Ibrahim's shoulder then leaned down and kissed Val on the cheek.

Ibrahim stood up from the fire. "It's a long season yet. There'll be plenty of more time for stories of Gerhardt Reichmann and his quest for Q. I shouldn't be at all surprised if by the end of our time together, I've managed to convert you two skeptics into disciples. Perhaps I'll plant a seed here beside the ruins of Tell Nebi Mend, and together we'll see what harvest it yields."

It didn't take Declan long to shovel away the sand and reclaim the small metal box he'd buried beneath the ruins of an ancient stone monument after Val died, in the sick, crazy days that had led him to the asylum. He'd locked it, buried it shallow like he buried everything now, and thrown away the key. That had been meant to put an end to it. To push Q once and for all out of his life.

Declan drew the knife from his boot and using its thick, broad blade like a prizing bar, ripped open the lock. It was all still inside, all still there. The sheaves of paper were all a bit yellower perhaps, a bit crisper around the edges and more wrinkled than he'd remembered, but otherwise unchanged.

He was surprised at how small a lot it really was. Like the man who returns to the house of his childhood and laments how time has shrunk it all down, so he was surprised at how little was actually there. But the arid sands of Tell Nebi Mend had been kind to the papers, as if the ruins had known that one day Declan Stewart would return for the things he'd left in their care. Reichmann's notebook, of course, sat atop the stack, its worn leather jacket still smugly proclaiming superiority over everything piled beneath it, the pitiful academic harvest of four lifetimes of failure in the quest for Q. The work papers—Declan's and Val's and even Ibrahim's. In the end, even Ibrahim himself, the old monk for whom Q had become nearly an obsession, had given up the quest. Val's death took care of that; it had taken care of them all, paid all accounts in full.

Declan thumbed through it all, recalling who had made a particular sketch, or where they had been when any of them had made a particular entry in their notebook. As the sun sagged low over the ruins, he sifted through it all—the bits and pieces of old maps, the helter-skelter drawings, the faded black and white photos—everything that he and Ibrahim had piled up and put inside then buried beneath the sand, as if that simple gesture might somehow bring Val back or magically make them both whole again. Perhaps that was why he'd dug it up, he told himself. Perhaps it was all about Val, touching again the things she'd touched, remembering better days, and holding her once again in his arms.

Once long ago, on the cusp of madness, he'd ridden into this place on horseback, just as he had done now. He'd placed the box on the sand and built a fire from the stump of a dead acacia tree and the scattered limbs of a juniper. He'd built it big and let the rising wind fan the flames into frenzy. He'd meant to burn it all, let the fire turn every last scrap of it to ash just as the fire had turned his wife and child to ash. With the tendrils of madness curling around him, he'd danced around the fire and howled up to the heavens. Then he pulled his knife, as he'd just done now, and crouched down beside the box and placed its heavy steel blade against the lock.

But as he lifted the lock and slipped the blade beneath the hasp, a churning mist rose up around him and encircled him, a cold, breath-sucking cloud. *Dark. Malevolent. Eternal.* Something unseen reached out of the darkness and stripped the knife from his hand. The box rose from the sand and went hurtling through space, circling in a tight spiral over his head, round and round and round again. The force that held him had no voice, but its grip was as hard as steel. Then another mist rose and another and another still, until, at last, a great fog filled the desert from horizon to horizon and blackened out the pale white light of the waning moon. The fog seeped into his ears, his mouth, his eyes. Like a wave, it washed over him again and again, seeking to make him its own. He felt himself falling under its spell. Anger and hatred welled up inside him. He felt the power of the darkness, of the spirits that held him down, and surrendered himself to them. But as he tumbled down the precipice of his hatred and madness, another hand reached out and pulled him back.

In the first stirrings of dawn, he had awakened on the sand, the battered metal box close beside him. The great, roaring fire of the night before had burned down to cinders, leaving a shallow black hole beneath it. So he'd taken his shovel and hollowed out the hole. Then he tossed the box inside and covered it with sand. If the power of his own obsession would not let him burn it, he would at least sentence it to an eternal exile. The quest for *Q* would end in the place where it had first begun, beside the haunted ruins of Tell Nebi Mend.

Hastily, Declan shoved the small cache of files into his saddle bag and set up camp for the night. In the morning, before dawn, he would leave this sinister place and put behind him the complex fabric of madness and memory that lay over it like a shroud. He would turn the mare back to the south then vector west toward the mountains. Then, he would enter another world, a world filled with its own ghosts and memories. A world he'd vowed never to enter again. He would slip through the narrow crack between the canyons called the *siq* and ride into the wrinkled maze of peaks and canyons that would lead him to the ancient monastery called Dier al-Shuhada. Then he would do what he had promised, but nothing more. With luck, he'd make the monastery by midday, get the girl and her son, and ride out of the madness and back toward the sea. The sea that had made him whole again. The sea that had kept him safe. But for tonight, he had no choice. He and the mare would have to make their peace with the ghosts of this place and the memories that haunted it.

CHAPTER XVIII

THE MONASTERY OF DIER AL-SHUHADA

"Hurry, girl! This way!" The voice that came from behind the flickering flame was soft and elfin, little more than a whisper.

Amala's heart raced as a trickle of sweat ran down her side and dampened the thin cotton of her night dress.

"I said quickly, child! There is no time to waste; they are almost upon us." Issa tugged her arm and drove them both forward toward the wavering drop of light.

Behind them, just beyond the closed door to the storeroom, another voice bellowed, the antithesis of the one that whispered from behind the candle.

"Bring the light and the fat priest. I can see the bottom of the stair, but we will need light in this devil's lair. Hurry!"

The other voice, the one behind the candle rang out. "Now child! You must come *now* or all of our lives shall be forfeit to the fire and the men who brought it."

"Follow the candle, Ommy." Issa's voice sounded like an echo to her, something that came from a place very far away. It steeled her

against the fear. Together, she and Issa navigated the river of darkness that separated them from the wavering dot. But just as they
reached it, the light went out. In its place came the smell of mildew
and stale, damp air. She started as a soft hand touched her arm then
closed its fingers tight about her and pulled her forward to a place
well beyond where the wall should have been. Then she heard the
sound of stone moving over stone and felt a gush of wind. The hand
released her arm. She stumbled down a short ramp, Issa in tow
behind her.

Again she heard a swooshing sound then a gentle pop. Drawing
Issa to her breast, she struggled to get her bearings. The hostile
voices seemed farther away now. She sensed the menace and danger,
but she could no longer understand what they were saying.

She felt warm breath on her neck then smelled the scent of garlic.

"Brother Crispus!"

"You and Issa will be safe here, child," he whispered softly in her
ear. His smell comforted her the way the scent of tobacco on Ibrahim's robes had comforted her on the day he'd ridden away.

"We have to keep our voices low and use only the one candle.
Light has a way of seeping out through the old stones if one is not
very careful. And the ears and eyes of those vicious jackals are sharp.
You mustn't be discovered."

"It's Ibrahim's map, isn't it? They've come for it."

"Yes, my child. They've come for the map. Already they've cut
the ears from Brother Elias and beaten Brother Serapion with the
butt of a rifle. I fear he's dead."

In the ragged oval of candlelight, Amala noticed a wide swath of
red across his forehead. He was bleeding.

"You're hurt, Brother," she whispered.

"Not badly. I was in the Basilica praying when they struck. The
walls of the old church are weak. When the missiles struck, they
tumbled down around me. My head is fine, but I think my shoulder
is broken. I managed to pull myself from the rubble. I knew I had to

find you and the boy. Something told me you'd come to the scriptorium. So I entered the tunnel and made my way here."

"The tunnel?"

"Yes, child. That's where we are now. The bones of the Brothers rest here. I imagine you smelled their scent as we entered. You and Issa mustn't fear these bones. They're all your friends."

"We don't fear them, Brother Crispus," Issa whispered, his hand dancing in the darkness. "We feel their spirits around us. They will protect us."

"Yes, Issa. There are indeed spirits here, good spirits. I promise they will keep you safe."

"Where does the tunnel lead? How did you enter it?" Amala strained her eyes against the darkness, looking for the other end.

"In the past there were many tunnels. But the earthquakes collapsed them long ago. Only this one remains. There are two entrances. The one we just passed through in the store room of the scriptorium, and one hidden in the wall of the refectory kitchen." Brother Crispus tucked the candle in a shallow stone nook imbedded in mortar.

"But there isn't time for history lessons now, child. You both must listen carefully. I can't stay here while my brothers are in peril. I'll exit the way I came in, then make my way to the stable and ride to the village for help. I don't know if I will succeed or fail. That will be for God to decide. But no matter what happens, you both must stay here. Keep as quiet as you can and limit your movements. Above all, don't try to leave by either door. It may be days before it's safe again. You understand?"

Issa rose up on the tips of his toes and studied the bleached white skull imbedded in the wall beside the burning candle. He probed the sockets of its eyes, then nodded to the dancing hand.

"Your job is to stay alive and wait. There's a cleft in the rocks at the other end of the tunnel where fresh water runs. Come, bring the candle. I'll show you." Together they followed the tiny dot of light until they came to the spring.

"There's a bag of food beside it. It isn't much, but I'm sure you can make the best of things for now. There are candles in each of the nooks, but use them sparingly. Let the silence and the darkness become your friends, just as the spirits that fill this chamber are your friends. If God is with us, in time either I or someone else will come for you."

Amala nodded.

"Brother, won't you stay here and wait with us? Surely, there's nothing you can do now and escape seems virtually impossible."

"I've lived forty years behind the walls of Dier al-Shuhada. My brothers are my only family. What kind of man would hide from the dangers his family faces? Who could live with the burden of knowing that he had hidden when his actions might have made a difference? I must go, child. I know you understand. Your job is to stay here and protect your son. Mine is to for my brothers what I can."

Brother Crispus pulled a lever beside the wall. A portal opened. He passed through it and vanished into the darkness beyond. With a deep groan of stone passing over stone, it closed behind him.

Amala and Issa were alone.

CHAPTER XIX

THE SYRIAN DESERT
TELL NEBI-MEND

Within an hour of first light, Declan had broken camp and readied himself for the long ride to Dier al-Shuhada.

It had been a difficult passage through the long hours of darkness, but he had managed the ordeal. The visual and olfactory hallucinations were coming more frequently now. He couldn't deny that. And with each new wave they grew not only more vivid and disturbing, but real. The desert was changing him. He was evolving backward, back into something else, but he wasn't sure what. It wasn't the man he had been before. That man was dead. He'd died on the sands of Khirbet Qumran. He was evolving backwards into something new and terrifying. And he sensed that if he wasn't extremely careful, he could end up losing himself again as he had done in the days before the asylum. And this time, he knew that he might never find himself again.

Declan felt himself a leaf drifting helplessly toward a waterfall. He needed to find an exit before it was too late. He needed to get to the monastery, retrieve the girl and her son, deposit them somewhere safe, then get himself out as quickly as he could. And, just like the leaf of his imaginings, he knew that if he didn't act fast enough, if he lingered too long or gave Q a way to worm its promises and lies back into his heart and his mind, he would go head first over the falls and crash into the rocks below. If he let it, Q and the madness that always came with it—the madness that had taken Reichmann long ago, the madness that had nearly taken him in the asylum in Damascus, the madness that had taken Val and their unborn son—would wash over him and bend him to its will like a sapling. He couldn't let that happen. He had to make sure that this was about the girl and her son, about only them and nothing more. Anything else and he would never again see the sanctuary of the stone cottage above the great reef the Westers had named Ghost Ships. If he hadn't known that before, he knew it now.

By late afternoon he'd reached the Siq, the Gate. That winding tunnel, barely wide enough to accommodate the mare, would take him into a maze of mountains and canyons and then at last to the monastery itself. For a long moment he lingered there before the Gate and contemplated what might lie ahead. He thought about the girl and her son, and wondered where he was going to take them, how he was going to keep them safe from the storms that Ibrahim's parchments had stirred from the clouds of the past. And wondered about the cache of papers, Reichmann's journal and all the rest, tucked in the saddle bag beside him. Why had he taken the shovel and dug them up? Was he already falling back under the spell? Was it already too late?

He patted the mare's neck, clicked his heels, and rode ahead. Flecks of dust swirled in the broad, broken streaks of sunlight that penetrated the dark bruise of lingering clouds. As he guided the mare through the narrow cleft and into a pool of shadow, the hairs on his neck tingled. He sensed a presence, something behind him. Declan turned and looked back over his shoulder toward the narrow gate behind him. But the path was empty. There was nothing there. He touched the holster at his side, adjusted it, then clicked his heels gently and eased along the painted red trail of gravel and stone.

It took him nearly three hours to work his way along the winding, narrow trail and through the labyrinth of towering peaks and sharp, descending canyons and arrive at last at the red mountain that signaled the end of the journey. As horse and rider approached that final peak, Declan had the sensation of riding into a vacuum. The air was still and lifeless. Other than the clopping of hooves on stone and the grunts of the mare's labored breathing, there was no sound of any kind. It was as if he had ridden into a tomb.

The mare snorted then twisted her head, tugging the reins and dancing in a restless circle. The velvety coat of fine hair along the back of Declan's neck stirred again, sending an anxious tingle down his spine all the way to his boots. He adjusted his grip and tightened the reins. Something wasn't right.

For a long moment he studied the high precipices that rose like jagged red tusks around him. He had the sense that, quietly and in the distance, someone or something was watching him. He took his time, scanning the ragged summits. In the distant sky just below the broken clouds, a carrion crow sailed the thermal winds. It soared in a long, straight line above the canyon then disappeared behind the mountain. The mare circled nervously. Declan's foot slipped out of the stirrup. He tightened the reins again then squeezed his knees to hold her steady. As he leaned down and slipped his foot back atop the smooth metal ring, he noticed a carpet of geometric patterns beneath him, the tread marks of heavy boots.

"What do you think, old girl? That's a lot of footprints for a forgotten trail deep in the desert mountains." The mare snorted, pulling her head left then right as she continued her nervous circle dance.

Declan scratched her ears. "Steady, steady," he whispered, shortening the reins and tightening his grip.

Declan leaned backward against the crest of the black leather saddle. He pushed his heels deep into the stirrups then reached his hand into his saddle bag. He removed the .32-caliber Walther he had bought from the trader in al-Qusayr. It occurred to him now that perhaps he should have bargained instead for the Glock. It would have packed more punch, and from the look of things, he might be needing that.

His chiseled features hardening, he racked the slide. A cartridge lodged in the blue steel barrel. With a slow, methodic gesture, he flicked his thumb and released the safety. Reaching back inside the saddle bag, he withdrew four nine shot clips, placed two into each pocket of his khaki jacket then buttoned the flaps. Turning his gaze back toward the high ridges around him, he tucked the pistol into the empty holster that dangled from his belt and guided the mare back up the trail. Slowly, they climbed the last ridge that separated them from the monastery called Dier al-Shuhada.

"Don't worry, girl," he whispered. "We're ready for whatever's over that ridge. You just go easy now. Slow and easy, okay girl?" Declan patted her again, then eased the reins and pressed her up the serpentine trail, a sheet of loose rocks and gravel cascading down the mountain behind them.

As they crested the ridge, Declan smelled the lingering acrid vestiges of gunpowder and smoke, and in the distance beyond, the sour scent of death. A tapestry of destruction unfurled itself before him. Large stretches of the monastery's walls lay in ruins, the supporting timbers smoldering beneath the clouds. The tall cedar gates at the north and west entrances were little more than splinters now, their timbers scattered like match sticks across the sands. The library, the refectory, and the hermitage were all in flames. Only the Fatimid mosque appeared to have been untouched, its gleaming gold crescent spire shining in the crown points of light that penetrated the broken layer of clouds. In the sky overhead, a murder of carrion crows circled, filling the void below with the chilling sounds of their hungry caws.

Declan didn't want to think about the scarlet canvas that awaited him amid the smoldering ruins of Dier al-Shuhada or what games his mind might play with him then. He didn't want to imagine what memories those scenes would stir from the dusts of his past or what dreams were yet to trouble him in the darkness to come. He'd escaped the memories of Tell Nebi Mend, but he would not be able to escape this.

Declan gazed skyward at the circling black wings and the shadows they cast in the cloud-streaked light of the afternoon. For a moment he felt as if he were flying beside them, floating high above the desert, his glimmering black wings pounding the thermal winds. It was an eerie sensation, as if he were a vulture, circling, watching the horse and rider far below, waiting for them to fall and make a meal for him. Then the sensation vanished. Declan took a sip of water from his canteen, then guided the mare through the ruins of what once had been a mighty fortress gate.

The bodies were there, just as he had known they would be, all laid out in a narrow, straight line before the smoking ruins of the basilica. Eleven men, each mutilated with knives and picked at by the carrion crows.

"No woman, no boy," he whispered. The mare snorted as she sniffed the foul stench of the wind. Declan considered the possibilities.

"Let's hope that means they either escaped or, God help me, that their bodies are somewhere else on the grounds. Better that than taken alive."

Declan knew exactly what the men who had done all this were capable of and he cringed at the thought. If they took them alive, a woman and a young boy, they would use their bodies for their own twisted pleasures, each in his turn. Then, in a few days when they'd sated their lust, they would draw the knife, slit their throats, and cast the remains into a ravine somewhere deep in the mountains where they'd never be found.

Declan tied the mare to an iron ring protruding from the battered stones of what had once been a wall, then walked slowly toward the carnage laid out before him. But it wasn't the images of torture and death that filled his mind now. It was the twin images of a woman and a child. The images he'd struggled all along to keep at bay. Even on the cliffs of Paparoa as he'd made his promise to Ibrahim—a promise to save a woman and a child—he'd done battle against those images.

Suddenly, Declan's body convulsed, stilled, then convulsed again. His head exploded with a fire that cut through to the very core of him. The images had allied themselves with the metal inside his head, and together they would have their way. Declan closed his eyes and tried to suppress the coming storm, but another spasm, this one more powerful and disturbing, shook him so violently that he fell to his knees. But the ground beneath him was no longer solid. Like a membrane, it stretched and hollowed beneath him until at last it broke. He went tumbling, end over end, through a lightless abyss. Declan opened his mouth and tried to scream, but the sound wouldn't come. The crescent scar burned like a branding iron. The very bones of his skull were melting, sending a wide, seething flow of lava over him.

"Valkyre," he cried out. "Valkyre!"

Look, everything's going to be fine here. Ibrahim and I will keep the work going till you return. And we'll call the hospital every day. I'll stay here until you tell me it's time for me to come." Declan kissed her cheek and pointed her toward the helipad. "The sooner you get going, the sooner we'll all be together again, including him." Declan placed his hand on the soft curve of her stomach.

Val feigned a smile, kissed him, then turned and walked away.

The Sikorsky trembled as it rose slowly into the cool morning sky. Its thundering rotors stirred a billowing storm cloud of sand over the limestone cliffs that lined the broad, sloping *wadi*. With one hand, Declan shielded his eyes from the sun and with the other waved goodbye. Through the swirling haze, he watched as it rose into the air. From behind her window, she was blowing him a kiss.

In the distance, Ibrahim waited beside the entrance to the cave. As the rotor wash faded away and the helicopter arched back toward the gleaming blue water of the Dead Sea, Declan turned and walked in that direction. Then suddenly a bolt of bright white light flashed on the far ridge ahead of him. A dancing trail of smoke streaked through the dry morning air. Declan turned around just as the SA-17 shoulder-fired missile hit the fuselage, igniting the fuel tanks and creating a massive ball of fire. The concussion blast ripped Declan from his boots and sent him flying backward, head over heels, through space. Arrows of flaming red shrapnel tore through his arms and legs. He hit the ground hard, shoulder first, shattering the bone. Blood gushed from his wounds as he rolled over and over across the sand. Then, at last, he struck a boulder and came to a stop.

Somehow, Declan struggled to his knees. A sheet of warm blood covered his face and spilled into his eyes. The world around him glowed softly in ominous shades of crimson and brown.

"Val!"

But he couldn't hear his own words. The blast had shattered his eardrums. The air reeked of burning flesh and aviation fuel. Declan reached his hands toward the sky, as if that gesture held the power to reverse the flow of time, as if he might somehow change destiny itself. A lightless chamber opened up before him. He screamed then tumbled into the void.

Declan focused on his breath and tried to regain his awareness of the here-and-now. He gazed at the bodies on the ground in front of him, the crows that circled overhead, the smoldering ruins of the monastery. Step by step, it began to make sense. No, not make sense. Nothing made sense any more. But at least he had managed to claw his way back to the present.

Declan pulled himself up and walked toward the mare. There was nothing left to do now but bury the dead and look for two more bodies that he hoped desperately he would find. The alternative was too chilling to consider.

CHAPTER XX

CALIPH'S DESERT COMPOUND
AL HAMAD DESERT, SYRIA

A surge of energy, sexual in its intensity, raced through Shari's body as the helicopter drifted down and settled onto the sands of Bi'ral Ulayyaniyah. As the rotors slowed and the howling engines dimmed to a muted hum, Shari admired the sharp crease of his military trousers and the way they broke crisply atop his glossy black boots. He unbuckled his seat belt, removed the headset, and donned a checkered keffiyeh. He squared his shoulders and stepped out into the bright sun of the remote Syrian desert.

"Everything is as you have ordered, Sayyidi." The soldier snapped a salute.

Shari nodded, returned the gesture, then turned and strode across the dunes toward the large tent that loomed in the distance.

He was pleased to find that everything was precisely as he had commanded it should be. A polished silver teapot and serving pieces were arranged neatly on the desk beside an unopened pack of Dunhills and a bulbous crystal ashtray. On one side of them sat the remote control for his music, on the other, a tidy stack of maps and books. Shari smiled, poured himself a cup of Earl Grey, and stirred in a spoonful of sugar. He tapped the remote control. The tent filled with the sound of strings.

"We await your command." The young jihadi grasped his Kalashnikov with one hand and touched his hand to his heart with the other. He then bowed deeply. Shari smiled again.

"Bring me the Syrian," he ordered, as he gently dropped his briefcase onto the table and took his chair. He closed his eyes and let the magic of the strings carry him far away from this awful desert. His imagination had to work especially hard here, but with a little effort, the images of London slowly appeared. He was in his salon in Knightsbridge. He savored the sensation.

At last the movement ended. He opened his eyes and saw a reflection of the Syrian in the polished silver mirror of the teapot.

"Upon your command, Sayyidi." The Syrian bowed and waited for Shari to reply.

"Have you my map, Commander?" Shari adjusted his keffiyeh to ensure that it hung evenly over both shoulders.

"Yes, Sayyidi. I have *the caliph's* map."

Shari took a deep breath and brushed the dust from his sleeve. Soon he would have to rid himself of this crude soldier that he sensed was a growing threat to his ambitions.

"And those who were at the monastery?"

"All dead."

"How many?"

"Eleven."

"All monks?"

"Yes."

"No one else?"

"No one else, Sayyidi."

Shari gestured toward the bag that hung from the Syrian's shoulder. "Let me see it."

The Syrian slipped the pouch from his shoulder and placed it on the desk. Shari tossed open the flap and removed a rectangular package wrapped in oiled skins. "Careless fools," he uttered to himself.

Shari tugged the white silk square from the top pocket of his military coat. Methodically, he polished the lenses of his spectacles in slow, circular motions.

"And the Jew?" Shari stressed the final word because such things were expected in the caliph's camps.

"He was taken in Zurich as you ordered and brought here."

"Any complications?"

"No, Sayyidi. His disappearance was reported in the European newspapers, but there's nothing to tie him to us. He awaits you in the prison tent."

"Good. I'll need time to study this." He tapped the package before him. "See that I'm not disturbed. But presently, I will want to see the Jew. I will call you when I'm ready."

"As you command, Sayyidi."

The Syrian pressed his hand to his heart, bowed, then took his leave. Shari tucked the silk cloth back into the top pocket of his jacket and drew a Dunhill from the fresh pack. Then he touched the remote control and again the tent filled with music. He closed his eyes and released a breath.

He would have to be careful with the Syrian. He was unrefined, but he was very cunning. He had the potential to create problems. Given all the danger his plans already entailed, the last thing Shari wanted was an added element of risk. Crossing the caliph was not something many had tried, and few had lived to tell of it. He was confident in his ability to work the strings of his opium-besotted puppet, but less so when it came to the Syrian.

Shari blew a thin column of slate-blue smoke into the air, then stubbed out his cigarette. Gently he removed the oiled skins and revealed the map. His heart fluttered with excitement. He'd never seen anything quite like it. Its state of preservation was incomprehensible.

Just as had been the case with the manuscript, it was supple and fresh, as if it had been prepared yesterday, not two thousand years ago. In all his years of treasure hunting, Shari had never encountered anything so magnificent. It was incomprehensible by any science he had ever known. Gently, he touched the edge of the map and felt a surge of electricity run through him. He was closer than he had ever been. So close now he could taste it. All that was left was to decipher the map. And that was where Judah Lowe came in.

CHAPTER XXI

THE MONASTERY OF DIER AL-SHUHADA

As Declan closed the last of the eleven graves, the sun sank beneath the horizon. Pastel hues of turquoise, rose, and tangerine bled from the sky, tinting the very landscape itself with the richness of their colors. Absently, he made his way to the well and washed the blood from his hands. When he finished and tossed the pail of red water onto the sand, he struck a match and ignited the lantern. He hoped that he still had two bodies to find.

Declan began his search in what was left of the refectory, the building closest to the graves, and one of the few besides the mosque that was still largely intact. When he entered, he saw that the assassins had been there ahead of him. Broken pottery, jars of olives, slices of barley bread, and the remnants of cucumbers, tomatoes, and dates were scattered across the stone floor. Otherwise, it seemed in good order. Plates and cups still stood neatly stacked on the counter, folded muslin cloths and a jumbled mass of wooden utensils beside them. Dented iron pots and skillets, their coal black metal absorbing the lantern light, still hung from curved metal hooks attached to the rafter beams. Fragrant branches of dried herbs, garlic, and gourds, punctuated intermittently by cheeses suspended in pear-shaped hammocks, lined the walls. Even the washing bowl still brimmed with soapy blue water.

Declan lowered the lantern and passed a beam of light across the floor. The tiny hairs on his neck stirred. A muted tingle scurried along his spine. It was the same sensation he had felt on the ridge above the monastery when he sensed something was not as it should be. It was a vague and subtle sensation, but not one to be ignored. Declan adjusted the knob and turned the lantern flame higher. Something scurried across his feet.

He squatted down and made a circle of light on the stone floor. Flecks of dust moved in a single direction, as if pushed along by a breeze. That was curious. With no windows and the only door closed behind him, the air inside the room should have been still and lifeless. But still the fine coating of dust floated toward the back wall.

Declan lay down on his side and tilted the lantern as far as it would go without upsetting it. He pressed his cheekbone against the smooth squares of limestone. The amber oval of light fanned out in front of him. The vague outlines of sandal prints and boot marks appeared, a thin veil of dust flecks flowing over them. Declan turned his face sideways and inched across the floor in the direction of the flow, dragging the lantern beside him.

When he at last came to a stone wall at the rear of the room, the dust flecks vanished. Like a subterranean river, that flowed into nothingness. Declan tilted the lantern up and studied the line of mortar that ran between the perpendicular planes of the wall and floor. The dust stirred evenly for two or three meters in each direction on either side of it then disappeared into a long hairline fissure at the base of the wall. He licked the back of his hand then squeezed it against the crack. A slow, steady flow of air cooled his damp skin. Unless he missed his guess, he had discovered a hidden door.

As with so many clever inventions, the Arabs had been the first to create them. It was said that the first, the *Bab al-sirr*, the hidden gate. It had been built in the ancient city of Aden at the command of the emir who wrought a secret sixth gate to his city, one that would be known only to him. No two were ever alike. The latches were often ingenious and nearly always invisible. Sometimes they were housed inside the door and accessed through a spider hole in the mortar. Other times the trigger was placed on the outside, hidden in plain sight, disguised as a brick, a metal hook, or some other entirely ordinary fixture.

With the aid of computerized devices and other modern tools, archaeologists usually uncovered their secrets quickly enough. But Declan would have to find the latch on his own. So he set the lantern on the floor beside him and painstakingly began to examine every stone. Only trial and error would show him the way.

An hour later, he found it. The latch was a two trigger device. Each trigger was hidden in a field of identical mortar holes at opposite ends of the wall. To open the door, one had to trip both mechanisms simultaneously. Declan rummaged through the kitchen and found a cache of metal skewers. He placed one into each hole. Then he drew a deep breath, and with his left hand and the heel of his right boot simultaneously applied pressure to them both. At first nothing happened. He adjusted the skewers and tried again. This time, the mechanisms clicked and something gave way. He pressed his shoulder into the wall and pushed. The wall groaned as it slowly opened.

Cool damp air and the smell of decay swept over his face and filled his nostrils. Then he heard the sound of a metal latch click again. A third mechanism had now automatically triggered. It was the counterweight. The load of the wall shifted. All he had to do was push. The sole of his boot skidded slightly on the loose dirt of the floor as he repositioned himself and pressed again. The immense portal moved steadily back upon itself and toward the inner wall. A deep, dark void that smelled of human decay opened before him.

"Amala, are you in there?" he whispered in Arabic. "It's Declan Stewart."

In the distance he heard the sounds of movement.

"Amala?"

Again, the sounds of shuffling feet. Someone was there in the darkness.

"Yes, we're here. We see the light." It was the voice of a child.

"Keep talking. I'll follow your voice." Declan lowered his head, slipped through the portal, and waded into the darkness.

"Here."

Declan followed the voice, the dim circle of light guiding his steps. Then along the wall, he saw the magic hand dancing in the air and moved toward it until, at last, he reached them, a woman and a boy huddled together beneath a wall of bones.

"Are you okay? Can you walk?"

"I think so." It was the woman's voice this time. "It's just that the darkness has made us a little disoriented."

Declan handed her the lantern. "Here, you hold this. I'll carry you."

"Ommy, it's just as I told you. The fire couldn't hurt us. The spirits of the Brothers kept us safe." Issa seemed at ease, unaffected by the ordeal.

"Come on. Let's get out of here." He still spoke in Arabic.

"My English is quite good, Dr. Stewart. We can speak English if you like."

Declan smiled. "Fine, no problem," he said, this time in his native tongue.

Declan placed one arm around Amala's waist and the other around the boy's shoulder, then led them out of the tunnel and back to the refectory.

When he saw that she was in her night dress, Declan instinctively peeled off his shirt and handed it to her. "It's not exactly clean, but it'll do. Now let's get some food and water into you two."

"Brother Crispus warned us not to leave the tunnel. I don't have any idea how long we've been inside. A couple of days, I think."

"That was good advice."

Issa smiled. He held his hand up and laughed as it danced.

"Don't pay any attention to him. He's a very polite and very smart boy, but sometimes he gets carried away with his little game. It occupied his mind while we were in the darkness."

Declan snatched a bag of dried fruit and pear shaped cheese from the rafters.

"They're gone then?"

"Yes, they're gone. Nothing left to fear here now."

"And Brother Crispus, did he make it to the village?"

Declan pretended not to have heard her question. With his knife he cut two slices from the mass of cheese and placed them on a plate. He added a handful of dried dates then sat down across the table from them.

"Eat that, but go easy, okay? When you feel up to it, I need you to tell me about all this. I need to know what happened, and when. I've got a pretty good idea about things, but details like timelines and any guesses about who did it will help."

"There isn't much to tell. The attack came before dawn. There were loud explosions and gunfire. Syrians, Afghans, maybe Algerians, I'm not sure. We made our way to the scriptorium and hid in the storage room. Brother Crispus showed us the tunnel, then he went for help. They came for the map, of course. I suppose you already know that."

"Then I'm sure they found it. If they hadn't, they'd still be here." Declan nodded as if speaking to himself.

Amala gazed at the outline of her bare feet on the smooth grey surface of the stone. "And the Brothers, Dr. Stewart. What of them?"

Declan rubbed the stubble on his chin and then let out a long, slow breath. "Do you want to send Issa to the well for a fresh pail of water? The night air might do him good."

"We'll go up together in a moment, Dr. Stewart. Issa is strong. He's a Palestinian, you know. He understands about war and death. That's why the dancing hand dances. Whatever you have to share, he can hear it, if he chooses to listen."

Declan arched an eyebrow, then nodded. He struggled for a moment with how to answer her. Then he simply spoke the truth.

"They're dead, eleven in all. I don't know about your Brother Crispus. Maybe he got out." He sipped the water as if it were a tonic against the memory of the mutilated bodies. As if it might ward off another episode. "I put them in the ground when I arrived."

"Eleven." Amala stared beyond the light of the lantern and nodded her head slowly. "Then Brother Crispus didn't get through. Eleven is everyone except Ibrahim."

Declan slowly exhaled, but said nothing.

"And what news have you of him, of Ibrahim?"

Declan didn't want to go there. He couldn't. Not tonight.

"Look, we both have a lot of questions. But I've just buried elev-en men. There'll be plenty of time to talk in the morning. Right now, we need to find a place to sleep. So why don't we head upstairs? It'll do you both good to breathe some fresh air after that dark hole. The *hamal* is in bloom, the moon is full. We can speak of Brother Ibrahim tomorrow."

Amala nodded and rose from the table. He had already given her the answer.

As they climbed the stairs and emerged into the stillness of the smoldering ruins, Amala pulled Declan's shirt close around her. "Do you think they'll return?"

"The ones who did all this? No, I don't think they're coming back. If they have the map and the manuscript, there's nothing left for them here. They're already looking forward, not backward."

"And if they didn't find the map?"

"Trust me, they have it. They never would have killed all the Brothers if they didn't. But in the morning, after you and the boy have had some rest, you can take me to the scriptorium and show me where Ibrahim hid it. Maybe we'll find something there that will tell us who's responsible for this. But for now, just sit here on these blankets. I'll find us a place to bed down. It won't take me long."

Amala found the sound of Declan's voice comforting. It was round and mellow and reminded her of better days. As he walked off into the moonlight, she studied the broad outline of his shoulders as it swayed back and forth. She liked the way the muscles of his back pressed against the white cotton of his t-shirt, still damp with sweat. And she especially liked the way he had covered her when he realized she was in her night clothes. For the first time in a very long time, Amala felt safe.

But she knew that even here in the care of a strong man, any sense of safety was just an illusion. She had learned that lesson well, as if her whole life had been designed to remind her of that one immutable fact. Danger was Amala's perpetual companion. Danger in Palestine. Danger in Israel. Now danger in Syria. How many times must she encounter the dark specter of death? she wondered. How many broken bodies and extinguished lives in the days past and the days yet to come?

The first had been in Gaza, when the Israelis came by night, beckoned by the katyushas Hamas had launched over the border into villages filled with settlers, their children peacefully at play in the fields behind the fences that pinned them in like cattle. They had ridden the skies like dark horsemen on the backs of the American made helicopters called Apaches, pouring their wrath down on the guilty and the innocent alike in a seemingly endless rain of missiles and fire.

And because the Hamas fighters had hidden behind them, the people had no place to run. Not the shopkeepers, nor the school children, not the infirm, the weary, or the resigned. Not even those who were willing to share the land. Gaza was so very small, a post-age stamp pressed against the turquoise sea, and so very crowded. Four hundred thousand people, most of them women and children, all packed into an area no more than forty-five square kilometers. So when fire fell from the sky and the men in uniforms crossed the border in their Merkva tanks, where was there to run? There was no charnel chamber in which to hide, no Declan Stewart to come and save them.

Then the Palestinians had turned on themselves. Brother against brother, chasing and firing and yelling their battle cries as Hamas and the Palestinian Authority did battle against each other. And still the shopkeepers and the children tried to run. And again, they had no place to hide. The danger was just as real, the death from a bullet or a bomb just as certain, whether it came from a Jew or an Arab. And now, here in the Monastery of the Martyrs, death had followed her once again. More blood, more loss, more sadness. But all things were God's will, were they not? He always had a plan for everyone, a divine destiny in all that was and in all that would be, whether or not she could comprehend its logic. She wondered whether God had a plan for Declan Stewart.

Amala was so very tired. She lay on her side beneath the olive tree and pulled Issa close to her, nestling his body in the nook beneath her breasts. She watched as Declan faded into the darkness. Slowly, she fell into a warm inviting pool kissed by moonlight. But she wasn't alone. Something circled around her, just beneath the surface. She was not afraid. It called to her from the depths. Its voice was strong and reassuring. It promised her safety from the dangers that lurked above if only she would let herself sink further. And so she let the darkness take her down, down into its cloistered realm of shadows and silence. As she descended, someone took her hand and guided her through the watery canyons of an alien world. But it was dark, much too dark to see. Unafraid, she let go and drifted into the void.

CHAPTER XXII

CALIPH'S DESERT COMPOUND
AL HAMAD DESERT, SYRIA

Judah Lowe was certain that he was about to die. He only hoped that the end would come quickly and that they would not use the knife.

"You must understand, *Doc-tor* Lowe, you aren't on the streets of Zurich. There are no policemen in clean blue uniforms here. There is no grand embassy filled with diplomats to rescue you. Here there is only desert. Here everything is jihad. There isn't anyone to save you from your fate now. Do you understand me, Jew?" The Syrian snarled as he pressed his face close to Judah Lowe's.

Judah gritted his teeth and tried to avoid the glare of his leering black eyes. He hoped his silence might be seen as a sign of resignation, even submission. But he had misjudged his captor. Lightning fast, the Syrian slapped him hard across the face and knocked him from his chair. He tumbled to the ground. The Syrian picked him up again. With a harsh jerk he plopped him back into the chair.

"Time is precious. The relic must be found. When you've deciphered the meaning of the manuscript and the map, you will tell only me. Is that understood? No one else, only me. If you don't follow this command, I will make you suffer in ways that you have never imagined, not even in your darkest nightmares. I assure you that I know how to keep a man alive for a very long time even as he begs for death. I can show you some of my tools if you like. The wires, the probes, and the drills, they're all here. And, there is always the knife," the Syrian touched the scabbard at his side. "I think you fear it most of all, don't you?" Slowly the Syrian drew the jambiya from his belt. Its curved blade glistened in the diffuse light inside the small tent. "Tell me now, will these things be necessary, *Doc-tor Ju-dah Lowe*?"

Judah Lowe was dazed, but he was not a fool. He had no idea what this was all about, but he was beginning to understand the rules of this particular engagement.

"After all, what does it matter to you, this relic? Give me what I seek and you are free to go, my cousin. Surely, this is a bargain a Jew can understand." The Syrian leaned down, grabbed a patch of the thin white hair at the back of Judah Lowe's scalp and jerked. Judah's head snapped back. Something popped but thankfully did not break. He pressed his knife tight against Judah's throat. Their eyes met. An icy-cold surge of fear swept through every fiber of Judah Lowe's being.

He was angry with himself. He had let his greed be his undoing. He should have been more careful, more suspicious. If not when the boy in the black leather jacket walked up behind him and called his name, then at least when he'd said there had been a change in plans. He'd been a fool. He'd let the Bentley and the promise of easy money blind him to the risks. He'd let his appetite for luxury in the winter of his life subdue his suspicious nature. The simple comforts—the crosswords by the fire on a snowy night and solitary walks along the Zurichsee; the crystal stems of inexpensive Barolo and the fragrance of flowers in bloom—should have been enough for him. But these men had gazed inside him and seen his weakness, then so very easily exploited it.

But there wasn't time now for recrimination. He had to find his voice.

"I have . . . no interest . . . whatsoever"—the words dribbled out. The sharp angle at which the Syrian held his head back against his spine had distended his larynx and made it difficult to speak—"in being tortured . . . or suffering in any . . . way." The Syrian released the thatch of hair. Judah gulped a breath of air, then swallowed. "I have no greater desire than to help you sort this out and to hope that you are, as you claim to be, a man of your word who will release me from this desert and return me to my home as soon as it's done."

The Syrian flashed a tight-lipped smile.

"But you must understand. This sort of endeavor is complex in the extreme. You say you have a manuscript and a map. But I've never seen them. I need to know about their provenance. I will need a means of placing them in time. But if you provide me with tools and time, I'm confident that if anyone can give you the answers you seek, it is beyond question the man who sits before you now. And if you will work with me instead of threatening me with things I am already quite adequately afraid of and deeply wish to avoid, I will do exactly as you say."

For a long moment laced with danger, the Syrian held the knife against Judah's skin and stared into his eyes. Once again, Judah Lowe sensed that his death was close at hand.

Then a voice came from the opening at the far side of the tent.

"Enough!" The word was a command, spoken in Arabic, with a slight accent Judah couldn't quite place.

The Syrian slowly withdrew the blade and turned around. An elegant man in a crisp military uniform, his white hair and black boots glimmering like mirrors, quickly stepped forward. The man raised his hand and shook his head. The Syrian stood up and turned slightly to face him. But he did not re-sheath his knife.

"I told you I would call for the Jew when I was ready, did I not?

You are in command of the camp, but I am in charge of the Jew. I am to handle his questioning, not you. Now put your knife away."

Judah at last had placed the accent. It was Farsi. The man was a Persian.

"Yes, Sayyidi." The Syrian's eyes glowed black and red as he eased his jambiya back into its sheath.

The man in the uniform walked toward Judah Lowe.

"I must apologize for the behavior of my colleague." He spoke to Judah in near-perfect German. "My name is Sharif, Doctor, and I'm in charge of you and of this expedition. Please disregard the barbarian and his knife. He has a limited role in this affair and oversteps his authority. I'm the one you will deal with. Me and no one other than me. Is that clear?"

Judah Lowe nodded crisply.

"The points you were making to our crude friend here are all well taken, Doctor. I'm quite aware of the reasonableness of your requests. First, you and I will spend some time with the manuscript and map. Then together we'll prepare a list of what you need to complete your work. I will ensure that you have everything, every last item you list, all the tools you require to complete the work we have assigned to you—books, computers, databases—you shall have them all. But know this, Dr. Lowe. Once you have these things, there won't be any room for excuses. There will be nothing to save you from the Syrian's knife should you fail. I trust we have an understanding?"

Judah nodded again.

"I am normally a patient man, Doctor, but in this matter time is painfully short. We work against the constant ticking of a small golden watch held by a most impatient and violent man in Beirut. He is the sponsor of our little expedition." He paused, then pulled up a chair and sat down beside Judah Lowe. Turning to the Syrian, he said in Arabic, "Cut his hands loose and have one of the men bring more tea and some food to my tent."

The Syrian stepped forward and with a flourish withdrew the jambiya. In a swift arcing motion, he severed Judah's ropes then slowly sheathed the knife. Judah rubbed his hands together, then massaged the bruised spot under his scalp where he'd hit the floor.

Then shifting once again to German, Shari said, "If you're wise, Doctor, you will do precisely what I say and speak only to me. If you do that and, of course assuming that you give me the answers I require, I imagine you shall live to someday tell your grandchildren of this grand adventure. Now, if you would kindly come with me, I want to show you the two most extraordinary parchments you will have ever seen. There is nothing like them in all the world. While we take our tea and study them together, I will tell you an amazing story, the story of a most delightful man, and a fellow Jew, I might add. He was a friend of mine. His name was Dr. Emile Zorn, also of Zurich, at least in a round-about way. I shall tell you a tale of obscure excavations, forgotten crates, a desert monastery, and, above all, a priceless treasure. A treasure that Dr. Zorn and I both unknow-ingly let slip right through our hands a very long time ago. It has taken me a lifetime to come as close to the treasure again. It is a treasure that awaits somewhere in the sheltering sands of an ancient desert that you, my good Doctor, shall show me how to find."

The young jihadi brought them yet another pot of tea. Was it the fourth or the sixth? Shari couldn't quite recall. He and Judah Lowe, working well into the night, had long ago lost any sense of time.

The aroma of bergamot filled his senses as he studied Dr. Lowe, who in turn studied the map and the manuscript on the table before them. The man's fear had vanished hours ago. In its place had come an academic's excitement and a deep curiosity. And, unless Shari missed his guess, an overwhelming desire for the prize.

"I will need a laptop and Internet access, of course. And a copy of

Balcombe's six-volume *Cartography of Ancient Lands and Lost Kingdoms* and al-Khoury's *Pre-Islamic Arabian Cartography and Nascent Map Culture*. Yes, both of those. And the Durabian Parchment. Above all, the Durabian Parchment. But that will be impossible. The original is in the Berlin Museum. That's too bad. The original would be so very useful."

"Please, Doctor, few things are impossible in my world. I ask you not to make assumptions about what is possible and what isn't. Simply write. Write it all down."

"And the Dilmun cartograph. Let's see, what else?"

Judah tapped his head with the pen. He was clearly working hard to get it all down. He took another sip of tea, then glanced up from the pad and smiled.

CHAPTER XXIII

MONASTERY OF THE MARTYRS
SYRIAN DESERT

Amala woke in the still, moist darkness of predawn. In the distance, jackals howled mournfully as if they feared the coming of the light. But they were powerless against the promise of a new day.

She lay on a cot, a coarse blanket wrapped around her from her shoulders to her feet. She lifted the cover. She still wore Declan's shirt just as she had when sleep took her beneath the moonlit branches of the olive tree.

Without moving, she scanned the tiny room. She was in the ante-chamber of the Fatimid mosque. On a separate cot pulled close beside her, Issa slept peacefully. On a small wooden table between them, the stub of a candle flickered dimly, casting dancing shadows on the walls around them.

Where was Declan Stewart? Quietly, she raised herself up on her elbows. Then she saw him, curled like an infant inside the womb, on the floor. Beside him lay his pistol and knife. The coarse brown blanket draped across his shoulders shook, as if he were trembling beneath it. She listened to the sound of his breathing. It was a ragged, restless sound that spoke of troubling dreams, of the terrors that come only at night. The breaths came in broken, erratic segments of time, his chest rising and falling like the surface of the sea when gusting winds make it restive and impatient. Just as she had counted her footsteps on the night of the attack, Amala counted his breaths. Unconsciously, she tried to bring her own breathing into rhythm with his, but she couldn't. It was too irregular. She took the candle from beside her and quietly slipped off the cot. In the flickering light, she saw the scar. It ran in the shape of a crescent from his cheekbone to his hairline.

Ibrahim had told her everything, of course. He'd told her about the tragedy, about what had happened at dawn a decade before on the sands of the Judean Desert. He'd told her what that day had done to Declan Stewart. How it had nearly taken his life. How in the end, it had sent him to the asylum in Damascus. How one day he had risen from his bed, stepped into the fog, and never been heard from again.

For a while she just stood there, not moving for fear of waking them. *What now*? she wondered. Now that the monks were dead and the map fallen into the hands of their murderers? What of the quest? What of *Q*? Had Declan Stewart come, as Ibrahim had called him to do, to unravel the secret of the parchments and to go in search of *Q*? Would he join the quest and do what Ibrahim had believed only he could? Would he bring the treasure out of darkness and into the light? Only time would tell.

Amala had been a student at the university in Amman when Jibril died. Issa was only four. It was supposed to have been a quick trip. His mother had taken ill. She needed someone to help. And so Jibril had boarded the bus at the Abdali station and gone to make arrangements for her. He arrived at Jerusalem Central Station on a day filled with bright sunshine. He'd gone to the market to do his mother's shopping. As he strolled the narrow lanes between tables laden with grains and fruits, pausing ever so briefly to test the ripeness of a cassava or the color of a tomato, an al-Aqsa teenager from Jenin released the button he held in hand, the button attached to the explosives-laden vest he wore beneath his coat. In an instant, Jibril had become a martyr.

Amala's neighbors in Amman celebrated. They said how blessed she was that Jibril had died for Palestine, even though he hadn't really died for Palestine at all. He'd only been reaching for a melon. They drank endless cups of mint tea and said things like "I know it's hard, but he gave his life for the people. He gave his life for the land. Many Zionists died. Be proud." They tilted the pot and filled their cups again, chattering like squirrels on their branches. "And who knows, perhaps one day your boy too will be a martyr for our home-land. Perhaps he too will die for Palestine." And that was when Amala knew they had to leave.

Ibrahim, her father's oldest and closest friend, came to her rescue, as he always did. With the permission of her father, he arranged an internship at Al-Azhar University. It was there that she learned the art and science of archival photography. Her wages were modest, but they helped her father support them. And more important still, she at last had a career and a way to fill the emptiness she felt inside.

Then, four years later, while the scars of her loss were still pain-fully fresh, the nightmare came again. This time it was the Israelis, not the martyrdom squads. Their missiles rained down on her father's apartment building like flaming stars that fell from the cold night sky. They destroyed the entire block, all the shops and homes, the cars and the street lamps. And her father. And her mother. And her brother. Suddenly she and Issa were alone. Suddenly they had no one left at all. Once again it was Ibrahim who came to help them.

Because there wasn't any place else to go, he took them with him to the monastery and set them up in the hermitage beside Brother Crispus's garden. When he first brought them to Dier al-Shuhada, Amala fell into a deep depression. For a long time, she and Issa were the only guests in the hermitage. The loneliness, the silence and the solemnity, only magnified her sorrows. But then one morning everything changed. She rose from her cot and listened to the desert wrens as they sang their cheerful song to the coming day. Outside, the brilliant white sun reflected off the golden cross of the Basilica and made the leaves of the olive trees shimmer. Slowly her sadness gave way to the beauty that surrounded her. She came to appreciate what she at first had despised. That was the day she had entered the scriptorium's storage room. That was the day that had changed the destinies of everyone.

The dawn sun scurried through the high windows of the minaret and stirred her from her memories. Softly, she crept past the doorway and made her way to the well. As she washed in the clear cold water, a brilliant sun beamed behind her, its rays streaking through the gnarled limbs of the olive grove. She picked her way through the ruins to what had been her quarters in the hermitage. She managed to find a few pieces of fresh clothing for herself and Issa. She discarded the soiled nightgown and changed into khaki pants and a white cotton shirt, then hurried back to the antechamber of the mosque. Issa and Declan were already up. The dancing hand danced as Declan fastened the last buttons of his shirt.

As he had suggested the evening before, she took Declan to the scriptorium and showed him the secret chamber where Ibrahim had hidden the map. The stones had been removed. The chamber was empty. Declan stayed behind and probed the wreckage for clues while Amala hurried to the refectory to arrange breakfast for them all. She found boiled eggs tucked into the cool recesses of the keeping cabinet, dried figs and apricots, hard-crusted bread, cheese, and a tin of coffee grounds. She even found Brother Crispus's secret cache of sweet biscuits.

Beneath the olive trees, Issa spun around like a dancer, his hands swerving this way and that, painting symbols in the air. As she set their places on the large stone table beside the fountain, Amala smiled. She found something reassuring in the golden rays of sunshine and the gentle rustling of the leaves. She dusted the woven reed seats of the chairs with her dish towel and wondered what was taking Declan so long. If he didn't hurry, the coffee would be cold. Then, over her shoulder, she heard his voice.

"Something smells good." Declan smiled and eased into the chair. Amala filled his cup with coffee.

"Did you find anything helpful?"

"Not really. Boot prints, the spent shells of cartridges, things like that. They used Kalashnikovs. There were fifteen, maybe twenty of them. Nothing much I didn't already know or at least already assumed. Nothing to tell me who did it. Nothing to suggest who sent them or where they've gone."

Declan bit into the leathery flesh of the dried fruit, tearing it in two with his front teeth. He sipped the hot coffee from the wooden cup and gazed at Issa and the stunning blue sky beyond him. It glowed serenely. Suddenly the shadows were gone. Only light remained.

Amala refilled his cup. Without looking up, she said, "Ibrahim's dead, isn't he?" as though she were commenting on the weather.

Declan's fine spirits dropped a notch. He encircled the wooden cup with his hands and gazed once more at the boy playing beneath the trees. The dancing hand intrigued Declan. It seemed never to rest. Then he turned round in his seat and looked up into Amala's eyes.

"I'm sorry."

"How did it happen?" The plates and the coffee pot didn't need moving, but Amala moved them anyway.

"He was murdered. I don't have any way of knowing for sure, but odds are good it's the same group that did this. The ones on the trail of Q. The ones who don't have the slightest apprehension about killing for it."

"Where did it happen?"

Declan turned his gaze back to the dancing hand. Then he said, as if speaking to himself, "A long way from here."

"In New Zealand?"

"Yes."

"Please, Dr. Stewart. I know this isn't a pleasant topic for either of us. But I have to know. Please, it's all right. You can tell me how it happened."

Declan instinctively touched the scar then expelled a long breath of resignation. "Not so much to tell. Assassins came by night. Ibrahim was shot. He died in the car on the way to the hospital. I buried him on a cliff above the sea because that's the only choice the assassins gave me. Then I came here because I promised him I would. I promised him that I'd come for you and Issa." Declan looked down at his plate, then mechanically, as if he had been programmed to follow the sequence, took a sip of coffee and another bite of fruit.

"Thank you, Dr. Stewart. Thank you for telling me." Amala placed her hand atop Declan's, then sat down beside him. For a while they sat in silence and watched Issa as he played beneath the trees.

Declan reached into his pocket and removed something. "Here, I thought you might want this, if not for yourself then for the boy."

He laid Ibrahim's rosary on the table before her, fanning out its dark wooden beads so that it made an oval.

Amala sat quietly for a moment and stared at the crucifix. She gazed at the image of Jesus etched into the smoothly worn metal. She could still see the outlines of anguish on his face. Slowly she reached out her hand and took hold of the black beads. She raised it up to the sun then slipped it into the pocket of her khakis.

"Thank you. It's good to have something of his, something to remind Issa and me of better days."

Declan nodded and circled his hands around the cup again.

"And so what happens now?" she asked.

Declan considered the question for a moment.

"Syria's a tinder box. My guess is that the Assad regime is finished, and as bad as all this is," he nodded toward the ruins around them, "it's about to get worse, much worse. If you have any friends or family, I'll get you to them. I've also brought some money for you. Once you're safe, I'm headed back home."

"We have no one. Now that Ibrahim and the Brothers are gone, there's no one left. No mother, no father, no brothers, no sisters. It's just Issa and me. But we'll be fine. We'll make do. Somehow we always have."

Declan drew another deep breath then slowly released it. "I understand. We'll just have to come up with another plan. Do you and Issa have passports?"

"Yes, we're Israeli citizens. Second class ones, but still citizens."

"Then maybe we'll go to Israel. Things aren't too bad there, so long as we stay away from Gaza. Anyway, I have a friend with a compound in the desert. He's a good man and a rich one. He has a great many connections and resources at his disposal. Maybe we'll go there for a few days and see if he can help us work something out for you both. The one thing I do know for sure, though, is that we can't stay here."

"And what about Q? What about Ibrahim's parchments?"

Declan swallowed hard then shrugged his shoulders. Beads of sweat formed along the line of his scalp.

"Nothing happens about Q."

"I don't understand."

"There's nothing to understand. I told Ibrahim to count me out. I wouldn't even be here now if I hadn't promised him that I'd get you and Issa to safety. Besides, there aren't any parchments. The assassins have the manuscript and the map. All I've got are photos of the manuscript that Ibrahim gave me at Ghost Ships. So the bad guys win. Ibrahim loses. That's just the way it works out sometimes. That's the way it always works out when it's about Q."

Declan lifted the coffee pot and with a gesture inquired whether she wanted more. Amala smiled and nodded. He filled her cup, then his own.

Amala's eyes hardened as she shifted the wooden cup back and forth.

"Forgive me, Dr. Stewart, but eleven men died here yesterday, the monastery was destroyed, and a friend who crossed the globe to find you is now buried in an alien land. You can't just leave it at that."

Declan felt a wave of anger well up within him. He slowed his breathing and tried to hold it back. "Look, I don't know what you want from me. I promised Ibrahim I would come find you. I did that. I promised him I'd get you to safety, and I'm going to do that. I'm doing everything that was asked of me, everything I promised to do. And you have no way of knowing how hard even that much has been. I shouldn't even be here. I don't belong here anymore. And the longer I stay here, the more danger I'm in. Not from this. I can handle this. From things you know nothing about, things that I'm not going to talk about, okay? I told Ibrahim not to lecture me. Now I'll tell you the same thing. I'll do what I promised him I'd do. Then I leave; then I have to leave. I don't have a choice if I ever want to make it back home."

"Ibrahim believed so deeply, so passionately, in a vision of the future that he willingly gave his life for it. I don't mourn his passing, I celebrate it. He gave himself to God, everything he had and everything he was. But he knew he wasn't the one. God didn't choose him to find Q, Dr. Stewart. God chose you. That's what Ibrahim believed, and he celebrated that. He rejoiced in the knowledge that you would be the one to unravel the mystery of the parchment, that it would be you who would follow the trail and find the scroll, that it would be *you* who would bring the world from darkness into light. And now, with so much blood spilled, so many lives sacrificed in that endeavor, you intend to just turn around and go home? Don't try to make this about Issa and me. We're fine. We'll be fine. This is about you, and about something much more important than Issa and me."

Declan pushed his chair back and stood up from the table.

"That's exactly what I intend to do. I intend to put you and Issa on one of those horses over there and the three of us area going to ride out of here. We leave in two hours. Make sure you're ready—both of you." Declan turned and walked away.

For a long while Amala sat alone in the shade of the olive grove, staring at the rosary and wondering what she had to do, what Ibrahim would want her to do. She owed Ibrahim her life and that of her son. And in a way, she owed the same thing to Declan Stewart. But she couldn't just stand by and let him walk away. This couldn't be the way God had intended it. So much loss, so much tragedy, only to end with bickering beneath an olive tree. For a long while she sat in silent contemplation. Then, at last, she rose from the table and went to find Declan Stewart.

CHAPTER XXIV

CALIPH'S DESERT COMPOUND
AL HAMAD DESERT, SYRIA

"Forgive me for interrupting your thoughts, Dr. Lowe. I trust you're making progress?" Shari's voice was soft and reassuring.

"Yes, after a fashion. Quite good progress."

"And the location of *Q*? How soon, Doctor?"

Judah pushed his chair back from the table and sipped the warm tea from his cup. It was Darjeeling. Somehow Shari had learned of his preference and quietly arranged it.

"It's a process. I'm closer now than I was an hour ago, and infinitely closer than I was three days ago. But the matter is astoundingly complex. The author of both the manuscript and the map created a code to obscure the location. It's intentional, and whoever created the code was very, very good. My challenge now is to find the key to his ingenious little anagrams."

Much to Judah Lowe's amazement, the quest for *Q* was proving to be the most alluring, challenging, and ultimately fulfilling endeavor he had ever undertaken. *Q* for *Quelle*— "the source." No one really knew for certain what *Q* was or whether it even existed at all. They'd reasoned that it must exist, but no one—until now—had any proof that it did exist. Until now, it had been nothing more than a theoretical construct. That's why there were so many conflicting theories and so much scholarly debate among the Christians and the Muslims, both of whom revered Jesus, albeit in radically different ways. And this manuscript and this map! They promised to settle the matter once and for all. They promised to change everything.

Judah didn't believe in God, and so he had no expectation at all that the revelation of *Q* would trigger a divine event. But there could be no doubt at all that it would make the man who found it exquisitely famous and astoundingly rich. The very contemplation of such a thing gave Judah Lowe goose flesh. Such mysteries and opportunities didn't come along even once in the lives of most scholars. At seventy-two, Judah Lowe would take the trade-offs that came with kidnapping, imprisonment, and uncertain duration of life to have the chance to be the man who made a find of this extraordinary magnitude. The fame alone would be worth that. But something told him that if he played his cards right, if he actually broke the code and helped the Persian to find the scroll, there was a tiny glimmer of hope that there might be much more in it than fame alone for the man who had made it all possible.

Shari had proved to be hospitable after a fashion. Once he was convinced that Judah Lowe had fully engaged in his work, he made sure that the soldiers left him alone. Sometimes, for no reason at all, Shari brought him apricots and raw cashews. Other times he shared a glass of sherry with him after dinner. When he had complained about how little sleep he managed on the canvas cot, Shari arranged a proper bed and mattress. A man could do worse, he speculated, especially under the circumstances.

Beyond his good manners, Shari was resourceful. True to his word, he had provided Judah Lowe all the research materials he had requested. Nothing he had asked for had been denied him.

Computers, printers, books—he now had it all. Even the Durabian Parchment, the *original*. How they had managed that trick, taking it right from under the noses of the curators in Berlin, he could not even begin to imagine. But Judah was beginning to appreciate that there was very little that was impossible for his new-found Persian collaborator.

When Judah made a passing comment regarding how helpful it would be were someone like Dr. Abu Assad there to discuss the precise meaning of an obscure symbol on the map, Shari had ordered the Syrian to have his men go and kidnap him. But in his zeal, Shari had failed to appreciate the fact that Judah had been speaking figuratively. Dr. Abu Assad had been dead for ten years. The Syrian had not responded well to that one, but Shari had laughed himself to tears with a loud raucous laugh that somehow did not quite seem to fit him.

The Persian was nothing like the jihadis that swirled around the camp. They never missed an opportunity to leer menacingly at Judah or to flash their weapons in his direction, as if to say, *"We can kill you any time we like."* His Jewry made him a magnet for such treatment. In the twisted logic of their hatred, all non-Muslims were enemies of Islam. And Judah Lowe was an infidel of the worst kind, which was to say, a Jew.

He marveled at the intellectual mystery of it all. How is it that they could ignore the importance of nuance? he wondered. How could they see the world only in stark monochromatic bars of black and white? He must remember to discuss the matter with Dr. Oberhoffer if he made it out alive. He was, after all, a physician, a psychiatrist, and a psychologist. He had delved deeply into the human psyche. Perhaps he knew where the human kindness in them all had gone, what had become of their empathy. It would be a captivating discussion on a snowy winter's day with spiced wine and a roaring fire. He hoped that he might live to have his answer.

Perhaps most curious to Judah Lowe was that it mattered not the least to his captors—other than the Persian for whom his Jewishness or the lack thereof was an irrelevancy—that he was not a practicing Jew. It mattered not in the least to them that he'd long ago exited the shadows of the old temple at number 10 Lowenstrasse, or that he hadn't attended a Seder, much less entered a synagogue, in more than fifty years. They cared not that he kept no traditions, maintained no faith, and for his own part found most Jews to be not at all to his liking. Those things weren't factors in the calculus of their hatred. He supposed that it was, for them, as it had been for the Nazis before them, merely a matter of genetics, names, facial features, and circumcised phalluses, all of which, he confessed, were part of his worldly constitution, markers that even his own best efforts at personal reinvention had been powerless to erase.

Judah Lowe had thought a great deal about Shari in these last days. He was an interesting and complex man who was clearly consumed by the quest for Q. But he didn't seem to belong in present company. He seemed more suited to the private clubs of London than to the deserts of jihad. He was a breed apart from the scrappy imbeciles with matted beards who roamed aimlessly through the camp fingering prayer beads and quoting from the caliph's latest video ramblings about the coming of the Mahdi and the end of days. He seemed to share so little in common with his comrades.

"Doctor," Shari removed a Dunhill from his pocket and lit it, "I realize that this is a complex matter. Were it entirely within my domain, I shouldn't rush you. I understand the complexity. My days at Harvard gave me a proper respect for the challenges of original though and scholarly endeavors. But my sponsor in Beirut is not a Harvard man, *Judah*." It was the first time he had called him by his first name.

"He and his warriors of Islam aren't men of letters. You may have noticed this. Perhaps most importantly, they aren't patient men. In their impatience, they may conclude that I have selected the wrong expert and assert themselves in ways I should prefer to avoid. Not only would their actions represent a threat to me, they most assuredly would not be welcomed by you."

Shari drew a long inhalation from the cigarette he held between the ring and middle fingers of his right hand. Thick streams of blue-white smoke flared from each of his nostrils.

Judah pushed his tea aside. "I understand completely. I'm under no delusions regarding my situation. I promise you that all that can be done is being done. You know yourself, I rarely rest. I work late into the night and am at it again before sunrise. I confess that the matter has captivated me. I give it my all. But it is extremely complex and overwhelmingly obscure. I don't wish to seem immodest, but I tell you plainly that no one else could have gotten you this far this fast."

"I agree, of course. After all, it was I who chose you for this affair. But time is the commodity we have the least of. Time is not our ally. Time is our enemy."

From the corner of his eye, Judah noticed a flicker of movement just outside the entrance to the tent. He turned his head. A fleeting shadow moved across the canvas then disappeared. Someone had been standing outside, listening to every word. Shari lightly tapped Judah Lowe's arm, then gestured toward the opening and touched his finger to his lips. He leaned forward and whispered,

"And time, I fear, is not our only enemy."

CHAPTER XXV

DIER AL-SHUHADA

She found Declan in the ruins of the stable. He had already saddled his mare and was in the process of tacking up one of the monastery's stallions. The horse's mane was matted and flecked with bits of straw that reflected the broken rays of the sun.

She knew that he had heard the sounds of her coming. But he did not turn around.

"I've seen the map many times." Her words were simple and to the point.

"Okay."

"I have a very good memory. It's almost photographic."

"Look, you'd better get packed. We're pulling out of here. Why don't you take those saddle bags over there and fill them with food and bottles of water. It's not that far to al-Qusayr, but it's a hard ride."

"I think I can reconstruct it."

"Reconstruct what?"

"The map."

Declan continued saddling he horses. "Then reconstruct it. When we get to my friend's place in Israel, you can show it to him. He's an archaeologist and a cartographer, one of the best. Maybe he can help you out."

"But he's not the one Ibrahim saw in his vision."

Declan tucked the cinch strap under the horse and slipped it through the rings. "You just won't quit, will you?" He still had not turned around.

"I can't quit. This isn't how it's supposed to end."

"How what's not supposed to end?"

"Don't play games with me, Dr. Stewart."

"My name is Declan."

"No, I think it's 'Dr. Stewart.'" She stared coldly at him.

"Fine, suit yourself." He tugged the cinch strap tight then tested the saddle.

Amala paused. Tentatively, she stepped toward him. "You know this isn't how Ibrahim's quest is supposed to end. It can't be. Not after everything that has happened."

Declan scratched the stubble of his beard and rotated his head on his shoulders, allowing the tight muscles of his neck to release some of their tension. Then he lashed the leather reins to the post and turned to face her.

"Look, even if your memory were photographic, ancient cartographs don't work that way. They're too complex, too subtle. You can't rely on memory alone. Sometimes something as seemingly insignificant as the slight curve in the shape of a letter or the placement of an extra ray line on a drawing of the sun or the orientation of an image can change everything. Even the best memory in the world can't take all that into account. It can't take the place of something you can touch and feel, see and study. It's the script itself, the characters, the way they were put on the parchment. It's always the script. Only the real thing will do. You have to have the map itself. Get it? Anything less and you've got nothing at all.

Unfortunately, there's only one map. And we both know who has that now. Let it go."

Amala's eyes drifted off in Issa's direction, a lock of charcoal hair drifting in the breeze. The boy had settled down beneath the tree. He was studying something he held in his hand.

"On the night the killers came, I was working on the computer, enhancing some of the photos I'd made of the map. Ibrahim wanted it all ready for you when you arrived. He knew you'd want to be able to enhance the images, zero in on specific letters and images. I had only just started. There were maybe two dozen shots of the map altogether. I work in phases. One set of shots, then enhance them, then another set of shots, and enhance them. That way I keep things in order. When the storm came, the lighting crashed my computer. I shut it down and left it on the table in the scriptorium. There's a chance it's still there."

Declan curled his lower lip over his teeth. He walked toward the manger, gathered a double handful of straw and then laid it on the ground in front of the horses.

"Look, I don't know what to tell you. It's the same thing I told Ibrahim. I'm not in the business any more. Besides, you need the whole map. A dozen snapshots won't do the trick. Part of it is no good. You have to have the full context. Ancient places are hard to find. Names change, geographic features change. It's like a puzzle, a riddle. It's easy to follow false leads, and missing pieces always lead to errors."

"I'm very good at what I do, Dr. Stewart. The photographs I took of the map were crisp and detailed, just like the images I made of the manuscript, the ones you've already seen. Thanks to those, we've got the whole manuscript. And if my computer's still in the scriptorium, we'd have most of the map. There's at least one wide-angle image of the entire parchment. It may be a little grainy, but with the other detailed shots, it ought to be enough."

Declan's heart rate quickened. He bit down on his lip and started to say something, something he knew he'd regret. But the glare of her penetrating black eyes held him back.

He walked across the stable and stopped in front of her. He pulled back the long strands of dark brown hair that ran on either side of his face and showed her the scar.

"Do you see this?"

Amala gazed at the rugged red gash that curled up from the high plane of his cheekbone and disappeared into the forest of his hair.

"Ibrahim would have understood. Now I'm asking you to understand. I can't do this. I can't let myself get tangled back up in this madness. There are a lot of reasons, and none of them much worth talking about. But nothing's holding you back. You're free to do whatever you want. I won't stop you. I'll even go back down to the scriptorium with you. If your computer's still there, I'll take a look at the images and tell you what I think. I'll do that much, but nothing more. But you have to agree that's it. Then you'll let this go and we all ride out of here today. Okay?"

Amala reflected for a moment, still studying the outline of the scar. At last, she nodded. Declan nodded in return. Together they walked toward the remnants of what once had been the greatest library in Christendom.

CHAPTER XXVI

CALIPH'S DESERT COMPOUND
AL HAMAD DESERT, SYRIA

Judah Lowe rolled up the sleeves of his crumpled white shirt. A thick carpet of coarse white hair obscured the ruddy skin beneath it. Hurriedly, as a greedy child might open a gift, he unfurled a large, aged map and draped it across the table.

"Come, I want to show you what I've found."

Shari placed his hands on the desk and leaned over the map. Judah switched on the cantilevered task light and adjusted its arc until a bright circle of light appeared east of the Red Sea in the southern quadrant of Saudi Arabia, north of the Yemen frontier.

Quivering with excitement, he guided a large magnifying glass up and down in search of the perfect angle. Then he tugged at Shari's arm and drew him down toward the glass.

"I've discovered some very interesting things." Judah lifted his cup and took a sip. The tea had gone cold. "At first, I thought your parchment was of a region of ancient Israel, perhaps the Sinai. That, of course, is only logical. The author, I believe, counted on us to make that assumption. That was the first of his very cunning deceptions. But the more I pursued that line of reasoning, the more things didn't fit. So I opened my mind to other possibilities. And that brought me to here." Judah tapped the map before them. "These are the great western mountains of the Saudi peninsula, the Sarawat Range. They look very much like the terrain drawn on the other map, Paul's map, don't they?" Shari leaned over the map, studied it for a moment, then nodded. "This entire area"—Judah circumscribed an imaginary arc with the closed tip of his pen, starting at the border of modern Israel on the north, then moving southward along the eastern shores of the Red Sea, encompassing thousands of square kilometers—"was the ancient land of Midian. You have heard of this land, I presume?"

"I am in my own small way a scholar."

"Of course, a Harvard man. Forgive me." Judah smiled. For a moment, it seemed, he was no longer a captive in a dangerous desert. He was a professor in his classroom instructing a curious mind. Increasingly, the sense of possibilities came to possess him.

"But do you know that to some Jews and even to some fundamentalist Christian sects, this mountain range, the entire area within a forty-kilometer circumference of the mountain known as Jabal al-Lawz, is considered sacred land? They believe that Moses and the Israelites first emerged from the forty years' exile in the desert here, not in Egypt. They believe that Jabal al-Lawz is in fact the Mount Sinai of the Bible, not Mar-Mousa in Egypt."

"Yes, I'm somewhat conversant with these theories."

"I'm impressed. These theories are a bit repugnant in most academic circles. But in fairness, there's some data to suggest that these speculations aren't as deranged as they might at first seem to the uninformed. At least in part, they may be true."

Shari gently shook a cigarette loose and lit it. He tossed the pack onto the table beside them.

"Please, carry on. I find this intriguing." The fragrance of tobacco smoke drifted lazily throughout the tent and swirled in rambling circles around them.

"The manuscript and map that you have are quite miraculous, as you already know. They're almost perfectly preserved. Truly, I've never seen anything like them in my entire career. But setting that extraordinary feature aside, they are also very confusing. Much of the geography seems to match this area, but the place names that are inscribed on it are all locations clearly established to have been in ancient Israel, not the Arabian Peninsula. So the pieces of the puzzle don't fit. Either the geography of the map is wrong or the names are wrong."

"Or there are other explanations still."

"Conceivable, yes. But probable? I think not. In any event, we know that Paul, the author of your manuscript and presumably your map, was not merely a disciple of Jesus. He was a Roman citizen, well-educated, articulate, and multi-lingual. Far from being the work of some illiterate, callous-handed fisherman of the Galilee, the manuscript and the map are the work of a man who was, to use a word, a genius, a master of language and, indeed, languages. So it's reasonable that in a matter of such gravity as the safety of a gospel written in the hand of Jesus himself, he would seek to mislead the unwary; that he would use deception to help protect his secret."

Shari gestured with the glowing ember of his Dunhill toward a series of multi-colored Post-it notes stuck at various intervals along the large chart. "What's this you've marked here along this area?"

"That is the region of Asir, the western mountains north of Yemen bordering the Red Sea."

"So you think the map is of this place?"

"I'm not yet sure, but I'm now inclined to think it is. Without getting too far ahead of ourselves, I believe it's likely that Paul hid Q somewhere in this general region. But, as I noted before, the place names don't match the geographical features. I now believe that this is some kind of code, a cipher, if you will. But a cipher without a

Rosetta Stone to help us unravel it."

Shari toyed with the golden signet ring on his finger as he drew another breath from his cigarette.

Judah took a laptop from the smaller table in the corner, placed it atop the map, and rotated toward Shari a screen filled with satellite images of the desert. "The Saudis call this the Empty Quarter. It was only in the late nineteenth century that this region was incorporated into Saudi Arabia. Before then, it had nothing to do with the Saudis. Its only inhabitants are a few ancient tribes—the Qahtan, Bal-Garn, Shamran, Rijal Alma, Rijal Al-Hajr, and the Bal-Ahmar. They're strange tribes with strange customs and practices. It's true that they call themselves Muslims today, but they're really pre-Islamic cultists. They keep some of the Muslim traditions, but in the quiet of their tents they follow far more ancient rituals. They pray to the desert spirits, the djinn. Their men see visions, their women brew potions. When you get right down to it, they don't really belong in the present Arab world. My best guess at this precise moment is that *our* treasure," Judah delicately tested the waters with his choice of pronoun, "is somewhere between this mountain called Zbyd and this mountain called Qurazimat, west of this desert valley and east of this long deep canyon that runs through these high escarpments." Judah circled the area with the tip of his pen. "But because the place names don't match, I can't be certain,"

"That's a massive area, Judah." The scholar's gambit had not gone unnoticed. "Even with a hundred times the men and resources I have at my disposal, we would never find *Q* in such a place as that." Shari drew again on his cigarette then stubbed it out in the bulbous, crystal ashtray on the table beside them.

"Yes, I know. I'm the first to admit it. Clearly, I'm missing something that Paul has hidden from us. There's a clue, or perhaps a number of clues, somewhere in this letter or on this map that I have yet to appreciate."

"You have to break the code, Judah. Already time and our enemies work against us. We have only a few days, if that."

The words didn't seem to register with Judah. His mind was on another matter that he was sure held the answer. "I keep asking myself, why a letter *and* a map? Why did Paul send both? There's something about that I haven't yet grasped. But I can feel it. I'm close. It's a disconcerting sensation to know that one is on the verge of something important without knowing quite what it is. But in time, it will come."

"For both our sakes, let us hope it comes quickly enough."

Judah nodded then returned to the map. He knew that he was close—closer than he intended to let the Persian, or anyone else, know.

CHAPTER XXVII

SYRIAN-JORDANIAN FRONTIER

"Amala? Are you awake?" Declan whispered softly from the front seat of the Toyota.

"More or less." Amala lowered the blanket and pulled herself up. In the back, Issa and the dancing hand slept the peaceful sleep of children and benevolent spirits.

"I think we've got trouble."

Declan slowed the engine and came to a stop. He clicked off the headlamps. In the distance, at the far end of the narrow caravan trail that crossed the barren desert south of At Tanf and north of Az Zalaf, a red warning light rotated atop an SUV.

"Are we across the border yet?"

"Maybe, but I can't be sure."

"So they could be from either side."

"They could be from any side. The Syrian Army, the police, the revolutionaries, the Jordanians, or they could just be thieves waiting for a caravan to rob. However you slice it, it's not good."

Declan unclipped the holster. He had been driving through the darkness along the rugged trail for hours. He was tired and hungry. He needed a bath, a meal, and some sleep. He had hoped they would have been deep into Jordan by now and well on their way to the border crossing at Taba. But the car he'd bought in al-Qusayr, the only car for sale, had been a problem, overheating twice and costing him precious hours that he couldn't afford. But he couldn't turn back now. There was nothing behind them. Nothing but a country slipping into the chaos of revolution. They had to find a way through.

For a moment, Declan weighed the situation, then turning to Amala, he said, "Hand me the bag on the floor beside you." Amala leaned down and recovered a canvas courier pack. Declan flipped the bag open and counted the bills.

"We've still got nearly ten thousand US. If they're Jordanian, they'll deal with us. Even if they're Syrians—pro-Assad or revolution—they'll still likely deal. Money, especially dollars, is the universal passport in these parts. And anyway, they're bound to have seen us. It's open desert in both directions for dozens of kilometers. Glaring headlights bouncing up and down over the dunes are pretty hard to miss out here. We can't turn around. That would be even more dangerous. We have to carry on and take our chances."

Amala nodded, but said nothing. Declan slipped the car back into gear and eased forward. Simultaneously, he removed the pistol from its holster, pulled up his shirt, and tucked it into the hollow place along the small of his back.

As they approached the flashing red light, the soft scarlet glow of pre-dawn appeared on the far horizon behind them. Declan didn't like it. He didn't like the idea of stopping. He didn't like the color of the sky. *Red sky at morning, sailors take warning*, the voice inside him sang. His father had said that as they floated on their boards, facing the double domes of the power plant at San Onofre, a red dawn rising behind the mountains. That seemed like a lifetime ago. What he wouldn't give to have the old Marine colonel from Camp Pendleton at his side again, the man who had taught him both how to

handle danger and how to ride the sea. But he was gone now, his
body turned to dust in the soft, sandy earth of the Oceanview Cemetery, high above the South Coast Highway. No one to help him now.
Just his instincts and memories of the distant past. He could only
hope that both would serve him well, as the old man had intended
they should.

Two men with machine guns, leveled and ready to fire, stood in
the middle of the faded flat ribbon that defined the Bedouin trail.
The powerful beam of their searchlight blinded Declan to their faces
and uniforms. He saw only the black silhouettes of threatening men
and weapons. The shadow of an arm pumped up and down, signaling him to stop. Declan gently pressed down on the brakes then
switched off the headlights. From the bag, he took a stack of bills
and stuffed them into his pocket.

"Wait here while I get this sorted. I'll leave the engine running. If
something bad happens, get behind the wheel and drive as fast as
you can back in the direction we came from. This isn't up for debate,
so just do it." He opened the door and stepped into the bright beam
of the searchlight. Then he slowly walked directly toward the men in
the shadows.

"Wait . . ." Amala whispered in Arabic. But it was too late. He
was gone.

Declan felt a cold rivulet of sweat run down his side. He was
evolving backward even further now, back into something primor-
dial, something hard and deadly. He was a creature possessed of only
one instinct, the instinct of survival. Not survival for himself, but for
the woman and child entrusted to his care by the man he had buried
above the sea. He had already decided what he would do. At the
slightest provocation, he would draw the pistol and kill them both.
He didn't care who they were or what side they were on. He didn't
want to know if they had wives or children of their own. He didn't
care about their names, their country, or their religion. They were
just the enemy now. They were a danger to the woman and the boy

he'd vowed to protect.

The machine guns loomed menacingly before him. They were leveled straight at his chest. One of the shadows nodded, and he stopped.

"*Marhaba*," Declan said firmly. "*Qaddaysh?*"

He wanted to start with just that, a casual hello, and then straight to the point. "How much?"

Black eyes glared at him from the shadows and began to ask questions. Who was he? What was a khawaja doing in this desert? Who did he have in the car with him? Were they armed? Where were they going? What did they want in Jordan and what were they fleeing from in Syria? Declan answered them in a series of lies that flowed out of him like water from a spring. He didn't even have to think about the answers. They just came.

Five minutes later, they had settled on a price that started at the absurd and gradually descended into a bargain. Slowly, the machine guns arced downward toward the ground. Declan passed a wad of bills to each of them and walked back to the car, never turning his face from them. He opened the door and slipped into this seat. He removed the pistol and laid it on the seat between his legs. "Keep your head down. We're not out of this yet."

Declan shifted the lever, put the car back into gear, and inched toward the men with the guns and the circling red light.

As they eased past the SUV, a green Jordanian flag fluttered softly as the wind gusted in anticipation of dawn. Declan eased his foot down and accelerated into the darkness.

"What happened?" Amala whispered.

"We got lucky."

By midday they had reached the border crossing at Taba and made their way into Israel. There was only one more desert to cross now, and Declan hoped it would hold no unwelcome surprises.

The Israelis called it Negev, from the Hebrew words for "dry" and "south." But the Arabs, more beautifully and more descriptively, called it al-Naqab, which means "the place without water." Abraham, father of all three monotheistic religions, built his home along the eastern edge of its inverted triangle. Through the center of its limestone mountains and canyons, the Nabateans built the Spice Road, a commercial corridor for their caravans laden with frankincense and gold. But all those people and their civilizations had vanished long ago. The desert claimed them and erased all traces of their existence. In the end, the desert beat them all. The way it always did.

"Ommy," Issa whispered as he fidgeted anxiously, rocking from side to side.

"Yes, Issa?"

"Are we there yet, Ommy?" He sang the words, as he often did.

"Maybe another half hour, not much more than that," Declan answered for her. He caught the boy's eye in the mirror and smiled.

"Will there be food?"

"We'll have to ask Dr. Stewart, about that."

Issa raised his dancing hand so that it might enjoy the view.

"Avi will feed us. He has only two passions in life. One is archeology. The other is food. But you should know he can be a difficult. He's had his share of trouble in this life. The money and the archaeology help, but there's still a hole. Just let it go if he says something."

"Like what?"

"Like about Palestinians."

"Oh."

Amala nodded, then turned to the window and looked out. As the rattling Toyota struggled out of the canyon and crested the ridge, the outline of a stone and mortar wall appeared atop a mountain on the distant horizon. A few hundred meters further along, they came to a gate. A massive painted sign read "Keep Out" in Hebrew, English, and Arabic.

Declan tapped the brakes, came to a stop, and got out. A galvanized chain was wrapped tightly across the post but the gate wasn't locked. In a series of quick, circular motions, he twisted the long strand of metal around and around until the chain fell free. He opened the gate and then, stretching the tight muscles of his back and legs, and breathed in the cool, fresh air. It felt good to be standing up, to have fresh blood flowing through him again. Declan scanned the ridge above him, half expecting to see an Uzi pointed down at him or to hear the challenge of Avi's or one of his son's deep-throated Hebrew voices. But he saw only sand and a few red anemones in bloom. He strode back to the car and drove through the gate.

The engine groaned as a puff of steam rose from under the hood. The old car somehow managed to hold together. Slowly, they ascended the steep switchback road. A thousand meters later they reached the high mesa that housed the compound. The metal roofs and shiny glass of the windows of the scattered buildings reflected the pink rays of the late afternoon sun into crystal shards all around the compound. Declan raised his hand to his forehead to shield his eyes. Then he saw him, standing in the shadows of the porch, arms akimbo. It was Avi Tzabari. Beside him stood his sons Levi and Dov. Each held an Uzi leveled at the hip.

"He's improved his security since the last time I was here."

"Or he simply heard the loud groans of our tired little car," Amala quipped, turning toward Declan with a smile.

The Tzabaris looked like a family of bears. All three were big men with full barrel chests. A heavy thatch of coarse, untrimmed beard covered their faces, their arms jungles of wool. Avi wore a khaki safari jacket and crumpled trousers. A broad-brimmed felt hat covered his balding head. They made for an intimidating trio.

Declan slowed the engine and lowered the window. He tapped on the brake then yelled out the window. "Avi! It's Declan Stewart. Save your ammunition. We may soon need it, old friend."

The man's face instantly changed from grim to ecstatic. He bounded down the porch steps and out onto the drive.

"It's a ghost!" Avi grabbed hold of the door with both hands and leaned into the window like a Great Dane welcoming his master home. "You should call before you come barreling up a private road, Declan. Things like that get a man killed out here. When my boys aim at something, they don't miss."

"Forgive me. You know that I would've called if I could have. But I've got some trouble, and I knew I could count on you to help."

"What's this all about?"

"It's a long story."

"We've got plenty of time. I like long stories. But it's sure good to see you! Reminds me of the old days." Avi smiled. He wrapped his arms around Declan, gave him quick embrace, then released his grip.

"And who's this you've brought with you? Your family?"

Declan grimaced. "No, just two friends. They're why I've come."

Avi was a Zionist to his very core. And in those brief windows of time when he was fully honest with himself, he would admit it—he didn't like Arabs and he especially didn't like Palestinians. Like Declan, Avi had suffered great loss in his own time and in his own way, as all men must sooner or later. His wife Talitha had been pregnant with their third son. Perhaps that was the real bond between Declan and Avi now, a shared loss of precious things. The papers had said that when the boy from Taba walked nervously through the restaurant's open double doors on a quiet Shabbat in the season of Sukkoth, his eyes had been full of fear. They said he had taken one, two, three steps, then made his move. Three because it was an odd number; an odd number because the Bedouin considered them lucky. Even numbers invited the mischief of the djinn. Such were the lessons taught in the camps. Then, the reporter had written, he cried out, "meekly" to use the journalist's term, as a boy might confess a sin to his mother, "Death to Zion". And with that, he had simply let go of the thin metal lever he held in the palm of his hand. In an instant, he had blown them all to kingdom come. And so a moment of shared tragedy had created a bond. That's why Declan had known that Avi would be there, arms open in greeting, ready to help him.

"Look Avi, I promise to tell you everything. But first, let me wash up and let's get something for these two to eat, okay? We've been on the road for the better part of two days, all the way from Dier al-Shuhada. The boy and his mother need some food and rest. We all do."

Avi patted Declan's shoulder then allowed his hand to linger there for a moment. "Dier al-Shuhada? All that way? And crossing the Syria border's not so easy these days. You'll have to tell me how you managed that in the middle of our bad boy Assad's little crisis. This must be about something important."

Declan nodded. "It is."

Avi turned around and called out, "Dov, Levi, give us a little help here. Show these two to the big bedroom by the garden. Get them soap and towels, then arrange some food." Avi smiled at Declan, but Declan didn't smile back.

"We need to talk, Avi." Declan turned his head to make sure Amala and Issa were not within earshot. "I've gotten myself into the middle of something bad. I need your help to get out of it."

Avi's smile softened and his eyes hardened.

"Okay."

"I have to get home, Avi. But first, I've got to get something arranged for them." Declan nodded toward Amala and Issa.

Avi puckered up his lips so that the hairs of his beard pointed straight out of his face in sharp white lines, then placed his arm across Declan's shoulders. Together they walked in synchronous steps toward the house. Already Declan felt his resolve unraveling. What was he doing here? Why had they come to this place, to the home of this man from his past, a man no less scarred by tragedy than Declan himself? He sensed the answer to those questions would be found in the saddle bag that lay in the dark recesses of the car behind, a bag filled with old documents, a madman's diary, and a laptop computer recovered from the wreckage of a monastery in ruins.

As they reached the house and ascended the steps that led to the doorway, the image of old bin-Mahfouz appeared on the canvas of Declan's troubled mind. They were in the faculty lounge in Cambridge, sipping coffee and debating ancient mysteries that no longer mattered to anyone.

"Who is powerful enough to escape his destiny, Declan?" the old Palestinian had asked rhetorically, running the palm of his hand across the salted plain of his thick, wavy hair from the tip of his forehead to the base of his neck.

In response, Declan had only smiled, then said he didn't know about destiny. And maybe it was true. Maybe he didn't then. Maybe time and the world hadn't taught him yet. But he sensed it now. He sensed the winds of destiny rising all around him. He was the leaf again, drifting toward the falls. He could see the contours of the disaster that awaited him, beckoning to him, but helplessly, unable to avoid it.

Dangerous fires already were burning inside Declan Stewart, fires of ambition and desire, and something more, something that he could not yet call by its name, something new and unfamiliar.

The flames were growing in their intensity, and he knew that if he didn't find a way to still them, they would destroy everything. And through the charred ruins the flames would leave in their wake, madness would rush in. Already he could feel the hot, hungry tongues of flame licking like ravenous dogs at his heels. But he had no way, perhaps no will, to stop them. They had the force of destiny with them. And just as old bin-Mahfouz had asked Declan so long ago, he now asked himself, *Who is powerful enough to escape his destiny?*

CHAPTER XXIII

CALIPH'S DESERT COMPOUND
AL HAMAD DESERT, SYRIA

"Sayyidi, forgive me for disturbing you, but the caliph commands your presence."

Shari instinctively sensed the work of the Syrian. He wondered whether Judah Lowe's time—and perhaps his own—had at last run out.

"The caliph is here, in the camp?"

"No, Sayyidi. He's on the video link from Beirut."

Shari checked the clock. Five minutes past three in the morning. The hour only stoked the flames of his suspicions. The opium-addicted prophet often roamed the small hours of the night. That was when the danger was greatest, when his mind was most confused, his behavior erratic and unpredictable. Whatever it was that had triggered this audience, he would have to be careful. Very, very careful.

Shari wiped sleep from his eyes and fumbled numbly for his boots. As he turned to go, he paused. He would need all his wits about him when he stepped in front of the camera.

"I trust you've followed the protocols? You've confirmed the audio and video encryption?"

"Yes, Sayyidi."

"On both ends?"

"Everything is arranged, just as the Syrian ordered."

Yes, the Syrian. Shari shoved his legs into his the khaki pants of his uniform then slipped first one foot then the other into his boots. Absently he reached for his comb.

"Have coffee brought to the communications tent immediately. I'll join you presently."

The messenger paused as if there were more.

"Well, what are you waiting for?"

"Respectfully, Sayyidi, it would be well to hurry."

"Yes, I understand. Go, fetch the coffee and meet me there. I'm on my way."

As soon as the boy had exited, Shari rushed to his desk and quickly tapped the keyboard of his computer. The printer hummed softly, then deposited a single sheet of paper into the tray. Instantly, Shari grabbed the document and tucked it inside his shirt. He sprang through the tent flap and out into the cool desert night.

A circle of jihadis were gathered in a tight knot outside the communications tent. The Syrian, a crooked smile on his face, stood quietly to the side of the large video screen. As Shari entered, the Syrian touched his hand to his knife and bowed.

"*Salaam,* Sayyidi. The caliph will see you best if you stand here." He gestured to a masking tape *X* in front of the camera.

Shari nodded, then placed the heels of his boots in the center of the mark. Instantly the image of a scowling man in a wheelchair flashed on the screen before him. Shari bowed. "*Masaa el-Khair,* Caliph. It is indeed welcome news to have such an unexpected audience in our desert camp."

"Welcome? And that's because you assume my message for you

will be a welcome one?" The caliph's voice was gravelly, the tone harsh and biting. Shari raised his eyes and studied the bright, looming image on the monitor. The red eyes merely confirmed what he already knew. He had taken the pipe, and recently.

"A small servant such as I, Caliph, can never know the thoughts of the great. Ours is to serve greatness, not ponder the depths of greatness."

There was a long pause. The caliph pursed his lips. Shari interpreted that favorably.

"Are you aware, Sharif"—it was telling, Shari noted, that he did not say "Shari" or "old friend," but rather "Sharif," his full name, the way his father, his uncle and even his beloved Emile Zorn had called him to account long ago—"that your Jew has not solved the mystery of the relic? How long must the prophecy wait? *How long*? And you coddle the Jew. You waste luxuries on him while precious hours slip away." The golden watch dangled from the caliph's clenched fist.

"I make many mistakes, great Caliph. Forgive me my errors. But have I not always done as I have promised? Have I not secured the manuscript and the map in service of the prophecy? The Jew grows closer to deciphering the map with each passing hour. I use the velvet glove, yes, this is true, Caliph. But only as an expedient to the prophecy's ends. The knife breeds fear; fear breeds confusion. A clouded mind cannot decipher the immense complexities of the code that reveals the secret of the relic's hiding place." Shari bowed deeply again

There was another long pause. Shari again weighed its implications as he measured the full range of his options.

Sensing a fleeting window of opportunity, he decided to play the card he had held close in anticipation of a time such as this. "To fail the prophecy is to fail the caliph. And to fail the caliph is to fail Allah. Failure indeed must command a price. Who among us would deny this?" Shari pivoted sharply on his heel and turned toward the Syrian.

"Not you, Abu al-Suri?"

"Not I, Sayyidi." The Syrian's eyes glimmered as he smiled, unaware of what lay in store.

"Great Caliph, I have no wish to diminish the honor of the Syrian's recovery of the map. This is a wondrous achievement in the quest for the relic, the fulfillment of the prophecy. But in his haste at Dier al-Shuhada, he allowed himself the luxury of focusing only on the relic and not on the true threat to the prophecy."

The Caliph leaned forward in his wheel chair, his face now filling the screen. "Tell me of threat."

Slowly, Shari felt the tide turning in his favor. He'd edged himself back closer toward control. Gently, he tugged the puppet's string.

"The stranger in the shadows of your vision, Caliph. Even now the danger grows. So, I ask, great Caliph, who has failed you? The Syrian who concerns himself with small matters such as the Jew and his luxuries, or I, who search not only for the relic, but for the shadow that threatens the prophecy?"

The Syrian touched the handle of his knife but did not draw it.

"So you know the name of the shadow?" The caliph arched his eyebrow then stared blankly into the camera. His words came from a place farther away now. His mind had turned to the dangerous specter that haunted his visions."

"The caliph has eyes in every land, eyes that seek not only the clues to the location of the relic, but the dangers that seek to deny destiny itself. Yesterday, I received *this* report"—Shari reached inside his shirt, removed the sheet of paper he'd taken from his printer, and held it up to the camera—"from a trader in a small village near the monastery of Dier al-Shuhada." A man passed through that village twice. An American with a woman and a child beside him who rode a horse bearing the monastery's brand. A man who bears a scar, great Caliph." Shari touched his thumb to his head and carved the shape of a crescent from his forehead to the high plain of his cheekbone. Shari stopped speaking then and let the silence do its work.

"A scar? You are certain?"

"I am certain, Caliph. And more than this, I know his name. It is Declan Stewart. And just as your vision foretold, he seeks the relic. So you see, my master, while the Syrian tries to make mischief over matters of little consequence to advance his own ambitions, I have not only uncovered the shadow, I have sent men to follow him.

"And so I ask again, great Caliph, who has failed you, the loyal servant who stands before or the one who would seek to sow the seeds of distrust between us?"

The caliph's eyes no longer focused on the camera. He stared into space, his fist raised to his chest, the sparkling chain of the golden watch dangling before him.

"The shadow must be destroyed even as the relic is retrieved. You must kill the shadow, Shari. You must not fail."

A shroud of silence enveloped the tent. Shari closed his eyes and let the low muted hum of the machinery fill his consciousness. Then he opened his eyes and, ignoring the Syrian's glare, spoke directly to the image on the screen.

"If the Syrian will do his job and leave me to mine, I will deliver to you both, my master. You will have not only the relic, but the head of the man who endangers the prophecy."

"He must not be allowed to escape."

The caliph lingered for a long moment over those words. Then he turned his head and stared directly into the camera. "Time grows short. I give you five days, Shari. Five days to find the relic. Five days to bring me the head of the shadow. Is it understood?"

Shari stared at the image that floated on the screen before him then bowed.

"It is understood, Caliph."

The caliph nodded, then the screen went dark.

The air inside the tent was filled with the smell of sweat and the electricity of conflict. Each of the soldiers stood his ground. They seemed to be waiting, uncertain of what to do next. They were waiting, but they weren't sure for what. Shari folded the paper and returned it to his pocket, then turned on his heel and moved toward the exit. The Syrian stepped in front of him and blocked the way. One hand rested on his jambiya and the other on the belt of ammunition strung across his chest.

"Five days, Sayyidi."

Shari pushed the Syrian aside and walked out into the night.

CHAPTER XXIX

TZABARI COMPOUND
SOUTHERN NEGEV, ISRAEL

As dusk settled over the Negev, Declan unfolded the fabric of his story, one step at a time, each segment flowing into the next. Occasionally he would rise from his chair and walk to the terrace where he would open the doors and let the perfumed breeze of evening wash over him. Then he would amble lethargically back to the comfort of the soft, leather chair and let the raspy monotone of his voice paint the canvas of Avi's mind.

"So that's it. Everything I know. All that's happened up to now."

Declan tilted his head back and stared at the ceiling. Fatigue was casting its net over him. His mind began to wander. He felt himself drifting into the void.

The baritone pipes of Avi's voice ushered him back. "That's quite a story. But you haven't shown me the photos, Declan."

Declan opened his eyes.

"Yes, of course, the photos. I've also got Reichmann's diary and all the research Ibrahim, Val, and I did over the years." Declan tugged the leather saddle bag from beneath his chair and handed it to Avi, whose massive frame loomed over him like a skyscraper.

How long, Declan wondered, had it been since Ibrahim had appeared on the high cliff above Ghost Ships, leaning on that bowing cane of his and calling out the name "Declan Stewart" like a crow from its perch? How long since the structure of Declan's life, everything he'd built since Val's death, had fallen apart and drifted like snowflakes in the wind? How long since the old man had first whispered the word *Q*? It seemed a lifetime ago now since the old monk had resurrected the curse and come to make his claim upon him. How many evolutionary cycles, backward and forward, had Declan passed through since then? How many more awaited him still?

"Perhaps I should admit this right up front, Avi." The mists of sleep curled around Declan and tugged at his sleeve. They urged him to let go, to surrender to his body's cry for rest. He took a deep breath and forced himself to push on.

"If our roles were reversed, if I sat there where you do now and if one of my old graduate students, no matter how bright or trusted or beloved, had showed up at my door, unannounced, a decade after he'd dropped off the map, and in a Joycean stream-of-consciousness told me of a lost map that leads to *Q*, of monasteries reduced to rubble, of bodies buried in the sands of Dier al-Shuhada . . . Well, let's just say that I would have my doubts."

The cold stub of Avi's cigar lay in the ashtray beside him. Absently, he reached inside the drawer of the table next to him and removed a pack of Gitanes. He tore away the cellophane, tapped out a cigarette, and lit it.

"You know me well enough not to misread my silence, Declan. I like to listen, to take everything in. I don't like to jump to conclusions." Avi blew a stream of fragrant cobalt smoke toward the ceiling, then picked errant bits of tobacco from his tongue. "It's not disbelief. It's digestion. The situation is complex. There are many parts to be considered."

Declan nodded. "You have a flair for understatement."

"For example, how do we know that the old monk didn't lie to you? And what about the girl and the boy? What do you really know about them and their role in all this? Sometimes it's not good business to trust Palestinians. Then there are the questions of who took the manuscript and the map, and who has them now. And we must consider *why* they have taken them, *why* they seek Q. Are they treasure hunters? Are they religious extremists? All these things and more we must ask ourselves." Avi planted his hand on the wispy hair of his scalp and let it linger there.

Declan rubbed his burning eyes. He would let the comment about Palestinians go. He didn't have the time or the energy for that kind of debate. "Some of those questions are easy, others more elusive. Let's deal with the easiest one first. Amala and Issa. They're only caught up in this by chance. One day she drops an ancient amphora and finds a manuscript and a map. Then things start to change, the way they always change when Q comes into the picture. The monastery is turned into a killing ground. They lose everything. They go to bed safe behind the walls of Dier al-Shuhada, then they wake up refugees with nowhere to go."

"You don't find it just a little curious that only the two of them survived the massacre?"

This time Declan's emotions were not so easily restrained. He could feel his grip tightening around the broad carved wood arms of the chair. "If you're suggesting they're part of the plot, that they had something to do with the destruction and the theft, you can bloody-well forget it. That's not where this thing leads us."

"*Okay, okay.* I'm not suggesting anything. I'm a scholar who's spent his entire life trying to unravel mysteries with far too few clues. So I consider the possibilities. All of them. I ask questions. It's my way. Especially when Palestinians are involved." Avi pursed his lips and stared into space.

Declan tried to hold himself back. He needed Avi's help. He

didn't want a row. But he was angry now. "What do you mean by that, Avi?"

"I mean just what I said. You have to be careful with Palestinians. They can't be trusted."

Declan rose from his chair and stepped firmly toward Avi.

"If I didn't need your help so badly, you know what I'd tell you to do, don't you?" Declan's eyes burned like coals in a raging furnace, but somehow he managed to keep control.

Avi took a breath, then rubbed his fingers across his face. "I can't deny what life has taught me, Declan. But let's not get into all that. I'm an old man. Old men sometimes say things they shouldn't. I apologize. I know they're your friends."

Declan turned his head and looked away. "Forget it. Let's just keep going." He sat back down in the chair. "I've lost the thread now."

"The old priest Ibrahim."

"Yeah, right. I knew Ibrahim. It seems like forever ago. We worked together on so many excavations over the years. He wasn't just a colleague. He was much more than that. He was there when," Declan winced, "when it happened."

Avi nodded. "So you don't have any doubts about him, about his story?"

"He's the one who took care of me. Then, when I was too far gone even for him, he made arrangements with the asylum. Without him, in more ways than I can count, I wouldn't be standing here now. And there's one more thing. You should know that Ibrahim was already dying when he came to see me. An old man with only a couple of months to live doesn't trek half way around the world to find a guy he hasn't seen in a decade just to tell him a lie. That one's a dead end too, Avi."

"Okay, so let's say we agree on that. But how do you know he wasn't wrong about the parchments? Maybe he reached faulty con- clusions despite the best of intentions. Just because he wasn't lying doesn't mean he was right."

Declan leaned across the table and removed the laptop from its case. He handed Avi the power cord and gestured to him to plug it in.

"So that brings us right back to the photos Amala made of the map and the diary and the other records I dug up at Tell Nebi Mend. Why don't you start with Amala's images, then reach your own conclusions about whether or not Ibrahim was right."

Avi attached the cord and plugged it into the receptacle. Declan reached over his shoulder and pressed the power button. A warm white circle appeared, then the screen sprang to life.

"Open the folder at the bottom of the screen. Inside you'll find all the images of the various map segments that Amala made. They're all quite good, though you'll have to work with one piece at a time since each image focuses on only one discrete area of the map. We should probably print out copies of this stuff now that we have access to a printer. That way we can mark things up as we go. In the folder next to that one, you'll find all the images she made of the manuscript—Paul's letter—or you can just look at the print-outs Ibrahim brought to show me. All things being equal, I'd rather have the originals, but the photos are exceptionally crisp and clean. And she isn't missing any pages or passages from the manuscript. She has that fully intact. Anyway, they're all there. Then you can turn to Reichmann's diary and the rest of it whenever you're ready. There are some interesting ramblings and a few sketches in those that I think you'll find particularly interesting. The rest are mostly random field notes that Val, Ibrahim, or I took at Qumran and the other digs."

"What about the parts of the map Amala didn't photograph?"

"Not too much we can do about that now. But there is one image of the complete map, though it's the worst of the lot. But she thinks that she can fill in any of the rough parts from memory. If you ask me, I say that's a tall order, but she says her memory's

close to photographic. I guess we'll find out as we get into this."
Declan shrugged his shoulders, leaned back in his chair, and closed
his eyes. He was drifting into sleep.

Avi stubbed out the cigarette then picked up a pair of reading
glasses and a large magnifying glass.

"Look, I'm going to need more than a quick spin through all this.
It's late. The girl and her boy are already sleeping. Why don't you do
likewise? We can start again in the morning after I've had a chance
to work through all this and see where it leads us."

As Declan walked toward the soft white chamber that awaited
him in the garden beyond, he felt as if he were floating on a cloud.
Collapsing on the bed, he had the sensation of drifting through time,
detached from the world around him, as if he had fallen loose from
world, a thing free and untethered.

Like a planet circling an errant sun, the room began to spin in
tight, concentric circles. As Declan worked to regain his bearings,
everything around him turned to dust and dissolved into the black-
ness of space. Suddenly, he found himself floating on a long board in
a shimmering sea of stars and cosmic dust. He drove his arms deep
into the white mists around him and pushed the board forward.
Slowly he glided toward an image in the distance. He stroked again,
and this time he closed the gap by half. Once more and the board
bumped into a door. It opened. In a smooth, arcing motion, he
turned the board, and entered the room.

He recognized the place immediately. The bars on the windows,
the metal frame of the cot, the faint hint of antiseptic told him he
was back in Damascus, in the asylum again.

"Declan." The soothing, dulcet tones of the voice came from the
corner beside the bed.

"Declan, come sit down here beside me. I have something to tell
you. Something you already know but I think you've forgotten."

Valkyre walked toward him then sat on the edge of the bed, the
pure white light of her image so translucent that for a moment he

was blinded.

"Roll off your board and swim to me. Come, we need to talk."

Declan was a sailor adrift in an alien sea enchanted by the siren's call. He let go of the rails and slipped into the shimmering ocean of starlight. He stroked once, twice, three times, then reached out and pulled himself up onto the bed.

"You remember this place, don't you, Declan? It's where I almost lost you."

"No. It's where I almost lost myself. You never lost me. I never lost you."

"Yes, we never lost each other. The currents of the universe just pulled us away for a while."

She extended her hand to his face and touched the scar. The sensation of her embrace filled him with comfort and remorse.

"You know why I've come, don't you, my darling?"

"You've come to set me free, to take me home."

"No. I wish I had that power, but I don't. But I have come to help you find your way home."

"But I don't want to stay here. I want to go. I want to be free of this world. It's hard and cold and lost, Val. Please help me to find peace again. I'm not strong enough for this world. I never was."

"But that's not your destiny, Declan. Not yet. The world *is* hard and cold and lost, my darling. That is why God has chosen you from all the men who ever lived from the beginning of time to lead it into the light. You will make it home, my love, but you can't leave the world behind. You have to show them the way, just as I have to show you the way. Their path into the light is your pathway home."

"But why, Val? Why me?"

"I don't know, Declan. There are some things none of us can know. I only know that it *is* you and that the only way back home is to follow your destiny."

The stars around him were fading now. Both they and Val were dissolving. Declan could no longer see her or feel the warm caress of her touch. Like a crumpled sheet of newspaper caught in a swirling gust of wind, he began to spin, slowly at first, then faster and faster. The fading sea of white starlight blurred into a blanket of foam. Beneath it lay only darkness.

The universe around him began slowly to spin. The sea of white light dimmed, then turned to darkness. The darkness, in turn, drew him into the depths of its churning vortex. He didn't try to fight it. He didn't have the strength. He let go and sank into the void beneath him. As he sank ever deeper into its realm, the only sound he heard was the faint, fading voice of Valkyre.

"Follow your destiny. . . ."

CHAPTER XXX

CALIPH'S DESERT COMPOUND
AL HAMAD DESERT, SYRIA

The Syrian sat atop the lonely dunes on the narrow spine of the high ridge above the encampment and contemplated the future. He had underestimated the Persian. He wouldn't make that mistake again.

He eased the Kalashnikov off his shoulder, laid it down beside him, then removed the long knife from his belt. The luminous moon, ripe and inviting, glowed on the horizon above the acacia trees. A lazy breeze hop-scotched across the sand. In the silver lunar glow, he studied the jambiya's sharp, curving edge and imagined it soaked in red from the Persian's neck. Absently, he tossed it into the air and watched it tumble end over end. Then before it could hit the sand, he reached out, caught it, and started the game again.

From the earliest days, the Syrian had been the right hand of the caliph. None dared to challenge him. Then the caliph had seen the vision of the relic and sent the Persian to go and find it. Slowly, as the years rolled by, the Persian had wormed his way inside the caliph's mind and heart. He had driven a wedge between the Syrian

and his master. The Syrian chastised himself for not realizing sooner
what was happening. Had he been more alert, he could have sorted
things out long ago. But the Persian was wily and his arts not easily
comprehended.

In the beginning, it would have been so easy to arrange an accident, even on the very streets of London itself. But those days were
behind him now. Now there was only one thing that could return
the Syrian to his rightful place and fulfill all his ambitions—the relic.
If he could somehow wrest it from the Persian's grip, if he could
place the relic in the caliph's hands, all would be as it should. Then
he, not the Persian, would share in the glory of the prophecy fulfilled. He would assume his rightful place.

The Jew was the key to everything, he decided. Only he could
solve the riddle and therefore only he could lead them to the relic. So
the key to all the Syrian's ambitions lay with him. If he was to break
the Persian's spell over the caliph, he must wrest control of the Jew
from the Persian. The Persian would have his five days, just at the
caliph had commanded. But it was time to make sure the Jew understood in whose hands the power of his destiny lay, for once he
understood that, the relic would surely follow. And with the relic,
the Syrian would remove the Persian thorn from his side once and
for all.

CHAPTER XXXI

TZABARI COMPOUND
SOUTHERN NEGEV, ISRAEL

Shortly after sunrise, Declan awoke to find Amala and Issa already in the garden. As was his habit, the boy played with the dancing hand. Amala sat in a circle of sunshine, watching him and drinking coffee.

Avi, as was his own habit, had worked through much of the night trying to assemble the jumbled mass of records into a comprehensible whole, trying to find some answers.

After breakfast they gathered in the great room that served as Avi's library, study, and sanctuary. He was ready to tell them what he had found. As the old bear spoke, he occasionally made notes with the stub of a pencil on a crumpled pad of paper. He'd remove his spectacles and turn to the computer or to the stack of photos or to the cache of documents from Tell Nebi Mend, then come back to his report, always moving ahead, but in a back-and-forth series of gyrations that made time seem out of kilter. But he began as he always did. He began with the fundamental questions.

"So, you ask what I think of all this. Now I'm going to tell you. We might haggle over the precise intent of a given word or the shape of a particular letter. More important," he raised his hand, the fingers tight against each other as if he were making a salute, motioning back and forth to underscore his point, "we might note that it's impossible from photos and digital images, no matter how clear, no matter how well made, to date parchment, to confirm the chemical make-up of the ink, to test for forger's arts, to assess the condition of the whole. And under other circumstances, I'd make all these objections and a great many more. I'd make them forcefully and with a lot of noise. But here, in this place, under these circumstances, I tell you without reservation that I believe both the manuscript and the map are genuine. And if you want, I'll tell you why."

Declan glanced at Amala and they nodded in unison.

"The syntax, the shape of the letters, the patina, the way the ink has faded. To achieve a forgery of this quality would be very difficult, my friend. Even for the best of Israel's many antiquities forgers, very difficult. And the provenance, such as it is, seems to me equally compelling. A forger, whether someone working with Emile Zorn back in the day or someone in the here and now, doesn't hide his handiwork in an obscure amphora. Forgers sell the things they forge. That's how they make their money. So not only because of what I see on this computer screen, but because of the facts and circumstances surrounding the parchments, I find it most difficult—not impossible, but most difficult—to imagine that this manuscript and this map are not what they purport to be. Whether they actually lead to a real place and whether Q is indeed hidden there, that is a different story, though there are some interesting corollaries between the map Amala photographed and the sketches in Reichmann's diary. And whether Q is a true revelation from God as your Brother Ibrahim believed, well that is something none of us can answer. That is something that will only be known if and when Q is found and its contents revealed."

Declan ran his fingers through the long strands of his salt-and-pepper hair and took a gulp from the mug that sat before him. The coffee was fresh and hot.

"Okay, that's a start, right? But I keep asking myself who would want Q so badly that they would destroy a monastery, kill a dozen men, send assassins all the way to New Zealand? Who has those kinds of resources and at the same time values parchment so highly and human life so little?"

"Those are infinitely more interesting questions, Declan." Avi shifted his weight back in his chair. "Infinitely more interesting and also more difficult. But before we tackle that, I want to ask you something, both of you." He bounced his stare back and forth between Declan and Amala. "It really doesn't matter to the analysis. I just want to know. But I don't want anybody to get bent out of shape, okay?" Avi arched an eyebrow and sought Declan's permission to proceed.

Declan glanced at Amala then back at Avi. "Sure. Fire away."

"Why are you doing this, both of you? Why are you wading into this? You got out of Syria. You're safely in Israel. You're okay now. You don't have to do any of this."

Declan wrapped his fingers around his neck and massaged the stiff muscles that ran up from his spine. But it was Amala who answered first.

"If for no other reason, because it was important to Ibrahim. But there's another reason. Suppose he was right. Suppose Q is a divine revelation that will change everything. Then it would be about much, much more than just seeing this thing through because of the men who gave their lives for it. It would be for a reason much bigger than that."

Avi nodded then turned his head and stared at Declan, waiting for his answer.

"Me, I'm not wading back into anything. I'm just trying to help Amala and Issa. I promised Ibrahim that I'd see them to safety. To figure out where safety is, I need to know something about who's behind all this. You make a promise to a dying man, you want to keep it. Simple as that."

"I get that part, Declan. But I already told you that I'll be happy to help arrange things for them. You don't need all this," he swept his hand in a broad arc over the table, "to do that."

Declan lowered his eyes. For a long moment they all sat in silence. Then he spoke. "Look, both of you need to know that I'm not built for this kind of thing anymore. Too many missing parts." Unconsciously he touched his finger to the scar. "Every instinct I have is telling me to run, to run as fast and as far as I can out of these deserts. But I can't do that, not yet. I didn't ask Ibrahim to come. I didn't ask to kill two men and bury a dozen more. I'm a surfer, not a soldier, but somehow I've landed right in the middle of all this. But above everything, I made a promise to a man who died with his head in my lap. And I intend to keep it."

Avi rubbed his beard and rocked forward. He didn't seem satisfied with Declan's answer, but apparently had decided to let the matter drop.

"If that's what you say, then okay. But I want to ask you something else then. This too doesn't really matter. But I'm curious. I already know the young lady's answer. It's written all over her face. But I don't know yours, Declan. Do you believe that *Q* is just a piece of parchment or do you believe that it's a divine revelation?"

"What do you think?"

"That's not what I asked. I asked what do *you* think?"

Declan hesitated for a moment then looked toward the ceiling and said, "Do you expect me to believe in myths?"

"Never answer a question with a question, Declan. That's for the politicians and the lawyers. Not for scholars. So twice you evade the question. Answer me with an answer or just tell me that you don't intend to give me an answer. Either's okay with me, just none of this dancing around bullshit."

The curtains stirred with a warm, fragrant desert breeze. The vacant space between Avi and Declan filled with the sounds of a songbird. Each man could hear the other's breathing. Each man refused to look away from the other's eyes.

"Look Avi, I came here for your help, not to be interrogated like some pimple-faced graduate student fresh off the plane from Harvard. I didn't come to debate whether there's a God, whether life has meaning and purpose, whether Q is this thing or that." Declan reached across the table, lifted Avi's cigarette from the tray, and stubbed it out. "I'm just trying to get two people to safety and myself home."

"You want my help, Declan. It has a price. A very small one, granted, but still a price. I ask only for an answer to my question."

Declan rose from his chair and started to speak. Then the song of the little bird caressed him like the breeze through the terrace doors. Its music reminded him of the tieke that had greeted Ibrahim at Ghost Ships. He took a long, measured breath and walked toward the sounds of the song. Parting the long, billowing curtains, he looked out into the cool of the morning, at the trees gently swaying and the flowers in bloom. A sleepy wind caressed his face. He breathed in the fragrances and the melody. Then slowly he turned back around and met Avi's stare.

"Do I *want* to believe in Q the way Ibrahim did, the way Amala does? Do I fervently *want* to believe that life has purpose and meaning and that in the end everything will work out right for everyone? That suffering and violence and madness and hardship will all magically vanish, that time will stop, and that thanks to a piece of parchment hidden somewhere in the desert we'll all enter a utopia free of all those things? What man could look inside his heart and head and say that he doesn't yearn for all that? Of course I want it to be true. I want it to be true with every drop of blood in my body. But wanting is not the same thing as believing, Avi. Do I believe that these things are true? The answer is no."

Avi shook a cigarette from the pack and lit it. He drew in a breath of smoke, let it linger within him, then set it free. Twisting the burning end up toward his face, he studied the glowing ember as if it held answers of its own.

"I'll take that answer. Consider the matter settled."

Declan nodded.

"So, now I'll turn to the question of who destroyed the monastery and killed the monks; who sent assassins to Ghost Ships, who is the architect of all these things? The answer to those questions lies in the motivations of the men involved. If the assassins believe like you do, Declan, that Q is only a rare parchment, then they see it simply as a form of currency. They're treasure hunters after a treasure. What do your instincts tell you? Is this a treasure hunt?"

Declan's shoulders slumped as he leaned forward in the chair. "No. My gut tells me it's more than that."

"I agree," Amala added. "You can believe it or not, as you wish. But in the weeks since I discovered the parchments, Ibrahim saw visions. An angel spoke to him. She sent him for Dr. Stewart. She warned him of the danger. It's not about treasure, Dr. Tzabari. It's about destiny."

Avi rose from his chair, curling his lip over his teeth, making a low-pitched whistling sound as he expelled his breath through the narrow gap between his teeth.

"Okay. So this is about something more than treasure, more than a rare artifact. Based on what I've seen so far, I agree with that. In that case, it really doesn't matter which one of you is right about Q and whatever place it may have in an eschatological view of the universe. What matters is what the assassins believe about it."

"We don't have any way of knowing that." Declan reached across the table and refilled his coffee.

"Go easy with the conclusions. If you reach them too early, you make mistakes. Let's just talk it through. Assuming Q exists, it's the single most important religious discovery of all time. Religion isn't only about a man's relationship with his God. It's about power here on earth. Whose power would *Q* threaten? Let's start close to home, with the Israeli government and the Department of Antiquities. If they felt threatened by something as simple as an ossuary marked 'James the Brother of Jesus,' what do you think they would do if someone showed up with a parchment purportedly written by Jesus Christ himself? You see my point?"

"The Israelis wouldn't kill a monastery full of harmless monks. They wouldn't send assassins to my home in New Zealand."

Amala arched an eyebrow, but it was Avi who responded.

"Now who's the one believing in myths, Declan?"

Declan fiddled with his watch, snapping the metal clasp open then shut. Then he rubbed the palms of his hands across the rugged stubble of his cheek.

"Okay. Point taken."

"They weren't Israelis, Dr. Tzabari. Not unless the Israelis are now working with Algerians, Syrians, and Afghans. Not unless they bomb churches and leave mosques standing."

"Don't be so sure about that. But okay, let's scratch possibility one and move on to the Muslims. For the strong men who control the masses, anything that threatens Islam threatens their power. Anything that might threaten their grip on the great masses of the Muslim world and the oil in the ground beneath their feet is a threat they won't take lightly. Power over a billion and a half people and most of the oil on the planet is something they'd gladly kill for, and regularly do. If they believed *Q* was a divine revelation, or maybe even if they didn't, they would want to hide it, destroy it, or find a way to turn it to their own purposes. Those are the three choices."

"Agreed."

"But let's get all the possibilities on the table before we start trying to narrow things down or reach conclusions. Last are the Christians themselves. There are many denominations, many sects each vying for power, influence, and wealth—just walk through the

Old City in Jerusalem and you'll get a taste of that in spades. The Orthodox, the Catholics, the Armenians, the Copts—they all vie for control of holy sites. It's not pretty. So, in the realm of power-based-on-religion, no one gets a pass. Everyone's got some dirt on his hands. Maybe even blood."

"Everything is so complex. More questions, fewer answers. Where does all this lead?" There was a sense of resignation in Amala's voice as she gazed out the window to the vineyard beyond.

"Well, we've established that ideology, not treasure, most likely is the motivator. And at the monastery, you heard Afghan, Syrian, and Algerian voices, right?"

"Yes."

"And Declan, in New Zealand, it was Yemenis, right?"

"Yeah, that's right. A pair of them."

"So, unless we're dealing with really clever guys, and I for sure put the Mossad in that category, we should start with the Islamic radical terrorists. They're typically made of men from diverse geographic regions, they're well-funded, and they're fanatical. The last, by definition, makes them merciless."

"And unfortunately there are legions, ranging from *al Qaeda* to the Taliban to hundreds of armies, groups, and gangs scattered across every continent."

"That, of course, is the challenge."

Something sparked in Declan's memory. "At Ghost Ships, the second assassin, the one who killed Ibrahim, he cried out something that didn't really register with me till now. As he rushed from the SUV and started shooting at me, he cried out '*Caliph, Akbar.*'"

Avi raised an eyebrow. "'The Caliph is great'?"

"Yeah—the caliph."

"Not '*Allahu Akbar*?' You're sure? Not '*God* is great'?"

"I'm sure. Why? Does that mean something to you?"

"Not at the moment, but I'll have the boys see what they can run down. In the meantime, I'd really like to return to these documents and spend some time with the two of you. Dov can help keep your boy entertained, if that works for you. And we can sit here together, the three of us, and work through all this a bit more. I don't know about divine revelations, but I do know about parchments and ancient cartography. I'd be lying if I didn't tell you I'm captivated by all this and what might lie at the end of it all. Anyway, I have some questions for Amala about the images, and about some sketches in Reichmann's diary for you, Declan."

Amala was the first to rise from her chair. For a moment she looked directly into Avi Tzabari's dark eyes, as if she sensed his suspicions and his prejudices, but did not fear them. Then, briskly, as if she were darting to the market, she crossed the room and sat down beside him.

"So let's get to work."

CHAPTER XXXII

CALIPH'S DESERT COMPOUND
AL HAMAD DESERT, SYRIA

Judah Lowe had broken the code. He was the only man in the entire world—only the second man in two millennia—who knew the location of Q.

His circumstance created within him the dual sensations of ecstasy and dread. Such knowledge was a dangerous and powerful thing. A single question swirled through the corridors of his mind. How would he use that knowledge to save himself from destruction and to profit from his discovery?

If there had been only the Persian to deal with things would have been easy, he sensed. The Persian was refined, educated, and sensible. He was, after all, a Harvard man. With a man such as that, one could reason, one could deal. But the Syrian was another matter entirely. Not only was he violent, crude, and vicious, but now he had been discredited and humbled. Perhaps the Persian saw that as a positive development, but Judah Lowe did not. From his vantage point, it was a dangerous new development that brought threats of its own, not only for Judah but for the Persian himself. His ignominy would make him more sinister and threatening. Already he marched about the camp like a wounded beast, restless and on the prowl, using the power he still held over the soldiers to send the message that he remained a force to be reckoned with. And he hoped that the Persian had not made the mistake of assuming that the soldiers were his men, under his control, for clearly they were not. They were the Syrian's men. That had been abundantly clear from the beginning. That wasn't good for the Persian, and by Judah Lowe's math, what wasn't good for the Persian wasn't good for Judah Lowe.

Judah was under no misapprehensions regarding his situation and his station. If it were up to the Syrian, things would have been much different all around, but especially so for him. He certainly wouldn't have had his tea and his mattress. He wouldn't have the apricots and the luxury of an evening stroll around the camp. He would be hungrier and dirtier. He might even have lost a finger, a hand, or—it gave him a chill to contemplate it—something more. And his chances of escaping, much less profiting, from his most extraordinary discovery would be, in a word, negligible.

Judah Lowe sensed that his ultimate time of trial would come in the mountains of the Arabian Peninsula after he'd recovered Q for them. That's when his value to them would be diminished, if not eliminated entirely. So the plan, it seemed to him, must have at least two parts. One was to give them enough information so that they might walk right up to the place, but not enough for them to actually find it unless he led them there himself. That would buy him more time, and more time meant more possibilities and opportunities. The second part of the plan would be to cement himself firmly to the only man who might actually see value in him beyond merely his value to lead him to Q. And that man was the Persian.

Judah hadn't quite worked it all out yet. But he knew that the Persian had a plan of his own, a plan that most definitely didn't involve the Syrian, and probably not even the man in Beirut. But a plan that just might involve a tenured Swiss professor with a remarkable set of skills.

Judah Lowe couldn't see all the twists and turns of the road ahead. But he could see far enough ahead to know that *his* only hope lay with the Persian. It seemed that destiny had, in a most curious fashion, joined them at the hip and assigned them a single fate. And so Judah pushed his chair back from the desk and went to tell the Persian what he had discovered.

At least as much of it as he intended to have him know for now.

"Forgive me, Commander." The young jihadi's voice startled the Syrian, awakening him from his contemplation.

"Yes, speak."

"The Sayyidi wishes to break camp. The Jew has deciphered the map."

The Syrian contemplated that news and weighed its implications. "Has the Sayyidi told you where we are to go?"

"We go to the Kingdom, Commander. We make for the frontier north of Yemen in the western mountains of the Rub al'Khali."

The Syrian stared into the boy's eyes. "Then we have a great distance to travel and unfriendly country to cross."

"Yes, Commander."

The Syrian rose from his haunches and turned back toward the camp. He glanced up at the sky. A cloud moved over the moon and obscured its radiance.

"Many things can happen on such a journey, can they not? Who can say what is the will of Allah?"

"All is the will of Allah, Commander. Nothing is that he has not ordained."

The Syrian locked his gaze on the dark horizon and smiled.

"What man is powerful enough to deny the will of Allah, my son?"

CHAPTER XXXIII

TZABARI COMPOUND
SOUTHERN NEGEV, ISRAEL

Declan Stewart had unraveled the mystery, and Reichmann's diary had proved to be the key.

Without the aid of the madman's sketches and notations, he might never have worked it out. The map had too many missing parts, and he lacked the originals of both parchments. But the diary had held the keys to overcoming those obstacles. It had been the map to the map itself, showing him the way to the Temple of the Redemption in the Valley of the Jackal. Showing him the way to *Q*. He could only hope that the assassins, with all the tools and resources at their disposal, somehow had missed the clues.

While Issa slept peacefully in the large bedroom just beyond the terrace doors, they had worked throughout the night, wading through Avi's books and charts, the contents of Amala's laptop, and Declan's pouch from the desert of Tell Nebi Mend. It had taken all night to work it out. But they didn't have everything. There was still much they didn't know. But they had just enough. They now knew within a few kilometers where Paul's map said *Q* would be found. The question now was what, if anything, they intended to do with that knowledge.

It had been just after midnight when Declan's breakthrough came. He knew at last that he had the answer. He couldn't restrain his joy. He spread across the table the print-outs of the digital images of the map. Like a puzzle, the segments were assembled in a pre-arranged order, leaving holes in the places where the images had been corrupted by the storm. Then he called them all together around it.

"I want you all to see something." Declan spoke softly, but his voice hummed with the electricity of excitement. When he had finished, he moved to the other table and unrolled one of Avi's own maps of the ancient Middle East. He placed a crystal ash tray at each corner to keep it flat, then ran the tip of his marker in a tight circle over an area near the bottom.

"What exactly is it we're looking at?" Amala asked softly, tucking an errant strand of hair behind her ear.

"What you're looking at is what I hope the assassins aren't look-ing at. What we're looking at is the place where someone is going to find *Q*."

Avi toyed with his tongue and the bottom of his lip. He readjusted his reading glasses and leaned closer to the map. Amala inched around the corner of the table to see what Declan had drawn. Dov and Levi glanced at each other, then back at Declan Stewart.

"We've all been focused only on Amala's images of the map. That's only natural because that's where the holes are. And since it's a map that purports to show the way to *Q*, anyone in their right mind would place all their energies there. Who needs to look at a manuscript if he has the map, right? *X* marks the spot, right? That's the way it works."

"The way it's supposed to work." The long strand of powdery ash broke close to the ember and cascaded down onto Avi's shirt.

"But maps aren't always what they appear to be. Especially when all the place names are abbreviated like they are in Paul's map. Abbreviations mean the map reader has to fill in some letters. It means he has to make some assumptions. But that situation is rich with possibilities for red herrings and mistakes. There are scores of devices the mapmaker can use to mislead and obscure. So, before I show you all this,"—Declan had returned to the first table and was making subtle adjustments to various pieces of his map puzzle—"tell me why Paul would write a letter in Hebrew? He was a Hellenized Jew. He was a Roman citizen. He'd been educated in Greek, he spoke in Greek, he wrote in Greek. All of his other letters are in Greek. So why now, when it comes to the most important undertaking of his entire life, why would he write it in Hebrew instead of Greek? To solve the mystery of his map, one must first answer that question."

Levi scratched his eyebrow, then with both hands rubbed his face. "So does anyone have the answer?"

"Well, Levi, let me ask you this: What's an interesting complexity of ancient Hebrew? Why has it been so difficult even to know with certainty that the name Yahweh is indeed just that?"

"No vowels for starters," Levi answered, a faint smile breaking through the wisps of his beard.

"Precisely. That makes it much better suited than Greek to creating a code. Okay, so now why don't you all come over here and take a look. Avi, look here on this image of this particular map fragment. Then look all around it and get your context as best you can, then tell me how you read this Hebrew word. What vowels do you fill in knowing it's a place in ancient Israel, and what missing letters do you insert given that this place name, like all the others on Paul's map, is an abbreviation?"

Avi leaned over his shoulder. "It's Bethsaida."

"Sure, that makes sense. Perfect sense. That's what Paul was counting on. Except thanks to Reichmann's diary, we know it's wrong. All of us have been thinking the same way Paul's enemies, the enemies of Christianity in the first century, would have thought. We assume the map has to be of Israel and its environs because that's the shape Paul drew, and because it makes sense. So naturally we see the name in Paul's abbreviation as the name of a city we expect to see. We see what Paul intended us to see."

"Intriguing. So what place do you say it is?"

"It's not so much what *I* say. It's what Reichmann's diary says. Before, that diary was just random drawings and crazed ramblings, including a lot of pro-Nazi dogma and totally unrelated stuff. It wasn't until all this came to light," Declan swept his arm in a broad, encompassing arc across the room, "that we had a proper lens through which we could then see that buried amid the insane rants were drawings of places that match Paul's map. Once all this started to come together in my head, it put Reichmann's sketches in a whole new light. A light that finally, after all these years, started to make sense. If you look at this image in Reichmann's diary," Declan laid back the leather cove and quickly fanned through the pages until he came to the one he wanted and then placed it atop the map, "then you come up with this. So how do you read it now, Avi?"

"Maybe Sayadah instead of Bethsaida. But there's no such place."

"Are you sure?"

"Not in the Israel of Paul's time."

Avi's eyes brightened. He arched a brushy eyebrow, smiled, then set his coffee cup on the table.

"You do what we all did. You narrow your horizons and it leads you to the wrong conclusion. We all made the mistake Paul wanted us to make. There was no Sayadah in ancient Israel. But there was." Declan turned back to the large map he'd marked on before. "Here."

Avi adjusted his reading glasses and leaned over the map.

"That's Saudi Arabia, Declan."

"You bet it is. Paul's great mystery, right? He went to Arabia for three years after his vision on the Damascus Road. No one knows why; no one has ever known why. None of his letters, no other source of any kind, says anything about the purpose of the trip or what he did there. That's very curious. He's struck blind and hears the voice of the risen Christ calling his name. It's a vision of such force and power that instantly it will change everything about him, even the very course of his destiny. And so what does a first-century man, an educated, intelligent, articulate man, do after something like that? Does he go to Jerusalem or Galilee? We could probably understand that. No, he goes '*immediately*'—that's the common translation of the word Paul himself uses—to Arabia. I'll read it to you." Declan shifted back to the other table, picked up a book, and opened it to the place he'd marked with a Post-it.

"'But when God, who had set me apart before I was born and called me through his grace, was pleased to reveal his Son to me, so that I might proclaim him among the Gentiles, I did not confer with any human being, nor did I go up to Jerusalem to those who were already apostles before me, but I went away *immediately* into Arabia.' Not to Jerusalem. Not to Galilee. Not even back to Damascus. To Arabia."

The wheels inside Declan's mind were turning faster now. A sense of excitement, was building within him.

"What about this word? How do you read it?"

"*Negra.*"

"But the map in Reichmann's diary says it is Nujayrah, not Negra. We don't have to know all the workings of Paul's Hebrew code. That could take us days that we probably don't have. But with Reichmann's map beside it, it all starts to make sense. Reichmann's map is the Rosetta Stone. It makes it possible for us to see Paul's map for what it really is, a map of a portion of the Arabian Peninsula along the Red Sea north of Yemen. That's where Paul went as soon as God spoke to him. The place where for two thousand years an ancient parchment, the most valuable one in the world, has been waiting for someone to come for it."

"What about *X*?" Dov asked, taking a slice of fruit and popping it in his mouth.

"What *X*?" Declan asked.

"The *X* you said always marks the spot."

"Yeah, well I didn't say that Reichmann gave us all the answers. That's where I think your knowledge," he turned on his heel and oriented his head in Amala's direction, "of the missing parts of the map has to come in. We can get close to *X* with the pieces we have and with Reichmann's drawings, but we can't know for sure. Reichmann shows us *X* but we don't have any way to compare it to Paul's map. That's one of the pieces that are missing. We can probably get within a few square kilometers of *X* with what we've got, but to know for sure precisely where *X* is we need your memory. I hope it's as good as you say."

CHAPTER XXXIV

CALIPH'S DESERT COMPOUND
AL HAMAD DESERT, SYRIA

"Get up. It's time to leave."

The soldier meant for his voice to be harsh and intimidating, but the high pitch sounded almost comical to Judah Lowe.

"The Syrian says you'll wear these from now on." He rattled a heavy pair of manacles and the rusted iron chain that connected them. Judah studied the boy's face. He had smeared dirt across his cheeks to obscure the patchy parts where his beard wouldn't grow. Judah put him at sixteen, if that.

When Judah didn't respond immediately, the boy shoved the barrel of his Kalashnikov into his belly and with an angry thrust pressed it hard against his solar plexus. "I said put this on, Jew."

"Is this really necessary? We're many kilometers in the desert. Where can I run? If your guns didn't kill me, your desert surely would."

The boy slapped Judah Lowe hard across the face with the butt of his rifle. The blow knocked the old man to the ground and sent his tea cup somersaulting. Judah tasted blood and the grit of sand. His vision blurred. His cheekbone began to swell and his jaw ached. He picked up the handcuffs and snapped them into place. In stunned silence, he sat on the ground, his arms dangling between his crossed legs, and awaited his next instruction.

"Do not move from this spot. I will return for you when it is time."

The young jihadi strode away. Judah Lowe gathered the blood and saliva inside his mouth into a ball and spit them onto the sands. The promise of possibilities seemed less likely now.

Judah Lowe sat on the sand, handcuffed to the truck. Dejectedly, he looked up at Shari.

"But why? I've done everything. I broke the code. I've given you the location. And once we actually get to the valley and can see the markers themselves, I'll be able to take you right to it. Why do this to me now?"

"Surely you realize, Judah, that this is the Syrian's doing, not mine. Because he cannot strike me, he strikes you. He knows that I don't approve, but also that because you are a Jew, I cannot object without compromising myself with the caliph. It really is surprisingly subtle and resourceful for the commander. I fear he is learning far more quickly than I might have preferred."

"I confess that the results of his education are not entirely to my liking."

"I am sorry, but I can't allow his treatment of you to lure me into a compromising position. That would serve neither of our ends, Judah. Unfortunately, for a short while longer, you must endure these indignations. But I assure you, I will settle things with the Syrian, and soon. This too shall pass, Judah." Shari knelt down beside him. With the edge of a linen handkerchief that smelled of vetiver and eucalyptus, he gently dabbed the fresh blood at his temple.

"Thank you." Judah licked his lips and spit over his shoulder. Shari filled a metal cup with water and placed it in Judah's hands.

"The Syrian thinks that he'll recover the relic and deliver it to the caliph. He fails to appreciate your importance, I'm afraid. After all, without you, none of us might ever find Q. I'm sure that this thought has occurred to you. If you should refuse to cooperate or fail to interpret the signs appropriately when we arrive at the valley, the caliph might never have his bauble. And as you may know, our caliph isn't a man who takes failure lightly, especially not in matters to which he assigns such great and overwhelming importance as the prophecy of the relic. But perhaps they think you wouldn't be so foolish."

Judah drank slowly, washing down clots of sand and blood as he swallowed. "Yes, after all, I could be lying or I could simply be wrong. Or more likely I could be holding one card back. Jews are not to be trusted, the Syrian is fond of saying. Perhaps he's right."

"That's very amusing. I'm glad to see you haven't lost your sense of humor."

Judah Lowe managed a broken smile, then nodded.

"But I'm certain you won't hold anything back from me. That wouldn't serve either of our interests. Now, for a while you must trust me. I have plans for you, Judah. Plans that go beyond the next few days. You will find rewards in this affair if you serve those worthy of your service. But for now, hold your tongue and do as you are told. The Syrian won't go so far as to kill you, but he may be inclined toward, shall we say, certain unpleasantness. Patience, Judah. All things in due time."

CHAPTER XXXV

TZABARI COMPOUND
SOUTHERN NEGEV, ISRAEL

"Dr. Stewart, wake up." Levi released Declan's shoulder and took a step back from the bed. "Forgive me, but my father says it's important."

Declan tossed aside the cover and sat up.

"What time is it?"

"It's early afternoon, but nobody got to bed till nearly dawn. Anyway, Papa's finally managed to get his video call through to General Eretz in Tel Aviv."

"What's a general got to do with this?"

"Papa will explain it all. You might want to hurry. These generals aren't so easy to get on the phone, even for someone as well connected as my dad."

"I'm right behind you."

Hurriedly, Declan laced up his boots and made his way to the library.

"Good. You're up. You want something to eat?" Avi paced nervously back and forth across the room.

Declan shook his head. As he walked toward the table where Avi sat, he ran his fingers through his sleep-tousled hair. "Just a cup of coffee."

"Jews always eat. It's the legacy of five thousand years of not knowing what lies around the next corner, whether there's a next meal there or not. Don't let me eat alone. Please, take something." Avi pushed a plate of fruit and pastries across the table to Declan. At the back of the room, Levi had donned a headset and was adjusting the video monitor. Dov sat quietly in the corner, cleaning his Uzi. Over his shoulder, Declan could hear the sound of metal parts being taken apart and reassembled. He had the sense that someone was expecting trouble.

"Maybe a little later, when I'm more awake. I thought Levi said there was a video call you wanted me on."

"You know military officers. They like to make people wait. It makes them feel like big shots. But this one's a good guy, an old friend. He'll call like he said he would. Probably just running a couple of minutes late."

"Who is he?"

"Former Mossad. Now regular army. He owes me a few favors. I thought he might have some answers for us."

"About a manuscript and a map?"

"No. About a massacre at a monastery and a man called the caliph."

Declan nodded. "Amala and Issa up yet?"

"The last time Dov checked on them they were still sleeping. Let them rest. We don't need them for this part. Besides, the general doesn't like Pales—well, anyway the rest will do them good."

Declan bit his tongue and let the comment pass.

Avi slid a carafe of juice and a glass across the table. "If you won't eat, at least try the juice. The coffee's still brewing."

Declan filled his glass then started to ask a question. But before he could, Levi snapped his fingers to get their attention.

"Dad, it's General Eretz. He's just confirming the encryption of our signal."

"Excellent. When he's ready, put him through."

The large monitor on the wall over Avi flashed blue then went dark for a moment. Then the crisp image of a heavy-set, middle aged man with a crew cut and a neck as wide as his head appeared on the screen. He wore an olive shirt open at the collar and a white crew neck t-shirt that barely restrained the forest of thick black hair beneath it. His epaulets bore the sword and laurel of a brigadier general in the Israeli Defense Forces.

"Natan, you've gotten fat!"

"If this is what you've gone to all this trouble to call me about, you must have a lot of time and money to waste. And by the way, you don't look so thin yourself."

Both men laughed aloud.

"It's been a long time, Natan. Too long."

"Time passes, men grow old. It's the way God made the world. Some sense of humor, he has. Now tell me why you're calling."

"I need your help, Natan. In the room with me are my two sons and an old student who is a close friend, Dr. Declan Stewart. We have some questions we thought you might be able to help with. Questions we don't want anyone to know we are asking, at least not right now."

General Eretz nodded then stroked his chin. "There are limits to what an IDF general can do, even for an old friend with good connections and a big pocketbook. But you tell me what you need to know. I'll see what I can do. But no promises."

"First, ever heard of someone called the Caliph?"

The general's expression changed slightly. The soft smile around the corners of his mouth was gone.

"Why do you want to know this, Avi?"

"Off the record?"

"There's a record?"

"A Christian monastery in Syria was attacked and destroyed a few days ago. You want the details or just the big picture?"

"Start with the big picture."

"Okay, so just about everyone was killed. A genuine massacre. Dr. Stewart discovered it. We don't have much to go on, but one thread we have is someone referred to as *the caliph*. That enough for now?"

"Enough to know that you and your Dr. Stewart are in over your heads."

"You want to elaborate?"

"You want to know about the caliph? I'll tell you about the caliph. You know al Qaeda and the Taliban and Hezbollah? Put them all together, you don't even come close to the caliph. Not in money, not in power, not in viciousness, not in crazy. If your friend is mixed up in something with the caliph, you can take it from me, he's screwed."

"That's not good, Natan."

"Who said it was? Look, this guy can't be touched. We've tried. The Americans have tried. The Brits have tried. The Pakistanis claim to have tried. Even the Russians tried. They were the only ones who came close, and that was a very long time ago. They managed to blow his legs off. He's gotten smarter since then. Since then, it's like he has some kind of protective shield around him. Nothing can touch him."

"So he'd think nothing about torching a monastery and killing monks."

"Not so much as a second thought, Avi."

"Where did this guy come from, Natan? How come I don't know about him?"

"Because that's the way he likes it. He first appeared on the scene in the late seventies when the Russians occupied Kabul. Except he wasn't the caliph then. He was just Siddiqul Islam, the son of Islam, his *nom de guerre*. Now he controls half the world's opium and heroin from his poppy fields in Asia. He's an addict himself. He uses the opium to conjure up religious visions. He thinks he's a prophet and so do the soldiers in his armies."

"So he heads a terrorist group?" Declan cleared his throat. His voice was hoarse and labored.

"Not like you're probably thinking. This guy, he doesn't seek the limelight. That's why you've never heard of him. He prefers the shadows. He works through proxies. He lets others take the credit, or the blame, but he's the one directing it all. He's not interested in general terror campaigns or the domination of a particular country. He leaves that to the others. To him those are just distractions. He hunts bigger game. He has a mission, a plan, a calling. He believes he's the *Mahdi* destined to take Mecca, to do battle with Satan, and then rule a world unified by a single religion which, not surprisingly, would be his particular brand of Islam." General Eretz paused for a moment to see the effect of his words.

"You know about the Mahdi, Declan?" Avi asked matter-of-factly.

"Islamist eschatology. He's the last of the twelve sacred Imams, a messiah, the redeemer of the world who comes in the end days to bring the Islamic version of justice to the earth. There is nothing after him. He's the harbinger of the end of time."

"We don't come across a Mahdi very often," the general continued. "He's not mentioned in the Koran. It's something like the Christian concept of the Rapture. There's nothing in the Bible about it, but the fundamentalists somehow latched on to the idea, and now it's a big deal."

Levi walked to the table and placed a carafe and two cups on it. After pouring coffee for them both, he joined the conversation, filling in some of the details of the general's story.

"It all started in the eighth century. Big power struggle between the Sunnis and the Shia. So somebody came up with the Mahdi thing. Now every few hundred years, somebody new pops up and says, 'Hey, I'm the Mahdi.' One showed up in the thirteenth century after Spain was reconquered by the Christians. Another one showed up during Napoleon's invasion of Egypt. In the late nineteenth century, a guy in Sudan called Muhammad Ahmad said he was the Mahdi, raised an army, took Khartoum, killed General Gordon, and hung his head from a tree. Maybe you remember that one. He's pretty famous. Then again in 1979, a guy called Abdullah Al-Qahtani attacked the Grand Mosque in Mecca and killed hundreds, maybe thousands. The Saudis worked hard to cover up the details and stats, so no one knows for sure. Anyway, he said he was the Mahdi."

"So you get the picture I'm painting here," General Eretz leaned forward so that his face filled the screen. "Look Avi, this guy is worse than any of the ones who came before. This guy is the real deal. He's an Afghan warlord whose poppies and opium have made him one of the richest men in the world. He's beholden to no one. His loyalty is to himself and his religious visions. He has his own treasury and his own armies. And he's got a son that some say is even worse than he is. In any event, he's powerful and well equipped. He's entirely his own man, and extremely unpredictable. Plus he's insane. How's that for a combination?"

Declan took a sip of coffee.

"So where does he fit in my story?"

"What story? Look, Dr. Stewart. Until a few minutes ago, I didn't even know you had a story. I'd never heard anything about a massacre at a Syrian monastery. They must have had a pretty tight lid on it because there isn't much that happens in this region I don't know about. But Syria's a special case these days given the open revolt against Assad. Our information out of there isn't as good as it used to be. The bottom line is that I can't tell you whether this caliph is your man, but I can tell you it is very interesting, the timing of your call."

"What do you mean?" Declan asked, arching his eyebrow and

tilting his eyes up toward the screen.

"I mean that two hours ago one of our satellites picked up six men crossing the Egyptian frontier and entering Israeli territory. A lot of Bedouins float back and forth over that border, so it might not be anything but a coincidence. But they are in a group, on foot, no camels or trucks. And they crossed south and east of El Kuntilla. Sound familiar?"

"You know it does," Avi answered. "It's just a few kilometers west of my compound."

"That's my point. Now you call and want to know about the caliph the same day some guys cross the border from Egypt near your compound. Curious, that's all I'm saying. In my business, a man has to be curious about coincidences."

"Curious is okay. Troubling is bad. Is it curious or is it troubling, Natan?"

"I don't know. There's a recon team monitoring them by satellite. Sit tight for a minute and let me see what I can find out. So just stand by." The screen went black.

Avi rotated his chair and turned toward Declan. "So, what do you think now?"

"I don't know what to think."

"This caliph fits our bill. He's an anachronism, a throwback to the eighth century. For him, the world and everything in it is ruled by divine forces. He thinks he's a prophet. You may struggle with the concept of Q as something more than a parchment, but a guy like this wouldn't. For him, such a thing would be easy to believe. Q would be a threat to his own divine destiny. He'd want that threat eliminated, the way the Philistines wanted the Ark of the Covenant eliminated. When a competing religion has a powerful relic, you want to crush it just to show everybody your god is the real god. Think about it. What greater power could there be than the power to destroy a god?"

Declan sipped at his coffee and reflected. "So your guess is that he searches for *Q* so that he can destroy it."

"That's my hunch."

Suddenly the video screen sprang back to life.

"Avi, I want you to listen to me. I don't know what kind of trouble you and your friend have gotten yourselves into, but I do know one thing. You need to leave the compound now."

"What? What are you talking about? This place is a like a fortress."

"Avi, I'm telling you as a friend, as a guy who owes you, get the hell out of there. The guys who crossed the border, they aren't Bedouins. I have the report right here in my hand. They're six commandos. You want to know their point of origin? It's the caliph's training camp at Wadi Umm Batima. They're armed and outfitted. They're on foot in hopes of not drawing our attention. But if they're on foot, they can't be planning to travel far. You're only thirty clicks from that border, Avi. And our satellite has their vector. They're headed straight for your compound."

CHAPTER XXXVI

TZABARI COMPOUND
SOUTHERN NEGEV, ISRAEL

The soldiers reached the Tzabari compound just past sunset. Easing along the ridge, they moved toward the plateau and the buildings that filled it. A hundred meters from the compound, all six slipped into a narrow cleft between the mountains. In a matter of minutes full darkness would settle over the land. It was then that they would make their move.

The Persian's orders had been precise and to the point. Kill everyone, then take the head of the man who bore a crescent scar. When they returned to the camp, a helicopter would be waiting. The head would be taken directly to the caliph. Only then could he be certain that the shadow would not haunt his visions.

With his infrared binoculars, the leader studied the compound. All the buildings were dark save one, the large one at the center. Table lamps burned softly in the windows and the faint sounds of music filled the air. That's where they would be. With luck, they would make short work of it and be back across the frontier before dawn.

The soldier set his field glasses aside and checked his wristwatch.

"We shoot to kill. We take no prisoners. We ask no questions." The soldiers nodded and prepared to fire.

Three RPG's hit the compound simultaneously and collapsed the front wall and the roof of the porch. Black smoke and flames filled the night air. A blistering rain of glass, steel, and burning wood fell in a circle fifty meters in diameter. Whole doors and windows hurtled through the air.

Their Kalashnikovs blazing, the caliph's men charged through the cloud of smoke and entered what remained of the building. Amid the flames, some crouched, others stood. Each fired his assault weapon in carefully choreographed bursts. Then, as if by divine command, simultaneously they each released their triggers and froze in place. An eerie stillness filled the room. Only the soft music of the radio and the crackling sounds of burning wood penetrated the silence of the desert night.

Declan and Avi stood before the monitors and studied the softly glowing screens of the surveillance cameras. Amala and Issa huddled like tortoises beneath the heavy wooden table while Levi and Dov, shoulder to shoulder, nervously fingered their Uzis. They had watched it all unfold on the series of video screens attached to the wall. And because the bunker they now occupied was less than fifty meters away from the chaos, they heard the noise and felt the thunder of the RPG's. But, at least for the moment, they were safe.

"Good thing we talked to Natan when we did. Otherwise, we'd be screwed right about now. As it is, we've drawn them in just like hungry alley cats to a saucer of warm milk."

Declan laid his hand on Avi's massive shoulder and gently squeezed. "Forgive me, old friend. I had no idea what I was getting you into."

Avi shrugged his massive shoulders. "Just be happy my call to

Natan went through when it did. Things could have been much, much worse."

"So what do we do now?" Declan asked.

"In about two seconds these guys will realize the fox's ruse. And it'll make them mad as hell, especially because it is a Jew that has tricked them. Then they'll start to search the compound. And they won't stop till they find us. Then they'll kill us. But first they'll probably torture us either to find out what we know about *Q* or just for the hell of it."

"I don't like Plan A. So give me Plan B."

"Plan B is I don't let them get that far. So I want you to get down on the floor with them." Avi nodded toward Amala and Issa. "Levi, Dov, you get down there too."

"But Papa, they're only six. We know the compound. Leave this to Dov and me. It won't take us long."

"I know you could. But all it takes is one lucky shot and I'm out a son. I'm not interested in that."

"But—"

"No 'buts'! Flesh and blood I can't replace. I have my own plan, and all it will cost us is some stones and mortar. I'm rich. It's insured. That's not much for a man to pay for the safety of sons, so just get down. Right now, I've got these bastards exactly where I want them. But they won't stay that way long. It's now or never."

Levi and Dov nodded grudgingly and settled onto the floor beside Declan, Amala and Issa. Avi removed a key from his pocket and unlocked a steel compartment embedded in the stone beside the large video monitor. From it he removed a square metal box with wires protruding from its sides. With a flick of his thumb, he opened the hinged cover. He pressed his index finger against the red metal window of the security scanner. A white LED atop the box began to flash.

"Cover your ears. This is going to be very loud."

Amala placed her hands on either side of Issa's head and pressed hard. Declan then gently placed his hands over her ears and leaned into her shoulder.

"Five, four, three, two, one . . ."

The explosion rocked the entire compound. Tiny pebbles and coarse grains of sand tumbled down the walls of the bunker and scattered like bits of hail all around them. Instantly, the room filled with a dense cloud of heavy red dust. Amala coughed. Issa burrowed his head into her lap and hid the magic hand beneath his shirt. Declan pressed his body close against Amala, protecting them from the cascading storm of debris. Then the vibrations ceased. The avalanche of stone and scree came to a stop. Slowly the thick cloud of dust settled and the air began to clear. The main building of the compound was completely gone.

General Eretz's AH-64 Apache circled the burning compound.

"I said put this damn bird on the ground, boy."

"But General, forgive my speaking freely. That building just blew sky high. That LZ looks pretty hot. It's too dark to know what I'd be putting you down in. The commandos are less than five minutes behind us. I suggest we wait for them to secure the area. My job is to make sure you're protected, sir."

"Your job, son, is to do exactly what I order you to do. If you don't set this chopper down immediately, I'll have your ass in irons before dawn. You got that?"

"Taking her down, sir."

The pilot gently guided the control stick forward. The helicopter made a lazy arc then settled onto the flat gravel of the motor court where only hours before Declan had steered the lumbering old Toyota toward Avi Tzabari and his sons.

The air was thick with sulfurous black smoke and swirling dust. Fires burned haphazardly across the front half of the compound. The most heavily damaged area was the main building and its surrounding grounds. Only scattered shreds of metal roofing and shattered timbers were left.

As the rotors slowed, General Natan Eretz, still dressed in the open-collar, olive shirt of his uniform, stepped out onto a carpet of softly burning rubble. The rotor wash caught the brim of his cap and sent it lofting high above the Apache.

"We're too late. Too damn late." He kicked the dirt with his boot and shook his head. Then in the near distance beside a small stone, he saw movement. Just as he unsnapped the holster and was about to remove his pistol, the man in the shadows called his name.

"Natan!"

"Avi! Son of a bitch! I thought you were dead."

"Not today, my friend. It's the caliph's jihadis that are dead, not us. They should have read the sign at the gate."

A broad smile of tobacco-stained teeth appeared on the rugged terrain of General Eretz's face. He grabbed Avi by the shoulders and pulled him to his chest. "You are one lucky son of a bitch!"

Avi patted Natan across the back. "You might want to work on your timing, Natan. I might have been able to save a few dollars if you'd gotten here a little quicker. But you get plenty of credit just for showing up! If I forgive you, will you lend us your helicopter?"

"Will I what?"

"Lend us your helicopter. My friends and I are in a hurry. We need a lift to Eilat."

"This isn't a taxi, Avi. It's government property."

"I know. And I just did the government a big favor. I took out six highly dangerous terrorists. For all your bosses know, they could have been on their way to Tel Aviv. And all I ask in return is a quick ride to Eilat. I'd say that's a bargain, Natan. Six terrorists for one short helicopter ride."

General Eretz shook his head then withdrew two cigars from his top pocket. He handed one to Avi then bit off the end of the other and popped it between his teeth.

"I want one thing straight, okay? I give you and your friends a lift, I'm out of this thing. You're one hundred percent on your own then, right?"

"No problem. No offense, but we'd actually prefer it that way ourselves."

The general nodded his head slowly then squeezed a manila portfolio into Avi's hands. "Take this. You can read it on the flight. I've marked the sections for you."

"What is it?"

"Ever heard of a guy called Judah Lowe?"

Avi bit the end off his cigar and spit it on the ground.

"Sure. Good ancient cartographer, bad Jew."

"He's gone missing."

"Interesting."

"Yeah. The coincidences just keep coming." Natan struck the match and lit first his cigar, then Avi's. "Look, I don't know what you're up to, Avi. But take my advice. Forget Eilat. Let me take you all back to Tel Aviv. Get a suite at the Intercontinental. Take it easy on the coast for a few days. Order some good food from room service. I'll put the whole thing on the Defense Forces' tab and mark it 'For services rendered.'"

"Maybe another time, Natan. Right now we've got business in Eilat."

"You and your Dr. Stewart friend are in way over your heads, my friend. Way the hell over your heads."

Avi glanced at the smoldering ruins of his compound.

"From God's mouth to your ear, Natan."

CHAPTER XXXVII

SAUDI DESERT
LONGITUDE 24° N-LATITUDE 46° E

The iron manacles dug into the flesh of Judah Lowe's wrists. But it felt good to be outside the camp, walking freely in the desert. A simple pleasure, but a most welcome series of sensations after the deprivations he'd suffered over the last two days.

He and Shari walked along the high ridge above the camp. The Persian had given him water and food and the blessing of a vacation, however brief, from his tormentors. In the distance, the Syrian and his jihadis refueled the vehicles and filled their containers with fresh water from the abandoned well deep in the Saudi desert. They were a long way off the beaten path. But that was precisely how they'd planned it to be. If they were going to make it to the Yemeni border unnoticed, they had to move like spirits across the sands.

"We are two men of the world, Judah," Shari said, pausing to study the Syrian and his men below. "We are 'of a certain age,' as the French so diplomatically say. We are educated men. We appreciate the finer things life has to offer. We are not so troubled, you and I, by ancient myths, by rumors of empty tombs, of prophets yet to come. We are men of intellect, not of omens and superstitions. You may find the characterization unflattering, but we are both in fact treasure hunters, albeit in slightly different ways and with different tools at our disposal."

Shari seemed to float between two great seas, one white below him, the other blue above him.

"Do you know Declan Stewart, Judah?"

The question had come from nowhere, and that did not go unnoticed by Judah Lowe. He wondered whether he should stop, or just keep walking, as the Persian had. He elected to carry on as if the question were of no importance. He brought his steps in rhythm with his companion's.

"*Dr.* Declan Stewart?"

"Yes, the eminent scholar, the one with the curious set of theories regarding *Q*."

"Of course, it's been a long time, but yes. I knew him. Everyone in the field did. His papers aroused a certain amount of controversy. That sort of thing usually leads to a degree of notoriety. Our paths crossed on a few occasions, nothing more than that. Why?"

"I was merely curious. We might be running into him. One never knows."

"I thought he was in an asylum or perhaps had died after that business at Khirbet Qumran."

"Like the phoenix long before him, Declan Stewart seems to have risen from his own ashes. He's quite alive, Professor. Mad, perhaps. But quite alive."

"And is this possibility of concern to you?"

"Should it be?"

"I can't possibly see how. The mystery is solved. Paul's map has been decoded. The relic's location is now known to us. We have only to go and fetch it. I should think the Syrian far more of a problem than Declan Stewart."

"Perhaps you're right. But still, it is curious. Twice I have sent men to kill Declan Stewart. Unfortunately, in neither instance were they as effective as the teams in Berlin I sent for the Durabian Parchment, or if you will forgive me for saying, or as the ones in Zurich who were sent to fetch you to us. The fact is, Judah, Declan Stewart has now gone missing altogether. If a lifetime of searching for Q has taught me anything at all, it is coincidences are uncommon. They often are omens of surprises yet to come. And with the Syrian still to be dealt with just as you say, a surprise is not something I would relish."

"But surely Declan Stewart can't possibly present the slightest problem for us." Judah used the pronoun intentionally. "We have the manuscript. We have the map. And above all, we know where Q is hidden. No one in the world, certainly not a man who has been in an asylum for who knows how long, can overcome all that."

"And if he had Avram Tzabari with him?"

This time Judah Lowe did stop. He looked at Shari, then despite the low state in which he'd come to find himself, erupted in laughter. "Avi Tzabari? You must be joking!"

"I assure you, Judah, in all matters regarding Q, I never joke." The high sheen of Shari's polished black boots glimmered in stark contrast to the pale white sand beneath his feet.

"Please forgive me, but I would be less than candid with you if I didn't say plainly that Avi Tzabari should be the last of your concerns. Declan Stewart, well, I at least can understand that one. But Avi Tzabari? He's nothing. He's just an old fool who hides in the Negev and fritters away his time and his fortune on unsound theories and amateur sleuthing. If you will forgive me, Shari, perhaps paranoia has gotten the better of you."

"Just because one is paranoid, my good Doctor, does not mean there isn't someone out to get him."

Judah considered the point then slowly nodded.

"So you find yourself between Scylla and Charybdis. On the one reef there is Avi Tzabari and Declan Stewart, and on the other, the Syrian. I would say that the Syrian is a real threat. Stewart and Tzabari, a most improbable one."

"Improbable things have been known to happen, Judah."

"Not often."

"No, but when they do, they can have profound consequences. If on the first of the month I had asked you to calculate the odds that you would be here in the desert, your hands chained like an animal in a cage, headed for a hidden valley no one has entered in two thousand years to find a manuscript that in all probability was written by the hand of Jesus Christ himself, how would you have judged that possibility, Judah?"

Judah Lowe stared at the steel manacles around his wrists.

"Improbable."

"Precisely."

CHAPTER XXXVIII

DAVID BEN-GURION HOTEL
EILAT, ISRAEL
RED SEA COAST

The last red rays of the sun disappeared beneath the broad lawns of the Gan Binyamin Central Park. The city of Eilat was eerily quiet.

"So take a look at this." Avi tossed the manila portfolio General Eretz had given him onto the table in front of Declan. Declan removed the papers and squinted at the tiny black print.

"Here, try these," he said, pushing a pair of lopsided eyeglasses across the desk toward Declan. "They don't have enough *umpf* for me anymore. They're ugly as hell, but at least you'll be able to see." Declan perched the horn-rimmed glasses low on his nose, as if he wished to make clear their temporary claim upon him.

Avi sat his cigarette on the edge of the ashtray and took a sip of coffee while Amala stared out the window onto the lifeless streets below. "Judah Lowe?" Declan uttered the words in a soft, slow whisper as if a light had gone on somewhere in his mind.

"So you remember him?"

"University of Zurich. Tenured. Respected. One of the best ancient cartographers and geographers anywhere. Top guy in his field. Massive ego. Thinks he's smarter than everyone else and always out to prove it. Do anything for a buck. Loves to read his name in the papers. I remember him."

"Yeah, and it says there he disappeared from Zurich. They think he was snatched right off the streets. That kind of thing doesn't happen very often in a place like Zurich."

"So you think Judah Lowe's disappearance is part of this?"

"The Mossad must think so. General Eretz gave me that paper before we boarded the helicopter and that's who he got it from. Remember what he said about coincidences? Ask yourself what you think. The disappearance of a prominent ancient cartographer from the sidewalks of Zurich on a fine fall evening no so long before Declan Stewart shows up at my door with his story of Q? The guy has no ex-wife. No disgruntled business partners. No bad habits like drugs or gambling. Very normal guy. All in all, a guy people like. Guys like that don't usually disappear into thin air. Now flip the page and look at the next one."

"'Rare Cartograph Stolen from Berlin Museum,'" Declan read aloud. "'The Durabian Parchment, an ancient map of the southern Arabian desert and northern Yemen dating from the first century C.E. was reported stolen.'"

"Coincidence?"

"I don't know, but that *is* amazing. That cartograph has its own room in the museum. Separate security monitors, twenty-four hour guards, pressure-sensitive casing. The guys who can steal that can probably do anything. So we at least know that we are dealing with men of extraordinary resources and cunning. But we probably knew that already."

"This just puts a point on it."

"And so they not only have the manuscript and the map. They have Judah Lowe to decipher it all, and they have the Durabian

Parchment and who knows what else." Declan shook his head, slumping down into the too-soft cushions of the hotel suite's arm-chair.

"That's about the size of it."

"So we may not be the only ones who have figured this out."

"We have no way of knowing, but with Judah Lowe, the Durabian Parchment, the original manuscript, and the map, that's a reasonably good guess. The only question is are they ahead of us or are they behind us? After all, we have Reichmann's diary, and that was the key. Without that, they'll have to do a lot more code breaking than we did. We had a shortcut. But how short we don't know. That's why we're in Eilat. I don't know about you, but I'm going after Q."

"With what?"

"I'm rich, Israel is small. With fewer than a half-dozen phone calls, I've got everything just about ready to go. The boat, the horses, the weapons, and the gear."

"So you're just going to sail down the coast, hop off at the mountains on the Saudi-Yemeni border, stroll into a maze of canyons and escarpments and go get it?"

"It's a bit more complex than that, but that's a fair summary."

"And what are you going to do if the caliph's men are already there?"

"That's why we're taking weapons and horses."

Declan stared at the large map Avi had spread across the table, the one he'd saved from the compound and brought with them. "You planning to enter on the Saudi side or the Yemeni side?"

"That depends on Amala's memory. Since the entrance to the valley we're looking for could be on either side based on Reichmann's drawing, we need her to tell us that. So the first thing we do is work from the computers here while the boat's being outfitted. Then we make that decision."

"Let's take a look at Google Earth and see what kind of satellite detail we can get of the coastline."

"Who needs Google Earth?" Avi quipped as he tapped an icon on his computer. "Say thank you to my friends at the Central Institute for Intelligence and Special Tasks."

"Which is to say, the Mossad," Dov translated as he unlaced his boot and leaned back onto the sofa.

With a few quick taps on the keyboard, Avi entered a restricted access database and zoomed in on the area shown on both Reichmann's and Paul's maps.

Avi pointed to a spot on the computer screen. "This is Umm Lajj. That's what Nujayarah is called today. The district of Sayadah." Avi shifted the cigarette to the right side of his mouth without touching it as Amala eased up beside him and leaned down to view the screen.

"The difficult part will be to find the canyon marked on the original map. We'll have to find some way to match up the descriptions on the ancient map, Reichmann's map and those on the satellite images," Amala noted, touching her finger to the shadow of mountains and crevices that filled the screen.

"Let's just take it one step at a time," counseled Declan. "We can keep circling the locations that match both Reichmann's diary and the images of Paul's map. That way we can narrow down the area to a manageable size and then see where we go from there."

"Okay, so let's put a circle around this area, then see if we can match up other points and begin to shrink the circle." Avi's cigarette dangled from his lips, a long ash suspended precariously from the glowing red tip.

With Amala's help, they began to make a series of marks within the circle they had drawn on Avi's map, indicating the location of the places that were referenced both on the images from Paul's map and from Reichmann's diary. Then they would pause and, using a ruler, draw triangulation lines to see where they intersected. Someone would raise a question or find an error. They would erase it all, brew a fresh pot of coffee, and start again. In that slow, halting fashion, they worked through much of the night. And little by little, the dimensions of their search area shrank.

By 2:00 a.m., they were all convinced that they had identified the spot they were looking for. If they were lucky and if Amala's memory proved true, they would find Q deep within a chain of high plateaus and interconnected escarpments between Mount Zbyd and Mount Qurazimat along the Saudi-Yemeni frontier. That was where the Valley of the Jackal lay. They still didn't know precisely where the Canyon of the Faithful Brothers would be, nor the exact location of the Temple of the Revelation. But in an area of less than four square kilometers, surrounded on every side by high mountains and sheer cliffs, they were certain to find them.

Avi, Levi, and Dov had made up their minds. They would leave Amala and Issa with a family in Eilat who would look after them, then they would board the vessel they'd chartered and go after Q. The only question now was whether Declan Stewart would be beside them.

CHAPTER XXXIX

BEIRUT, LEBANON

The bright afternoon sun warmed the naked stumps of the caliph's legs. From his perch on the broad terrace above the city, he gazed at the distant horizon and listened to the ticking of the clock inside his head.

"The shadow troubles me, my son."

"The shadow has no power to stop you, my father. Mecca calls your name. The Prophet has revealed your destiny to you. The city beckons you, does it not, my father? It calls your name. It begs you to liberate it from its oppression. The shadow can't stop you. You don't even require the relic. Weapons and soldiers are more powerful than shadows and parchments. Weapons and soldiers are the keys to your destiny."

"But we must have the relic. I have seen its power in my visions. It alone can deny the Mahdi his destiny. Destroy the relic, and we destroy the shadow. They are joined, one to the other. If either is extinguished, both will perish. Only when this happens can the prophecy be fulfilled."

"But Father, how can a shadow and a crumbling sheet of parchment buried beneath the sands keep us—keep *you*—from your destiny?"

The caliph's eyes were red from the opium smoke. His voice was harsh and angry now. "Are *you* the Mahdi? Have *you* seen the vision? Has the prophet called *your* name? What do you know of omens and of the work the djinn? What do you know of true power, of power so great that no weapon can ever deny it? You are a fool."

"Forgive me, Father. You are the Mahdi. I am your servant. Come, let's go back inside. Take the pipe. Your vision will guide you. It will show you what is to be done. For only *you* are the chosen one." He bowed low before his father.

The caliph removed the shawl from the table beside him and covered the scarred stumps of flesh. With a wave of his hand, he instructed his son to make it so.

From the desk drawer he withdrew the pipe and filled its bowl with the pungent black tar. He placed the briar between his father's lips. Quickly he struck the match. The caliph drew deeply, sucking the flame down and filling his lungs with a heavy cloud of harsh blue smoke. For a moment, he held it captive inside him. He closed his eyes and let the narcotic seep into the fabric of his body. Then he tilted his head back, blew out, and took another draw on the pipe.

When he had finished, the caliph snatched the small gold watch from his vest pocket. He opened the case and watched the tiny black hand speed remorselessly around the dial.

"So little time."

"Then why wait? The Persian has the manuscript and the map. He and his Jew have deciphered its secrets. Already he crosses the desert. Soon he will arrive at its place of hiding. The destiny of the relic is no longer uncertain. In three days, no more, it will burn and the shadow will burn with it. There is no reason to delay. Consult the Prophet in your vision. Surely the Prophet will command you to strike now."

"Only the relic can change the course of my destiny and only the shadow can threaten our quest for it."

"Of course. It is precisely as you say. But it is only three days. And the omens are good, are they not? All the Saudi ministers and sheiks are assembled in Mecca for the conference. A single blow, swift and without mercy, will behead the beast. If we wait until the Persian has confirmed his recovery of the relic and the death of the shadow, our blow may come too late."

"Not without the relic, my son. Not until the shadow is no more." He snapped the watch shut and returned it to his pocket. Then closing his eyes, he entered his dream. There in the distance, beyond the gleaming blue dome of the mosque, floated the scroll, and close beside it, closer than he had ever been before, the man with a crescent scar.

וְיָדָעְ֣וּ וְשִׁ֗י

וְיָדָעְלַבְמוּ וְדָי־לָעַ הָיָהֽנ לְ

יֽחֽ־וָיָה וב הָיָֽהנ רְשֶׁא־לָכ הָיֽ

CHAPTER XL

DAVID BEN-GURION HOTEL
EILAT, ISRAEL
RED SEA COAST

It had been a long night troubled by uneasy dreams and the contemplation of questions for which Declan had no answers. This journey had never been about Q, he told himself in the quiet, black hours of the night as the luminous dial of the clock beside him ticked off the minutes as if they were hours. But then, in the half consciousness that filled the chasm between waking and sleep, the lie had lost its power and he had seen the truth. The journey had always been about Q. Not about Amala. Not about Issa. Not about a promise to a dying man. But always—only—about Q. From the very instant he'd spotted Ibrahim on the high cliff above Ghost Ships. Declan had known even then that it wasn't the old priest calling his name. It was Q and the promise of what might be. Q come to re-ignite the flame. Q come to wake him from his dream. Q come to reclaim the one man to whom it was bound by a bond that could not be explained.

As the first pale rays of dawn brightened the window of his room,

Declan breathed in the cool sea air and studied the thin cotton curtains that danced like Issa's magic hand. The long night was over. The dawn had come. And in that moment, Declan's mind cleared. He knew what he had to do. He knew that he could no longer lie to the Tzabaris, to Amala, or to Issa. But most of all, he knew that he could no longer lie to himself. It was time for him to do what he had always been meant to do. He had to sail south through the Straits of Tiran along the coast of a hostile and unforgiving land. He had to enter the Valley of the Jackal and find the Canyon of the Faithful Brothers. He had to locate the temple hidden deep within, find Q and make it his own. Only then would the flame be extinguished. Only then would he find the peace that had eluded him all his life. It was the only way to end the addiction once and for all. It was the only way he would ever find his way back home. That's what Val had been trying to tell him all along. She couldn't take him home, but she could show him the way.

As hard as it was to accept all that, the hardest part was yet to come. He would have to tell Amala and Issa that they couldn't come with him, that they would have to stay behind with the family Avi had arranged to care for them. Nothing would be harder than that— to tell the person who had lost it all to the quest, that *her* quest was at an end, that she would not see the difficult road she had tread through to its end. After all, it had been Amala, not Declan, who had discovered the manuscript and the map. In a very real way, they belonged to her. And so did Q. But not even those considerations could justify the risk. There would be danger along the road ahead just as there had been danger on the road behind. The killing at the monastery, at Ghost Ships, and at Avi's compound assured them of that. The contours and the dimensions of the danger were unknowable. But its ferocity and barbarity had already been well defined. Declan couldn't change the past. He couldn't take away the losses and the sorrows. But he could change the future. He could do just as he had promised Ibrahim he would do. He could get Amala and Issa to safety. Declan had already sacrificed one woman and one boy to the quest for *Q*. He could not, would not, allow that to happen again.

As the last day before the journey unfolded around them, Declan said nothing. He simply went about the business of securing horses and supplies while Avi and the boys arranged the boat and Amala continued to study the computer images and the maps. He had decided that it would be better that way. Less time for debate. Less time to argue. The boat would leave at midnight. He'd tell her then, at the last moment before they left the hotel and went their separate ways.

But unlike the night before when the minutes had seemed like hours, the final day sped past him like a bullet train, and suddenly he found himself watching from the doorway as Amala gathered her things together and packed her bags. Issa sat beside her playing games. At the table in the corner of the sitting room, Avi and his sons made the final arrangements for the journey. They would leave in an hour. And still Declan hadn't told her. He'd put it off, intentionally waiting till the last minute, hoping against hope that she would reach the same conclusion herself and save him from that awkward moment yet to come. But of course she hadn't. How could she? Was it not her quest as much it was his own? And now there was no place left to hide. He'd run out of time.

"Amala, you aren't going with us. Avi has made arrangements with a local family. You and Issa are staying here."

She looked up from the little canvas duffel she'd bought at the market in the hours after breakfast.

"What?"

"I'm sorry, Amala. But it's just too dangerous. As difficult at the last days have been, the days ahead will be worse. There's no way of knowing if we'll even make it back."

"But you need me. There are still so many questions about the map. Without me, your chances of finding *Q* go down. I'm the only one who has actually seen the original map. Without me, you wouldn't have been able to narrow things down as far as you have."

"And what of Issa, Amala? What about him?"

"Where I go, Issa goes. We're not splitting up."

"I can't let that happen, Amala. I can't let you—either of you—go on this trip." Declan's voice was firm, his words coming in short, harsh clips. But that's the way he'd meant them to be. He couldn't afford to be gentle. He couldn't afford to be kind. There was no way he was going to allow her to get on that boat. She needed to understand that.

"No."

"You're staying. The arrangements have already been made. You'll wait here in Eilat for us to return. That's all there is to it." Declan turned his back to her and started to walk away.

Anger flashed in Amala's eyes. "But I'm the one who found the map in the first place. I'm the cause of all this. You know that without me you don't have a chance. There will undoubtedly be markers along the trail, signs that Paul put there to lead and to mislead. If you run into something unexpected, something that you've misinterpreted from the computer images, what do you do then? You'll never find the temple without me. All this"—she gestured at the maps, the photographs, the provisions, everything scattered throughout the room—"will have been for nothing. Ibrahim's death will have been for nothing. The monks' deaths will have been for nothing. The destruction of Dier al-Shuhada will have been for nothing. The loss of your friend's home will have been for nothing. Is that what you want? "

Declan stopped, pivoted on his heel, and started to speak, but Avi cut him off.

"This family you'll be staying with, Amala, they're good people. They have kids Issa's age. He'll have someone to play with. He'll have good food. He'll have a warm bed. He'll be in a safe house with locks on the doors. Trust me, it's the right place for you two till we return. Where we're going just isn't any place for a woman and child. It would be reckless and unforgivable of us all."

Amala ignored him. She stared directly at Declan and refused to look away.

"Without us, *both* of us, none of this would ever have happened. I discovered the manuscript and the map. Before the caliph's men stole them, I produced the photos that gave us a chance. If Issa hadn't had the idea for us to hide in the storage room when the assassins came, we'd both be dead and you wouldn't even have the partial images of the map you have now. No one has given more in the quest for *Q* than Issa and me. No one has lost more than us. Ibrahim is dead. The monks of Dier al-Shuhada are dead. The monastery—our home, our *only* home—is in ruins. Everything and everyone is gone!"

"I can't change the past. All I can do is be smart about the future."

"You still don't understand. You can't do anything about the future. Don't you see? Ibrahim was right. *Q* is your destiny. For all of us, this quest is *our* destiny. Not for some of us. For all of us. We each have a role to play in what is to come. How can you dare to tell us we stay behind?"

"That's bullshit desert talk. I don't want to hear any more about destiny!" Declan was yelling now. His face was burning and his heart pounding. He started to say something more, then stopped. He realized he'd already said too much. In a plea for help, he turned his eyes toward Avi. Avi nodded gently. He rose from his seat at the table and walked toward the center of the room.

"Look, I know this is your issue. It's between the two of you, I mean. The boys and I, this isn't our place. So I think we should take Issa downstairs with us and get some dinner. That okay with you, Amala? That way you two can talk this over alone. But do me a favor, okay? Think about the massacre at Dier al-Shuhada. Think about the destruction there. Think about eleven graves, twelve counting Ibrahim. Think about my compound, about all we've learned about the caliph and all the resources he has. Then ask yourself what's the right thing to do. And ask yourself one last thing. Ask yourself what happens if when we get where we're going, the caliph and his men are already there. Whatever you two decide, I'll go along with. But just do that for me."

Avi rubbed his beard then nodded to Levi and Dov, gesturing for them to bring Issa and hurry along. Avi opened the door and together the four of them walked outside. The room filled with the perfume of juniper and lilac and the moist, organic smell of the sea. In the distance a ship's horn bellowed. In the blue-black skies beyond the fluttering curtains, silver stars shimmered like flecks of crystal. Then the soft click of the door echoed in the room. Declan and Amala were alone.

Declan paced awkwardly to and fro, intentionally avoiding Amala's stare. When at last he spoke, he had soothed the fires of his anger. His voice was barely more than a whisper.

"Look, I know how you must feel. But try to see this from my perspective. I promised Ibrahim that if I did nothing else, I would make sure that you and Issa were safe. And you will be safe with Avi's friends. You don't have to stay in Eilat. It's just for a while. I have a good feeling about this trip," he lied. "I think we'll be in and out quickly. We'll be back in less than two weeks, maybe less than ten days."

Amala said nothing. Like a statue, she stood straight and proud. Her steely gaze spoke for her.

"So you can give me the silent treatment if you want to. I've spent a lifetime in these deserts. I know all the tricks. But you don't understand. You can't understand. Q isn't what you think it is. It isn't about the light. It's about the darkness. I've pursued this damn parchment my whole life. That's what it does to you. It takes you over. It's like a drug, a vicious, addictive, deadly narcotic. It makes good men do bad things and bad men do terrible things."

"You know Ibrahim didn't believe that. He believed the manuscript would bring peace and harmony, that it would end conflict and suffering forever."

"So what? And to be precise, he believed both. He knew first-hand how dangerous and alluring it is. But he also had convinced himself that it was something more. Fools have believed one version or another of Ibrahim's myth since the beginning of time. Not because it's true, but because they want it to be true. I already admitted it to you and Avi at the compound that I want it to be true too, but that doesn't mean it is. It doesn't magically make it happen. What it *does* do is ensure that madmen chase it. Killers like those who came to Dier al-Shuhada. People like me who are weak and who think they'll find answers that don't exist, answers that can't exist. Don't do this to yourself, Amala. Don't do this to Issa. Neither of you has a place on this journey. I don't even belong here. But I don't have the strength to get off the drug. I can't walk away."

For a long moment she gazed into Declan's eyes.

"You're so very different tonight from the way you were at the monastery when you saved us. You sound nothing like the Declan Stewart I saw then, nothing like the Declan Stewart Ibrahim loved and trusted."

"I'm sorry if I disappoint you. I'm sorry if I disappoint him. But, I'm just talking sense."

"You want to know the truth? I will tell you. An angel spoke to Ibrahim in a vision. She told him that God has chosen you from all the people who have ever lived from the beginning of time to be the man who brings an end to all that is evil in the world. She told him that God has chosen you to reveal *Q*. Maybe he told you that. Maybe he didn't. But it's true. So now maybe you're telling yourself that Amala is talking more 'desert bullshit,' that you don't believe in angels. Maybe you're telling yourself you don't even believe in God. But I can see it in your eyes. I've known it from the first moment I met you. You do believe. You believe everything, just as Ibrahim did. Only your pain and your loss hold you back."

"Don't go there. You don't know anything about my losses, Amala.

You have no idea what I've lost."

"I know what I need to know. I know your destiny is what it is. I know that nothing you do now, nothing anyone does, can change it. Our destiny, Issa's and mine, is what it is and nothing can change that either. Our destiny is inextricably bound to yours. Don't try to deny us our destiny the way you seek to deny your own."

"So, what do you want me to say? Did you find the manuscript and the map? Yes. Could we have gotten this far without you? No. Do you have a right to come? Maybe. But that's not enough. That can't be enough. It was enough once, and I paid the price. I already have innocent blood on my hands because of this addiction I have, this lust, for Q. I already sacrificed one woman and one child to my weakness. I won't do it again. You can't ask me to do that again. You don't have that right."

A gust of wind blew in from the terrace door and stirred the curtain. It smelled of night flowers and the promise of rain.

"I'm not asking you to. You say you know our culture. So then I'll put it culturally. You're not my father or brother. You're not my husband. You don't have the right to make decisions for me. All I am asking is that you not stand in my way. Unlike you, Issa and I not only know our destiny, we gladly embrace it."

"Bullshit. A kid can't be allowed to make a decision like that. You're telling me that you would risk your life and Issa's for a parchment?"

"Issa is part of this, all this. He's much more a part of it than you know. In time, you'll see. Ibrahim believed in Q. He believed in it so much that he gave his life for it, and he did so willingly, without regret. Brother Crispus could have saved himself. But instead he gave his life to protect Issa and me. How could I be willing to do any less? Do you not feel the winds of destiny? Do you not realize that the hand of God is upon us all here in this place, in this time? Surely it's not only I who senses this. Surely it's not only I who has seen things in my dreams. You above all of us must know."

"Destiny is a myth."

"You don't believe that, it's just something you say. None of us knows what will happen when the manuscript is revealed, but I know that Issa and I must go with you into the Valley of the Jackal. You know that too don't you, *Declan?*"

The syllables echoed inside Declan's mind. It was the first time he'd had ever heard her say his name.

Amala took a step toward him and raised her hands, inviting him to take them. Declan gazed into the glimmering jewels of her eyes. Then he looked down at her hands. They were so small, yet so strong. She raised them higher, but still he refused to touch her.

"You have no responsibility for what Issa and I do, Declan. It isn't your choice, it's ours. So regardless of what happens, you have nothing to punish yourself for."

"You don't know who I am. You don't know what I've been through, nor what I lost because of Q. Is an old monk's dream going to give me back my wife? Is it going to give me back my son? Tell me why I should give a damn what happens to this world."

"Tell me why you still follow the quest for Q."

"Because I'm a fool."

"We're not so different, you and I. We've known sorrows beyond our due. We've lost more than is our share. We've borne burdens none should be called to bear. And still, if we speak from our hearts, we know that God hasn't abandoned us. We know what he has called us, all of us, to do."

She reached across the narrow chasm of space that separated them and touched his crescent scar. A crystal tear slipped from the corner of Declan's eye and tumbled like a raindrop down to the dark wooden planks of the floor. Amala followed its trail with her finger then drew him close to her.

"You aren't the only one who's lost precious things, Declan. You aren't alone anymore. God sheds tears beside you, beside both of us. That's why he's sent Q to save us. Won't you believe as you once did? What's the harm? If Q is only ink on a parchment then you won't have sacrificed anything. But if it's what Ibrahim believed it to be, imagine the wonders of the great awakening." Amala squeezed his hand. Tears cascaded down her cheeks, etching a path across the delicate line of her neck.

Declan gazed into her eyes. Suddenly, the entire universe spread out before him. Stars sparkled in the distant mists of swirling galaxies. Suns, surrounded by blue and white planets, burned in the distance. He was no longer in the room above the sea. He floated weightlessly in the black void of space. Slowly, a pale green mist arose and obscured the twinkling of the stars. He turned his gaze back toward Amala. She too now floated in space beside him, but her movements had slowed to a crawl, like the motions of a revolving figurine atop a music box that had wound down.

Declan closed his eyes and inhaled the mist. It was warm and fragrant and stirred old memories in him. Then he sensed another presence close beside him. Slowly, he turned around.

"Don't hold back, Declan. Let this moment be. "

"No, Val. I can't. I won't."

"But you must, my darling. You've been alone in your exile too long. It's time for your mourning to come to an end. Amala and Issa need you now. And you need them. Don't be afraid, Declan. Everything is as it should be. Everything will be is as it is meant to be. But you have to stop fighting it. All you have to do is let go."

"I'm not the one, Val. I can't be. Please, take me with you, take me home. I can't do this. I'm changing, and I'm afraid of what I might become."

"There is only one way home. You know that now, don't you? You don't need me anymore, my darling. You now know what you must do. Just let go."

Val's image faded into the mist. Declan turned back toward Amala, and suddenly the universe folded back in on itself. The stars and the planets and the fog vanished. They were back in the room, facing each other, the curtains stirring restlessly in the evening breeze that blew in from the sea. She placed her arms around him and drew him close to her. Declan closed his eyes, and let go.

CHAPTER XLI

SAUDI SOUTHERN DESERT
LONGITUDE 15° N-LATITUDE 44° E

The sun was low on the western horizon behind them when Judah tapped Shari's shoulder and pointed to the ridge.

"That's what we've been looking for." The image was unmistakable. A single cylinder of stone that cantilevered horizontally from the sheer face of the cliff and two sharp vertical stones that pointed toward the heavens. Together they formed the likeness of a jackal.

Heavy clouds filled the darkening skies as Judah set up his table and laid out the computer and the maps. Without the marker, even Judah Lowe might never have found it. The gap in the canyon wall was subtle and obscure; so narrow that only one man would be able to pass through it at a time. The complex geometry of interconnected escarpments that towered above the ragged, narrow gash in the cliff face made it nearly invisible. The shadows created a maze that acted like camouflage. Paul had chosen his hiding place well.

"We've got another hour or so of daylight. How far beyond the entrance do you expect to find it?" Shari's sense of excitement was palpable.

Though Judah no longer wore the manacles, his arms ached from his elbow all the way down to the tips of his fingers. The iron shackles had rubbed the skin raw and left sores along the undersides of his wrists.

Judah contemplated for a moment, working the calculus of how best to answer without giving too much away. "We don't have much to go on from this point forward. The map indicates the trail, but it no longer seems to take account of scale. I'm certain that there will be more markers along the way. Markers like the jackal, but the map doesn't ascribe a form to those markers. We'll need to be alert to them. And we'll need light."

"And what of the satellite images? Surely we can use them to supplement the clues contained in the map."

"Unfortunately, they'll be virtually useless beyond that gate. It will be like stepping onto the surface of a distant planet. The escarpments bend and curve at harsh angles up, down, sideways. They rise up to the sky then drop off into darkness. The deep defiles, the steep ridges devoid of plateaus, the scattered boulders as big as buildings, it's all going to make a camouflage of shadows as thick and impenetrable as the Amazonian forests. It's almost as if all of this was carved by the hand of God with a single purpose in mind—to hide that valley and everything within it."

Shari lifted his eyes to the escarpment and the thin, ragged crease that defined the entry to the valley beyond.

"Then give me your best guess, Doctor." Judah sensed that Shari's use of the honorific was meant to underscore his growing impatience.

"Ten kilometers."

"Could it be farther?"

"Anything is possible once we're beyond that gate. But I very

much doubt it. As the crow flies, it can't be more than three kilometers. But we're not crows. We can't just fly across the valley.
We'll have to cling to whatever ribbons of trail we find in there,
probably clawing to the side of the cliffs as we go, wrapping back
and forth over our trail as we try to make our way down to the
valley floor. It will be like a crumpled sheet of paper." Judah wadded
the paper beside him, unfolded it again then dropped it to the table,
making his point more clearly than words alone could do. "So we
have to expect a lot of ascents and descents and more than our fair
share of doubling back over ground we will already have covered.
That adds both distance and time to the journey. Once we're actually
inside the valley itself, I'll be able to make a better estimation."

"So what do you recommend?"

"I recommend we make camp here and wait for dawn."

"Time is short, Doctor."

"Would you prefer to enter that godforsaken place now and in an
hour find ourselves covered by a veil of darkness? Would you take
the risk that we'll miss a marker or worse still step off a cliff? I have
no idea what lies beyond that gate. Whatever advantages might be
gained by passing through it now could easily be lost with a single
misstep, a single sign unnoticed in the darkness. You asked my rec-
ommendation. I gave it. We should wait for dawn."

Shari appeared to contemplate that idea. He debated the issue
with himself, weighing the advantages of moving quickly against the
dangers of the darkness. "Perhaps you're right. We've come too far
and accomplished too much to risk it over a few more hours.
Besides, I have the sense that a night under these heavy clouds might
actually work to our advantage. The soldiers are restless. You can
see that even now. Look at them. They clearly don't like it here. If
they weren't so afraid of the Syrian, I don't think they would ever set
foot beyond that gate. These are all uneducated villagers who can't
even read the Arabic of the Korans they carry. They're superstitious
boys from superstitious lands."

Shari studied the map for a moment, paused, then lit a cigarette. "It would be quite useful if there were another way out of that valley, a way that didn't require one to return through this gate. A way that the Syrian and his men might be unaware of."

Judah nodded in agreement. "Yes, that thought has already occurred to me." Judah tapped his pen on the far side of the image that filled the computer screen.

"Just here on the west side of the escarpment, there appears to be another way into—and out of—that valley. It isn't certain and most assuredly will not be easy. But if it's there at all, it's actually closer to where the valley and, by definition, the temple should be."

The Persian nodded and smiled.

"We're thirteen men now, Judah, including the two of us. The nearer we come to the manuscript, the greater the danger will be. The Syrian has great influence with these boy soldiers, but even he isn't strong enough to overcome the power of ancient superstitions. We'll need to use that to our advantage. While I can't know precisely what the Syrian's plans entail, I am certain of one thing. He doesn't intend to let either of us walk out of that valley alive. A another way out, one known only to us, may come in handy."

"The odds would seem to be decidedly in the Syrian's favor."

"Perhaps, but odds can change, and sometimes very quickly. For example, there will be no moon tonight, Judah. The soldiers won't like that. Moonless nights are a bad omen to them. They believe that the djinn walk abroad on moonless nights. We're only two, my friend, but I sense that we have invisible allies all around us."

Shari placed his hand on Judah's shoulder and smiled.

CHAPTER XLII

THE RED SEA, SOUTH BY SOUTHEAST
LONGITUDE 20° N-LATITUDE 39° E

The trawler sped silently through the Straits of Tiran. To the west, the rose-hued buildings of Sharm-el Sheikh dotted the horizon. The helmsman guided the boat between the island and the peninsula, turned south-by-southeast, then took the engines up to twenty knots.

Declan Stewart stood alone at the rusted iron railing and gazed out across the wind-rippled waters of the Red Sea. Silver gulls called out in high-pitched caws then dove low over the deck before banking hard and ascending again. As the weary evening sun melted on the western horizon behind him, Declan watched the waves break on the shore. They were children's waves, waist-high rollers that broke on the shallow sands along the bottom then quickly dissipated. They wouldn't be the same tomorrow. The sands would shift overnight. Then the waves would break differently, on a different shore. The sea was always changing, evolving both above and below the surface. Just like Declan Stewart.

Declan closed his eyes and let his mind wander. He tried to conjure Val from the mists that lurked inside him. He needed to ask her
what it was he had done, what it was he was doing now. But she
didn't come, only the images of waves and an air filled with fog. He
was back at San Onfre now, back in the sea with his dad floating on
the board beside him. It was a winter's day, cold and misty. They
had the whole ocean to themselves. The long, thin ribbon of beach
all the way from Pipes to Trestles was deserted.

*"Not everything in life has to be big and grand, Declan. Sometimes it's
just nice to stroke once or twice then pop up and ride for a long, long time,
especially on a day like this when there's no one around to crowd you. Sort
of like a car passing through a school zone. It gives you time to enjoy
things, time to really see what's going on around you. That's why I like the
fog. It brings emptiness and peace, time to reflect and just be."*

*The deep marine layer had distorted the world around them into a place
where the customary laws of physics were less reliable, less sure. Seated
atop his long board, Declan had the sensation that he was floating in a
dream. He adjusted his ankle leash then turned and tried to find his dad.
But he had vanished in the fog. He was only a voice now, a voice that came
from deep within the swirling white clouds that clung to the sea. .*

"You know who the best surfer in the world is, don't you, Declan?"

"I don't know, Dad. Maybe Tom Curren."

"He's pretty good, but it's not him."

"Laird Hamilton, then."

"He's pretty good too. But, no, it's not him either."

"Then who?"

*"It's the one the sea chooses, Declan. She gets to decide. Once in a gen-
eration, she picks one, just one. It's no one anybody heard of, because the
guys who ride the circuit for money are already too far gone for her. They've
forgotten what brought them into the water in the first place."*

Declan bobbed like a cork on the sea, the fog billowing in great
white sheets all around him. He couldn't see anything now, not his
father, not the horizon behind or the beach ahead.

"Can't see much, Dad."

"Don't need to see much, Declan. All we need to do is trust the sea. Just let go and be in harmony with what's around us. That's the trick to life. Knowing when to let go."

Declan opened his eyes. The skies around him were dry and clear, like the desert itself. But still he felt like that boy floating in the fog. He wasn't sure what was behind him or what lay ahead of him. He wished the old man were standing beside him now, leaning over the railing and looking out to sea. The old man would've known. The old man would've shown him the way. But he was gone now, buried on his own ridge above the sea. He was just a memory, something stored in Declan's mind, buried beneath the sands of time. Just like Valkyre and the boy. Just like everyone he had ever loved. Blink an eye, the world changes. Blink an eye, everyone's gone. And now, like a fool, he had proved to himself that he hadn't learned anything. Like a fool, he had dared to love again.

He hadn't meant for it to happen. He'd done everything he could to keep it from happening. But Amala had touched his soul. She understood his pain and she shared it. He didn't have to tell her about loss and fear. He didn't have to tell her what it had done to him. She already knew. When he looked into her eyes, he saw himself.

But none of that excused what he had done now. Despite everything the world had taught Declan Stewart, he had let it happen again. Now, against every instinct he possessed, he was taking a woman and a child straight into the heart of danger. And the knowledge of that frightened him to his core. Soon the smuggler's trawler would turn back to the north and disappear into a secret harbor on the foreboding coast of a lawless land. New and fearsome dangers would await them on the road ahead, and no one knew where that road would lead.

Declan sensed that he wasn't alone. He turned his head into the wind, toward the bow of the ship. On the weather deck, the sea breeze playing games with the loose strands of his hair, sat Issa. His collar whipsawed back and forth in the wind. As if he too had sensed a presence, he looked up at Declan and smiled.

Suddenly, Declan found that he had let go of the rails and was walking toward the boy. He hadn't willed it to be so. It had just happened, automatically, as if the boy had summoned him. He drifted along the catwalk and down the short metal ladder, landing at last beside the boy. But Issa wasn't looking at Declan any more. He was playing the game of the dancing hand and sniffing the ocean breeze. Somehow he seemed different now, older and more mature, as if the journey were changing him, just as it was changing Declan Stewart.

"Ever been to sea?" Declan asked without intending to.

Issa gave no sign that the words had registered, and for a moment Declan thought that the sounds of the gliding wind and the lapping waves might have swallowed up his words. But instead of asking again, Declan just sat quietly and gazed at the cresting mountains beyond the water. Then the dancing hand stopped and Issa turned his eyes toward his other hand, clenched in a fist. He kept the hand close to his chest and shielded it from the wind. Then at last he looked up at Declan and gestured toward his hand, inviting Declan to come closer, to see what he held inside. Gradually, Issa opened his fingers. A small green beetle stirred beneath the shelter of his hands.

"He knows secrets." Issa whispered the words as if he were inside a church.

A tiny bead of sweat cascaded down from Declan's hairline and touched the crescent scar. He turned and looked at Issa, but his gaze was fixed on the beetle. As if he alone could speak the language of insects.

"Those beetles and I are old friends. We have a history, your companion and I."

Declan noticed a slight upward tilt of the head, an arching of the ear in his direction. The gesture was subtle but telling. He had caught the boy's attention. The connection Declan had hoped for had been established.

"This friend of yours is the *Kheper aegyptiorum*. That's the name the entomologists, the men who study insects, gave him long ago. But you and I, Issa, we need not be so formal with my old friend. You and I may call him by his nickname; I'm certain he won't mind. In fact, he likes it when we say the word *scarab*. I like the sound of that word, don't you? *Sca-rab*. It slithers and slides off the tongue, the same way our little friend moves across the desert sands. Try it. *Scarab*."

Issa grinned. "*Sca-rab*." He arched his ear and tilted his head so that the threads of black hair no longer dangled in the sea breeze. Instead, they settled over a curious eye that glimmered, just like the metallic shell of the beetle, in the red rays of the sun. Declan's lip curled into a smile.

"Rotate your palm in that ray of light, Issa. You'll see something spectacular. You'll see his shell catch the sunlight then turn it gold and green. When the ancient Egyptians saw that the scarab could do that, they proclaimed him divine. They had concluded that our little friend and their god Ra, the sun god, were kinsmen."

Issa raised up his hand. He tilted the beetle toward the sun. With his other hand, the boy made a shield from the wind. Then suddenly, the beetle exploded like a jewel of sparkling black, gold, green, and blue. Even Declan was enthralled by its splendor.

"People don't believe that anymore. They say the beetle is just a beetle and the sun is just the sun. But now you have seen for yourself, so you can judge whether our friend is god or merely an insect." The boy glanced up at Declan, and Declan smiled.

"The Egyptians saw that each night the sun died on the western horizon and then in the morning was born anew in the east. And the scarab did the same. Each night he disappeared into a hole in the earth, just like the sun. Then each morning he reappeared, again just like the sun. That's how they knew that he and Ra were brothers.

That's how they knew the beetle was divine. So they made great statues, some as tall as a building, to honor him. They scattered his image all across the great expanse of their realm. The pharaohs even had scarabs buried beside them in their tombs. They hoped he might take them with him when he rose into new life on the far horizon."

Issa arched an eyebrow. The dancing hand corkscrewed through the wind, the beetle safe in its cradle beside it.

"It's an ancient secret, something lost in the past. It's the kind of thing only old archeologists like me remember. Only men who spend their lives in the past even care about such things now. But now you know too. You know the true story of the scarab. Perhaps one day, long after I'm gone, you'll tell it to your son. In that way, the story will live on and won't be forgotten. Like the beetle, perhaps it will live forever."

"Is it true or is it a myth?" Issa asked, placing his hand back inside the pocket of his jacket.

"Who can say? But does it really matter so much? After all, just because a myth isn't true doesn't mean that the truth is not in the myth."

"The truth is always in the myth, Dr. Stewart."

Declan nodded. Then, from the corner of his eye, he noticed the captain. He had been standing there all along, listening.

Avi, Declan, and Amala, huddled together in the grimy light of a galley that smelled of fish guts and smoke. Declan looked troubled.

"Don't get me wrong, Avi. All I'm asking is, can we trust him?"

Levi walked through the doorway and sat down at the table beside Amala. He had a cup of coffee in one hand and a cigarette in the other. "Do you want me to guess who you're talking about?"

"We're talking about the captain," Amala whispered.

"And all I'm saying is that there's something about him. Something I don't like. I'm not indicting him. I'm just asking if you're sure we can trust him."

Avi shrugged. "Look, I know it's not a fancy cruise ship and that Ephrom isn't anyone's idea of a cruise ship captain. But what we have is what we ordered. We have to blend in, not draw attention, and this old tub is the best way to do that. It makes us a grain of sand in the desert, and that's what we want to be." Avi scissored his fingers at Levi. Levi passed the cigarette to him as Amala refilled all their cups with fresh coffee.

Declan grimaced. "I get all that, Avi. I have no complaints about the boat. I'm asking about the captain of this vessel. Can we trust him?"

"Can we trust him? I can't look inside the man's heart and his head and know what's really in there. Ephrom's an Orthodox Jew. I knew his uncle. If we were all Gentiles, I'd be worried. He'd cheat us, because that's what his rabbi says you can do. He says a Jew can cheat a Gentile. But not another Jew. Besides, we're not just three Jews. We're three Jews with three Uzis. I think our secrets will be safe with him, but if it's guarantees you want, you should've hooked up with a banker."

"Does it really matter at this point?" Amala asked. "I mean, we're already committed. There's no turning back. Whatever things are, they are."

"The girl has a point, Dr. Stewart. At this point, Ephrom's the only game in town." Levi drew a fresh cigarette then tossed the pack onto the table.

"Okay, so forget I asked. But I think it would be smart if all of us kept an eye out just the same."

Avi nodded and bent forward in the chair, stretching the muscles of his lower back. "Look, there are a thousand things we could worry about. But what's the point? Most of them are well beyond our control. Our time would be better spent going back over our plan. We'll hit the cove tomorrow night, and it's going to be tricky and dangerous once we set foot on Saudi soil. There won't be time to start reworking things. So let's just walk through it again while we still have time."

Levi drew a breath from his cigarette. "We better have a good plan. Jews aren't welcome where we're going. In fact, neither are Christians. Even Palestinian ones, if you don't mind me saying." Levi smiled at Amala, making a gesture of apology. "If we're caught . . ." Levi grimaced and passed his thumb across the flesh of this throat.

No one commented. They didn't need to.

Declan removed the rolled map from his shoulder bag and spread it on the galley table. Amala placed her cup on one corner and sugar dispenser on the other to hold it in place.

"We're on our way to here," Declan pointed to the rugged mountain range and a tiny nick in the coast line. "Our smuggler's boat has a pretty shallow draft. If we're lucky, we can go right up to the shore. That'll speed our unloading substantially and let us get into the mountain canyons quickly."

"Please, Declan, you must call him Captain Ephrom. He *is* a smuggler, but he doesn't like to be called one, especially not on his own boat." Avi blew a heavy cloud of blue smoke toward the ceiling of the cramped compartment.

Declan ignored the comment. "It's a little more than a thousand kilometers from Eilat." Declan laid the point of his pencil down on what appeared to be a tiny cove north of the Yemeni border. "That's a long way, but now that we're in open water, *Captain* Ephrom claims we'll make thirty-five knots, maybe more. I have my doubts, but we'll see."

Avi picked at his lower lip then wiped what he'd found there on the leg of his khaki trousers. "Trust me, we'll make that speed or better it. It's another reason I chose the captain. This ship is made for smuggling. He'd have been caught long ago if not for the dual engines. When other ships are around, we chug along like the rest of the rust buckets. That way we don't stand out. But when we're alone in open water, we make time."

Declan reworked the math in his head. "Let's assume all that's right. That means we should make landfall at the cove north of Qutuf al Misri before dawn on the third day."

"Nice allusion," Levi quipped.

"I don't get it," Dov uttered, lazily.

"'On the third day, Abraham looked up and saw the place in the distance,'" Avi whispered absently, quoting from the Book of Genesis. He turned from the table and stared out the porthole at the darkness of the night. "So who's Isaac?"

No one laughed.

"'He suffered death and was buried, and on the third day, he rose again,'" Amala added softly, shifting her gaze to the broad expanse of sea roiling outside the portal.

For a moment they all sat in silence. Then Avi crushed out his cigarette and feigned a cough. He didn't like the mood that had settled over the wretched little galley.

"It's a good place, that cove. Larger vessels can't get in. It's too narrow and shallow. And the captain says the mountains wrap around it like a giant fist." Avi illustrated with his hand. "The whole place is one big shadow. That kind of cover you can't buy. It gives us exactly what we need."

"How much do you think they've figured out, Declan?" Amala stirred a spoonful of sugar into her cup.

Declan absently tapped his pen on the table. "I wish I knew. Judah Lowe is very smart and very good, but he doesn't have Reichmann's diary."

"But he does have the original manuscript, the map, the Durabian Parchment, and presumably a lot of other resources," Amala added.

"Yeah, but will he use them? He was brought into this by force. He didn't volunteer."

"Trust me," Avi said. "He'll do everything within his power to help them. He won't have a choice if he wants to stay alive and in one piece. The caliph's men will know how to motivate him."

"That's probably so. In any event, we have to assume that the caliph's men know as much as we do. If we're lucky and they don't, great. If they do and they're there, we won't be surprised." Declan got up from the table and walked to the porthole. He undid the latch and let the sea breeze in.

"Paul's map marks the entrance to the Valley of the Jackal on the southeast side. But Reichmann's map says the entrance he found was up here to the north and west, the way we're headed. If the caliph's men are coming, it's almost certain they'll come from the direction marked on Paul's map, not the one on Reichmann's."

"So if that's right," Avi observed, "they won't come by sea. They'll take the land route down through the deserts north through Hafar al Batan. But they won't want to bring any attention to themselves. That's the last thing they want. They'll weave back and forth across the desert, stopping for water at the small way stations the Bedouins use. Then if they're smart, they'll cross into Yemen, probably south of Khamis Mushayt. They'll go west and double back, working north through the mountains. That'll bring them to the same series of escarpments we're headed for, only they'll come by land from the southeast, and we'll come by sea from the northwest."

Declan studied the satellite images. "It looks like they'll have to stair-step up just like us, but since we enter from the west, we'll have half as many escarpments to traverse. It'll take some time for them to cover that much ground."

Declan heard a cracking sound and looked up to the skylight above the table. A shadow passed over the smudged glass of the marine skylight. He couldn't be sure, but he had the feeling someone had been listening to every word they said.

CHAPTER XLIII

SAUDI SOUTHERN DESERT
LONGITUDE 15° N-LATITUDE 44° E

At dawn the caliph's men passed through the narrow gate and began the last phase of the journey. With luck, they would reach the Valley of the Jackal by sunset and then enter the temple at dawn.

The soldiers had been restless and anxious all throughout the night before. But that was nothing compared to the eerie sense of danger that took hold of them now. Nothing around them was familiar, everything seemed filled with omens and the promise of dangers to come. The plants, the color of the stones, even the shadows and the shape of the sky were alien and ominous. The Bedouins nodded to each other and scanned the ridges around them. They had known all along. They had sensed it the moment they saw the boulders in the shape of a jackal. All of it—the stones, the invisible gateway hidden in the side of a sheer wall of stone, the narrow ribbon of trail they now trekked along—was the work of a djinn.

Shari was the first to enter the valley. He had intended it as a subtle message to the soldiers. A message that he was a man of intellect, not of superstition. That he had no fear of whatever lurked beyond the long, narrow crack in the canyon wall. And so he took it with a measure of pride that he should be the first man in two thousand years to enter that strange and haunted domain. At long last, *Q* was within his reach. The quest that had consumed a lifetime was nearly at an end. Emile Zorn would have smiled.

An eerie stillness settled over them as they pushed beyond the gate and descended into the realm of darkness and shadow. The twisted corridors of stone were filled with swirling winds and the damp, fragrant mist that comes before a rain. Heavy clouds troubled the western sky. They all feared the coming of the rain.

Throughout the long day they marched, a slow, plodding caravan of fearful men moving across a rugged trail of loose gravel and fragile shale ledges. The soldiers, weighed down by heavy loads of water, ammunition, and other supplies, inched along the narrow trail that clung like a thread to the walls of the sheer cliffs that were the only way down. Then one missed a step. A noisy barrage of loose stones cascaded down the deep, black crevice. He grasped at a branch that protruded from the rock, but it had decayed from within and crumbled in his hands. The load of his heavy pack shifted and he lost his balance entirely. First his right foot, then his left, slipped off the ribbon of trail and into the nothingness of empty space. Shrieking, he went plummeting over the edge. In tight, ugly circles he tumbled down into the void. The screeching sounds of his passing echoed throughout the labyrinth again and again and again. Then there was only the sound of the wind whistling through the portals of the stone walls that surrounded them. As if they were a single, integrated being, the soldiers that remained touched their amulets in unison then whispered prayers as they turned their eyes away from the limp red body impaled on the sharp rock below.

Shari smiled. The Syrian now had only nine.

The soldier's sudden death—one moment he had been there, the next he was gone—only fueled the fires of superstition and terror.

Already skittish from the omen of the moonless night before, the death had almost shaken them free of their fear of the Syrian. Some of the soldiers began to whisper among themselves that they must turn back, that evil waited for them in the valley below. It had been wrong to pass beyond the gate, they whispered. The stone image of the jackal had warned them. But no one said such things within earshot of the Syrian.

Two hours before sunset, they came to a small plateau. Judah Lowe set up the table and consulted his maps.

"In two hours, this maze will be filled with darkness, Judah." Shari's words were delivered in an even, flat monotone. "The trail breaks in two directions now, there to the west and this way to the north. Which one do we take, Judah? Which one leads to the canyon and the temple?"

Judah gazed up uneasily at the towering walls of stone around him. "You have to remember that the map's primary purpose and its greatest details were focused on leading us to the entrance to the valley itself. Now that we're inside, it's harder to know for certain. Remember, our only guide is a two thousand year old map. And this whole area is an active seismic region filled with volcanoes, troubled by the earthquakes that come with them. Many things can change in two thousand years. But even if it's all just as it was, look at this maze of stone and shadow that surrounds us. We could be right on top of the canyon, even the temple itself, and not even know it."

Shari removed the bandana from around his neck and wiped the sweat from his face and neck. A mist had begun to rise around them. It was as if the rain clouds above were sucking the moisture out of the ground, as if the world were raining backwards.

"So do you recommend that we carry on or do we make camp and wait for dawn?"

Judah tilted his head toward the sky and bit his lower lip. "We have to be close. We're just not seeing it. If my calculations are correct, there simply has to be a small, deep canyon somewhere down there. Give me one more hour. We have enough light left for that. If I haven't found it by then, we can make camp."

"Another hour means they'll be setting up camp in darkness. That will make the Syrian's men more anxious still. I think I like your plan, Judah. One more hour it is."

Shari snapped his bandana, rolled it back over itself, then reattached it to his neck. "Commander," he shouted over his shoulder, "Gather the men. We continue on."

For a long moment the Syrian stared at Shari and said nothing. They were dueling now, each man using all his skill and cunning to ensure that he, not the other, walked out of that valley with the prize. The Syrian touched the handle of his jambiya. For a moment he held his fingers there. Then, as if he had holstered his emotions, he nodded.

An hour later as the sunlight faded and the billowing mass of clouds gathered strength, Judah Lowe discovered the canyon. It lay deep within the veil of mists, hidden by steep walls of stone on the eastern face of the escarpment. They would need the light of day to attempt the descent. They would make camp there and wait for dawn.

Murder wasn't exactly in Shari's line, at least not directly, not by his own hand. But he had the skills; he knew how it was done. After all, had he not, by the caliph's command, spent a season in his training camps? Had he not learned the dark arts of the twisted old prophet's version of jihad? He'd hated those long days filled with propaganda and the lessons of war. But he had endured them, as he had endured everything. He endured them because they were just one more installment in the price of Q.

Had the circumstances been different, he would have ended it quickly with a short burst of machine fire, the toss of a grenade, a single shot to the head. But those were not options now. Now he had to take account of the soldiers. They might be afraid, and indeed they were, but they would not let his assassination of the Syrian go unpunished. So just as Emile Zorn had counseled him so long ago, Shari once again would have to rely on intellect and cunning to achieve his ends. He would have to be wily and deft in his handling of the affair, because even a slight miscalculation could lead to disaster. It could mean the loss of everything. The loss of the treasure he'd worked a lifetime to find.

As the jihadis made camp, they whispered spells against the omens and the spirits that filled the valley. They were fools, just like the people of the village he'd been born to, the dusty, impoverished village at the edge of the Persian desert, the village he'd left behind when he was only twelve. The village he'd never seen since. It had been a hollow and lifeless existence there, devoid of culture and learning, filled with gossip and the tedium of repetition. And what did they get for it all? Only three handfuls of sand cast upon a grave, he answered. Three because Allah blessed the odd numbers. The even ones were unlucky.

"Your name is not Shari. It is Sharif." His father's angry voice had boomed like thunder through the house. *"It is a proud and ancient name. You will not whittle it down to a stump."* Then he raised the cane, its thin, arcing body whistling through the dry desert air, and extracted a price.

He had never belonged there. He knew that from his earliest memories. He belonged to another time and place. He was a gazelle in a land of plow cattle. Yet no one seemed to care. In a way, he was grateful for all the torture he had endured, first at the hand of his father in the village at the edge of the desert, then later at the equally brutal hand of his uncle in Palestine. They all ostracized him because he was different. But he was thankful for that now. Being different in a place where sameness was cherished was what had made him who he was. Only Emile Zorn had appreciated him for that. Emile Zorn had led him out of the wilderness and shown him the way. He was the only man who had ever shown Shari kindness and expected nothing in return. He was the only man Shari had ever truly loved.

When this affair was concluded, when he at last held *Q* in his own two hands, he would return to Capernaum. He'd make sure that Emile Zorn, in a small way, shared in the riches and in the glory. He'd build a monument to him there. He'd make sure the old cripple managed at last to get the respect that had eluded him all his life.

But before that day might come, there was much left to do and many obstacles to be overcome. He had to find the path that would lead him down into the canyon. And he had to kill the Syrian and all the men around him. He still hadn't made up his mind about Judah Lowe. Something pawed at his consciousness and told him that the frail academic with horn-rimmed reading glasses, badly fitted suits, and a taste for the finer things, might yet have further value to him.

CHAPTER XLIV

SAUDI-YEMENI FRONTIER
LONGITUDE 15°N–LATITUDE 43°E

"This is an omen," Captain Ephrom said, scowling. "My mother is Sephardic, from Iraq. She knows the Kabbalah. You should always heed an omen, she says. To do otherwise is to tempt fate."

Avi stared up at the sky, but said nothing.

Only moments before the silver moon had floated like a ripe golden melon above them. Then as they passed through the narrow entrance to the cove, a dark armada of clouds appeared from nowhere. The moon and platinum stars vanished into the impenetrable black void. Only shadows remained.

"You're sure you want to go through with this?"

"Omens I don't know about, Captain. But this darkness? It's okay with me. I'll take it. It's good camouflage." Avi tugged at his ear and thought for a moment. "And it's a little late to be asking myself whether I'm sure I want to go through with this."

Not for the first time, Avi contemplated Declan's question. *Are you sure we can trust him?* There was something about Captain Ephrom.

He wasn't like his uncle. He wasn't like any Orthodox Jew Avi had ever dealt with before. He always seemed to be ogling Amala as if she were a trinket he intended to steal. Or perhaps it was the way he counted the money when Avi paid him the first installment. Or maybe it was just Avi's fear rising up in him and playing games with his mind now that they had crossed the point of no return.

As the captain had promised, the trawler's shallow draft allowed them to squeeze the gunwales of the ship close alongside a natural stone jetty that protruded from the cliff. It took less than an hour to unload it all—the horses, the weapons, the ammunition, and the supplies. When they had finished, Declan and the others fanned out across the shore in search of a trail. They needed to get into the mountains quickly and set up camp for the night. Only Avi had stayed behind with Captain Ephrom. There was something he wanted to get straight.

"So, it's your ass, my friend. Who am I to tell you what to do? But you look smarter than this to me. Maybe you should just pay me off now and tell me to turn this ship around and take you back to Eilat. You're a Jew, my friend. A Jew is not a good thing to be any-where these days, but especially not here."

Avi pursed his lips and started to light a cigarette. Captain Eph-rom raised his hand and shook his head. "You want a cigarette, you wait till I'm out of this cove. That light can be seen from a long way off in this kind of darkness." Avi slipped the lighter back into this pocket and tossed the cigarette into the sea.

"Remember, if they catch you, you never heard of me, and you don't know anything about this vessel. I lose it, I'm screwed."

"I don't plan to get caught."

"No one ever does, my friend."

"Just be sure you're back here in five days. Exact same time, exact same place."

"I was thinking about that. When we discussed my fee, I didn't know all the things I know now."

"Such as?"

"Such as you and your mates there. You're after a treasure."

"Is that what you think?"

"It's a small ship. You don't need walls with ears to know what's what."

Avi intentionally delayed his response. He wanted to be sure the smuggler understood precisely what he was about to say.

"So, let me be straight with you, Ephrom, one Jew to another. The fee is double if you're back here in five days. Got it? That's a very good deal for you. But if you're not here then, my boys won't like that so much. They don't like missed appointments. If you miss this appointment, just know that an accident will happen to your boat. Or maybe your house will catch fire. Maybe you'll be walking through a dockyard one night and simply disappear. My mother wasn't Sephardic. I don't know omens. I don't know the Kabbalah. But see, I can tell the future. It's an open book to me. You understand what I'm saying, don't you? One Jew to another."

Ephrom smiled. "Double is good. You pay half now, though. In cash."

Avi didn't like that idea, but he didn't imagine he had much of a choice. He nodded then counted out the bills.

"Five days. Exactly. No more. No less. I'll be here, same time, same place. But you make sure you're here. Because if you're not, I won't wait. That's the deal. I come back, you're here, okay. I come back, you're not here, I'm gone. And for good. No return passage, no second coming."

"Indeed."

The old smuggler eased the trawler back from the jetty then vanished into the darkness.

They were three Jews and three Christians in a land that didn't like Jews and Christians. And they knew it. They could feel the vibrations of hostility in the air, as if it leaked like a vapor from the very stones that surrounded them. They didn't like the way the darkness made them feel, but they were grateful for its cover. Quietly they advanced in a single line toward the cleft in the cliffs, each horse tied caravan-style to the one in front of it.

As they slipped through the narrow fissure and entered the deep maze of mountains and canyons beyond, Declan felt as if he had stepped through a window, tumbled through space, and landed in another world. The sounds of the sea behind them were gone. Only a stark, bullying silence remained. There was no stirring of the wind, no buzz of insects or the crackling sound of mammals scurrying in the darkness. Even the storm clouds seemed to have been swallowed up by the absolute darkness beyond the shore. It was a vacuum, a sealed chamber out of sync with the ordinary world. And there was something more. Declan had the feeling they weren't alone.

"We don't need to go far," Declan whispered. "Now that we're away from the coast, we just need to find a spot to get some rest while we wait for dawn."

Levi was the first to notice. His voice came from the rugged line of boulders to Declan's right. "Dr. Stewart. There's another crevice here. It looks like there's a flat, open area that fans out on the other side. It might do us for tonight."

"Here, take this and check it out." Declan tossed him a flashlight from the saddlebag. "But be careful." Levi nodded, then both he and the dull beam of his flashlight disappeared down the corridor of stone. A few moments later, they both reappeared.

"It's perfect. Large, flat area protected by high cliffs on every side. You want to see?" He gestured his light at Declan's feet, inviting him to see for himself.

"No, I'll take your word for it. Lead the horses in. We'll make camp there for the night."

After they had fed the horses and laid out their bedrolls, Amala asked, "Shall I make a fire?"

"No fires till morning."

"That means dinner from cold tins. I hope that's okay."

"Yep, and nothing but water to drink tonight." Declan rubbed Issa's head and managed a smile. The dancing hand seemed undisturbed by the eeriness of their surroundings. "But we can have a fire and coffee once the sun's up."

The smell of rain drifted down from the rumbling clouds that massed in heavy columns above them. But the rain refused to come, as if it were waiting for a sign.

As he unlaced his boots, it occurred to Declan that they were all like Issa now. They had entered their own secret world of the dancing hand. Each was alone, trapped in a prison cell filled with his own thoughts and recriminations, doubts, fears, and ambitions. They were sailors shipwrecked on a hostile shore. The safety of home— how he wished he were there—was a memory to them now, an ember in the dying fire of their consciousness. Everything in every direction as far as a man might wander held the promise of devastation and the hint of misfortune. There was no way to know which actions might lead to safety and which to harm. They only had their instincts to guide them.

Declan gently pulled his bedroll up beside Amala and lay down. Issa squeezed his bag in between them, smiled first at Declan then at Amala, and slowly closed his eyes.

Declan at last had decided that he would no longer lie to himself. Not about Amala, and not about Q. He was no longer afraid to be who he was. He knew now that if he were given the chance to turn back from either of them, to walk out of this and back to his cottage above the sea, he wouldn't do it. Love called to him now, just as Q had called to him all along. It wasn't the voice of madness he heard now, it was a voice of peace, and guidance, saving him from the madness. It was Val. Val had given him the strength to be who he was. She had prepared him for whatever lay ahead. And when this thing was done, when all that now lay ahead was behind, she would help him find his way back again, back to where he belonged. Wherever that might now be.

Amala was the first to rise. She made breakfast while the men fed the horses and packed their bedrolls. In the distance thunder rumbled so heavily that Declan could feel it in his chest; they all could. Even the ground beneath them trembled at its command.

Across the canyon floor, beside a looming boulder that etched its way vertically toward the purple sky, Issa sat alone playing the game of the dancing hand and consulting, as if he were an oracle, the scarab beetle. The haunting tune the boy hummed seemed to hang in the air. It mingled with the deep growl of the thunder and the subtle fragrances of coffee brewing over the open fire.

Declan squatted down beside the flame and warmed his hands. Avi and the boys had already gathered there. The alluring aroma of coffee and the inviting warmth of the small fire had been too much for them to resist. As he leaned over to pick up a tin cup for his coffee, he kissed Amala lightly on the cheek. "Good morning."

Amala smiled then filled his cup from the metal pot, its speckled shell glimmering blue and white on the grate above the glowing red embers of the fire. Their eyes met for a moment then they both turned away.

"We have exactly five days before Captain Ephrom returns to our little jetty," Declan said matter-of-factly. "If we're not there, he turns back around and goes home. We never see him again. So our number one priority is not to miss our ride home. We have five days to find the temple, get Q, and get out. That's a tall order, but it is what it is. So I want to be sure we're all on the same page. We do what we came to do if we can, but by hook or by crook, we're back here in time to meet the ship."

Declan glanced quickly at the faces around him. Each in turn nodded.

"Horses all set?" Declan asked, turning his gaze toward Levi.

"They're loaded," Levi responded casually. "I've already scouted an animal trail over the ridge. It's not great, but it takes us exactly in the direction the map says we need to go. I don't know how far it goes or how long it'll last, but it's a good way to start the day." Levi adjusted the shoulder strap of his Uzi then took a gulp of coffee.

"That's good work. In an hour we need to be out of here and on that trail. We move quickly, but we move quietly. For all we know, the caliph's men may be over the next ridge."

Avi nodded then tossed the cold, bitter residue of his coffee to the ground. He leaned down and placed the empty cup on the rock beside him.

"Five days," Amala said to herself as she extinguished the fire and began putting the utensils away.

Declan looked skyward toward the rumbling black clouds. "If the monsoon rains open up, it could be pretty slow going. But if the weather holds, we'll get more than half-way there today. I'm counting on us reaching the valley sometime tomorrow in the late afternoon or early evening. That means two days to get in, two days to get out, one day to find Q. It's not much margin of error. So before sunset tomorrow, we better be sitting before the Temple of the Revelation, whatever it may be, and hopefully we'll be sitting there alone."

Suddenly, a dry crack echoed from the ridge above the spot where Issa played. On its heels came a tinkling rain of loose rock cascading down the canyon wall. Instantly, they froze and didn't make a sound. Declan looked at Amala and touched his finger to his lips. She nodded then repeated the gesture to Issa. Then, with the open palm of his hand, Declan gestured toward the ground, signaling her to slip down behind the boulder. She shook her head and gestured toward Issa. Declan nodded. Amala crept delicately toward him. Declan whistled softly and caught Issa's attention. He signaled the boy to get on the ground and wait for his mother. The dancing hand stopped. Issa returned the scarab beetle to his pocket. Avi signaled to Levi to circle around and approach the ridge from the west. He then made the same sign to Dov, signaling him to approach it from the east. Noiselessly, each slipped a clip into his Uzi then, crouching low over his boots, crept toward the ridge.

Gingerly, Declan placed his tin cup on the ground and unfastened the soft leather flap of his holster. As he studied the tangle of arid desert shrubs around them, Declan removed the pistol and switched off the safety. From the corner of his eye, he glimpsed movement and pivoted on his heel. For a moment, he studied the cluttered ridge line. Then he saw what had moved. It was Levi, sliding into place beside a giant boulder, his Uzi leveled and ready. Dov was another thirty meters beyond, climbing up from the east.

The horses were skittish and sensed danger. Their bulbous, liquid eyes darted nervously in every direction as they snorted the cool morning air. They danced in a tight circle, straining against their reins. Declan's heart pounded inside his chest. He had only one thing on his mind. He had to protect Amala and Issa.

Then they heard another cracking sound, this time just beyond the crest of the ridge. It was closer than the one before. Declan dropped to his knee and leveled his pistol, pointing it in the direction of the sound.

Damn it, why don't they show themselves? Impatiently, he waited and watched, glancing anxiously back toward where Amala and Issa lay.

Something moved again. This time Declan saw an image on the ridge. It moved in fits and starts just beyond the slope of the mountain. A tall, looming shadow was coming toward them. He touched his finger to the metal of the trigger but did not squeeze. He still couldn't see what it was.

"Don't shoot."

Declan eased his finger back a few millimeters.

"It's me." Dov's voice was calm, almost playful.

"What the hell are you doing? Get down!"

"Don't worry, he's gone."

"Who's gone?"

"The leopard. It was a leopard like I've never seen before. Big and beautiful, with eyes as green as acacia leaves. Crazy spooky, though. When I first got a glimpse of him, I thought he was walking upright, like a man. Then its eyes flashed at me like a couple of headlights, and suddenly he was a leopard. Never saw anything like that before. I took aim and was going to shoot him. Better safe than sorry, right? But then he looked right at me and I couldn't pull the trigger. The muscle in my finger wouldn't move. It was like looking into the eyes of a ghost."

For a moment, they stood quietly and let the tension drain out of them. Then Avi at last broke the silence. "Which direction did it go?"

"He followed the trail, the one we're taking. I figure that's his trail." Dov moved cautiously back toward the horses turning his head back over his shoulder and surveying the ridge.

"Not so good if he comes back for a meal," Levi carped.

"He won't be back."

"You sound pretty sure of yourself."

"Look, if we see him again up the trail, I'll shoot him, okay? But he could've taken me if he'd intended to. He was that close. He's not looking for food. It was like he wanted to be sure we'd found the trail and knew which way to go." Dov lifted the coffee from the fire and poured a cup. "I'm starting to sound a little crazy, huh? I guess this place is getting to me."

"Enough with the omens and crazy talk," Avi growled, hiking up his pants then popping a cigarette between his teeth. He drew a deep breath of smoke then expelled a tight narrow stream while he wiped his head with his bandana. "Let's get moving."

Dov shrugged then adjusted his Uzi.

"Amala, you and Issa okay?" Declan spoke in Arabic. It had become the language of their intimacy.

"Yes, Declan. We're fine." The hint of a smile crossed her lips.

"*We're fine,*" Issa mimicked as the magic hand danced in the air beside him.

Declan holstered his pistol and snapped the flap back into place.

"Let's hope this is all we run into," Avi uttered.

Declan nodded, then walked toward the horses. He wondered where the caliph's men might be and how much Judah Lowe had already deciphered. He hoped they had learned little and were still a long way off. But something in his gut told him not to count on it. Something told him they were close.

CHAPTER XLV

THE VALLEY OF THE JACKAL

"Sayyidi, forgive me. There's a caravan on the western escarpment three kilometers from here. They're on the ridge just above the canyon. From there they can surely see the temple."

Shari and Judah Lowe sat together with an array of satellite images before them. They and the men had searched all day for the entrance to the Canyon of the Faithful Brothers. But still it eluded them. If they were going to reach the temple, they had to find a way into that canyon.

"How many?"

"It's difficult to say, Sayyidi. The sun is low and the ridge is covered in brush. Perhaps four, maybe others. And at least three horses."

Shari nodded. "Have they seen us?"

"Insha'Allah, no, Sayyidi. We noticed their movements through the field glasses, but there's no sign they saw us."

"Perhaps it's a band of Bedouins," Judah Lowe suggested hopefully.

The soldier ignored him.

"Well?" Shari demanded.

"I think not, Sayyidi. Bedouins wouldn't travel in a haunted place such as this. They too fear . . . the djinn." His voice grew softer as he uttered the word, as if he were afraid to utter it aloud.

"Did they wear keffiyeh?"

"No, Sayyidi. They wore hats."

"And I imagine you've already told this to the Syrian?"

"Abu al-Suri is not in camp, Sayyidi."

"Indeed? That's rather interesting. So where is he?"

"The commander doesn't advise me of his movements, Sayyidi. I know only that he's not in the camp."

"Because you looked for him first before coming and reporting this to me?"

"Yes, Sayyidi,"

Shari touched his finger to his chin. "A betting man would wager he's off looking for a trail that leads into that canyon and the temple beyond." Shari's mind already was assessing the possibilities. "An unexpected caravan in the middle of a haunted valley. The Syrian gone missing from the camp. Allah works in mysterious ways, is this not the teaching of the madrassas?" Shari arched his eyebrow toward the boy.

"Allah's ways are his own, Sayyidi. He reveals to us only what he would have us know."

Shari clasped his hands together and nodded at Judah Lowe.

"Yes, and Allah has revealed to me that Declan Stewart has come to call. It's amazing the power of an ancient parchment. After all this time and so much tragedy, he still follows the trail. The question for us now is rather simple, isn't it? Do we allow him to continue his quest and see what he comes up with? There is, after all, a chance that he knows something we don't. Or do we strike preemptively and eliminate the risk?"

"We have the manuscript, we have the map." Judah spoke casually as if he were in his study considering a matter he'd read in the evening paper. "It's highly unlikely Declan Stewart has anything we need."

"Yet, somehow, like a ghost, a specter, he's made it this far. He has to know something to have accomplished that feat. He's a resourceful and persistent fellow. I think it's unwise to underestimate him."

"Why bother with him at all? What trouble can he possibly cause us now?" Judah lazily circled an area on the map.

If Shari heard Judah Lowe, he didn't acknowledge it. Instead, he turned back to the soldier. "Go now and find the Syrian for me. Bring him here."

"As you command, Sayyidi." The soldier pivoted on his heel and strode briskly away.

"This is an interesting situation, my dear Doctor. I'm beginning to have a renewed respect for Declan Stewart. But more importantly, I'm beginning to see possibilities in his return. Possibilities that may help us deal with our Syrian friend and his little flock of followers." Shari took a Dunhill from his jacket and lit it. He drew languidly on the cigarette then let the cloud of smoke wander lazily from his lips and up toward the threatening, black clouds that filled the sky.

"I don't see your point, Shari."

"You will, Judah. Trust me. You will."

CHAPTER XLVI

THE CANYON OF THE FAITHFUL BROTHERS

Declan Stewart had made a critical error. And unless he could find a
way to correct it, their quest for *Q* was at an end.

Arms akimbo, he stared down into the Canyon of the Faithful
Brothers. Beneath him, a solid wall of stone dropped in a dizzyingly
sheer descent for three hundred meters. Without ropes and sophisti-
cated climbing equipment, there wasn't any way to get down it.
Now he understood why Paul had placed his marker to the east
across the open expanse between the escarpments. It was the only
way in.

Declan had assumed that their challenge would be to find their
way into the Valley of the Jackal. It never occurred to him that once
inside there wouldn't be a way to enter the canyon that housed the
temple. He was slipping, he scolded himself. He should have
expected it. His heart sank. There was only one choice now. They
would have to find a way across to the other side. They would have
to scrape and claw their way across the shoulders of the broad,

rugged escarpment and enter from the southeast. And there was no way they had time for that. Captain Ephrom would have come and gone well before then. He had to be sure they were on that trawler when Ephrom returned. He had to be sure they'd make it home.

He'd already made up his mind. He would send the others back; he would carry on alone. All he would need was a few days more. Then Avi could send the ship back for him. If they were to have any hope of finding and retrieving Q, that was the way it would have to be. There wasn't a third way. Strangely, the notion of staying behind in this valley didn't frighten him. There was something hauntingly familiar about it all. In a way he couldn't fully understand, it felt like home.

The temple was carved directly into the sheer face of a solid granite mountain. It had no foundations, no building blocks, no keystones or mortar. Just a miraculous hollowing out of the side of a limestone mountain. A serpentine deck of red granite steps snaked their way up from the floor of the deep canyon and led directly to the entrance. As he gazed through the binoculars, Declan had the odd sensation that he'd walked that path before.

How could Paul have managed all this? he wondered. It would have taken masons and carpenters, food, water, and a hundred other logistical details to build that temple, to carve something like that into the face of a solid stone cliff. How could three years of self-imposed exile in Arabia be enough to accomplish everything he now surveyed? Perhaps the answer lay in the name of this place. The Canyon of the Faithful Brothers. How many of them must there have been? Essenes, Galileans, Arabians? Who could now say? Something told him they had come long before Paul, that they had come because God had called them to build this temple. And when they had completed their labors, they had stayed behind. Something told him that somewhere in that temple, he would find their remains.

Declan panned the binoculars from one side of the temple to the other, then down along the steep walls of the canyon. It was easy for him to understand how the narrow gorge had kept its secrets so long. The valley that housed it was nearly impenetrable. There were only two ways in. As for the canyon, it was so obscure that a man might walk by the entrance a thousand times and never notice it. The overhanging ledges of the escarpments acted like camouflage for the temple. To all practical effect, they were invisible.

Amala had made all this possible. Without her, he wouldn't be standing there now on the ridge high above their tiny camp, the temple looming in the distance beyond. She, not Declan Stewart, had found the manuscript and the map. She, not he, had entered the storage room and opened the crate. She had dropped the amphora and uncovered its secrets. She was the true discoverer of the Temple of the Revelation. She was the one who had come to awaken Q from its long centuries of sleep, not Declan Stewart. And if by some incomprehensible wonder of divine workings Q was what Ibrahim believed it to be, then she would be the true harbinger of the great awakening. She would be the savior of the fallen world.

Declan twisted the dial of the field glasses. On either side of the temple entrance there was an identical image, but he couldn't make it out. He turned the dial again, this time ever so slightly to the right. Then he saw them, two angels, beautiful and alluring, inviting those who ascended the steps to enter. Declan sensed that these were not dark angels of warning. They were creatures of the light.

Again, Declan felt the strange sensation that he'd been there before, that he wasn't seeing those images for the first time. Suddenly, a vision stronger than memory itself filled his mind. He was no longer on the cliff looking down. He was inside the temple, following a darkened hallway carved from the stone. Quickly, he strode through an open portal. He counted his steps then turned to the right. He counted his steps again then turned left. Then he saw it. Before him, atop a terse flight of narrow steps, sat a box wrapped in a glimmering band of copper. Declan had only to reach out his hand and take it. A powerful sensation of warmth and goodness surged inside him. He extended his arm. He touched the box.

Without warning, a thundering explosion erupted and sent Declan tumbling to the ground. His foot slipped. His body moved downward and over the cliff. Desperately, he dug his fingers into the flinty soil and tried to hold on. He kicked his feet, struggling to find a foothold in the sheer face of the cliff. With the steel toe of his boot, he managed to make a foothold. Cautiously, he pushed the weight of his body down and stabilized himself. For a long moment, he dangled there, three hundred meters of mist separating him from the canyon floor below. If he let go, nothing could save him. It was a sure, straight drop to the ragged boulders below.

The binoculars cascaded down, end over end. He tried not to look. He had to focus on his hands and his feet. Somehow he had to pull himself back up onto that ledge. Declan flexed the muscles of his arm and back and pulled. Slowly he inched back up toward safety. When he had cleared the ledge, he dug his elbows into the earth and dragged himself away from the precipice.

Then, even before he could get his wits back about him, the sound of gunshots rang out. The camp was under attack. His heart stopped. It was the high *rat-tat-tat* ping of a Kalashnikov. The caliph's men had beaten them to Q. Amala and Issa were in danger.

Declan drew his pistol from the holster and slapped an ammo clip into place. He threw a bullet into the chamber then sprang like a gazelle, almost free falling through space as he raced back down the trail toward the camp. He hadn't a moment to lose. He had to close the distance between him and the men firing the shots. Half running, half tumbling, he charged toward the sound of the guns. Ten seconds, thirty seconds, a minute. The gunshots and the voices came ever closer. He could make them out now. Syrians and Egyptians. They barked and growled like feral dogs.

"Hurry. Kill them all!"

Declan had to move. He had to get there in time.

He leapt over a gully and lost his footing on the loose shale. His knee buckled. He bounced, legs first along the ground. The force of the impact tore the fabric of his pants. He felt something sharp scrape across his kneecap. But somehow he recovered his balance and kept going. Pure bursts of adrenaline surged through his body. Faster, he ran toward the voices and the gunfire below.

"Quickly. Spare no one. *Allahu Akbar! Caliph Akbar!*" It was the blood-curdling voice of a Syrian.

Gunfire erupted to his right. But this time it wasn't a Kalashnikov. It was an Uzi. A voice called out from the boulder a few meters ahead of him.

"Declan, get down!"

Declan ducked just in time to avoid the spray of bullets that came on the heels of the *rat-tat-tat* of the Russian made assault weapons. He felt the wind from the bullets as they whizzed past his head. He heard the high pitched whistle of their passing. Declan lowered his shoulder and rolled laterally as if he were careening over a waterfall. He fired three rounds then slipped behind the stump of an acacia tree.

"Quickly, to your right!" Avi's voice was sharp and crisp.

Declan dived into the narrow recess behind the boulder. Avi lay on the ground beside him. He pointed his Uzi toward the ridge. There were blood stains on his thigh and a seeping wound in his shoulder.

"We'll be completely surrounded soon. They've got one ridge now. It won't take them long to take the second, then after that the third. Once they have the final ridge, it's all over, Declan."

"Amala and Issa?" Declan's words came briskly in a clipped staccato of vowels and syllables as he struggled to catch his breath.

"The boy found a cave at the foot of the defile. The trail behind us goes down that way. If you hurry you can just make it."

Six shots came in rapid succession, glancing off the boulder and sending shards of stone flying like shrapnel through the air.

"Dammit! We've got to do something. We're like fish in a barrel here. What about Levi and Dov? Where are they?"

"Levi's on the high ridge where the leopard's trail ended. But I don't know how much ammo he's got left. Dov is squeezed into the face of the cliff just beyond the camp. They're pinned down pretty good."

"What about the grenades?"

"It's too bad I've got all of them here. We'd be better off if the boys had a couple up there. They could turn this thing around from there."

Declan nodded. "Any guess how many of them there are?"

"Eight, ten. Hard to tell. They came so fast and out of nowhere. If the horses hadn't bolted first, we'd have been killed before we even knew they were there. They hit the camp with an RPG only a minute after we got out of there."

"Give me a couple of those grenades. I'll see if I can make it up the ridge to Levi. Let's see if we can get back to even."

"You need to go to the girl. She and Issa are alone in that cave. They don't even have a gun. Someone's got to look out for them. They're fine for the moment, but they won't be for long."

"If we don't take these guys out, nobody's gonna be fine. I'll go to them just as soon as I get those grenades up to Levi." Another burst of gunfire came from the ridge above.

"That was an Uzi. Maybe Levi's doing okay without the grenades. He's a good shot, that kid."

"We both know what has to be done and you're in no shape to make it up that trail."

Avi nodded grudgingly. "Okay, but hurry. You need to get to Amala and Issa. As soon as you toss the bag to Levi, follow the gap between the boulders to the bottom of the gorge. The cave entrance is like the eye of a needle. But look for footprints in the dirt. You'll find it. Before you squeeze in, use a branch and brush them away. No sense advertising to these guys where you are."

Declan nodded then turned his eyes back toward the ridge where the shots had come from.

"And Declan, listen to me. This is important. You can't let these animals take them alive. You know what they will do to the girl and the boy too. You can't let that happen. You have to be strong enough to do what has to be done if it comes to that. You have to be strong enough to make that cave their Masada."

Declan nodded sharply. "Look, give me the grenades. I'll make it up the ridge and get them to Levi. Then we'll see what happens."

"It's a risk."

"Life's a risk. That's one of the first things you ever taught me, old friend. We both know if I can get these grenades to Levi, maybe we all get out of this and nobody does a Masada. Anyway, that's the way it's going to be, so let's don't waste any more time arguing."

Avi shook his head then handed Declan a canvas courier bag containing four Belgian made NR-423s.

"Count three, then run like the wind. I'll cover you. Whatever you do, you've got to make it back to Amala and the boy. And Declan, you were right, and I was wrong. They're okay."

Declan knew that Avi meant, *"even though they're Palestinian."* He slipped the bag over his shoulder, took a deep breath, then counted off the sequence: "Three, two, one . . ."

Avi leaned forward and unleashed a rain of gunfire. In Hebrew he called to Levi and Dov to fire. Bullets zipped by Declan's ears and ignited the ground at his feet. At the end of the trail he grabbed hold of a boulder and pulled himself up. A round struck the canyon wall less than a meter in front him. His hand slipped, and he tumbled backward. Quickly, he pulled himself up and started again. This time he made it.

"Here, Dr. Stewart. Here!" Levi called out from a crevice in the ridge.

Declan dove in at his feet. For a moment the gunfire came to halt. "That was hairy."

"But a nice job. You're very quick for an old guy." Levi smiled as if they were merely two men in a bar telling stories. He slipped the strap off his shoulder and laid the bag at Levi's feet.

"There are four grenades in there. Make the most of them."

"No worries. I'll use them to get Papa out of the trap he's gotten himself into."

"What about Dov?"

Levi's light smile faded. Declan noticed a large circle of blood on the boy's arm.

"Are you sure you're okay? Are you sure you can make it to Avi and Dov?"

"Look, Dr. Stewart, my brother's dead, see? It's just us. My dad, you, me, the girl, and the boy. That doesn't leave many options. You get back down the ridge to Amala and Issa. Did Papa tell you how to find them?"

"Yes."

"So that's where you belong. That's your family now. That's your job. This one's mine. I know what I have to do. You know what you have to do. So let's just leave it at that. You want a grenade?"

"It'll do more good up here with you. I have plenty of ammo."

Levi nodded. He understood the dark meaning imbedded in those words.

"Then I'll use one to lay down the cover for you. That should shut down their Kalashnikovs long enough for you to get to the cave. But you have to hurry. They're moving to that ridge now. When they get there, this thing will pretty much be over. But I've got a few tricks up my sleeve. I'll take plenty of them with me. Maybe that will give you the chance you need to get Amala and little Issa back to the coast. Anyway, time to go. I'll lay down the cover. You make tracks."

"Levi—"

"*Go!*"

Declan bit hard into the soft flesh of his lip. Destiny had fore-closed the options. There was no alternative. "God be with you.

Forgive me."

"You don't make the destiny of men, Dr. Stewart. Only God has that power. Now, please, go."

Levi pulled the grenade from the pouch, lifted the pin, counted three, then heaved it across the open canyon to the ridge beyond.

The explosion rocked the canyon. A cloud of brown smoke rose into the air. In that brief moment of haze and confusion, Declan slid back down to the trail. He quickly snaked his way between the boulders to the bottom of the gorge. Madly, he searched for the entrance to the cave. But he couldn't find it. Then gunfire once again erupted behind him. He got down on his hands and knees and tried again. He felt his way along the wall while he studied the ground that ran alongside it. Then at last he saw it. A tiny footprint beside a clump of desert shrubs. Declan quickly grabbed a dead branch and brushed the ground around him as he squeezed into the tiny gap behind the thorny branches.

"Amala . . . Issa . . . it's me, Declan." His voice echoed. That was a good sign. It meant that somewhere ahead the cave opened up.

"Here."

Amala's voice was strong. That too was a good sign.

"Here, keep coming. Crawl on your stomach. You'll have to press very hard to squeeze through. Just keep crawling. In a few meters, you'll be able to stand."

Declan crawled toward a beam of light flickering at the far end of the tomblike tunnel. Behind him he heard the explosion of another grenade, then several bursts of gunfire. It was the high pitched *rat-tat-tat* of Kalashnikovs. The Uzis had fallen silent. Declan expelled all his breath then forced himself through the eye of the needle. At last he emerged into the chamber. He knew that behind him, three friends had died. Levi hadn't even managed to use the last of the grenades.

"Are you all right? How did you find this place?" Declan stood up and dusted himself off. Amala's light shined at his feet.

"Issa found it. He said the beetle showed him the way."

Declan bent over backwards to loosen the tight knot in his back, then checked to make sure his knife and pistol were still in place. "The what?"

"The beetle. The scarab. He said you told him to 'follow him into a hole in the ground when the sun sets, and at sunrise you'll come out on the other side in a bright new world.' He said you told him to listen to the beetle. He says the beetle showed him this cave."

Declan nodded. "Then we owe the beetle one."

"Where are the others?"

Declan locked his eyes on hers. He shook his head.

"They're with God now," Issa whispered.

Declan's heart was breaking, but he didn't have time for mourning. He had to protect Amala and Issa. He had to make a plan.

"Is that flashlight all you have?"

"Yes. The attack came out of nowhere. We didn't have time for weapons or water or anything else. Only time to run."

Declan thought for a moment. "Okay, first we need to block this entrance. Issa, you gather up as many small rocks and pebbles as you can find. Amala, you can help me move these larger ones."

Issa placed the beetle back into the match box and returned it to his pocket. Then, using his hands like tiny shovels, he scooped up mounds of dirt and gravel and deposited them in the narrow gap of the entrance. Then he scuttled inside and kicked the pile as far as his legs would reach. Then he would return to the cave and start the sequence over again. When at last he had finished, Declan and Amala slid four small boulders in place and sealed the opening. He hoped they weren't sealing their own tomb.

"It's not perfect, but it's the best we can do with the time and the materials we've got. We're lucky only one person can enter that tunnel at a time. On his belly and squeezed like that, he'll have a hard time clearing the way. Not impossible, but difficult and time consuming, especially if he has a Kalashnikov on his back."

"What now?"

"Ommy, the beetle says to go this way. He says to trust him, he knows the way."

Amala turned the flashlight toward Declan. He checked his ammunition. "We've got plenty of shells if we need them. Let's hope we don't."

"So what do we do now?" Amala raised her shoulders and tilted her head back, strands of black hair disappearing into the shadows.

"Issa's suggestion is as good as any. After all, the beetle got us this far." Declan forced a smile.

Issa took the box from his pocket and placed the beetle into the palm of his hand. Its shell glimmered blue, gold, and green in the faint light.

"The scarab says this way, Declan."

It was the first time Issa had ever called him by his name.

CHAPTER XLVII

THE VALLEY OF THE JACKAL

Shari could barely restrain his excitement. His plan had worked precisely as he had intended it should. Well, perhaps not precisely. After all, the Syrian was still alive. But that was an account he would settle in due time. For now, he would take a moment and enjoy the fruits of his labor.

"It appears that Declan Stewart and his band of Jews were good fighters, Commander. They appear to have outsmarted you at nearly every turn, save the last one, of course. You are, after all, still alive."

Understandably, the Syrian had imagined that four men, a girl, and a child would be easy fruit to harvest. An RPG, a few harsh words, a burst of gunfire, and it would all be done. But he had made one critical error. He had not only underestimated the Jews, he had underestimated Declan Stewart. And few knew better than Shari the consequences of that. Perhaps most telling was that three of the Syrian's men had been lost to grenades set as a booby trap under the bodies of the Jews. The others had been killed in more or less straight-up fashion, expert shots right through the head and from a distance. Declan, it seemed, had chosen his friends well.

"Amazing," Shari commented as he drew gently on the cigarette and worked the math. His odds of walking out of that valley, Q in hand, were definitely improving.

"They lost three men. You lost seven. Declan Stewart, the woman, and the child somehow managed to escape."

Shari studied the glowing ember of his cigarette then gazed into the Syrian's dark eyes.

"In fairness I should tell you, Commander, that I myself tried to kill Declan Stewart once long ago. Then, I even sent men to kill him just the other day. *Twice,* in fact. But they had no better luck than you. For reasons I have never fully understood, Declan Stewart is not an easy man to kill. He has nine lives, as they say." The Syrian glared, but held his tongue.

"So here we are. Our great force is reduced to two Bedouins, one Jew, a Persian, and a Syrian. That makes five. As for Declan Stewart, they are three, but one is a woman and one is a child. His weapons status is uncertain. Whether he is well or wounded is uncertain. Whether he has food or water is uncertain. How he got here and managed to find this place is also uncertain. Precisely how he managed to escape and precisely where he is now are complete mysteries to us. I do have that right, don't I?"

"Declan Stewart is unimportant, Sayyidi. Infidels may be killed at any time. All that matters is the relic. Once the caliph possesses the relic, he will launch the attack. Mecca will fall. The Mahdi will be proclaimed. There is only the relic. Everything else is illusion." The dark jewels of the Syrian's eyes glowed in the soft lantern light.

Shari drew a breath from the Dunhill then extinguished it.

"You are, of course, correct. The relic is all that matters. It's only eight hours till dawn. At first light, we'll make our way into the canyon, enter the temple, and take the relic. We can worry about Declan Stewart afterwards. I'm so pleased we have at last found something we agree on."

"If we don't take him, the desert will. There's no water in this land. He no longer has his horses or supplies. He has no sanctuary. There's no place for him to hide."

"You are mistaken, Commander. There is one ideal place for him to hide."

"And where is that, Sayyidi?"

"You would have to ask Declan Stewart. At present, he is the only one who knows."

CHAPTER XLIII

THE VALLEY OF THE JACKAL

Declan checked the faintly glowing dial of his wristwatch. They had been inside the cave for two hours, inching along through the inky darkness, the flashlight's white oval beam their only guide.

Declan had no way of knowing how far they had come or even if they had been followed. He only knew that they had to keep moving forward through the twisting black coil of the tunnel. The tunnel was their only hope. Ahead, there was at least the promise of escape; behind, only the dead men they hadn't buried and the ones who had killed them.

Declan picked up a rock. With his knife he scratched a mark on it.

"What's that for? We don't plan on going back." Amala's voice was soft and comforting.

"I don't like to foreclose options. This is just in case we change our minds."

Amala touched his hand, but said nothing. Issa looked curiously at them both and then at the beetle. He shoved his open palm into the flashlight's beam.

"There's another way out. The scarab knows. He will show us."

Declan and Amala glanced at each other. They hoped Issa was right. Then together they continued down the dark, winding tunnel.

Half an hour later, they came upon a tiny waterfall and a bubbling pool of crystal blue water. Declan felt waves of excitement ripple through him. The pool showed signs of human hands. It had been enlarged and shaped with metal tools. Perhaps the beetle was right.

Issa had already lain down on the smooth stone beside the water. His little body was exhausted. He needed rest. They all did.

"Let's hole up here for a bit. We've covered a lot of ground. It's okay if we just settle in for a while; give our bodies some time to rest." Declan studied the stone edge of the pool and the markings on it.

Amala nodded. The soothing sounds of falling water had already lulled her into a trance. She eased up beside Issa, raised his head, and placed it in her lap.

"It's time to sleep, Ommy."

"Yes, time to sleep, Issa."

Like nodding kittens lodged beside the subterranean spring, Amala and Issa surrendered themselves to sleep. Declan slipped behind them and placed his arm around Amala's torso. He squeezed gently then kissed her neck. In Arabic he whispered, "We're going to make it. I promise you, we're going to make it."

"I know. Everything is going to be all right." Her words trailed off into the darkness. She closed her eyes. Declan held her close and then they both drifted off to sleep.

They had gone less than a hundred meters from the underground spring when Declan noticed it.

"Look." He moved the flashlight's beam across the wall, pausing to highlight the chisel marks. "This passage has been enlarged with tools."

"Just like the pool behind us."

"The same. Human hands did that work; human hands did this work."

"Then the tunnel leads somewhere."

"But where?"

Issa smiled. The beetle rotated its head and twitched. Issa raised his palm to his ear.

"The scarab says go a little further along, Declan. He says he knows the way. He says you know it too, but you've forgotten. He says he'll show you." Issa now spoke in English.

In the dim column of yellow light, flecks of dust swirling around them, they advanced another two hundred meters down the tunnel. Then Declan noticed a peculiar sensation.

"Something's different. What is it?"

Amala reflected for a moment. "I don't notice anything," she replied.

Issa placed the beetle beside his ear.

"The scarab says you know. He says there's no need for him to tell you things anymore. He says you must tell us. He says he's tired now and has to rest."

Declan thought for a moment. Then the fog in his mind cleared. He knew what it was.

"It's the air. It's drier and no longer still. Feel it? That soft, slow breeze on our faces?"

"Yes," Amala said. "It's not moist like it was down by the spring. And the smell. It's a scent, a sweet perfume. Is it juniper?" Amala breathed in deeply, probing the recesses of her memory.

"Sandalwood," Declan said absently. "It's incense. We're near the temple. This tunnel leads directly into the Temple of the Revelation. I don't know how I know it, I just know it."

"Then we follow the scent of the sandalwood. That's where our destiny awaits us."

Declan touched the pistol at his side. "If the caliph's men already entered the temple, this tunnel's going to take us straight into their laps. We can't take that chance, not with all of us anyway. I want you two to stay here and—"

"No, Declan. We're in this together. All of us. We're coming with you."

"Sure, that's what I'm saying too. It's just that I want to do some reconnaissance. You won't have to wait long. I'll come right back for you."

Amala didn't appear entirely convinced, but she nodded.

"As soon as I know it's safe, I'll come back and get you. If we're lucky, we've beaten them to the temple. I don't think they would have attacked us if they already had Q. Anyway, I'm glad I marked the trail. We might just have a shot of making it back to the boat in time, and with Q in our hands."

"And if it's not safe in the temple?" Amala asked, squeezing his hand.

Declan shrugged. "Surfers are lucky. They have to be. I'm betting they haven't made it there yet."

"But what if they have?"

"That's why I'm doing the reconnaissance. If they're there, I'll make sure they don't see me. I'll turn around and come straight back. If they already have Q, things actually get a whole lot easier. They'll have what they came for and won't wait around for us. Either way I'll be back. But promise me that you'll wait here. Under no circumstances are you to leave this place till I get back. Just like the secret room at Dier al-Shuhada, okay?"

Amala nodded.

"And here, I want you to keep the pistol. I won't need it out there. It's just a recon mission. You know how to use it?"

Amala took the Walther PPK in her hand and slid a bullet into the chamber.

"I know how to use it."

"Good, and take this too." Declan handed her the flashlight. "I have my pocket light. It'll have to do for what I need. Now you two go back down to the spring and wait for me there."

Declan smiled and kissed her cheek.

"Be careful. We need you. You realize that now, don't you? The three of us, we need each other."

"I won't disappoint you. I promise to be careful, and I promise to come back."

"That's a lot of promises."

"I always keep my promises."

Declan held her tightly the way he had held Val in better days. Then he picked Issa up in his arms and squeezed him to his chest.

"Take care of your Ommy, okay? And look after that beetle too. He's my new hero."

Declan pivoted on his heel and walked away.

וַיָּ֫שֶׂם

לְ וַיְדָעְלַבְמוֹ וְדִי־לַע הָיָהְב לְ

יהּ־וָיְהַ וּב הָיָהְנ רְשֵׁא־לָכ הָיְ

CHAPTER XLIX

THE VALLEY OF THE JACKAL

Judah Lowe, dreaming of winter fires and spiced wine, didn't hear the Syrian as he entered his tent and crept up beside the cot. But when the cold steel of the jambiya scraped the delicate skin of his throat, he knew immediately who had come to take him.

"Don't move. Don't make a sound, Jew. If you're not as quiet as the night itself, I will slit your throat. You will die with the taste of blood and dirt in your mouth."

Judah twitched to show that he had understood. A warm, scarlet thread rolled down the ridge of his neck. Perspiration pooled under his arms and along his sides.

"Now get up, and quietly put on your boots. Then together we're going to go to the temple. It's time to retrieve the relic."

Judah Lowe twitched once more. His fear had returned. The same fear he'd felt in the darkness of the plane as it jetted him toward the desert. Silently and without shame, he prayed. He prayed to the god of Number 10 Lowenstrasse, the god of the tribe whose bonds to him he had worked so hard to sever. He prayed that he might make it back alive. That he might find himself in his office in Zurich, breathing the warm dust and leather-scented air of history around him. Not history like this. Not history as it was being made. Not history lived in real time. He'd had enough of that. Now he wanted only to be back home. The allure of Q was gone. There was only the cold reality that death was at hand.

Noiselessly, they exited the tent and stepped out into the swirling mists and rain. By the light of the Syrian's lantern, they headed toward the hidden trail that he had discovered three hours before sunset. The trail that led down into the Canyon of the Faithful Brothers and to the temple beyond. The two Bedouins, the last of the Syrian's little army, stood alone by the fire. As he and Judah Lowe strode quietly by them, the Syrian nodded toward them. The tall one raised a hand and nodded in return. A signal had been given. A signal had been received.

At dawn, the Bedouins rose from their posts and crept toward Shari's tent. They were frightened of the djinn, but they were more frightened of the Syrian. They could only hope that their amulets and the images they had etched in the dirt beside the fire would keep them safe.

Silently, each drew his blade then together they slipped inside the tent. A lantern hung from the support pole and burned a faint light. The tallest of the Bedouins eased up beside the bed, raised his knife then struck quickly.

But something was not right. He had killed many men in the service of the caliph, and most of them with the knife. He knew the feel of steel piercing flesh and bone. He knew the force it took to drive the blade deep into the body of a man. This time, the blade had pierced its target too easily. Quickly, he struck again. But again, he had the same odd sensation. Angrily, he tore away the blanket and tossed it to the ground. On the cot lay a bundle of clothing tied with belts.

"*Waa Faqri!* It's a trick," he screamed, sheathing his knife. "The Sayyidi is gone." Instinctively, he reached up and turned the dial of the lantern.

When he heard the dull click, he knew immediately his mistake. He cursed himself for his carelessness. He cursed Bashir for not stopping him. But above all, he cursed the djinn. All this was their doing. In that brief moment that seemed to him an eternity, the Bedouin realized that all his symbols and talismans had been power-less against them. He should never have tempted fate on a moonless night. When the Syrian had given him his orders, he should have nodded, waited for his image to fade on the horizon, then turned around and run for home. What after all was the power of a man when measured against the dark magic of the djinn.

He closed his eyes. The tent exploded. A giant ball of fire rose into the damp night sky.

The Syrian and Judah Lowe had already reached the steps of the temple when a flash of fire lit the dark, storm-clouded sky behind them. The sound was muffled. But the Syrian knew that meant nothing. It was the brightness of the light that told a soldier what he needed to know. It had flashed with a golden intensity then turned red with tips of blue.

"Grenades and a canister of petrol," he said aloud.

But why a single explosion? he asked himself. If Declan Stewart had attacked the camp, why launch only one grenade? And why no gunfire? But even before the questions had fully formed in his mind, he knew the answer. This was the Persian's doing. But even the Persian could not deny the will of Allah. The Syrian would have the relic, and nothing could stop him now.

CHAPTER L

TEMPLE OF THE REVELATION

Declan reached the end of the tunnel only to find his way blocked by a barrier of heavy wooden timbers and stone. In the narrow beam of his penlight, he studied the contours of the obstacle and ran his hand along the crease that separated the stone wall from the broad beam of wood that defined the edge of the barrier. A narrow ribbon of air rushed past his fingers.

Declan tucked the light into his belt, squared himself, placed both hands in the middle of the barrier, and pushed. Nothing happened. Readjusting his feet and his hands, he lowered his shoulder and pushed again, this time using the strength of his legs to drive forward. Suddenly the barrier moved and the sweet smell of incense filled his nostrils.

A slit opened up as the barrier slid into the stone wall of the tunnel. Slowly, Declan squeezed into the gap.

For a few moments he stood in total darkness watching and listening for signs of the caliph's men. But nothing moved. Declan raised the narrow amber beam of his light and panned across the space. As he did so, the small hairs on the back of his neck tingled and a powerful sense of déjà vu overwhelmed him. He had been in this place before. The carvings of angels, the altar, the high ceilings sculpted from the very stone of the mountain were all familiar to him. But it was the doorway at the far end of the room that sent a jolt of electricity down his spine. He had walked through that door before and navigated the dark maze of hallways that lay beyond. Declan knew instantly that through that door lay the path of his destiny. Through that door lay his way home.

Just as he moved toward the door, Declan's light flickered. He tapped it against his palm. The beam of light steadied but refused to brighten. Quickly, he scanned the walls from the high rafters to the floor. Then he saw the twin caste iron brackets on either side of the doorway. Wasting no time, he moved across the room and removed one of the torches. The broom sedge wrapped with leather thongs was crisp and dry, as was the heavy coat of pine tar and pitch that covered the bundled branches.

Declan reached into the pocket of his khakis and withdrew a square metal lighter. He struck the flint wheel, made a flame, and held it up to the torch. But the heat given off by the wisp of flame wasn't enough to ignite the pitch.

Hurriedly, he removed his knife from its scabbard and dragged the ragged edge across the surface of the hardened pitch, making a coating of loose flecks. Then he struck the flint wheel again and touched the flame to the fine coat of powder he'd created across the surface of the torch. The flecks crackled and sparked, then at last the torch sprang to life. The chamber filled with flickering yellow light.

Declan's feet seemed to know the way even if his consciousness didn't. He glided through the shadowy corridors, guided by a memory he couldn't explain. He knew instinctively that he was headed toward the chamber he'd seen in his vision as he gazed down at the temple from the high ridge. He was headed toward the simple stone altar he'd seen in that vision. He was headed straight for Q.

Declan felt excitement building within him. Soon he would have
Q and the long nightmare of his obsession would be at an end. What
lay beyond the discovery, only time would tell. The only thing he
knew for sure was that Q's power over him would finally be at an
end. He, Amala, and Issa would put the past behind them. Together
they would find the peace and happiness that had eluded them all for
so very long. Together, they would find their way home.

Suddenly, Declan's feet stopped. Before him lay the sunken rec-
tangle of what once had been a ritual bath. It was only dust and
stone now, but in his mind's eye Declan saw it differently. He saw
the empty pool glimmering with clear blue water from the subterranean spring. He saw men washing themselves, preparing to enter the
chamber that held the sacred manuscript, the epistle to all mankind
written in the hand of the living God.

A cloud of incense floated on the still surface of the translucent
water. Slowly the cloud expanded, rising into the air, filling the
room with its smoke and its perfume. The crescent scar throbbed.
Declan raised his hand and touched it. Strangely, there was no sensation. He closed his eyes and breathed in the soothing, warm
fragrance. When he opened his eyes again, he was no longer alone.
He was surrounded by bearded men with glimmering black eyes,
their white robes stirring as if caught in a gust of wind. They stood in
silence, as if they were waiting for him to say or do something. Then
the torchbearer who stood among them lowered his flame and illuminated the portal beyond the baths. He looked at Declan and
gestured toward it.

"Enter, my brother, and be careful. We have waited long for your
coming. Our vigil is now at its end."

Declan glanced over his shoulder at the portal, then turned back
toward the figure. But he and all those who had stood beside him
had vanished. Declan Stewart was alone.

He took a deep breath and turned in the direction of the portal.
"You were right all along, Ibrahim. You shouldn't have had to come

so far to tell me what I already knew. I promise you now that everything will be as the angel told you it must. I won't let you down this time. I promise to bring Q into the light. I promise to give it to the whole world."

Declan lowered his head and entered the darkness. It was the moment he had dreamed of all his life.

"Dr. Stewart, I thought that might be you. How very resourceful you are."

The voice echoed harshly off the stone walls.

"You see, I knew you would come. I knew that the Syrian was no match for you. I knew that nothing could stop you once you were this close. Nothing would keep you from Q. But I am afraid that once again, you have come too late."

The man raised a small wooden box encircled in a copper band up with one hand and a pistol with the other. Its barrel was pointed directly at the heart of Declan Stewart.

Declan stood in stunned silence. Then at last he uttered, "The caliph—"

"Oh you do me a great injustice, Dr. Stewart. I am not a zealot. I am a treasure hunter. Surely you remember me from the desert at Khirbet Qumran? The caliph believes that he must destroy Q to fulfill a prophecy. Do I look like a man who would destroy the most valuable artifact in the entire history of the world because of a prophecy? I have worked far too long for this moment to give it up to a fanatic who has come to believe his own myths."

"*Traitor!*"

Declan turned toward the deep voice that rang out from the doorway behind him. There were two men, one brandishing a knife with a long, curving edge, the other a prisoner, crouched on his knees beside him. Declan immediately recognized the voice of the Syrian who had commanded the attack on the camp.

"Commander, you too are more resourceful than I gave you credit for. And I see you have brought Dr. Lowe all crumpled in a ball at your feet. You haven't harmed him I hope. I have plans for him. But regardless, I suppose you have come for this." He held the box up before him. "But I see you brought only a knife. And this, dear Syr-ian, is a gun fight."

Shari changed the angle of his pistol and prepared to fire. The Syr-ian's eyes flashed. In a dazzling flash of motion, he snatched the Glock hidden along the small of his back and fired three shots. The man beside the altar dropped to his knees, then tumbled down the hard stone steps and landed in pool of darkness. At the same time, the prisoner sprang to his feet and ran full tilt through the portal. His footsteps echoed in the chamber as he disappeared into the darkness.

Instinctively, Declan reached for his pistol, but the holster was empty. The Walther was with Amala and the boy. His mind raced across the landscape of possibilities, searching desperately for a glimmer of hope, something that held the promise of escape.

Suddenly another shot rang out. A sharp, high-pitched ring. It wasn't the sound of the Syrian's gun, but of a Walther. Declan's Walther. He studied the fading trail of the muzzle flash. It had come from the antechamber behind them. Someone else had joined the fray. Then he heard a groan. The Syrian had been hit.

"Declan, hurry." It was Amala's voice. She had ignored his peti-tions. She had followed his trail.

"*Sharmoota!*" the Syrian cried.

Two more gunshots rang out. This time it was the Glock. Now Declan knew there wasn't time for the gun. His knife would have to do. He snatched it from his boot and sprang to his feet, charging toward the darkened pool where the Syrian's voice and his shots had come from.

"Amala! Stay down," Declan cried.

Then a third shot rang out. Declan stumbled. The force of the Glock's bullet spun him around, like a charging leopard struck by the force of the hunter's heavy shell. Somehow he managed to keep his feet. Warm blood oozed from his leg and pooled inside his boot. A fire burned up the length of his spine. But he was a wild animal now. Nothing short of death could stop him.

He dove head-first into the shadows. With a thud, he hit his mark. The Syrian tumbled over and banged into the ground. Locked together, they rolled to the edge of the empty ritual bath. Declan felt blood on the Syrian's shoulder. Amala had hit her target, but it was only a flesh wound, one that had only made him more vicious and more lethal. The Syrian was on top of him now. He had the better angle. Declan had to do something. He had to work himself free.

The Syrian pressed the barrel of his Glock upward against the pressure of Declan's wrist. A few more degrees, and it would be pointed directly at his temple. It would be over.

Declan felt the flames inside him rising higher and higher. He was growing stronger. He stiffened his arms, then with a swift, hammer-like motion, he drove his forehead into the Syrian's face. Quickly, Delcan wrapped his legs around the Syrian's torso and spun him around.

"Die, you son of a bitch," Declan gasped, raising the knife.

But the Syrian was too quick. He drove the palm of his hand into Declan's nose and threw him off balance. A searing bolt of pain rain through Declan's face, but with it came a surge of adrenaline that cleared his mind.

With a quick, short motion of his knife, Declan slashed the Syrian's wrist. The Glock clattered to the ground. Seizing the moment, he grabbed the Syrian's keffiyeh and wrapped it around his neck like a garrote. Declan jerked hard. The Syrian groaned. He jerked harder still. Then something broke. He grabbed the Syrian's head from behind and plowed it into the stone that lined the ritual pool. He banged it hard.

Declan pulled his head back and pressed his blade to the Syrian's throat. He pressed down hard and sliced a deep gash. But it hadn't been enough, not for what Declan had in mind. He drew the knife back and made the motion again. This time the blade cut all the way to his spine. With a final jerk and slash, Declan severed the Syrian's head from his body. For a moment he held it suspended like a dark red moon before him. Then he smelled the faint scent of sandalwood. He let go. The Syrian's head rolled across the stones and tumbled into the darkness recesses of the ritual bath.

Declan swept up the Syrian's lantern.

"Amala!" he cried.

He raised the lantern high above his head and searched the empty spaces around him. Amala lay like a broken doll at the entrance to the antechamber, a red pool forming a dark circle around her. The Syrian's bullet had found its mark.

"No! Not again! Not again . . ."

Declan tossed the knife aside. In the soft glow of the lantern light, its blood-red blade glimmered like a ruby. For the first time, he saw her wound. His heart shattered. The bullet had struck her just below the chest, ripping a jagged hole that ran all the way through her. Blood flowed down her side. The crimson pool grew ever larger beneath her, its dark waters flowing across the stones and empting into the same pool where the Syrian's head now rested. Her precious life sanctified the font that the Syrian's body had defiled.

Declan sat the lantern aside and carefully slid his arm under Amala's neck. His vision blurred in a flood of tears. Gently, he lifted her head and placed it in the cradle of his lap. Raven strands mixed with blood clung to her skin. But she was more beautiful to him than she had ever been. He no longer felt the pain of the bullet wound in his leg. All he could feel was the burning fire of the crescent scar. He was falling into a deep pit filled only with darkness.

"Amala."

Strangely, she smiled.

"God is everywhere, Declan. In life, in death. His hand guides everything. Nothing happens that is not the will of God."

"I curse him. I curse God."

"No, you must never say that. You must never think that. Life has purpose and meaning, Declan, and so does death. There are many paths, but only one destination. I follow my path, the one the angel showed me long ago. Now you must follow yours. Bring Q into the light. This has always been your destiny. Ibrahim knew it. The angel foretold it. And in your heart, you know it too."

She coughed. A ribbon of blood ran down her cheek. She struggled to find her breath.

"But now you have another destiny as well. You must be a father. Take Issa as your son, our son, and raise him up to be strong. He's special, Declan, in ways you haven't yet imagined. Even now, he's changing. And in time you'll know the truth. But for now, you must make of him the best of what you are, of what you have always been."

Declan felt a great wave of pain and fear wash over him. He felt as if his skin were being slowly peeled from him with a jagged shard of glass. His howl of agony echoed through the lightless chamber.

"Here, take this Declan. It's yours now." She squeezed the silver crucifix of Ibrahim's rosary into his hand. "Remember me."

Declan begged her not to die. He cried out to God, "Take me. Take me instead." Then he wept. He had promised to keep her safe, to make for her and Issa a home. But, just as with Val so very long ago, he hadn't been strong enough. He never had been.

"I love you."

His words trailed off into the darkness. Declan squeezed the rosary in his right hand and her tiny fingers in his left. But there was nothing. She was gone. Declan was alone.

EPILOGUE

GHOST SHIPS BREAK
SOUTH ISLAND, NEW ZEALAND

The gentle offshore breeze toyed with Declan's hair, alternately hiding and revealing the jagged contours of the crescent scar. His eyes were focused on the western horizon and the boy who bobbed in the shallow waters near the shore.

Issa sat patiently atop the tri-fin and waited.

"Get ready," Declan called out from the beach. "Here it comes."

Issa paddled hard against the back draft of the rushing water. As he gathered speed, the soft white wave lifted the tail of his board and drove him toward the beach. Issa popped up to his feet then crouched low. Declan smiled. It pleased him to know that the boy rode the same way he did, right foot forward, face to the wind.

Already it had been a good day for Issa. He had ridden a dozen waves and still wanted more. They were gentle rollers that broke inside, close to the rocks, like the waves of the Red Sea that Declan had watched from the rusting rails of Ephrom's trawler. They weren't big. It wasn't much. But it was a start. By the end of summer, Declan imagined the boy would be ready for the outside break. But there was no hurry. The sea would tell them when it was time.

It had been a quiet ride through desolate mountains on hungry horses made skittish by the storm. But the rain clouds had vanished. Sunlight had been their companion each step along the way back to the secret cove. The old smuggler had come, just as he promised he would. When he learned that Avi and his sons were dead, he arranged their passage back to New Zealand with the captain of a Maltese freighter who required no papers and asked no questions.

It had been a somber passage. In all the long weeks at sea, the dancing hand refused to dance. The beetle, who still glimmered in the golden sunlight, fell silent and no longer shared his secrets. All of them—Declan, Issa, the dancing hand, and the scarab beetle—had given themselves over to their mourning.

But when they at last reached the stone cottage on the top of the cliff above the great reef of Ghost Ships, something changed. Each felt his heavy burden of pain grow a little lighter. A new day had dawned for them all. A new beginning had come to lay its claim upon them.

Declan had buried Amala just outside the entrance to the Temple of the Revelation in a patch of earth where a sliver of light shone through the shadowy veil of the high escarpments. He couldn't give her the sea, but at least he could give her the light. Then he took Issa's hand in his. Together they prayed. Ibrahim had been right about many things, but in one respect he hadn't been right at all. Declan Stewart had never truly lost his faith. It was just that his sorrow had blinded him for a while.

Lazily, Issa lounged atop his board and rode the gentle white foam to the shore. Once there, he dragged the board up close beside him and made his way to Declan.

"Declan, did you see that? Did you see me turn?"

"You bet!" he called back with a smile. "That was great."

"Come back in the water. Now it's your turn. One more wave,

please? I want to watch you ride. I want to watch you ride the big one."

Declan breathed in the fresh salt spray as he wrapped the leash back around his ankle and grabbed his board.

Summer had come early to the southern hemisphere. Yet Declan still hadn't solved the mystery of the box. It had proved to be as enigmatic in discovery as it had been in its obscurity. He had tried every trick he'd ever learned about ancient technologies, looking but not finding a tiny *bab al-sir* that might be the key. But still its secrets eluded him. It had no portal, no opening, and no chamber of any kind. It was a seamless wooden block surrounded by an inlaid band of copper that had no beginning and no end; a perfect unbroken circle. The symbols etched into the band of copper were untranslatable. They were unique, alien, unrelated to any human language he or anyone else had ever seen. Only the carving in each end of the box was recognizable. It was the haunting image of the angel, the one from the temple.

"Are you sad?"

"No, Issa. Just thinking. How could I be sad on a glorious day such as this with you at my side?"

"You were thinking about the box?"

"About the box, yes. I still can't open it. To tell you the truth, Issa, I'm not even sure I want to."

"Don't be afraid of the box. It brings the light, the light that will come when it's time."

"That's what Ibrahim thought too."

"And Ommy, and the angel."

"Well, maybe one day we'll find the secret that opens it. Maybe one day we'll see if they were right about the light. But now I promised to ride a wave for you, and I always keep my promises. Enjoy the sun. When I get back, we'll go up to the cottage and make some lunch."

"When you get to the reef, Declan, wait. The beetle doesn't like to be alone. I'll run to the house and get him. Then he can watch you too. He likes the sea."

"Okay, you do that. I'll wait on the point till I see you wave from the cliffs."

Issa sprang from the boulder and dashed like a hare up the trail toward the house.

When he arrived there, a stranger was waiting on the porch. She sat in the wicker chair beside the table and looked out to sea. On the table before her lay the box.

"I've been waiting for you, Issa. I've been watching you ride the waves. You've learned a great deal in a short time."

"The beetle and I have been waiting for you to come. We knew you would. The beetle told me."

"Yes, he knows many things, our glimmering little friend. I sent him to you."

"You look just like I knew you would," Issa smiled. "You look like Ommy except your hair is golden."

"That makes me very happy. Thank you for that compliment."

"You've come about the box, haven't you?"

"In a way."

"You've come to show Declan how to open it, haven't you?"

"No. I've come to show you how to open it."

"But what about Declan?"

"Once the box is opened, there isn't any turning back. Things will start to happen, and very quickly, I'm afraid. Some bad things, but eventually some very, very good things. Declan will need help. He'll need your help . . . and mine. That's why I've come. I've come because he needs us both. I've come because now he has no one but us."

"But I already know how to open the box."

"Yes, I know you do. You only needed someone to tell you that it was time, didn't you? I have come to tell you just that. It is time."

Issa reached across the table and picked up the box. He touched the images of the angels on either end. They began to glow softly. Then he pressed the alien symbols along the copper band in a complex sequence of back-and-forth movements so fast his fingers blurred. Then he stopped and sat the box down on the table again.

The encircling copper band glowed, then like a mist, evaporated. Like holograms, the images of the angels drifted into the air. The box was open. A bright light emanated from within the chamber. Issa slipped his fingers inside and removed a small parchment scroll.

"Very good. I couldn't have done it better myself. Now hurry back down to the beach. Let your father finish his last wave. It's a special one. No one else but he could ride it. Then tell him the box is open and the scroll awaits him. Tell him also that a friend has come to help."

Issa leaned across the table and kissed her cheek. Then, like a marmoset late for his supper, he scurried off toward the sea.

COMING SOON

Book Two of the Q Series

Q: APOCALYPSE

As the world descends into chaos, triggered by terrorist acts of unspeakable proportions, Declan is drawn ever deeper into a realm of danger and intrigue where he encounters new mysteries, new challenges and the darkness of his own desires.

Accompanied by Issa and the alluring, enigmatic Siobhan, Declan follows an arduous trail that leads him across storm tossed seas to the San Thome Basilica in Chennai, India. Inside the crumbling walls of the ancient cathedral, he uncovers important new clues to the meaning of Q and the role he must play in the fulfillment of its destiny. But Declan isn't alone in his quest. He never has been. At each step along his perilous adventure, he and his companions are shadowed not only by the Caliph and his scheming son Bahran Chah, but in an unexpected turn of events, by Judah Lowe and his new sponsors from the Central Intelligence Agency.

Picking up where *Q: Awakening* leaves off, the second book in this captivating trilogy takes the reader on a fast-paced, thought provoking journey into the innermost regions of human desire and longing. Confronting the demons of his heart and the sinister forces that would turn the power of Q to their own twisted ends, Declan must find the strength and courage within himself to overcome them all and in so doing, to bring Q, and all of humanity, into the light.

GLOSSARY

Aasalaamu Aleikum: (Arabic) A traditional Muslim greeting, typically translated as "may Allah's grace be upon you."

Caliph: (Arabic) A title historically taken by some Islamic rulers that asserts both political and religious authority to rule passed down from Muhammad. A number of contemporary Islamist groups have advocated for the restoration of the caliphate by uniting Muslim nations, either through force of arms or political action.

Cucciolo: (Italian) Cub, pup, puppy. A term of endearment often used between a mother and a child.

Che cazzo stai dicendo: (Italian) A slang term generally translated as "what are you talking about?" or "what the devil do you mean?"

Dier al-Shuhada: (Arabic) Monastery of the Martyrs. There are a number of ancient monasteries throughout the Middle East that correspond to the fictional one contained in the novel. Among these are Dier Mar-Moussa in the Syrian Desert near Nabak and St. Catherine's Monastery deep in the Sinai.

Djinn: (Arabic) In Arabic tradition predating Islamic culture, a spirit capable of assuming human or animal form and possessing supernatural power, usually evil, over the lives and fortunes of human beings. In Arab lore, the universe is inhabited by only three sentient beings, humans, angels and djinn. Ancient carvings in the northwest of Saudi Arabia and in the southern deserts of Jordan near Wadi Rum and Petra indicate that some pre-Islamic cultures worshipped djinn.

Dove siete: (Italian) Where are you?

Insha'Allah: (Arabic) "God willing" or "if God wills." In Arab regions the term is common and is frequently used not only by

Muslims, but non-Muslims as well.

Jaddah: (Arabic) Grandfather, grandpa.

Jalabiya: (Arabic) A traditional, loose-fitting garment typically made of cotton. Most commonly it is collarless, ankle length, and of a single color.

Jambiya: (Arabic) A traditional desert dagger with a wide, curving blade, typically housed in a scabbard worn from a belt or attached to a robe.

Judengasse: (German) Literally "Jew's alley." In the Germanic speaking cities of the Jewish Diaspora, this term referred to area of the city traditionally set aside for the Jewish population. A ghetto. The descriptions in the novel of the Zurich Judengasse, and the events surrounding the Juden tax and the Black Plague, are historically accurate.

Judenhut: (German) A tall, conical hat (typically yellow) that served in Germanic countries as a distinguishing mark for Jews. The concept originated with the decrees of the fourth Lateran Council (1215) and was reaffirmed by the Synod of Vienna (1267).

Keffiyeh: (Arabic) Traditional Arab headdress worn particularly in arid desert regions. It is commonly fashioned from a single square of cotton or other woven fabric.

Khawaja: (Persian origin but now adopted as an Arabic word) A common slang phrase used throughout the Middle East to refer to any foreigner regardless of his nationality or ethnicity.

La Nebbia: (Italian). The fog.

Mahdi: (Arabic). Typically pronounced as three syllables [Ma-ha-di]. Often translated as "the rightly guided one," who, according to Islamic Hadiths (traditions, as opposed to scriptures), will come before the end of time to rid the world of wrongdoing, injustice and tyranny. The historical references contained in the novel to those claiming over the centuries to be the Mahdi are accurate.

Malviventi: (Italian). Tough guys, gangsters.

Marhaba: (Arabic) One of the most common greetings in the

Middle East, meaning "hello" or "welcome."

Massa el-Kahir: (Arabic) Good evening.

Ommy: (Arabic) Mommy.

Qaddaysh: (Arabic) How much?

Quelle: (German) The source. The term was first adopted by the nineteenth-century German theologian Johannes Weiss to refer to the one, original, proto-Gospel, now commonly referred to as *Q*. While no trace of *Q* has ever been found, British biblical scholar, Oxford graduate, and member of the Archbishop's High Commission on Doctrine in the Church of England, B. H. Streeter first formulated the view that *Q* must exist as a written document and not merely an oral tradition. He postulated that it was composed in Greek and that some of its contents could be found in the Gospels of Matthew and Luke. Streeter refused to speculate publicly regarding who could have authored such a text, but it is rumored that he privately embraced the theory that it could have been written in the hand of Jesus himself. Gerhardt Reichmann, whose quest for *Q* is described in the novel, is a fictional character.

Ruach: (Hebrew) Spirit or wind, but used throughout the Hebrew scriptures to describe the divine breath of God, the force that moved over the waters at the time of creation, and that animates all life. The term is used repeatedly throughout the Old Testament to refer to God's divine power and dominion over the universe and everything in it.

Salaam: (Arabic) Peace, or peace be upon you. Although an Arabic phrase, it is widely used throughout the Middle East by members of all nations, religions, and cultures.

Sayyidi: (Arabic). A more formal honorific title roughly equivalent to "sir," "lord," or "master."

Shukran: (Arabic) Thank you.

Waa Faqri: (Arabic) Slang phrase typically translated as "Damn" or "Dammit."

THE HISTORY OF Q AND THE
MAKING OF A STORY

Q is the name ascribed to "the one and original" gospel of Jesus that some scholars believe must have existed but of which no trace has ever been found. Q stands for "*Quelle*," the German word for source, a designation first adopted by the nineteenth-century German theologian Johannes Weiss, New Testament scholar at the University of Heidelberg. Weiss and others believed that Q had circulated widely, at least as an oral tradition, among the earliest Christian communities.

British biblical scholar, Oxford professor, and member of the Archbishop's High Commission on Doctrine in the Church of England, B. H. Streeter was the first to express the view that Q was an actual written document and not merely an oral tradition. Streeter asserted that Q had been composed in Greek and preserved as a parchment codex and, as such, someday it might be found. He also believed that some of its contents had been incorporated into the Gospels of Matthew and Luke. Streeter never publicly speculated regarding who could have authored Q, but rumors circulated that he believed it had been written by the hand of Jesus himself. This rumor, and the theories and history behind it, were the genesis for this novel and the two that will follow it.

In 1945, two Bedouins wandering the deserts near Nag Hammadi in southern Egypt (the same deserts I wandered in researching this book) stumbled across a cache of ancient documents hidden in a heavy earthen jar. The vessel contained twelve Coptic codices bound in gazelle skin that have come to be known as the Nag Hammadi Library. In and of itself, their discovery ranks as one of the most important archaeological finds of all time. For Q scholars, on the other hand, the

Nag Hammadi Library offered something much more alluring; it offered the first tangible evidence of the existence of Q.

That evidence came in the form of a complete copy of the Gospel of Didymos Judas Thomas, commonly referred to as the Gospel of Thomas. Before Nag Hammadi, only fragments of that gospel had even been found. However, armed with the complete Coptic translation of the work, New Testament scholars were able to reconstruct the Greek version, the language in which the work had originally been composed, in its entirety. And it was there, in the Gospel of Thomas, that the first solid clues to the existence of Q emerged.

As Weiss and Streeter had believed was the case with Q, the Gospel of Thomas was not a narrative story. Instead, it was a simple collection of 114 sayings attributed to Jesus, each beginning with the phrase "And Jesus said. . . ."

When scholars compared these sayings to the Gospels as we know them today, they found that a number of them had been incorporated into the books of Matthew and of Luke. This fueled new excitement because it indicated that each of these ancient authors had possessed an even earlier document, a proto-Gospel that could only have been Q.

The plot of *Q: Awakening* and its protagonist Dr. Declan Stewart are entirely creations of my imagination. So too are Dr. Judah Lowe of Zurich, the gnostic scholar Gerhardt Reichmann of Berlin, and the endearing scoundrel Emile Zorn. Indeed all the characters and their ambitions, tragedies and destinies are fictional. Yet, the places they travel and much of the history upon which the story is constructed are derived from real places and real events.

In the course of writing this novel, I went to great pains, during dangerous and tumultuous times in the Arab world, to travel extensively throughout the Middle East to conduct research on location and to interview Bedouins, monks, scholars, and many others. I wanted the story to be as genuine and as real as I could make it while at the same time retaining all the entertainment and excitement of a fast-paced international thriller.

With the aid of Israelis, Palestinians, Syrians, Yemenis and Saudi Arabians, I visited nearly all of the lands I have written about. I crossed the Sinai from the Straits of Tiran to reach the library of the oldest monastery in Christendom, St. Catherine's (the template for the fictional Dier al Shuhada and its scriptorium). Aided by Bedouins (who placed their arms across my shoulders and whispered "Or-o-ence, Or-o-ence, your forefather was a great man. He helped us. With honor, we now help you"), I crossed desolate stretches of wilderness in post-revolution Egypt, passed through tense security check posts manned by ill-omened soldiers armed with Uzis and grenades, and even slipped across the unmarked border that separates Jordan from Syria in the throes of chaos. We sipped sweet mint tea around midnight campfires and talked of the desert, of God, and of destiny, as I shared with them the story of Q and my fictionalization of it.

I benefited from the knowledge and assistance of Israelis, including a former IDF "black ops" colonel, who wandered beside me as we crossed the deserts of the Negev (the home of my fictional scholar Avi Tzabari and his sons Levi and Dov), explored the caves and ritual baths of Qumran, walked along the edge of the unimaginably blue waters of the Dead Sea, and drank coffee in the cafes of Jerusalem's Old City. And with the colonel, much as I had done with the Bedouins before, we pondered the intricacies of Middle East affairs, the vastness of the universe, the insoluble mysteries of the human condition, and the universal quest for purpose and meaning in life.

Two other places loom large in this novel—Zurich and New Zealand. Zurich is the home of both Judah Lowe and Emile Zorn, each an important character in his own right. In my travels to that fine, genteel city beside the Zurichsee, I visited the old synagogue at Number 10 Lowenstrasse where Judah Lowe had come of age, struggling to define who he was and who he might become. There, I learned the history of the city's Jewish diaspora. I walked the cobbled streets of the old *Judengasse* and talked with bearded elders about the *Judenhut*, the conical hat that Jews had been forced to wear in times long past. Together we calculated the magnitude of the *Juden* tax they had been forced to pay.

And when we had finished, I knelt in the candlelit sanctuary of the Fraumunster Church and prayed for those who had suffered and died.

Lastly, there is New Zealand, home-in-exile to the man who stands at the very heart of my story—Declan Stewart. With my good friend Bruce Hopkins (the actor who portrayed Gamling, General of Rohan in the *Lord of the Rings* films) beside me every step of the way, I walked Declan's desolate, storm-tossed beaches on the western edge of the South Island near the fictional town of Graves Bay. I surfed the waters of the Tasman Sea that Declan surfed. And in the quiet moments, as the antipodal summer sun vanished into the endless ocean, I contemplated the mysteries of God, Q, and humankind, all as Declan does in this tale. Most special of all, Bruce and I got to know one of the South Island's legendary surfers, Barry O'Dae, who aided me greatly in conceptualizing the fictional reef break called Ghost Ships. Even now in the autumn of his life, haunted by the specter of Parkinson's disease, Barry surfs the waves of Tauranga Bay and Nine Mile as if he were only a boy. Like Declan, indeed like me, the sea defines him and makes him who he is.

As I studied the history of Q, wandered across many varied lands, and came to know the diverse peoples and cultures that are so very much a part of the Q saga, I felt the same eerie sensation with each step along the way. I felt that I wasn't so much writing a story as I was recording a story that was being revealed to me. Is this what it's like to be a prophet? I wondered. To sense revelation, to be shown something important, and then be duty bound to share it with the world? I don't know. But anyone who tells you that stories can't change us, can't script new and divergent destinies for us all, tells you lies. Stories make us who we are and shape who we might become. And so it is with the story of the world-weary voyager Declan Stewart and the elusive, alluring promise of the manuscript called Q.